PRAISE FOR
UNBOUND

Part quest fantasy, part dark adventure, with a splash of vampires and horror thrown in the mix, and this story turned out to be such a cool blend of so much of what I love in a killer read.

—Out of This World SFF

Paladin Unbound feels like I've witnessed an entire homebrew D&D campaign wrapped up into 334 pages. And I'm here for it.

– Zack Argyle, Author of *Threadlight*

Paladin Unbound was a fun read, combining the feeling of real stakes, with the nostalgia of classical quest fantasy and the chaos of a D&D game.

– Beneath a Thousand Skies

Paladin Unbound is a richly imagined fantasy novel packed with adventure, creatures, gods, friendship, and goodness.

– A Pocket Full of Tomes

If books were table games, *Paladin Unbound* would be Dungeons and Dragons when everything else is simply Chutes and Ladders! This bright action-fantasy book is superbly imagined and skillfully executed, particularly with its evocative and immersive imagery.

– Indies Today

You'll devour this book and end up wanting for more.

– The Medjay of Fayium

All in all, this is easily one of the best books I have read in the past decade, and tying for my favorite fantasy book of this year with Dragon Mage is no small feat.

– Bookwyrm Speaks

Mr. Speight's world building is fabulous as he brings Evelium to life for us. I highly recommend *Paladin Unbound*. You will not be disappointed.

– Book and Nature Professor

There are powerful stakes, heart-breaking scenes, quality writing prose and amazing combat scenes. I really enjoyed this. It's a 10/10 from me!

– Al Alhambra Book Reviews

When people ask for books I'd recommend to a fantasy newbie, ones that represent all the wonderful things the genre has to offer, I have a few go-tos. *The Hobbit*, obviously, and the Dragonlance Chronicles (really, is anyone surprised?), and, more recently, *The Ventifact Colossus*. Now I'm adding *Paladin Unbound* to that list, because this book would make anyone fall in love with fantasy.

– Witty and Sarcastic Bookclub

Paladin Unbound really made an impression on me. I devoured it in the way I haven't devoured a book in a long time. I could feel the author's passion on each page. More, it reminded me of my early fantasy days when I would devour book after book, reading late into the night just so I could enjoy one more chapter.

– Bookworm Blues

To Rowena,

Thanks so much for all your help and enthusiasm!

May Vaila's light shine upon you!

Best,

MYSTIC REBORN

Jeffrey Speight

Literary Wanderlust | Denver, Colorado

Published in the United States by Literary Wanderlust LLC Denver, Colorado.

www.LiteraryWanderlust.com

ISBN Print: 978-1-956615-20-3
ISBN Digital: 978-1-956615-21-0

Library of Congress Control Number: 2022951632

Cover illustration: Ömer Burak Önal
Map illustration: Thomas Rey

Printed in the United States of America

MYSTIC REBORN
AN ARCHIVES OF EVELIUM TALE

Evelium
a continent of Tyveriel

Amarthian Sea

Winterashe

Meriden

Naur's Rune

Lazarus Woods

Amnesty

Retribution

Ilathril Mountains

Silverheart Pass

Lindamere

Whitewood Knoll

Lake Wanda

Stone Rift

Pyra's Thimble

Ember's Watch

Windswept

Mount Anvil

Lernmar

Testament

Seorsian

Wyrmald River

Isle of the Twelve Mares

Festbury

Mirina's Path

Clearwell

Telridor's Keep

Moaning's Hope

Sea of Widows

Astar Crossing

Amaris

Maryk's Cove

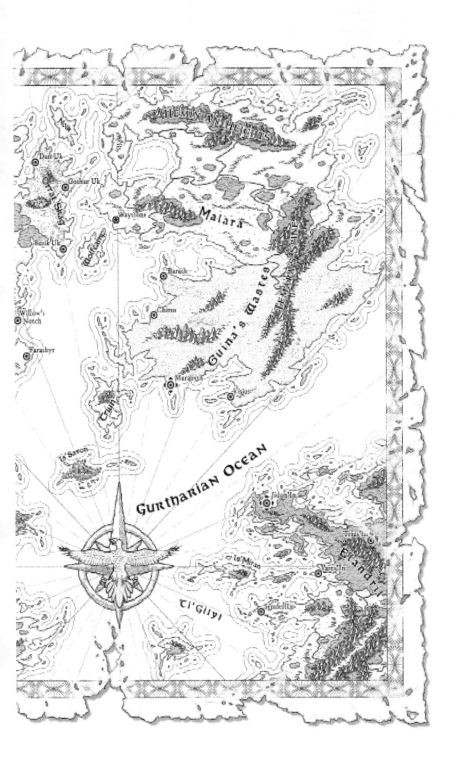

DEDICATION

For Missy

Every child should have a mother who loves them
unconditionally.

I'm glad ours have you.

PROLOGUE

Deep within the interior of the ruins, I found him. With a simple offering, he returned to the world of the living.

—*Telsidor's Missives*
Diary entry dated 1ˢᵗ of Anar, 60 AF. Unearthed from the Ruins of Anaris, the month of Emin, 1156 AT

—▲—

Spara awoke on the forest floor, leaf litter and dirt caked to the warm blood that streamed down her face. An intense shooting pain coursed through her head. She gingerly felt the vacuous cavities that were once her eyes and shook violently at the realization they were gone. What would she do without her sight? Why had her god left her this way? She took as deep a breath as her panic would allow and tried to clear her mind of the fear.

She was unsure how long she had been unconscious since witnessing Vaila's rift consume Naur, the God of Fire, and banish him to the hells of Pragarus for eternity. Crickets chirped not far from where she had fallen. In her mind, she could now only perceive the natural energy of the living since the burst of energy from Vaila's rift had seared her eyes. The crickets now resembled tiny fireballs amidst the shadows of the dense forest undergrowth.

A vision flashed in her mind. Purple fire engulfed a great castle, its spires crumbling into the city below. A young woman with grey skin accepted a glimmering gold circlet upon her raven-blue hair. The young woman peered out over a throng of subjects. Her eyes were pupilless, with amber irises, and ringed in black. The Grey Queen.

Vaila must have wanted Spara to see this vision. To see the ramifications of impending chaos and the despairing future of the mortal races. It was as though Vaila wanted to be certain someone would know the true impact of Naur's selfishness. Like lighting the wick of a candle, Naur's plot to claim Tyveriel as his own now set into motion an inevitability. Just as the candle burns bright only to eventually flicker out, so would the Age of Man.

Spara gripped the rhodium orb she wore around her neck on a simple but unbreakable chain and took a deep breath. The pain radiating through her head faded along with the vision. She cried, not from the pain of her wounds or the loss of her sight, but for the end of the Age of Grace; Vaila vanquished Naur and then she ascended to Kalmindon's idyllic heavens in a burst of celestial energy, while her brothers, Kemyn and Brinthor, relinquished much of their godly powers in favor of remaining on Tyveriel. The end of the Age of Grace meant gods would no longer walk alongside the mortal races. They would no longer maintain the balance between man and beast.

By now, the other Mystics, her fellow demigods, must have sensed Vaila drift beyond the veil which hung between heaven and earth. The Mystics would, no doubt, convene at Ember's Watch which was always their plan should the gods find resolution to their perpetual war. Spara hoped they would await her return before they ascended themselves. Surely, Atalan would. She must get to her love.

Hot tears streaked down Spara's face, the pain of her injuries competing for her attention with the anguish that gnawed at her gut. She licked her lips, salt tinged with the ferrous taste of blood coating her tongue. Wiping her face clean, she dried her hands across the front of her gown, imagining the sorry state of the celadon silk, pushed the errant sweat-soaked wisps of ebony hair from her cheeks, and set off through the forest.

Spara burst from the Lazarus Woods, tripping over the rugged earth. Root and rock tore at her bare feet, every step accompanied by a twinge of pain propelling her onward.

Finally, the sun warmed her face and she fell to her knees, thankful to be in its presence. She fumbled with her rhodium icon. Her hands shaking, she held the orb, and ran her thumbs over its engraved surface.

"Vaila, I need you now more than ever." She touched her forehead to the ground. "How could you leave us like this? Did we not deserve better treatment for our devotion? Did *I* not deserve better than to be left blind and disfigured?"

She lay silent for a moment, her burning forehead welcoming the cool earth. She tried to come to terms with her current situation. She took a deep breath, suppressing the tears.

"Atalan will know what to do," Spara said.

She pulled herself up to her feet and took off in a sprint, the muted auras of the field's tall grasses racing by her in a blur. She needed to get to Ember's Watch and reunite with the other Mystics before they ascended to Kalmindon to escape the Age of Chaos in favor of living amongst their gods. She gained speed, and two stark white angelic wings sprouted from her back. With two strong beats, the wings lifted her off her feet. She flew upward into the heavens and made southeast through the cloud-filled sky.

She flew with purpose despite not seeing the way before her. Drawn to the other Mystics by the growing chirping sound resonating in her mind, she allowed the compulsion to guide her flight where her sight no longer could.

"Atalan, hear me." She sensed her proximity to Ember's Watch where the Mystics would gather in preparation of their ascension. "I need your help."

▲

Warda was the first of the Mystics to run from the central keep of Ember's Watch into the open field surrounding the stone tower. She shuddered at the alarming speed at which Spara, whose form left a trail of green ether, plummeted toward her. The others followed, guarding their eyes against the blinding sun.

Spara's approach was awkward and uneven. Her descent too steep. Coming up short of the gathering, she crashed into the earth, casting a shower of dirt and rock into the air like a small meteor colliding with Tyveriel's fertile surface .

Atalan gasped. "Spara, no." He ran to Spara's side with the others a step behind. He was the largest of the Mystics, standing nearly seven feet tall. He donned sleeveless robes of saffron and red, and leather bracers studded with rubies to match his robes, his hulking forearms bulging from beneath.

Atalan jumped into the crater Spara's impact had created and found her tangled body lying face-down, half buried in rubble. Warda slid down the loose dirt wall in close pursuit, rocks and soil shifting beneath her feet. When she reached Atalan, he was holding Spara's limp body in a brawny arm, wiping the hair and grime from her face. Her wings had receded.

"Her eyes," Atalan's face was pallid, his eyebrows furrowed. "A great power has seared them from her face. We must commune over her immediately."

"Of course," Warda said, dropping to her knees beside him.

Ember, Mirina, Torrent, and Pyra joined them and surrounded Spara in the middle of the crater. The Mystics closed their eyes and grasped their matching rhodium orbs. They prayed together, speaking in a celestial tongue. Light emanated from the bloodied holes where Spara's eyes once glistened as green as the fresh growth of moss after the Sowing Moon. The glow intensified until two vibrant beams of light shot up into the late afternoon sky. Spara's eye lids blinked open. The light flowed from her sockets and revealed smoky grey orbs that swirled as though they each contained a burgeoning storm.

"We failed." Warda hung her head. "How could this be?"

"We didn't fail," Atalan said, his voice gravelly with despair. "The magic that took her eyes was far stronger than anything we can counter."

Atalan helped Spara sit up and placed his hands on her face and kissed her. "I'm glad you found your way back to us before it was too late. What happened?"

Spara told them of the events that led to her blindness.

"This is both fantastic and deeply troubling news," Mirina said, climbing to her feet and dusting off her pale-yellow gown with delicate hands. She tangled her fingers in her short red hair and gazed into the distance. "If Vaila has truly ascended, as Spara says, we must decide if we are to stay in Tyveriel and weather the Age of Chaos with the few remaining mortals or follow her to Kalmindon ourselves."

"Yes," Ember said. "There is much to consider."

"There's more," Spara said. "The same force that took my eyes granted me a vision of the future. In that moment, I saw the Grey Queen. She is coming. I don't know when, but Vaila showed me Tyveriel's destiny."

"You are confused, child." Torrent said, still on one knee as he stroked his white beard. "The Grey Queen is nothing more than a children's story. A fiction from a bygone era."

"I know what I saw. And my mind is clear," Spara said, her eyes flashing, a storm raging within them. "She's coming. Vaila showed me. She wanted us to know what the future holds in store for Tyveriel. Perhaps to make our decision less of a burden."

Warda stood, taking Spara by the hand. "Come my dear, let's go inside so you may get some rest. Free your mind from these troubles." She smiled as if expecting Spara to see her expression, then grimaced. She helped Spara to her feet and put her arm around her, the vibrant red of her gown contrasting with Spara's celadon silk which had been reduced to soiled rags.

Warda guided Spara into the great hall of Ember's Watch. Its stone walls were unadorned but for a series of crimson beads of light in the shape of a cross on the far side of the oblong room. They mounted the stairs, Warda's hand firm on Spara's back. At the third floor of the watchtower, Warda threw open the first door on her left, revealing a quaint bedroom with pastel linens and fresh-cut flowers carefully arranged in several vases placed throughout.

"It's nice to be home." Spara drew in a deep breath and faltered to the edge of her bed.

Warda gathered a washbasin and a clean cloth. "First, let's get you cleaned up and changed. Then I'd like you to take some rest. It will help you recover," she said, unbuttoning Spara's gown along the side of the bodice.

"Yes. I need sleep. Promise me you won't make any decisions in my absence."

Spara's gown fell to the floor, and she slipped her amulet over her head and handed it to Warda, who placed it on the bedside table.

"We wouldn't think of it, my dear," Warda said. "You've sacrificed much for our benefit. We will take good care of you."

Spara smiled as Warda washed the smears of dried blood and caked dirt from her cheeks.

"What?" Warda asked as a shallow smile graced Spara's face.

"Nothing. I'm just feeling better."

"Good." Warda untied Spara's bun and brushed her long, black hair. She placed the brush down and helped Spara to bed.

Warda sat at Spara's side for some time, watching her sleep and listening to her nervous murmurs. "Poor child," she whispered, stroking Spara's hair. "You are a harbinger of inevitable change for which I find myself ill prepared. I can sense Vaila has left Tyveriel, so I have no choice but to believe your story. My only question is, what is the right path forward?"

Assured that Spara was sleeping soundly, Warda plucked Spara's amulet off the side table and left to rejoin the others. They sat around a circular wooden table at the center of the great hall. Pyra was pensive and watched Warda as she descended the stairs and approached the table.

"How are we to believe her account, when she clearly has lost her faculties?" Ember asked.

"Surely, you can feel the gods have departed Tyveriel," Mirina said. "Unless you have lost yours as well, Ember."

"Yes, I've felt the void and it besieges me. I wasn't sure of it until I saw Spara's eyes. And even then, I didn't want to believe it."

"None of us do," Warda said, tossing Spara's rhodium orb on the table, the chain attached to it coming to rest in Atalan's hand. The chain matched each of their own. "She's in no condition to go with us. Today's events have drawn too much of her power and it will take time for her to heal. We must sequester her on Tyveriel and ascend immediately. We would be foolish to wait and allow the dragons the opportunity to hunt us now that our gods have left. Surely, they too have sensed Vaila's departure."

"I won't leave her behind." Atalan pushed himself back from the table in disgust. "How can you even consider such a betrayal?"

"What other choice do we have?" Torrent asked, leaning back in his chair with his feet crossed upon the table. "I know you love her, but this is what's best for us and Tyveriel. Without her icon to give her power, we can easily contain her in this realm."

Atalan strode across the room, the walls bulging around him from the force of his indignation. "I know you are right, but my heart breaks. Can we at least ensure she will receive the care she deserves? She's a Mystic, is she not? I will not tolerate any harm coming to her."

Pyra ambled to Atalan's side. She grasped one of his huge hands in both of hers and the walls returned to their normal state. She pushed up to the tips of her toes and whispered in his ear. Atalan placed his free hand on the dome of his bald head. "Very well. Pyra will see to Spara's accommodations. We must take great care to hide her away. There are many who would seek to abuse her power. She's not to become a tool for mortal conquest."

"Of course," Ember said. "None of us want to see her hurt further. We simply cannot risk waiting for her. Pyra will attend to Spara's needs, while the rest of us prepare for ascension. Make haste to your Waystones and await Pyra's signal. We ascend together."

Pyra placed her right hand on Atalan's broad chest. "You have my word, Atalan. I will treat her with the utmost care."

Atalan nodded and took his leave, bounding up the stairs. The door to his room slammed shut. Pyra turned to the others. "There's much to do before we ascend."

"You can never let him know where you hide her," Warda said. "Don't let any of us know. He will tear the heavens apart to get back to her."

"Of course." Pyra scowled. "I know better than any how much she means to him. I promise, only I will know what becomes of her."

CHAPTER 1

It is told that the Creator Gods, themselves, chose Tyveriel
upon which to set free the spark of life. The first of their grand
experiments.

—*The Gatekeeper's Abridged History of Tyveriel*
Vol. 1, Chapter 1 – Unearthed from the Ruins of Meriden, the
month of Anar, 1217 AT

—▲—

Umhra the Peacebreaker sat on Splinter's back, peering across the snow-covered fields to the ruins of Antiikin. The mist of his breath hung in the air between him and the towering spires of the ancient Evenese city which formed a jagged silhouette against the low afternoon sun. The half-Orc drank from his water skin—slaking his thirst—and nudged Splinter off Mirina's Path. With a snort, the horse trotted down the embankment and into the tall grass.

Umhra threw back the hood of his heavy sable fur cloak and surveyed the frozen landscape, the air biting at his face. He pushed an errant lock of hair from his eyes and rubbed his hands together to warm them from the bitter cold.

The memories of his confrontation with King Eleazar two years earlier came rushing back to him, and his skin prickled.

At the onset of their meeting, the ghost king had been less than hospitable, preferring to clash swords and refer to Umhra as a mongrel on account of his half-Orc blood. Ultimately, however, the king conceded to Umhra keeping Forsetae, the Evenese sword, in his possession until he put an end to the Brothers of Resurrection and their plan to summon Naur from the hells of Pragarus. Umhra hoped, now that he was returning Forsetae as promised, their second meeting would prove more amicable. Regardless, his stomach twisted.

He felt stronger than ever, having regained the strength and weight he had lost while trapped between the mortal plane and the hells of Pragarus where he and Vaila defeated Naur, but his anxiety remained with him. It was as much a part of him as the rhodium pyramid that hung around his neck. The rhodium pyramid that identified him as a Mystic, having completed his final Suffusion months earlier. Other than the improved strength and the ability to summon Forsetae at his will, he was still unsure what it meant to have achieved Mysticism.

The ruins were quiet, almost beckoning him forward. He guided Splinter through the overgrown rubble of the fallen city—a maze of ruins leading to Forsetae's home. They weaved in and out of the shadows of the buildings still standing, reaching the city's central tower from which King Eleazar and the other spirit warriors of Antiikin had come when he was last here. Umhra reined Splinter to a halt and peered up, following the smooth façade of the jade spire into the heavens.

"No telling how long this will take." Umhra patted Splinter on his muscular neck and dismounted. "Stay here as long as it's safe."

Splinter snorted and twitched.

Umhra crept toward the two colossal doors of the tower. They were completely smooth, with no handles or visible hardware, and were perfectly flush with the building's façade. Made of the same fine jade construction, even at this close range, the building's glossy finish seemed near perfect and reflected the sun's light back at the surrounding terrain.

He inspected the doors, looking for a means of entry. Not seeing any, he put a shoulder to them, but they did not move. He grimaced and summoned Forsetae to his hand. The sword glowed a vibrant blue as it took material form.

Ah. My final resting place. You intend to return me to these halls of the dead. The sword's voice resonated in Umhra's mind.

I intend to keep my promise. I have no desire to lose you as my companion, Umhra said.

Then approach the doorway with me in hand. I shall grant you passage into the Great Tower of Antiikin. I am welcome here.

Umhra had learned to trust in the sword's judgement and held Forsetae out in front of him. Forsetae met with the surface of the doors, and passed through them, a pulse of energy rippling along the structure's surface like a still pond disrupted by the first drop of rain. Umhra's arm followed, and then the rest of him until the tower swallowed him entirely.

It was dim and uncomfortably hot within the ancient building. The air was stale despite waves of heat buffeting Umhra's face. Forsetae alit and revealed a great hall with jade pillars reaching up to a vaulted ceiling high overhead. How glorious it must have been before the War of Rescission, when it was a place of the living—the center of a great society. Now, a thick layer of dust covered every surface, obscuring any ornamentation once visible.

By Forsetae's glow, Umhra proceeded into the room, passing banquet tables and suits of armor fashioned from green glass. Swords, pole arms, and other weapons of the old Evenese style adorned the walls. In the center of the room was a large firepit with a pyre of wood prepared for burning. Beyond the firepit, the room extended past Umhra's field of vision, unveiled to mortal eyes for the first time in nearly two millennia as he crept.

Straight ahead. In the undercrofts we shall find what we seek. A forge room with a fire undying, despite being long neglected. My birthplace.

Umhra held Forsetae above his head to cast its radiance further. At the far end of the room, a wide stone stairwell led down to the undercrofts. A chill ran up Umhra's spine.

At the bottom of the staircase, a long hallway led toward a door which emanated a warm orange glow. Umhra followed the light and passed through the door, holding Forsetae before him as his key. On the other side, the undercroft opened into an expansive room with a large forge glowing hot along the far wall and an equally impressive anvil of black steel at its center. Ancient Evenese glyphs flickering with preternatural vigor surrounded the yawning hearth.

Along both side walls, there were six white marble plinths, each holding an ancient Evenese weapon resting on violet silk. Umhra circled the room and passed an ornate helm of gold with a single horn arcing from its right side, a pair of bracers adorned with opalescent gems that swirled with discontent, a dagger of green glass, and a bow made of black wood with scribing that glowed frost white. Artifacts of a bygone age.

The final two tables were devoid of their displays. Umhra kneeled and retrieved a pile of dusty silk fabric laying at the foot of one. He shook it out, sending a cloud of dust billowing into the air, and returned it to its rightful place. Carved upon the plinth's apron in old Evenese was the name, *Forsetae.*

"The clerics of Antiikin gave one of them to Modig Forene so he could return order to Evelium," a voice said from over Umhra's shoulder. "The other, you hold in your hand, mongrel. Stolen from our keep ages ago, by a man jealous and undeserving."

Umhra turned to see the ethereal form of King Eleazar. He remained quiet, waiting for the spirit to continue.

"But you have kept your word and brought the mighty Forsetae home. And, against your desire to keep it for yourself," Eleazar said. "It has not been my experience for your kind to withstand temptation in favor of fulfilling a promise."

"King Eleazar." Umhra took a deep bow, ignoring the insults. "You were wise enough to let me keep Forsetae in my possession so I could complete my quest and save Evelium from certain destruction. Forsetae served me well, and I was successful only with its help. I now return the fabled blade to your possession as promised, despite the powerful bond we have formed." Umhra turned the blade and presented it to the king, pommel out.

King Eleazar drifted forward and reached out for the sword. "I witnessed this success you speak of. For a time, you crossed over into my purview, the realm between the living and the dead. A journey from which you have not fully recovered. Or is it something else that weighs upon you?"

"Everything has changed. Everyone wants something from me. Life, my life was less complicated when we last met."

"The true cost of heroism. Do you think the life of a king is any different? I know your path all too well. If I should travel it today, I would value this sword beyond all else and yet, here you stand before me ready to relinquish a most powerful ally. I must admit, you are quite unique."

"Yes. Forsetae proves to be an invaluable ally, and I admit there is a piece of me that wishes to keep the blade for myself," Umhra said. "But I'm a man of my word and so return it to a much-deserved rest beside your glowing forge."

King Eleazar gripped the handle and lifted Forsetae from Umhra's grasp. The blade's glow shifted to green as it attuned with its king. "It has been a long time since I last held this weapon. And yet, its feel is familiar to me. As though it had never left my side."

The king inspected the sword, turning it in his hand. "Its form has changed while in your possession. And, for the better."

With exceptional speed, King Eleazar swung Forsetae down upon Umhra. As the blade arched toward him, Umhra's armor materialized. Unlike when the two clashed in the fields outside Antiikin two years ago, the plates were now smaller and shaped like diamonds, interlocking in a pattern which gave them the appearance of dragon scales. The armor's color was a pure silver-white and its surface more reflective than before.

Umhra stood his ground as Forsetae stopped just shy of his face. King Eleazar gritted his teeth as he willed the blade to his target. The green radiance Forsetae assumed in Eleazar's phantasmal hand gave way to blue, the color of Umhra's aura.

King Eleazar retracted the sword from Umhra's space. "Most rare," he said. "This explains why Forsetae favors you. You have completed your Rhodium Suffusion and ascended to Mysticism. You are an angel among men and now walk the bridge between mortality and divinity. Odug is, to this day, no fool."

"He has shared much with me about the ways of the Paladins of old."

"Yes. He was a great warrior, reaching his Platinum Suffusion as you had when we met last. He sacrificed much for Tyveriel—including bequeathing his soul to this blade. You have rewarded him with the honor and prestige he deserved in life."

"What can you tell me of Mysticism?" Umhra asked. "I have no idea as to the ramifications of this achievement, only that Vaila willed it."

"There is only so much I can impart upon you as I never pursued such a path in my mortal life. To realize the extent of your powers, you must find the one other of your kind left on Tyveriel. Unfortunately, she remains hidden from me," Eleazar said.

"Of whom do you speak?"

The spectral king smiled at the asymmetry of the information between them. Despite Umhra's apparent power, his lack of knowledge and experience betrayed him. Eleazar lowered Forsetae and glided over to the table where the great sword had lain for ages, gesturing for Umhra to join him.

"Spara, of course," he said.

"The Mystic? I thought they all ascended to Kalmindon at the end of the War of Rescission." Umhra's armor dissipated like smoke from a snuffed-out fire.

"Not all. For reasons unknown to me, the others left Spara behind when they ascended. They took great care in hiding her away for all eternity. But that is only because there has never been another to achieve a Rhodium Suffusion until now. If you know what to listen for, you will hear her calling to you. She will have witnessed your achievement and will seek you out with the hopes you will free her."

"Calling to me," Umhra said. "I should go to her, then?"

"Only if you want to understand your full potential. But I caution you against the burden. You have already become more powerful than any man on Tyveriel. Why would you seek more?"

"So, I could better protect it," Umhra said. "There are yet threats to our land."

"There will always be threats. But, if you must, listen for her call, Paladin of Vaila. And, do not return to these halls of the dead. You no longer have use for them, nor they of you."

He offered Forsetae to Umhra. "I have no need of this weapon. It is mine alone to give, though Telsidor denied me that right so many ages ago. Consider your oath to me kept and Forsetae a sign of my respect. I only ask you think of me and my kind should you reach Kalmindon. We grow weary of being trapped in this world."

"Thank you, King Eleazar," Umhra said, grateful to have Forsetae back in his possession, "You have proven yourself a great ally, and I shall never forget your graciousness. I promise to do what I can on your behalf should the day come."

King Eleazar nodded, his form fading, leaving Umhra alone in the forge room with its antiquities.

His task completed, Umhra left the forge room and made his way back upstairs to the tower's main doors, Forsetae lighting his path. The Paladins of Antiikin appeared as Umhra walked, forming a line on either side of the great hall. They held their swords high.

My brothers come to bid me farewell. Forsetae said. *They have not forgotten me after all these years.*

Umhra came before the enormous doors, stopped. He turned to face the Paladins, thrust Forsetae into the air.

"The spirit of Antiikin lives on," the apparitions bellowed in unison.

"The spirit of Antiikin lives on," Umhra said, nodding.

The ghosts vanished, leaving Umhra and Forsetae alone once more. Umhra turned his attention back to the door. Placing his shoulder against its smooth jade surface, he pushed the door open and stepped out into the frigid evening air. Umhra closed the door behind him.

Splinter waited a few feet from where Umhra had left him, digging at the snow with a hoof. Umhra eyed the tower, squinting against the falling sun.

As he approached his steed, the rhythmic beat of his heart resonated in his right ear. He rubbed the ear, exercising his jaw back and forth in an effort to rid himself of the annoyance. With the persistence of an Orc drummer leading an army into battle, the thrum continued.

He climbed upon his saddle and the pulsing faded. He turned Splinter in a full circle. The thrumming in his ear amplifying and fading as though it were the needle of a compass. Could this be Spara, the Mystic, calling out to him as King Eleazar had foretold? There was only one way to find out.

"We head north," he said, pulling the reins to the left. "We'll make camp once we put some distance between us and Antiikin."

Splinter snorted and trod forward.

The pair rode out of the fields and back onto Mirina's Path, turning onto Englen Penn Way toward Vanyareign. All the while the persistent rhythm grew in Umhra's ear.

CHAPTER 2

Within its confines, I can never be found. Here I may pursue my work undisturbed.

—*Entry from Aldresor's Journal*
Undated. Discovered in the Tower of Is' Savon, month of Riet, 1444 AT

Alessa Elmont lounged in an oversized canopy bed surrounded by plush canary-yellow pillows and billowing silk curtains. She had grown accustomed to life within the confines of Castle Forene but now, nine-months pregnant, Cleric Dynava had prescribed bed rest due to Alessa's proclivity for early contractions and dizzying headaches. She had taken to embroidery to pass the time, but she found time did not pass quickly enough. The grey stone walls of her ample bedroom seemed to be slowly closing in on her.

Alessa had enjoyed her pregnancy despite not loving King Arving and receiving no love from him in return. Their arrangement was one of practicality—the king needed a healthy heir and Alessa needed a stay of execution for her eldest brother. Only a sovereign could deliver such a reprieve and the king's promise of naming her queen upon the birth of their child was an assurance she could not come by otherwise.

The idea of delivering unto Evelium the next of the Forene bloodline and the possibility of helping sculpt the kingdom's future as its queen had grown on her but neither were her aspirations prior to the king's proposal. She had had other dreams. Dreams of seeing the world outside Vanyareign. Dreams of traveling to far-off continents with exotic cultures and foreign landscapes. Tyveriel offered so much more than this.

Ever since the Barrow's Pact rescued her from the clutches of Varina the Decayer and the Morion Coven, her family was welcomed at court and grew close with the king. Her parents saw it as a means to gain stature for the Elmont name and to marry Alessa off to a wealthy young lord. Unfortunately, her brother, Fineus, saw it as an opportunity to further his penchant for gambling and other untoward behavior. When the broken body of another young aristocrat was found on Castle Forene's battlements with Fineus's dagger lodged between his ribs, Fineus was brought before the Elders Syndicate and sentenced to death by hanging.

A knock on the door snapped Alessa from her ruminations. She pushed herself up in bed and adjusted the pillows behind her. She hastily fixed her tousled ebony hair and folded her hands atop her protruding stomach.

"Come in."

The door swung open, and a guard entered the room. "My Lady." He offered a shallow bow. "The king wishes to join you presently."

"Of course. Please, don't keep him waiting another moment."

The guard stepped aside and stood at attention. King Arving swept in from the hallway. His skin was fair and his hair was dark, and he possessed the pointed ears and high cheekbones of an Evenese pureblood. He wore emerald green robes and a simple gold circlet that crossed the middle of his forehead.

"That will be all," he said to the guard who bowed and pulled the door closed behind him as he left.

The king turned toward Alessa. "My dear. How are you fairing? Dynava informed me you have been put on bed rest until the child arrives." He came to the side of the bed.

"Yes. Most unfortunate. An abundance of caution, I'm sure. I feel quite well other than the occasional headache."

"Dynava is a knowledgeable cleric. Heed her words. Is there anything we can do to make you more comfortable? I hope your midwife is attending to your needs."

"She is. And the chambermaids have been most attentive." She stifled a yawn.

"I am a bit bored, however." She held her current embroidery project toward him. It was a delicate patch of foxglove, pink and lavender flowers arising from a patch of elegant greenery. "There are only so many flowers I can stitch."

The king took the hoop and inspected the design on the stretched almond-colored fabric. "You have a natural ability. I would not have the patience for it, myself. How would you like to hear a story? Maybe it would break the monotony a bit."

Alessa was surprised by the gesture. She shifted over on the bed to make room for the king. "That would be lovely."

King Arving placed the embroidery hoop on the bedside table and sat beside Alessa. He took one of her hands in his and stroked it. His touch was kind, gentle. Alessa drew in a deep breath and exhaled slowly, allowing herself to relax.

"Have you heard the Legend of the Grey Queen?" King Arving asked.

"I have, my Lord. My parents told me when I was I child. I should think every child in Evelium has been frightened by that tale."

The king smiled. "Excellent. I would like to share with you the truth behind the legend."

Alessa felt a flutter in her chest. She leaned toward King Arving and gazed into his chestnut eyes.

The king cleared his throat. "As you know, the Legend of the Grey Queen harkens back to the Age of Grace when gods walked Tyveriel with the mortal races. It was told that one day, men would inherit Tyveriel and usher in an age of tranquility and prosperity. This age would continue until the birth of the Grey Queen who would set civilization as we know it ablaze and bring mankind to its knees."

"Yes. I know the legend well."

"Of course. But what you don't know . . . what so few outside the Forene family know is, on the day of his coronation, Modig Forene, the father of Evelium, hosted a great banquet to celebrate the onset of a new age and share his vision for Evelium with his most trusted advisors. Amidst the ceremony and merriment, the banquet was interrupted by a powerful fate who appeared from thin air in the middle of the great hall. The room was captivated as this ancient witch in tattered black trinket covered robes perused the room. When her gaze settled upon Modig Forene, she pointed a crooked finger and beckoned him toward her. He strode forth and met her in the center of the great room, surrounded by his closest confidants. It was then she cursed him for his transgressions against the wild things of Evelium during the War of Dominion. As recompense for the death he wrought to end the Age of Chaos, neither he nor his descendants would ever sire a healthy daughter. This is the reason the Forene line of kings is just that. A line of kings devoid of queens and princesses. Every female child born to the family has died. In essence, they were each grey queens. You see . . . the tale your parents told you is a metaphor for the curse upon my family which lasts to this day."

"What of your sister?"

King Arving sighed. "A most delicate subject I implore you to keep between us."

"Of course." Alessa leaned further toward the king, her round stomach interfering.

"Jenta does not bear the Mark of Forene. My father so

desperately wanted a daughter which he knew he could never have. In fact, he was so desperate that he arranged for my mother to conceive in secret by another sire, with the hope she would have a girl. All of Evelium celebrated Jenta's birth . . . the one and only Forene princess. Outside of myself, and now you, only the Elders Syndicate is aware of her illegitimacy."

Alessa's mind whirred. "And why do you share this sensitive information with me now?"

"Partly to entertain you in your current state, partly to share with you a secret I've never been able to express, and partly to guide you in prayer for the birth of a healthy son. I'm afraid that if our child is a girl, she will be stillborn, or worse."

Alessa's stomach knotted at the thought, but she feigned a smile. "Worry not. This baby kicks me with a vengeance. Here . . . feel." She placed the king's hand on her belly. The baby thumped within her.

A smile of true delight spread across King Arving's face.

"If you tap my belly, he will tap back. I have no doubt he will be a great king like his forefathers."

"Tap your belly?"

"Is the king shy?" Alessa asked coyly. "Yes, tap my belly."

King Arving raised a finger and tapped. The baby kicked the same spot in reply.

"Oh, he is fierce! A warrior! He possesses the spirit of a Forene."

"Did you expect anything less? The child is your heir."

The king nodded, withdrew his palm from Alessa's stomach. "It is getting late. I should let you rest."

"You are welcome to spend the night. I would enjoy the company."

"Thank you. I'm afraid Cleric Dynava would not approve of me keeping you any later than I already have. You need your strength. I will check on you in the morning." King Arving stood and strode for the door.

"My King?" Alessa asked as he opened the door. "Any news

of my brother?"

King Arving kept his back toward Alessa. "His guards have been instructed to treat him as they would the brother of their queen. Should all go well with the child, he shall be released as soon as my heir is named. I will keep my promise as you have kept yours."

"Thank you. I hate to think of him languishing in the dungeon for a crime he's adamant he did not commit. He has many faults, but murder is not among them."

"Please, don't trouble your mind about such things now. Focus on your health and that of our child. All else will be seen to in good time."

Alessa nodded. It was impossible for her not to think of Fineus and his freedom being held over her head. The birth of her child and her brother's fate were inextricably intertwined. For nearly a year, he'd been locked in a cell awaiting the gallows. She hoped he knew how much she sacrificed on his behalf. That, maybe, his time imprisoned would not be in vain but rather he would redirect his life toward virtue.

"Good night, Alessa." King Arving slipped through the doorway leaving her alone.

"Good night, My King."

Alessa's head ached. The room spun. Frustrated, she threw herself back against the pillows. She too was imprisoned. This room was her dungeon, this bed her cell, this child her sentence. Hopefully, it would all be worth it in the end.

CHAPTER 3

*Inexplicably, the boy . . . this Adyti as the Elandrians call him,
could transform matter at his will. I would not have believed
it if I hadn't seen it myself.*

—*A Traveler's Guide to the Odd and Obscure by Sentina Vake*
Chapter 23 – Unearthed from the Homestead in Maryk's Cay,
month of Riet, 1407 AT

—▲—

Umhra slowed Splinter to a trot as they entered Travesty's
east gate. He had not returned to the city where he grew
up since the death of his adoptive father, Ivory Lapping, and
had no intention of ever doing so until King Eleazar told him of
Spara's presence and the thrumming in his ear drew him back
home. The pulsing had grown with every stride Splinter took
toward Travesty and now resonated in his mind as an almost
deafening roar. He dismounted, favoring to walk the streets,
and tread to the temple where he once lived.

Umhra paused at the temple gate—a flood of memories
rushing back to him. He could envision his younger self running
across the courtyard, several monks chasing him as he laughed.
A smile broke across his face—such a simple time. He sighed
and then looped Splinter's reins around a fence post.

"I hope this won't take long," he said, patting the side of Splinter's neck. "Behave yourself."

Umhra had forgotten how bitterly cold it could get this far north into the province of Winterashe. Umhra's cloak billowed in the frigid breeze as a light flurry of snow fell. He shook off the chill and crossed the empty courtyard to the heavy wooden doors leading to the nave, snow crunching beneath his feet. He opened the doors and welcomed the burst of warm air that hit his face. He drew in a deep breath and entered the temple.

The temple was as quiet as he remembered. There were rows of pews on either side of a central aisle, and a myriad of candles dripped wax on the stone floor. Several people sat toward the front of the nave, praying before the large wrought iron triangle suspended from the vaulted ceiling high overhead.

Umhra threw back his hood and strode to a young monk who had just entered from the east transept. Noticing the half-Orc's approach, the monk stiffened his spine and cleared his throat.

"May I help you?" He asked in a soft voice that feigned acceptance.

"Can you let Father Rius know Umhra the Peacebreaker seeks an audience with him? He will know the name."

"Know the name? I should say so," the young monk said a bit too loudly. The others within the church glared back at him. A broad smile broke across his face. "The older fathers still share stories of you whenever something causes a disturbance on temple grounds," he whispered.

"I suppose I left an impression then," Umhra said. "Could you fetch Father Rius for me? I'm here with urgency."

"Right away. Please make yourself comfortable until I return."

The monk left by the door through which he had entered. Umhra untied his cloak, placed it on a pew, and sat beside it. He shut his eyes and gave himself a moment of peace. In the temple's quiet, the steady pulsing returned to his right ear. He rubbed his temple, hoping the nuisance would abate, but it persisted—a slow, rhythmic thrumming.

"Brother Umhra," the monk said. "Father Rius will see you presently."

"Thank you," Umhra said, the pulsing fading into the background. He followed the monk out of the nave and down a long window-lined hallway connecting the temple proper to the monastery's dorter. They continued up a narrow flight of candlelit stairs and into a quaint library.

"Father Rius will be here shortly. Please make yourself at home. I must get back to my duties."

"Thank you, brother."

"Think nothing if it. I was happy to help, Brother Umhra." The monk left Umhra in the library.

Umhra walked the perimeter of the room, perusing the books that filled the oak shelves lining its walls. Two large windows gave the library an airy feel, uncharacteristic of most he had visited. He ran his fingers across a multitude of leather bindings and thought of the last time he had been in this very room.

Ivory sat alone at the oval table in the middle of the room. He hunched over a book as Umhra bound in to get him, as it was past time for their daily training session.

"Umhra, before we go downstairs, come and sit with me for a moment," Ivory said.

Umhra rolled his eyes but obliged, sitting in the chair beside his adoptive father.

"This book," Ivory said, holding an olive-green leather text up for Umhra to see. "I have just finished studying it for the ninth or tenth time. It is a compilation of ancient texts and my own learnings. In the future, it will prove invaluable to you. When you do not know how to proceed, return here and read it."

"What's it called?" Umhra asked.

"It does not have a name. It is safer that way. It will only

have meaning for you and only when the time is right."

"Umhra," Father Rius said, entering the room. "My you have filled out nicely."

Umhra snapped away from the wall of books he was staring at and greeted Father Rius with a broad smile. "Father Rius, it's wonderful to see you. I'm glad to see the years have been kind to you."

The tall Evenese man approached and put his hands on Umhra's shoulders, inspecting him with hazel eyes. "It seems Brother Ivory was right. You were destined to become a good man. I dare say great. I can read it on your face."

"Thank you, Father. I trust all is well with you?"

"I have no complaints other than the normal aches and pains that come with age. And those, I choose to look at as a reminder of all the blessings the gods have bestowed upon me. Otherwise, Travesty continues to grow and our flock along with it."

"That's good news," Umhra said.

"Tell me, son. What brings you back to us unannounced on this frosty morning? Is everything alright?"

"A book, actually. One from my father's collection. I thought of it recently and was wondering if you still had it in your possession."

"Of course. We kept all of Ivory's things in case you should someday come back for them as he hoped. I am glad you have. But you will not find his books in this library. We packed them and all his possessions away in your training room downstairs. Take any of Ivory's belongings you see fit. He bequeathed them all to you."

"Thank you, Father. I shouldn't take up anymore of your time."

"I would offer you an early lunch, but I am needed in the temple for service," Father Rius said. "If you care to spend the night, I welcome you as my guest for dinner."

"I appreciate the offer, but I'm not expecting to stay the

night. Perhaps, if I am still here late in the day, I will change my plans and join you."

"Fair enough." Father Rius smiled. "You remember your way to the undercroft, don't you?"

"Like it was yesterday, Father. It was nice seeing you."

"And you as well, Umhra. May Vaila shine her light upon you."

"She does. And may she for you as well."

Father Rius left the room, his long tan robes dragging behind him. Umhra gave him a moment and then left the library, nearly breaking into a run down the hallway. He hurried down a staircase, past the ground floor, and into the undercroft below. At the base of the stairs was an open door leading down another hallway with three doors along its right wall. He went to the last of the three. His heart raced with childish excitement at the prospect of returning to his old training room.

He grabbed an oil lantern from the wall and threw open the door. He walked inside and closed the door behind him. Other than several crates piled along the wall next to Ivory's desk, nothing had changed.

Umhra looked the room over and recalled all the wonderful times he had within its confines. The rack of silvered weapons he used to practice with still graced the wall behind his training pit. The wood training dummy still stood in the center of the sand-filled pit, awaiting its next battle. Everything was in its place other than Ivory.

Shifting his attention over to the desk and the crates beside it, Umhra forced the memories and emotions that accompanied his returning to this room back into the recesses of his mind and turned toward the future.

The crates were each labeled. Umhra searched the pile until he found one marked *Books*. He moved a couple crates that sat upon it to the side and hauled the heavy crate from its place and rested it on the floor. The lid was nailed shut.

Umhra focused on the rhodium pyramid he wore on full

display around his neck. He searched for his god, Vaila, in his mind and welcomed the surge of warmth that coursed through his body. The etchings of wind currents on the pyramid's sides alit. Vibrant blue ether danced into the air. The pulsing in his right ear returned, this time somewhat more intense than earlier. He shrugged off the annoyance and placed his left hand at the top corner of the crate. Summoning Forsetae to his hand, he sheared the lid of the crate from the base.

Umhra opened his hand and the blade vanished as quickly as it had appeared. He tossed the lid aside and removed some straw packed atop the crate's contents. He lifted out the first handful of books and placed them on the ground beside him. Checking their bindings, all were titled, none matched the muted olive tone he recalled. He reached back into the crate, retrieving a second stack of books. Still, no matches. After a third stack also disappointed, Umhra stomach churned. He tore into the rest of the books, casting aside one after another. Digging through the straw at the bottom of the empty crate, his hand brushed over one last book which he had missed in his frenzy. It was olive-green and had an unmarked binding just as Umhra remembered.

With a sigh of relief, he leaned against a stone pillar and slid to the ground, staring at the drab cover. He eagerly leafed through the pages. To his initial surprise, they were all blank. He worked his lower lip over one of his tusks, closed the book and focused again on his icon. The pyramid glowed a vibrant blue and a matching symbol appeared on the book's cover. Umhra reopened the book, and the words inscribed on its discolored pages coalesced before him.

My Dearest Umhra,

If you are reading these words, my soul has departed Tyveriel and you have achieved your Rhodium Suffusion. I cannot tell you how proud I am to have had the opportunity to be your father, even though only through adoption. From the moment I saw you at the edge of Wicked's Pass, I knew you were capable of things the rest of Tyveriel would not understand and, eventually, your path would move beyond the knowledge of man. As such, I compiled as many learnings as I could from the ancient texts relating to Mysticism. It is far from complete but should point you in the right direction. I hope in a direction toward the only other of your kind still on Tyveriel. Begin your search at Ember's Watch, where the Mystics convened on the eve of their ascension. I wish you luck, my son. I miss you.

Love, Ivory

Hot tears ran down Umhra's face as he read. Then, the knowledge that Ivory understood his destiny all those years ago eased his aching heart. He sat on the cold stone floor for several hours, taking in the contents of *Ivory's Nameless Tome,* as it would come to be known, and knew what he needed to do next.

Closing the book, Umhra placed it on the desk along with his cloak and repacked the rest of the books he had pulled from the crate. He returned the crate to its place along the wall, covering it with its damaged lid and the other crates he had moved to the side. He put his cloak around his shoulders and slipped the book into one of its ample interior pockets.

Umhra took one last look about the room and drew in a deep breath, as if to fill himself with the scents of his past. He retrieved the oil lamp, pulled the door shut, and returned the oil lamp to its mount on the wall.

He bound up the stairs and through the dorter. He found the monk who had summoned Father Rius for him earlier. The monk was joined by three others all dressed in taupe robes. They chattered like school children. One of the monks tapped him on the arm as Umhra approached, and gestured toward him with a tilt of his head.

"Brother Umhra," the monk said. "May I help you with something else today?" The other monks stood aside, eyes wide.

Umhra looked them over. Nodded. "Um. Yes. I need to get message to Anaris. Does the temple still have birds for such purposes?"

"Of course. I'd be happy to facilitate. Please, follow me. Although I'm sure you know the way."

"I'll follow your lead, if it's all the same."

The monk marched forward, a sense of purpose in his steps.

"You broke the wall in my room." One of the monks blurted out excitedly. "Crack's still there."

Umhra nodded, bit his bottom lip. "Sorry about that. I broke a lot of things when I lived here. I must be going."

He hurried from the room to catch up with his guide who was holding a door open down the hall. As Umhra neared, the monk entered a stairwell cloaked in shadow. He climbed the stairs with Umhra a step behind.

"As I'm sure you recall, the birds are kept in the north tower. The church uses them to communicate between our disparate locations. We have several that regularly fly between here and Anaris."

"I'll just be needing the use of one."

"Of course."

They came to a landing and walked out into the open air of what looked like a bell chamber. An arched window spanning each of the tower's walls allowed for excellent views of Travesty and beyond. Instead of a bell at the chamber's center there were six cages on a worn wood table, each filled with mourning doves. The birds cooed vigorously as the men approached.

The monk opened a cage door and picked a bird with a blue ribbon wrapped around one of its ankles. "You can write your message on one of those strips of parchment. He can set flight once we bind it to his ankle."

Umhra took a slip of parchment from a bowl on the table

beside the cages and plucked a quill from the adjacent ink jar.

Laudin

– In Travesty.

On my way to Ember's Watch.

I need your help.

Meet me there when you can.

U.

The monk removed the ribbon from the bird's ankle, coiled Umhra's message around the ankle, and affixed it with the ribbon. He then walked to the east-facing archway and released the bird.

Umhra watched as the bird flew from site toward Anaris, its wings whistling.

CHAPTER 4

Her psychosis deepening, Spara was locked away. She had become a danger to herself and others.

—*The Tome of Mystics*
Unknown Origin. Unearthed from the Ruins of Oda Norde, month of Bracken, 1320 AT

—▲—

Alessa threw herself against the plush yellow pillows piled high at her back and wiped the sweat from her brow with the back of her hand. A dim candlelight flickered at the bedside, underlighting the chambermaids dressed in ochre robes that buzzed about the room. For the delivery, they wore fitted wimples that only allowed their faces to show which gave them an air of superiority. Another woman sat on a wooden cross frame chair in the far corner, her legs crossed beneath a forest green gown.

"I can't do it." Alessa huffed, a stab of pain in her lower back.

"What choice do you have, child?" The woman sitting in the corner picked at a bothersome fingernail. "You've come this far and must deliver to the king a healthy heir."

Alessa buried her face in her hands and wiped away the

tears. Her entire body longed for the labor to end.

Her midwife came to her side and stroked her hand. "You're almost done, my Lady," She had a kind face that poked out from under her wimple, which buttoned below her chin. Her robes were a stark white with ornate silver embroidery on the cuffs of her sleeves. "One more push and we should see the child's head."

Alessa felt a surge of energy from the words of encouragement. The last twelve hours had been so overwhelming . . . exhausting, but finally, there was a glimmer of hope the travail would soon be over. She took a deep breath, pushed a tangle of dark hair from her face, and twisted the fine white linens in her hands in anticipation of the next contraction.

The cramp began in her lower back, spreading around her sides and into her abdomen. Her body compelled her to push. She bore down, the pain growing in concert with her effort.

"I can see the child, my Lady."

Alessa fell back against the pillow, her lungs burning as she struggled to catch her breath. The pain resumed almost immediately, giving her no time to recover. She scrunched her face and blacked out the room. She pushed again, every muscle in her body trembling, a ring of fire between her legs.

With a final push, the pressure released, and the pain and exhaustion morphed into intense worry as she noticed the silence in the room.

Then, the baby cried. Alessa collapsed against the bed once more, her chest heaving. She buried her face in her hands and sobbed. Her baby's wailing was strong, and Alessa's worry gave way to a rush of butterflies in her stomach.

The midwife gasped.

"What's wrong?" Alessa asked, still breathless from the labor.

"Nothing, my Lady," the midwife said. "You've birthed a healthy daughter." She waved for the woman seated in the corner to join her.

Cleric Dynava stepped into the light, revealing a gold icon around her neck. It was in the shape of a diamond, with a unique symbol engraved on each of its eight facets. "Ladies, may we have a moment, please?"

The swarm of chambermaids dropped what they were doing and filed out of the room.

The child's crying continued.

Alessa craned her neck to catch a glimpse of the newborn. Cleric Dynava positioned herself between Alessa and the midwife, blocking her view.

"Why won't you let me see her?" Alessa asked. She had never felt so protective of anything in her life, and she had not even yet laid eyes on her child.

The midwife wrapped the baby in a navy-blue blanket and held her up to the cleric. Cleric Dynava chewed on her bottom lip. She placed one hand on the child's head and the other on her icon. She closed her eyes and a bright light surrounded them, causing a nervous Alessa to shield her eyes.

The light dissipated . . . the crying ceased. The cleric and the midwife huddled around the child and continued to obstruct Alessa's view. Alessa pushed herself up on her palms to get a sense of what was wrong, but her arms gave out, and she sunk back into the bed. The women whispered to one another out of Alessa's earshot.

"I will inform the king of the child's birth," Cleric Dynava said, shaking her head and striding for the door.

The midwife, still holding the swaddled infant, turned to Alessa. "My Lady, I present to you, your daughter. She is healthy despite her complexion."

The midwife approached—Alessa wiping the sweat from her eyes—and leaned in to show Alessa her daughter. Amidst the sea of blue, the baby slept, her mouth open, a hand smooshing her grey cheek. The child's eyelids were ringed in black and the hair caked to the side of her face was raven-blue.

Alessa gasped, held the midwife at bay with an open palm.

"What's wrong with her? Is it some sort of illness?"

"Cleric Dynava assured me the baby is not ill. She does not, however, know precisely how to explain the child's peculiarities."

"What does that mean?"

"It means, you have a healthy daughter who needs her mother. Don't concern yourself with anything else at the moment. A mother does not have the luxury of choosing her challenges."

Alessa dropped her hand and smiled. "You're right. May I hold her?"

"Of course, my Lady." The midwife placed the bundle of blue in the crook of Alessa's arm. The baby yawned.

Alessa peaked beneath the blanket at the infant's chest.

"There is no need for modesty. A good mother knows every inch of their child's body."

Alessa nodded and unwrapped the blanket revealing a tiny grey body. She placed her hand on the infant's chest and felt her heartbeat, her chest rising and falling with each breath. Alessa stroked the baby's cheek and carefully inspected her hands and feet. Alessa then swaddled her baby in the blanket, loose edges everywhere.

"No, like this, my Lady." The midwife showed Alessa how to fold the blanket snuggly around the baby. "They like to feel secure."

Alessa nodded, her gaze not leaving the baby's ashen face, which stood in stark contrast to the warm bronze of the arm that cradled her. The child's eyes blinked open, revealing golden pupilless irises. Alessa tilted her head, smiled. "She's beautiful!"

"Yes, my Lady, she's quite unique," the midwife said. "Now is a good time to see if she will take to the breast."

"Of course," Alessa said. She unlaced the top of her gown, exposing her left breast, and brought her child close. The baby's mouth opened, her head wagging from side-to-side.

She latched on to her mother and suckled. Alessa smiled again, tilting toward the midwife to boast.

"A natural, my Lady. You will serve your daughter well. Cleric Dynava has gone to fetch the king."

"The king." Alessa suddenly felt as though an anvil sat on her chest. "I had forgotten about the king. He won't be happy. He'll think she's cursed."

"Cursed? Why cursed? What have you done?"

"What have I done?" Alessa could not believe the accusatory tone in the midwife's voice and answered with a bite in her words. "All I've done is keep my promise to the king and provide him the heir he so desperately desires."

The midwife took a step back from the bed and averted her eyes from the would-be queen.

The door creaked open and Cleric Dynava entered the room, her cheeks flushed. "The king is on his way. Prepare your child, my Lady."

Alessa sat upright and re-laced her gown. She dabbed the baby's mouth with the edge of her sleeve, cradled her in her left arm, and righted herself on the bed to sit as tall as possible. Cleric Dynava and the midwife stood on opposite sides of the bed, their hands folded, facing the door.

The fleeting moment seemed like an eternity, Alessa's stomach a twisted ball of nerves. The door swung open, revealing two guards standing against the stone wall on the far side of the hallway. Around the corner came King Shale Arving. He wore auburn robes trimmed with gold and his circlet across his forehead. His eyes were glossy, hopeful, and he brandished a prideful smile. One of his guards pulled the door closed behind him.

"Alessa, my dear," he said. "How are you?"

Cleric Dynava and the midwife bowed. Alessa nodded along with them.

"I am well, my King. Thank you for your concern. Would you like to see our child?"

"I would," King Arving said. "Dynava told me she has a distinctive quality to her. Much like we discussed the other night."

"She does, my King." Alessa placed the child on the bed beside her. Her hands shook as she unwrapped the baby to show the king his daughter's full body.

King Arving approached the bed and stared down at the child. He rolled her over on her stomach, inspecting her back. At the nape of her neck there was a faint birthmark resembling the shape of an outstretched raptor's talon. He ran his finger over the mark and then returned the child to her back. He rubbed his cheek and sighed. "She bears the Mark of Forene . . . the same birthmark each of Evelium's rulers has shared with Modig Forene, himself."

"I am told she is healthy." Alessa's voice cracked. Never had she felt so much hang in the balance. She knew a daughter with grey skin was exactly what the king feared—that he would be beholden to his family's ridiculous fairytale. How could something so helpless and sweet bring about the reckoning of such entrenched power?

"I am pleased to hear it." The king's frown contradicted the sentiment. "I am, however, unable to name your child as my heir. The entire kingdom as well as the rest of the continent would be sent into an uproar should I offer them a future queen with her peculiarity."

"You mean our child, my King," Alessa said, her jaw clenched. "You would be so weak as to deny your heir her place based on a myth and the color of her skin?"

"My Lady, that is no way to speak to your king," Cleric Dynava said.

King Arving held his hand in the air to stifle the cleric's protest. "It's okay, Dynava. She deserves a moment of candor. My dear, there is nothing wrong with the child. She is quite beautiful in her own way, but I will not be the king that risks bringing about our reckoning by my seed. How I wish it could be different. How I wish I could love her."

"She's not the first, is she?" A fury welled up within Alessa. "This has happened before."

"Yes. You are not at fault. It would seem my very seed is corrupted as the legend foretold. The Forene Dynasty dies with me."

"You would prefer the certitude of your family's rule ending over the possibility our daughter is the fabled Grey Queen?"

"I would." King Arving hung his head. "I do not expect you to understand. Thank you for all you have done. Your brother shall be released as promised and absolved of his crimes." He turned and walked for the door.

"What's in store for us, then?" Alessa asked. The king opened the door and paused in the threshold. Then, without a word, he departed.

"I don't understand," Alessa said, looking up at Cleric Dynava and the midwife, neither of whom would meet her gaze. "Can either of you explain this superstitious idiocy?"

"My Lady," the midwife said after a long silence, "I don't pretend to understand the ways of kings and their politics. I have, however, always known King Arving to be a just man. I'm sure he will treat you both with the utmost care. We will leave you to bond with your child. You did well today and should be proud."

Both women exited the room, leaving Alessa on the bed with her infant daughter. Alessa stared at the door, her mouth agape. The baby cried. Alessa scooped her up, swaddled her as the midwife had shown, and embraced her.

"We are going to have to look out for each other," she said. "It doesn't seem anyone else will."

CHAPTER 5

*Knowing we have but one chance, we travel to our Waystones
and hope for salvation.*

—*The Tome of Mystics*
Unknown Origin. Unearthed from the Ruins of Oda Norde,
month of Bracken, 1320 AT

—▲—

Laudin sat on a windowsill of his quarters at Peacebreaker Keep, one eye on the nascent morning and the other on Naivara, who slept tangled in his bedding. The hour was early, and the moon still shone, although fading against the burgeoning sun. The Iminti ranger rubbed the scar that ran the length of his cheek. Below, a dense fog rolled across the property and rendered the surrounding gardens with their marble statues of the Bloodbound, Umhra's fallen band of half-Orc sellswords, but a memory.

Taivaron, Laudin's faithful harrier companion, had woken him up before he was ready, chirping at the window as he was known to do when desiring an early-morning hunt. Laudin's mind was plagued by Umhra's prolonged absence and, this morning, his worry kept him from returning to the warmth of his bed. Umhra had set out for Antiikin over a month ago, insisting on going alone—something he did more and more frequently since completing his Rhodium Suffusion and becoming a Mystic. It was as though he realized his destiny lie on a path apart from his friends and distanced himself intentionally. Laudin was not ready to let him go.

From through the mist, Taivaron appeared. Fog spiraling from his form with every beat of his wings. The raptor approached with his quarry clutched in his claws. Laudin held out his arm and welcomed the familiar pinch of Taivaron's talons, and brought the bird within the room.

"What did you find there boy? Looks like you won't need to hunt again for days."

Taivaron picked at the feathers of a mourning dove. A strip of parchment was bound to the dove's ankle by a blue ribbon.

Laudin returned Taivaron to his perch and untied the thread. The ranger read the note and embraced the butterflies which always fluttered in his stomach at the onset of a new adventure. He'd never been to Ember's Watch. The only known ruin of the Mystics predated Antiikin and was a treacherous and cursed place. Nobody in their right mind would go there willingly. Nobody except Umhra and the Barrow's Pact.

Taivaron picked more feathers from the dove and chirped. Laudin smiled. "Yes, you did well. I'm sure the church has other messengers. There's no telling how long it would have taken them to get this to us if you hadn't interceded."

"Have you finally heard from Umhra?" Naivara asked, leaning on an elbow so her auburn hair cascaded onto the bed, a pointed ear poking out from between her locks. The Reshinta might not have been deemed a beauty by her own people, but to Laudin there was no more beautiful woman in the world.

"Yes. Finally. He's been gone for too long. His note says he made his way to Travesty and now wishes for us to meet him at Ember's Watch."

"That explains the grin on your face. A new and dangerous place to explore."

"Seeing you explains the grin on my face. I worry for Umhra. He journeys into uncharted waters. Those ruins haven't been inhabited since the Age of Grace. Who knows what terrible things lurk there, attracted to its magic."

"I think Umhra can take care of himself. He's far more powerful than the rest of us combined. And possibly, any creature on Tyveriel."

"And he attracts that much more trouble, as a result, it seems."

Naivara laughed, her freckled nose scrunching. "Very true. What do you think he wants at Ember's Watch?"

"He likely seeks knowledge of the Mystics of old. I would do the same if I were in his situation. I can't imagine being so much in the dark about my destiny. If his quest brought him back to Travesty, I'm not sure he'd see Ember's Watch as being any worse."

"Well, he has a long trip ahead of him if he comes from Travesty. Let's talk with Gromley, Shadow, and Nicholas and make arrangements to set out this afternoon."

"Agreed. That should put us outside the ruins a day or so before him," Laudin said, sauntering bedside.

Naivara smiled and lifted the sheets as an invitation. "We have a bit of a journey ahead of us as well. Come back to bed and get some rest . . . at least until the sun fills the room."

"As you wish, My Lady." Laudin climbed back beneath the covers and nestled up against Naivara, her warmth in stark contrast to the surrounding room. He kissed her lips and closed his eyes, welcoming the weight of her weary head on his chest.

▲

Gromley and Shadow were finishing breakfast when Laudin and Naivara joined them downstairs in the dining room. Shadow was dressed in black leathers from head-to-toe, his stark white hair shorn close at the sides and left long on top. His ashen skin gleamed in the sunlight streaking in through the eastern window and his lilac eyes glimmered with their usual sense of mischief. He leaned back in his chair, his feet elevated on the table before him. "So, what kind of mess are you getting us into this time?" he asked, absently flipping a dagger in the air and catching it.

"What makes you ask that?" Laudin asked.

"We know you well enough, Laudin," Shadow said. "You have that look in your eye. The one that's only there when we are heading out into the wild . . . toward the unknown. Toward danger."

"I didn't know I was that transparent."

"It's really something you should work on."

"I've received word from Umhra. He needs us to meet him at Ember's Watch."

"For Anar's sake," Gromley said, chewing a last piece of bacon as he stroked his ebony beard. The Zeristar cleric was notably shorter than his dining partner but what he lacked in height, he made up for with strong, broad shoulders. "Did he say what he wants with that insidious place?"

"No. The message arrived from Travesty early this morning. It said nothing more than he would need our help."

"Then, we should probably leave as soon as possible," Naivara said, making herself a quick plate of food and sitting down at a chair flooded by the early morning sun to join Gromley and Shadow. "But, where's Nicholas? He should have a say in this."

"He's out back readying to head into Anaris to see his brother," Shadow said, "They were planning to have lunch. You better catch him before he leaves. There's no telling how long that lunch could go."

Laudin plucked a few strips of bacon from a pewter platter and jammed one in his mouth. "I'll have the horses readied in anticipation of our departure while I'm out there. Prepare to move out."

Laudin left the keep through the rear door in the kitchen,

barely noticing the help who each wished him good morning as he passed. He had been feeling idle, spending so much time here since King Arving bestowed the restored Telsidor's Keep upon the Barrow's Pact after they returned triumphant from Meriden. He was eager to travel—to once again find adventure rather than responsibility. From across the expansive yard, he waved to the stable hand to get her attention.

"Miara, has Nicholas departed yet?"

"No, my Lord. He's still in the stables. You know how he likes to talk with Munch before they head out on the road."

Laudin smiled. "I do. While I have you, would you ready the other horses? We are to set off as soon as practicable."

"Yes, my Lord. I was just preparing to take Kimbal out for a ride. I suppose Lady Naivara will handle that then?"

"She will."

Miara nodded and went back to her chores as Laudin hurried for the stables. Opening the stable door, the smell of hay and manure filled his nostrils. From the farthest stall he could hear the murmurs of a one-sided conversation. He approached.

"It's only lunch. I don't know why you need to make such a big deal about it."

Laudin peaked over the stall door to see Nicholas Barnswallow reclined in the hay beside his speckled pony, Munch, who snorted and stomped obstinately. No larger than an eight-year-old human boy, the Farestere's tangle of red hair was littered with straw.

"Sorry to interrupt," Laudin said, resting his arms atop the stall door. "We received word from Umhra this morning. He needs our assistance."

Nicholas popped up from the straw. "I'm glad you interrupted. Munch wasn't really in the mood for the trip to Anaris anyway. I can be ready to leave within the hour. Nathaniel will understand."

"I thought you would be so inclined. I'll fill you in on the road. The others are already making their preparations."

Munch nickered.

"Well, that's what you get for complaining about going to Anaris for lunch. Off on another adventure we go. I'm sure I'll be needing the saddle bags."

The pony snorted.

In agreement, Laudin and Nicholas returned to the keep, Laudin heading directly for the armory and Nicholas to his room. Gromley's war hammer greeted Laudin as it hung on the far wall of the ample armory, resting on two iron brackets. Laudin slung his quiver over his shoulder and grabbed his bow. He ran his fingers along the string to ensure its quality. Convinced of its condition, he gathered his scimitar and a few other items from about the room.

He reconvened with the rest of the Barrow's Pact, or at least what was left of it—with Umhra off on the his own and Talus having returned to duty in service of King Arving. Laudin was so proud of this adventuring party that had come together by happenstance and stayed together by choice. They had done great things for Evelium and, no doubt, would do much more.

They raided the kitchen, stuffing their satchels with provisions for the journey ahead. Their preparations complete, they went out to the yard where the horses were now waiting, saddled and eager to begin a new adventure.

The Barrow's Pact mounted their steeds and rode for Ember's Keep.

CHAPTER 6

The pestilence ravaged the cities of the north. Nary a soul
could be found that wasn't affected by its deadly touch.

—*The Gatekeeper's Abridged History of Tyveriel*
Vol. 1, Chapter 1 – Unearthed from the Ruins of Meriden, the
month of Anar, 1217 AT

—▲—

A week had passed since Alessa gave birth to a healthy,
but admittedly unique, heir to the Raptor's Throne. Her
daughter bore the Mark of Forene and yet, there were no
celebrations of the child's arrival nor mention of her great
future as ruler of Evelium. In fact, nobody had the care to even
ask Alessa the baby's name.

Only her chambermaids came to her room, and then only to
tend to her most basic needs. Even her midwife, who had been
so supportive during her pregnancy, had vanished without a
trace. She was entirely alone with her infant . . . locked in her
room within Castle Forene which she had grown to despise.

She had not seen or heard from King Arving since the night
of the delivery when he so plainly shared his disappointment
with the daughter she bore. She had no communication with
the outside world and was unsure if her parents knew what

became of her or that they were grandparents.

At least, she was feeling better. The bleeding had stopped and her energy had returned. She was able to get out of bed and exercise when the baby was sleeping. She'd had enough embroidery to last her a lifetime.

A part of her still hoped King Arving would reconsider his position and come seeking forgiveness, welcoming them both into his life and sharing their daughter with the world. But she knew better. Her situation was less than ideal and she was the only one who could do anything about it.

She paced the room, unable to sleep as her mind ruminated upon her options. The tinny clanking of armor neared her door from down the long hallway outside. It was well into the early hours of morning, and the guards were changing shifts. She put an ear to the door to eavesdrop on any conversation the guards might have in the process.

"Well, aren't you lucky," the guard outside her door said to the other as they approached. "You drew the short straw, didn't yah?"

"Yeah. I'll have nothing to do but stand outside this door until breakfast. Gonna make for a long night. Where you off to?"

"I'm off until tomorrow. Maybe, I'll hang around until Brienna shows up to get breakfast started. Then I'm off to the barracks."

"You haven't given up on her yet? She told yah she wasn't interested."

"Know of anything better to do?"

"Nah. I just hope the king will give the order and put these two out of their misery so we can get on with things."

Alessa leaped back from the door with a start. Her mind whirred. How could she be so blind as to not have seen that her isolation was pretense to the king ridding himself of this nuisance? An unwanted heir . . . an unkept promise. She had to think fast and plan her escape. There was no time to waste.

She looked around the room. Everything came at her too fast. She couldn't focus.

She dashed to the window and threw open the sash. She leaned out, peering down onto the battlements far below. The extraordinary height made her head spin, her stomach twist in knots. She pulled the window closed—not an option.

The only way out was through the door . . . the door which was guarded at all times. She'd tried opening it several times over the past week and, each time, she found it locked from the outside. If she was going to get out, she would need to lure someone in first.

Again, she went to the door and listened. The guard outside whistled off key obviously not concerned anyone would hear.

Alessa went to her wardrobe and retrieved a simple gown of dark green wool. It was far from her favorite but it was warm and practical. She gathered her few belongings and stuffed them into the oversized pockets of a matching cloak which she folded on the foot of her bed.

The baby slept peacefully. Alessa blew out a candle on the table beside the bassinet and removed the candle from the ornate silver candlestick. The molten wax running down its side burned the palm of her hand. She dropped the candle and kicked it out of sight beneath the bassinet. She picked up the candlestick and felt its heft in her hand. Replacing the candlestick on the table, she took a step back and drew in a deep breath to steel her nerves.

Alessa rushed to the door and pounded on it, furiously. "Help," she screamed, her tone shrill with panic. "My baby isn't breathing. Help me. She isn't breathing."

The lock on the door clicked and the door swung open, the guard entering the room. He was tall, with a thick frame and grimy brown hair.

Alessa tugged at the sleeve of his blue tunic. "You must help me. She isn't breathing. Something's wrong."

Far too slowly for a man who cared about the fate of a

newborn child, the guard lumbered to the side of the bassinet and peered down upon the baby. "It seems fine to me. I mean, as fine as the little abomination can be."

Alessa grabbed the candlestick and hit the guard in the back of his head with all the force she could muster. His skull split, blood spraying from a deep gash.

The guard spun around, his hand searching for support on the table beside him. He slid, taking a couple awkward steps along the length of the table, his face twisted in a look that somehow conveyed shock, pain, and anger all at once. "What the fu—"

Alessa swung again, this time connecting with the side of the guard's head just above the temple. His eyes rolled back so only the whites were visible and his body went limp. He fell like a tree succumbing to the ax and hit the floor with a thud.

Alessa stared at him, dropped the bloodied candlestick on the floor. Her baby cried, snapping her out of her trance. She kneeled at the guard's side and removed the keyring and dagger from his belt. She then rushed to the bed, threw the cloak around her shoulders and fastened its clasp at her sternum. Dropping the dagger and keyring into a crowded pocket of her cloak, she retrieved her crying baby and held her close to her chest.

"Shhh. Everything's alright." Her voice trembled. "I need you to be quiet for a bit. Can you do that for me?"

The baby's crying ceased in her mother's arms.

Alessa stepped over the unconscious guard and stalked toward the door. She poked her head out into the hallway, the oil lamps flickering down its length confirming it was empty. Alessa pulled the door closed behind her, locked it, and hurried down the hallway to the spiraling staircase at its end.

She crept down the stairs, careful to stay in the shadows as she passed floor after floor. Coming to a familiar landing she paused and listened as two men spoke around the bend of the stairs. Alessa's heart raced. They were guarding the throne room and blocked her path to the stables and courtyard below.

She doubled back up the steps to the next floor and entered another corridor. To her left, two guards stood at the far end on either side of the entrance to the king's living quarters. That meant there was another stairwell to her right that would place her at the rear of the castle grounds. From there, she could make it to her parents' home. They would know what to do.

With the stairwell in sight, Alessa quickened her pace then froze. A man came up the stairs, his head hung out of sorrow or exhaustion. He had a tall, muscular build and meticulously groomed blond hair. He wore an unassuming set of brown leathers but the sword at his hip spoke to his importance. From its grip, golden eagle wings extended up the base of the blade, and its pommel boasted a flawless sapphire that gleamed in the lamp light.

Alessa ducked into the recess of a doorway and searched the pocket of her cloak for the dagger she took off the unconscious guard. She drew the blade and prayed to the gods the man would pass her by without notice. His steps were heavy and he groaned as if each were a tremendous effort.

He rounded the corner at the doorway, one hand on the back of his neck, and walked into the tip of Alessa's dagger. The delicate point bit into his leathers. He sighed.

"I don't want to hurt you, so take a step back and I'll be on my way." Alessa emerged from the shadows and walked the man backward into the hallway.

In a flash, he grabbed Alessa's wrist, bearing down on a nerve at the base of her thumb. Fire shot through her arm, her fingers went numb, and the dagger clattered to the ground. The man raised his other fist. Alessa winced, anticipating the blow that would end her escape.

"Alessa Elmont?"

His voice was kind, if not confused. He lowered his fist.

Alessa worked up the nerve to look upon him and recognized him as Talus Jochen, a member of the Raptor's Grasp, the special forces division of the king's army, and affiliate of the Barrow's Pact who had saved her from the clutches of the hag, Varina the Decayer, just over two years ago. She felt the blood rush to her cheeks in embarrassment and smiled sheepishly.

"Sir Jochen, I am so very glad to see a familiar face."

"May I ask why you are hiding outside my room in the dark hours of the morning with a dagger and what I can only guess is a baby?"

The absurdity of it would have made her laugh if it were not for the sheer desperation eating her from within. "We're in trouble." Alessa nodded to the child. "We need to get out of this castle . . . out of Vanyareign."

Talus furrowed his brow, his cobalt blue eyes staring into Alessa's. "I can take you to the king in the morning. He will be able to help you."

"No!" Alessa fell to her knees. Her body trembled, she cried freely. "He's exactly who we run from."

Talus peered down the hallway, Alessa's gaze following. Shadows flashed across the cold stone walls.

Talus held out his hand. "Quickly. To my quarters. We can talk there."

Alessa took his hand and allowed him to help her to her feet.

Talus snatched up the fallen dagger and whisked Alessa into his room. He closed the door behind them, careful to control the latch to a soft click.

The room was austere. Other than a map of Evelium on the wall, there was little more than a table with four chairs. Beyond it, there was a modest bedroom.

"Would you like to put the child down and tell me what's going on?"

"No. I'll hold her, if it's all the same to you."

Talus shrugged and pulled a chair back from the table. "I can't offer you anything more comfortable than this."

"It will be fine." Alessa took a seat at the table. "Thank you."

Talus sat across from her and rested his head against the back of his chair. He yawned and rubbed bloodshot eyes. "Go on. I'm all ears."

▲

Talus strode to King Arving's throne room. Rarely was he summoned so early but, this morning, being called upon by the king came as no surprise. He had not slept in two days, having just returned from the city of Requiem on business for the crown, and a nagging headache throbbed behind his eyes.

The two soldiers standing guard at the door stepped aside and saluted on Talus's approach. He returned the salutation, not breaking his stride as he threw the door open and entered the expansive room. Despite the early morning sun streaming through towering windows, the oil lamps remained lit from the night prior.

Talus came to the side of the Raptor's Throne, the golden chair from which each king of Evelium had ruled the kingdom. King Arving sat upon the throne, enveloped by the wings of the great eagle that formed its back, his foot propped up on the head of the blight grasped in one of the eagle's claws. He clasped a heavy leather-bound tome on his lap. Before him stood two guards, sullen expressions on their faces, and one with a blood-stained bandage wrapped around his head.

"You sent for me, my King?" Talus asked.

King Arving held a hand in the air, calling for Talus's silence. He leaned toward the guards before him. "How, exactly, did the young lady manage to render a soldier in the king's army unconscious and escape the castle unnoticed?"

The bloodied guard stared at his feet. "She claimed the child wasn't breathing. I rushed in to provide aid and she caught me off guard."

"As to her escape," the other guard said, "it was the middle of the night. All stations were manned and patrols completed. She, somehow, eluded us . . . or, she's hiding within the castle still. We have called in all available hands to search the grounds. I'm confident we will find her."

"Confident?" King Arving threw his book at the guard. The book tumbled through the air and struck the guard on his shoulder. It fell to the ground, splayed open. "I don't want confidence—I want results. Get out."

The guards bowed and hurried from the throne room, leaving Talus and King Arving alone.

"Talus?" The king beckoned Talus forward, his tone calmer.

"Yes, My King?" The kings' face was gaunt. He looked as tired as Talus felt. The scowl he wore accentuated his Evenese features. "I know you have plans to return to Anaris, but there is a delicate matter I need seen to. A matter so sensitive, I am only comfortable entrusting it to you."

"You know I'm here for you, my Lord. What weighs on you so heavily?"

"I have fathered another child. It has the same, shall we say, idiosyncrasies as the others."

"My condolences, my King. I know how desperately you seek a worthy heir."

"I have given up on that dream. It would seem I'm not destined to sire anything but abominations. The Forene bloodline will default to my bastard cousin and his progeny."

"I can only fathom your struggle with the possibility," Talus said. "What would you have me do to ease your worried mind?"

King Arving's eyes narrowed. "I doubt you can understand anything about my struggle. The weight of my kingdom does not sit upon your shoulders. I would not have you worry about such matters." He sighed. "Regardless, this morning my predicament has complicated further, with the mother having escaped with the child. As I cannot have my heir's existence come to light, I request that you locate the pair and dispose of them. I cannot rule with this threat hanging over me. Also, see to it the cleric and midwife understand that their discretion is of the utmost importance. They are the only others to know of this."

"Not to question your judgment or wishes, my King, but are you sure you wouldn't prefer to preserve the optionality the child offers? It survived the delivery, no?" Talus asked.

"Yet you question both," King Arving said, his tone cold. "If you cannot follow my simple orders, I will have your men attend to my needs and see you relieved of your service to the crown."

"No transgression intended, my King." Talus bowed and stared wide-eyed at the floor. "I'll see to your orders as I always have. Should you want confirmation when I complete the deed?"

"No. Your word shall suffice. Just see to it with expedience. I wish to rid myself of this burden. Now, leave me to my thoughts." King Arving waved Talus out of the throne room.

Talus bowed and withdrew.

Returning to his quarters, he found Alessa and her baby sleeping in his bed where he had left them. He contemplated the risk he took in harboring her. In all his years in service of the king, he had never found himself so torn between duty and morality. He no longer knew where his loyalty should lie—with the king he'd served so faithfully for so many years, or the rightful heir to the Forene bloodline and the Raptor's Throne. He would need time to decide and, in order to have that time, needed to get Alessa and her baby to safety.

Alessa startled awake. She swung her dagger through the empty air and settled on the form moving toward her, the blade shaking.

"It's me. You're safe . . . for now."

Alessa lowered the blade and brushed an errant tangle of hair from her eyes. "Do you believe me now?"

"Unfortunately, yes. The king confirmed both that the child is his and he wants you both dead. He tasked me with hunting you down and carrying out the order, personally."

Alessa squirmed, her skin going pale. "So, what now?"

"Later this morning, I will lead a search party to your parents' home. We will perform a thorough inspection of the property and interrogate your parents. Upon my return, I will notify the king they know nothing of your whereabouts and that we will need to expand our search throughout the city and beyond. Tonight, under cover of darkness, I will get you out of Vanyareign. I believe it safest to get you out of Evelium and start a new life elsewhere in order to ensure your safety and preserve the child's claim to the throne."

"Out of Evelium? New life? I can't believe this is happening."

"Unfortunately, all Evelium holds for you is death," Talus said. "For both you and your daughter."

Alessa's gaze searched Talus's face. He knew too well the wrath of an angry king. He knew there was no victory for Alessa and her baby, only degrees of defeat.

"You are serious?" she asked.

"I've never been more so. Be ready to leave tonight when I return."

CHAPTER 7

I was certain it was him. After two-hundred years, he once again walked among the living. Seeing nothing but fury in his eyes, I fled.

—*Entry from Aldresor's Journal*
Undated. Discovered in the Tower of Is' Savon, month of Riet,
1444 AT
—▲—

Umhra reined Splinter to a halt as Ember's Watch pierced the horizon, the pulsing in his ear growing in the presence of the ruins. Beyond the stone tower of the central keep, a plume of thick grey smoke rose into the air, a streak of black against a clear, dusky sky. He smiled at the thought of reconnecting with the Barrow's Pact. With a gentle kick from his heals, he prodded Splinter into a trot.

Keeping his distance from the ruins, he coursed through the open plains all the while closing in on the overt trail of smoke. He took in the expansive grounds of the watch. Many of the buildings which surrounded the central tower were little more than shells of their former selves. The outer wall was intact, but its two gates had rusted away. A chill ran up his spine.

Laudin was the first to spot Umhra, standing from his seat

beside a fire of fresh pine branches and waiving vigorously. The others joined in but it was Nicholas who ran to greet him. Umhra slowed Splinter and dropped down from his saddle before the young Farestere who crashed into him with a fervent hug around Umhra's waist.

"It's good to see you too, Nicholas." Umhra put an arm around Nicholas's shoulders and squeezed him tight. "I hope I didn't keep you long."

"Not at all," Nicholas said, releasing his friend. "We just got here yesterday evening. Enough time to set up camp and have Shadow and Laudin scout the place out. Everyone wonders why you called us here."

"Of course. Now that we are together, I will share everything I learned while in Antiikin and Travesty. I still have more questions than answers but I'm making progress."

"Wonderful news. Come, let's get to the warmth of the fire."

Umhra nodded and followed Nicholas into camp, towing Splinter behind him. He met Laudin, Naivara, Gromley, and Shadow with warm embraces and tethered Splinter alongside the other horses. He stretched his aching muscles and joined the others around the fire which Laudin now fed with dry hardwood.

Gromley returned to defeathering a pheasant and Shadow and Nicholas to a game of dice. Umhra retrieved Ivory's Nameless Tome from the inner pocket of his cloak and passed it to Naivara who sat beside him. She leafed through the pages, a curious expression on her face, and passed it on to Laudin.

"I know you are all curious about why I called you here and what business I have at Ember's Watch. After visiting King Eleazar, I was drawn back home to Travesty where I located Ivory's belongings. I recalled him telling me about this book and that, one day, it would help me unlock a mystery."

"But its pages are blank," Naivara said.

"To me they were as well. That was, until I reached out to Vaila as a Mystic. When I opened my eyes, the words within were plain to me."

"What does the book say?" Nicholas asked, having abandoned his game of dice in favor of inspecting the book for himself.

"I've barely begun to uncover its teachings, as I'm a slow reader, but it is a guide of sorts. A guide to everything Ivory knew of what it means to be a Mystic. It contains samples of ancient texts and his own notes. He somehow knew I would achieve my Rhodium Suffusion or, at the very least, that there was a good chance I would. Expecting I would be the only one of my kind, he compiled whatever he could from the historical tomes and had the book enchanted to hide its contents from mortal eyes."

"And what you read pointed you here?" Shadow asked.

Umhra nodded. "Apparently, Ember's Watch is the last place the Mystics are known to have gathered before their ascension to Kalmindon. All but one of them, that is. It seems, the Mystic, Spara, was left behind on Tyveriel for some reason. I was hoping to find a clue here that might lead me to her current location."

Gromley slid a spit through the plucked pheasant and placed it over the fire. "I have read every known text on the Age of Grace and its final days and none of them mention anything of Spara being left behind. This is a meaningful revision to history . . . to our understanding of the gods and the Kormaic faith."

"Yes, the implications are no doubt consequential but I leave that to others. My immediate concern is locating Spara and learning what it means to be a Mystic. I have no idea as to the extent of my abilities."

"And, you think we'll find something here that will set you on that path?" Laudin asked.

"I am hopeful that will be the case."

"Then, we head into the ruins tomorrow morning." Laudin turned the spit revealing a flame-kissed pheasant leg. "For now, let's enjoy being together and a fine meal under the stars."

Everyone around the fire nodded in agreement.

"Thank you," Umhra said. "For everything. I wouldn't be where I am without your friendship and support."

"You know we can't resist the peril you offer on so regular a basis." Gromley said, crossing the campsite to Umhra and returning his book. "This path you are on is one of great significance. We are honored to do our part . . . however small."

Gromley sat beside Umhra. "Will you share some of the book with us? Maybe something you saw relevant to Ember's Watch or Spara being left behind."

"I don't see the harm in that." Umhra cracked open the book, passing over Ivory's inscription to the first blank page. He closed his eyes and reached out with his mind to connect with Vaila. Her presence warmed him from within. When he opened his eyes, his pyramid icon glowed a vibrant blue and words filled the page. In the firelight the words glowed with a pearlescent sheen. He read aloud.

"It is told, on the day Vaila, Brinthor, and Kemyn banished Naur to the hells of Pragarus that Vaila ascended to Kalmindon, leaving her brothers on the mortal plane as per their wishes. According to a tome left behind by the Mystics, themselves, Spara was also in the Lazarus Woods that day and witnessed this act that ended the War of Rescission and the Age of Grace. She returned to Ember's Watch where the other Mystics had gathered but, due to some malady, was unable to ascend to Kalmindon with them. Alas, the Mystics were not willing to wait for Spara and weather the onset of the Age of Chaos, and ascended to Kalmindon, sequestering Spara in Tyveriel for eternity. To this day, Spara's whereabouts remain a mystery."

Gromley rubbed his forehead. "A tome left behind by the Mystics! I should like to see this someday. I've never heard mention of such a text. Do you have any idea where it resides?"

"Unfortunately, no. It's possible Ivory will have mentioned its location somewhere within these pages, though. I will let you know."

"I expect there is a treasure trove of information within."

Umhra nodded. He closed the book and slipped it within his cloak. A pang of hunger gripped his stomach. "When's that pheasant going to be ready?"

"It'll be a bit, yet." Laudin turned the spit again. "If I rush it, it'll be tough."

At the moment, Umhra could have been convinced to eat it raw. He hadn't eaten since the morning and found the aroma of the roasting fowl nearly more than he could bear.

Laudin tossed him a chunk of rustic bread. "This will take the edge off."

Umhra tore into the bread like a lion would its prey.

Soon enough, dinner was ready and the Barrow's Pact celebrated into the night. As the moon rose high in the star-filled sky, they prepared camp. Umhra unfurled his bedroll, lay down, and leafed through Ivory's Nameless Tome. He wondered what tomorrow held in store.

The morning brought a stiff wind and a driven snow. Umhra awoke to see Gromley stoking the fire which fluttered in an effort to stay lit. He rubbed his eyes and came fireside trying to warm his freezing hands. The rest of the Barrow's Pact were still asleep, huddled together in a pile of furs.

"That was miserable." He took a swig from his waterskin.

Gromley laughed. "Aye. It was a long night. Did you get any rest?"

"Some. Naivara throws a mean elbow when she sleeps, though. Want to get some breakfast started?"

"I'm sure they'd appreciate waking up to something warm." Gromley pulled a sachet of loose tea and a bundle of parchment from his satchel. "Bacon. I can't think of anything else I'd rather wake up to."

Soon, the smell of sizzling bacon woke the others and the wind and snow ebbed, lifting everyone's spirits. The party made quick work of breakfast and readied themselves for the plunge into Ember's Watch. The days were growing short as the Reaping Moon neared, and there was little interest to be caught among the ruins after nightfall.

Umhra stamped out the fire and the Barrow's Pact began their hike to the ancient keep. "Shadow and I got as close as the southern gate," Laudin said. "We didn't notice anything suspect but dared not enter the grounds."

"Alright." Umhra peered over the unassuming wall marking the edge of compound. "We enter through the southern gate. I will enter first and let you know when to follow."

They crouched at the entrance, the remnants of a rusted gate clanking against the stone with each gust of wind. Umhra inspected the property, his gaze following the pea stone path to the central tower. Clumps of tall grass now dotted the once-manicured yard and the outer buildings were overcome with twisted vines and errant trees. It was an unwelcoming place.

Umhra crept through the gate, his head on a swivel. He came to the corner of a crumbling building and peered through the window, the glass long since broken out. The roof had caved in and ages of dirt and debris climbed up the interior walls. He put his back to the wall and waved the Barrow's Pact within the compound and motioned for them to keep to the path.

Laudin led the team in with his scimitar in hand. They stalked across the field toward the shadowed doorway of the central tower. As they passed the building where Umhra crouched, the ground trembled. The building lurched, scraping against Umhra's back. He dove to the ground as the building pulled itself free from earth.

The walls cracked and ancient mortar crumbled away. Rocks shifted, ground against one another, and the building took on a humanoid form twice Umhra's height. Umhra summoned his armor. Rhodium scales materialized in a wave around him and Forsetae came to his hand in a cloud of blue ether. He struck out at the golem and sent a shower of sparks flying as he carved a deep gouge into the construct's side.

The golem glared at him—its eyes balls of red arcane fury—but it did not reciprocate. Instead, it turned and lumbered toward the rest of the Barrow's Pact.

"Run!" Umhra yelled.

The others dashed for the central tower, the golem picking up speed in pursuit. Umhra ran after it, barely keeping pace.

Across the yard, two other buildings pulled free from the earth and transformed into stone behemoths. They honed in on the Barrow's Pact, one coming between them and the tower, the other attacking from their flank.

Gromley met the golem before them with a blow from his war hammer. The entity stumbled backward, a shard of stone falling from its chest. The third golem charged at Shadow and Nicholas. They dove as both of the construct's enormous fists swung past them and met with the gravel path. Shadow's daggers flew. The blades careened off the golem's form and returned to Shadow's hand, his target unscathed.

The golem Umhra chased charged at Laudin who ducked beneath its attack and carved through the golem's lower back with his scimitar. The golem spun, its glare transfixed on Laudin. The construct's eyes flashed and it struck out again.

Laudin's reactions were slowed and he was met with the full force of the golems fist. He careened through the air and crashed into Umhra. Umhra skidded backward and the soles of his boots found purchase in the loamy soil. He kneeled with Laudin cradled in his arms. The golem raced toward them and reared its arms overhead.

"No," Umhra said, holding a hand toward the charging golem.

The golem slowed and came to rest before Umhra.

Laudin cringed and grabbed his ribs. Umhra focused on his icon and blue ether wafted from the wind currents carved into its surface. He placed a hand upon Laudin's chest and the ether flowed from his icon into Laudin's body. Laudin relaxed.

"You alright?"

"Better now, thanks."

"It seems, for some reason, they listen to me." Umhra nodded to the golem who stood idly before them. "I'm going to try to get the other two under control."

"Please do."

Umhra stood and turned back toward the fray just as an auburn-furred mammoth crashed into the idle golem and drove it to the ground between giant curved ivory tusks. The beast continued its momentum and trampled the golem underfoot. Rock scattered in all directions. The mammoth trumpeted a victory cry and turned toward the other threats.

"She's amazing," Umhra said, watching Naivara in mammoth form charge back toward the path.

"I couldn't agree more." Laudin choked. "Go. Put an end to this if you can."

Umhra ran toward the battle. Gromley was trading blows with his golem and Nicholas and Shadow dodged their adversary and countered with daggers and the occasional fireball from Nicholas's ruby ring which detonated on the construct's formidable torso.

The golems poised for attack, Umhra rushed into the middle of the scrum and held a hand at each of them.

"Stop. Both of you, stop."

He spun to Naivara. "Stop."

The great mammoth skidded to a halt and snorted. The golems dropped their arms and waited.

"They are with me." Umhra approached the golems. "They mean no harm. They pose no threat."

The golems' eyes dimmed to a muted garnet. Umhra motioned the party into the tower. "I'm not sure how long this will work. Let's go."

Gromley rushed over to Laudin who now limped toward the party, his face pale and covered in sweat. The cleric placed a hand upon Laudin and a white celestial glow emanated from beneath it. The color flooded back to Laudin's face. He nodded in appreciation.

Together, they jogged for the tower. Naivara and Umhra pulled up the rear to assure the golems would not interfere. The others stood at the yawning entrance of the tower, and Naivara dropped her mammoth form and joined them.

Umhra peered into the dark interior of the tower. "We'll need some light in here, Gromley."

Gromley pulled an orb from his satchel and set it hovering before the party. It drifted through the doorway, came to light, and illuminated the room within. The foyer opened into an expansive oblong room with a large wooden table at its center. The chairs meant to surround it were toppled and strewn about the room, some in pieces. The table itself was scarred with gouges in its thick pedestal and top. At the far side of the room, a stairway led up into the tower and, beyond it, a door lay torn from its hinges and similarly scarred.

The Barrow's Pact fanned out across the room and followed Gromley's orb. Umhra took a step up the stairs. A light snow danced in the stairwell from a broken window on a landing above. The pulsing in his ear returned, causing him to stop. It called him to a sundered doorway. He turned to the party. "Whatever I came here for is this way." He pushed past the others who had gathered behind him at the base of the stairs and proceeded into the next room.

The glow of Gromley's orb caught up to Umhra and pushed light into the room. Cast iron pots hung on a rack along the near wall, a butcher block toppled over beneath them. Knives were strewn across the stone floor.

An acrid odor burned Umhra's nostrils and intensified as he crossed the room. He couldn't place the smell. It was not that of death or decay, nor was it alchemical. Another door torn from its frame met him beyond an open hearth and a brick oven. A trail of black ichor disappeared into the darkness.

"I don't like the look of that." He pointed to the trail as the rest of the Barrow's Pact filled in behind him.

Shadow kneeled and investigated the ichor closely. "I'm guessing it's exactly where we need to go, though."

"I'm afraid it is." Umhra stepped over the trail and continued on, coming to a stairwell leading to the undercroft. He paused, picking up an erratic clicking sound coming from the darkness below.

Umhra waved Gromley toward him and directed his orb down the stairwell. As he turned back to the undercroft, a creature with two curved dagger-like appendages leaped up the stairs, screeching against Umhra's armor. Umhra fell back against the wall.

The creature landed before him and stamped its forelegs into the floor, sending chips of stone flying. It was black and the size of a wolf. Its body was part chitinous carapace and part ragged fur. Behind its razor-sharp forelegs it had another ten smaller legs and a stinger at the end of its short, bulbous tail.

Hissing threateningly from a rat-like mouth filled with sharp teeth, it spit black ichor onto Umhra's armor. Like glue, it clung to him. The creature lashed out again, but Umhra kicked it down the stairs. The creature shrieked from the shadows.

More clattering answered its call. Gromley sent his orb down the stairs and illuminated the room below. Several of the creatures skittered from the light.

"Melacrites," Shadow said, coming to Umhra's side. "Nasty little things from the Sepyltyr. I can't imagine how they got up here to the surface but they are fairly common among the colonies of my people below the Ilathril."

Umhra started down the stairs. "If they come from the Sepyltyr, they must have tunnels. We can drive them back with light long enough to search the rooms below. I have no interest in killing more than necessary. Naivara?"

"I'm ready when you are." Naivara stepped to the fore, her gold circlet already glowing with green radiance.

Umhra and Naivara sent forth beams of pure-white light, flooding the space below. They led the party down the stairs and into the arched undercroft. The melacrites scrambled from their path as the light hit them and dove into holes that lined the walls in irregular intervals. Their incessant chattering faded. The room was empty.

Umhra closed his eyes. The pulsing in his ear grew. Whatever it was he was meant to find resided beneath him.

There was no obvious path below the undercroft—no entrance to a root cellar or crypt. "I'm going down one of the melacrite tunnels. I need to get beneath this room."

"Are you sure that's wise?" Nicholas asked. "There's no telling how many of those things are down there."

"I'll be fine. We know they run from light." Umhra kneeled by the nearest tunnel entrance and peered into it with the help of his radiant aura.

Laudin kneeled beside him. "Call for us if you need anything."

Umhra nodded and allowed Forsetae and his armor to dissipate so he could better fit within the tunnel. Headfirst, he delved. Every surface was coated with melacrite tar which stuck to him as if warning him to go no further.

The stench was abhorrent and he could not tell if the passage grew warmer as he went or if he sweat from nerves and exertion. Melacrites scuttled from his light, fleeing down the right side of a fork in the tunnel. Umhra paused . . . nearly vomited. Paying heed to his ear, he took the left branch.

On his elbows and stomach, Umhra labored through the slime-coated tunnel until it emptied into an octagonal room of identical construction to those above but with no obvious means of access as part of its design. He slithered from the tunnel and wiped sticky ichor from his face. Strings of it clung to his skin, draped in gentle curves between his hands and face.

Umhra scanned the room. Similar strands covered the walls and floor. They converged in twisted, pulsating piles, each containing numerous black eggs that glistened with a pearlescent sheen that reminded him of caviar he had once shared with Xavier Pell in the greenroom of his apple orchard. Umhra had found the delicacy repugnant but ate his fill, nonetheless, as not to offend. Next time, he would politely decline.

The beating in his ear ceased and was replaced by a shooting pain. Umhra dropped to a knee and rubbed the side of his head trying to assuage the pang. The room spun. Umhra closed his eyes and focused on his icon, calling out to his god. When he opened his eyes, he caught a glimmer of metal amidst one of the nests.

He crawled to the item, melacrite ichor begrudgingly yielding to his progress. He tore away the section of nest that had claimed the object. The eggs quivered as if one with the nest. Umhra wrested a rhodium jewelry box free from the nest's grip. The pain in his head subsided. He relaxed, worked his jaw about to relieve the tension.

Umhra placed the jewelry box in his satchel, climbed to his feet, and trod back to the tunnel entrance. He climbed into the tunnel and began his ascent to the room above where the Barrow's Pact awaited his return. Exhausted, he neared the fork in the tunnel, the aura around him expiring and leaving him in complete darkness. He felt his way around the turn and saw the bead of vibrant light ahead that was Naivara's spell.

The skittering of melacrites once again became audible, their untold numbers regrouping in the absence of Umhra's celestial light. He labored to quicken his pace but the melacrite ichor worked against him. The clicking of chitinous claws on hard stone grew louder. He wasn't going to reach the others in time.

"Light," he yelled, a melacrite hissing only feet behind him. "I need light."

He heard no reply. A shooting pain in his calf was followed by the familiar warmth of blood pouring from a new wound as a melacrite stabbed him again and again. He kicked with his other leg, the sole of his boot connecting with the face of the melacrite behind him. The creature howled. Umhra kicked again, this time not finding anything within range.

Umhra gritted his teeth and dragged himself forward, his calf aching. The clicking of the melacrite once again drew closer. As Umhra kicked once more, a radiant light shone down the tunnel.

Umhra's hulking frame blocked the light. He pressed himself onto the floor of the tunnel and buried his face in the crook of his elbow. The creature behind him screamed and turned from its pursuit, clambering back down the tunnel from which it came.

Umhra pushed himself back onto his elbows and climbed as fast as he could, not knowing when Naivara's spell would lapse. He reached the end of the tunnel and Laudin and Gromley pulled him from its grip, a trail of blood in his wake.

"He's wounded," Laudin said. "His calf."

They sat Umhra on the floor and Gromley laid his hands upon the wound. The cleric closed his eyes and Umhra's body flooded with warmth. He sighed and welcomed the momentary peace.

"Thank you."

"Don't mention it, lad. Did you get what you came for?"

"I did." Umhra held his hands out wide. "I hope it was worth the trouble."

The sound of stone shifting drew his attention to Naivara who drew the sides of the tunnel inward and closed the tunnel's entrance. "It won't take them long to find their way to one of the other openings. I suggest we go."

"Agreed," said Nicholas. "I don't care to confront a swarm of them."

Gromley helped Umhra to his feet and waved the others up the stairs. "Let's be on our way, then."

Shadow and Laudin led the way up the stairs followed by Nicholas and Naivara. Umhra limped behind them and Gromley waited so his orb would light the room as long as possible. The party continued through the kitchen and great hall and out into the fresh air.

The golems had returned to their resting places, one of the out buildings now in considerably more disrepair than when the Barrow's Pact had arrived. The sun fought through a blanket of winter clouds as the party returned to their camp.

"So, what did you find?" Laudin asked as he carefully arranged tinder to start a new fire.

Umhra sat on his bedroll. His entire body ached. He pulled the rhodium jewelry box from his satchel. It gleamed as if untouched by age or, unlike himself, melacrite excretions. Its lid had beveled edges but, otherwise, it was flawless in its simplicity.

"It's locked," Umhra said, passing it to Shadow. "Can you do something about that?"

"I'd be happy to." Shadow smiled and placed the box across his knees. He rubbed his hands, blew into them, and cracked his knuckles. He inspected the box.

"Nicholas, would you mind giving me a hand. The box is warded as well."

Nicholas shuffled over on his knees and joined Shadow in looking the box over. "You're right, it is."

Nicholas pulled a sachet of herbs from his bag and crushed them over the box. His ruby ring flashed with arcane energy. "That should do it."

"Thank you." Shadow retrieved a pick set from his belt and inserted the tension wrench into the base of the lock. He followed with the pick and gingerly set the pins within. With a click, the lid popped open. He handed the box back to Umhra.

Umhra opened the lid wide and found a rhodium orb attached to a simple but unbreakable chain. He lifted it by the chain and showed the party.

"The icon of a Mystic," Naivara said breathlessly.

"Spara's, I suppose." Umhra stared at the icon's gleaming surface, the pounding of his heart returning to his ear. "I'm one step closer to finding her."

"What's next?" Shadow asked.

"I head north."

"Can we help you?"

"No. This is something I have to do on my own."

CHAPTER 8

Deep in the jungle we discovered the great temple for which we searched. We lost three of our men before we could escape the wrath of the serpent who called it home.

—*A Traveler's Guide to the Odd and Obscure by Sentina Vake*
Chapter 23 – Unearthed from the Homestead in Maryk's Cay,
month of Riet, 1407 AT

—▲—

The sun hanging low on the horizon, Talus prodded Maelstrom up King's Walk, a squad of mounted soldiers falling in behind him. They galloped along the spiraling road in their ascent of Mount Orys to Castle Forene high above. At the sound of their thunderous approach, carts that ferried visitors to and from the castle pulled aside to let them pass.

Talus waved a young soldier with sandy hair and green eyes who rode at his flank to come ride alongside him. "We head to the king with our report. Be prepared to speak honestly about what you witnessed. It is imperative you develop a level of comfort with expressing your insights to His Majesty."

The soldier nodded. "I will, Sir Jochen. Thank you for the opportunity."

"It's not an opportunity. As a member of the Raptor's

Grasp, it is your duty. We are also the king's eyes and ears, not just the edge of his blade. He can only rule justly if we provide him sound and thorough information."

"I understand, sir. I will give a full and detailed report."

The squad slowed to a trot as they crossed beneath the portcullis of the castle gate. The wind howled and the emerald green banners adorning the grounds snapped wildly. They continued past the keep's entrance and made for the stables.

Following Talus's lead, the soldiers dismounted and passed their reins to the stable hands who rushed to gather the lathered mounts. They bound up the stairs and entered the king's throne room.

The Elders Syndicate was in session. They were gathered around their stone table arguing over taxes to be gathered before the end of the year. King Arving sat in his throne awaiting their counsel.

The squad came to a halt behind the Raptor's Throne, Talus and his protégé at the fore. The soldiers snapped to attention and held a prolonged salute.

King Arving held a hand in the air and the Elders Syndicate halted their debate. "A moment, if you will. This should not take long."

The elders each bowed before the throne and filed out of the room.

"Come before your king."

Talus led the squad to the front of the throne. They bowed.

"Did you visit the Elmont estate?"

"We did, my Lord," Talus said. "We executed a thorough search of the property and interviewed the family."

"And?"

"Sir Alimede. Will you please report to the king our findings?"

The protégé cleared his throat and took a step toward the throne. "My Lord." He bowed. "In our physical search of the premises, there was no evidence the Lady Elmont had returned to her parents' home. Upon questioning the family, they were convincing to their lack of knowledge of the lady's whereabouts or condition. They maintain they had not heard from her in nearly a month which coincides with our records of their last contact. Unfortunately, we are, as of yet, unable to locate the Lady Elmont."

King Arving rubbed his chin. "Talus, you also found their account plausible."

"Quite, my Lord."

"I have always known the Elmont family, with the exclusion of their son, to be people of integrity. With this in mind, you may close your investigation into their involvement in the lady's escape and disappearance. I am yet to understand how she has eluded us for this long, however. Double your efforts in your search of the castle grounds and the city."

"Yes, my Lord." Captain Alimede bowed. "We will not let you down."

"I should hope not. You are dismissed."

The soldiers pivoted to form a single line and followed Talus from the throne room. Once outside, Talus stopped and addressed them. "Alimede, you and I will head up the search of the castle grounds. Inform Bisyk he is to have twice the manpower in sweeping the city."

"Yes sir. Right away, sir."

"I'll meet up with you in the bailey shortly. We can split up from there."

Captain Alimede saluted and hurried down the stairs. The rest of the soldiers followed him.

Talus bound up the stairs, returned to his quarters, and locked the door behind him. It was quiet, which had been a difficult state to achieve with an infant in the room but, somehow, Alessa managed to keep her baby comfortable and not call attention to their presence. Still, his heart pounded at the thought they had been discovered in his absence. He bound into the bedroom.

It was empty. He kneeled and peered under the bed. There, Alessa and her child huddled, Alessa's eyes wide with fear.

"Have you been there all day?" Talus extended a hand and helped Alessa shuffle out from beneath the bedframe.

"Much of it." Alessa shrugged. "She actually slept quite well under there. Did you see my parents?"

"Yes, and your brother. He is home as the king promised. They worry for you."

"And, rightfully so." Alessa placed the baby on Talus's bed and brushed the dust from her gown"

"They gave convincing testimony that they know nothing of your whereabouts. The official report will free them of any responsibility."

"How was my mother? Did you tell her I was alright?"

"No. She is, obviously, quite worried. I thought it better she knows nothing of our plan. I may be able to explain things once you are safe."

Alessa's eyes welled with tears. "And, we leave tonight?"

"Yes. We've been lucky to go undiscovered this long. Tonight, when the castle is still, I will call on a young member of the Raptor's Grasp who was with me at your parents' home today. I will bring him here so there is proof of your capture and have him tell the king I have taken you and the child outside Vanyareign to fulfill his orders. You and I will then head to the stables, gather Maelstrom and ride for Tayrelis."

"Why Tayrelis?"

"I have people there I can trust to keep you safe while I convince the king that you met your end. If all goes well, I will return to you within a couple days and we will be on our way."

Alessa nodded. "How will you do it?"

"Do what?"

"Kill us. How will you tell the king you did it?"

Talus considered the macabre question. "I don't see how."

"It's a simple question, Sir Jochen. I'd like to know what you will tell the king of our demise."

"I am going to tell him I ran you through with Aquila." He put a hand to the handle of his sword, the sapphire embedded in its pommel glinting. "He will find it palatable that you both met a swift death at the blade of his ancestors. He's not a cruel man by nature."

"You know nothing of his cruelty." Alessa's words dripped with anguish.

"I suppose you are right. I apologize. Gromley always says I need to work on looking at things from other perspectives."

"Tell me. What happened to the other women in my situation? Those that failed the king as I have."

"Until now, I understood they each died in childbirth along with their infants. I admit, you cause me to wonder otherwise. I certainly had nothing to do with them."

Alessa pursed her lips and ran her tongue over her teeth. "I believe you."

"What choice do you have?"

"None. I haven't had a choice in quite some time. I just wanted you to know."

"Let's get through tonight. Let's get you two out of Vanyareign. You will taste freedom again. For now, I have to meet up with the others and resume our search for you. Keep the child quiet. There may be others roaming these halls besides me."

"She's been a good sleeper so far. I think we will be alright until you return."

"Good. I'll return late tonight. Try to get some rest. We have a long trip ahead of us."

"Back under the bed I go."

Talus chuckled. "If it makes you feel better. But everyone checks under the bed when turning a room."

He left Alessa standing bedside, staring at the floor, and swept out into the hallway. He locked the door and bound down the stairs, through the stables, and out into the crisp evening air. Hurrying to the bailey, he found Captain Alimede and the rest of the search party waiting for him.

"There's a very good chance Lady Elmont is still on castle grounds despite our earlier searches coming up empty," Talus said, eschewing formality with his men. "If any of you find her, bring her directly to my quarters. I will handle matters from there . . . unceremoniously as the king wishes. I'll see your wages doubled for a month should you find her."

The soldiers went into an uproar at the notion of some extra coin in their pockets.

"Alright." Captain Alimede held his hands in the air and the soldiers quieted. "Sir Talus and I will search the main keep as to not disturb the king. The rest of you, here are your assignments."

"I better not get the latrines again, Alimede" a soldier easily twice Captain Alimede's age but inferior in rank complained. "You always stick me with the crap jobs."

The soldiers laughed.

"No latrines this time, Pollum. I've upgraded you to the dungeon."

The soldier frowned. "She couldn't get down there if she tried. You're an ass."

"I'm your superior officer," Captain Alimede said. "Off you all go."

The group dispersed, headed to their assigned locations.

"Are you agreeable to taking North Hall?" Captain Alimede asked. "You live over there and the king will be more comfortable with you searching around his private quarters. I'll take the kitchen and South Hall."

"Makes no difference to me. We'll start with the ground floor and work our way up."

The men went their separate ways. Talus began in the grand vestibule and executed his search with zeal. He enquired with everyone he passed as to whether they had seen the Lady Elmont or heard a baby crying at any point in the last day. He looked under tables and within each recess the castle offered.

After hours of feigned exploration, Talus returned to his room.

Alessa was asleep in his bed, the baby cradled beside her.

Talus cleared his throat and Alessa startled awake.

Talus approached the bed. "I'm sorry to wake you but it's time."

Alessa sat up and rubbed her weary eyes. "Alright. What do you need me to do?"

"I will bring my comrade here to see you for himself. He will likely interview you regarding our whereabouts. Tell him you were on the fifth floor of the north tower. I was just there and much of it is empty. Otherwise, just look distraught like you did when we ran into each other last night. Once he is convinced, we will be on our way."

"I await your return. Fifth floor of the north tower."

"Exactly."

Talus left the room and ran for South Hall. He found Captain Alimede searching a storage room filled with clutter. Talus's chest heaved. "Alimede, I'm glad I found you. I caught her."

"Where is she?" Captain Alimede stepped over a pile of fabric bolts.

"She's locked in my quarters. I'll fill you in on the way there."

Captain Alimede nodded excitedly and followed Talus back to his room, a baby's cry greeting them as they neared.

When Talus opened the door, Alessa had hung the sheets from his bed out the window and stood peering out into the darkness, her hair a bird's nest, her dress disheveled. Her baby lay on the bed behind her, wailing.

"Don't get any ideas," Captain Alimede said, rushing toward her. "You wouldn't survive the drop, anyway."

He wrested Alessa from the window, reeled the sheets into the room, and pulled the sash closed. "Now, shut that thing up."

Alessa scooped up her baby and flashed Talus a look he could only interpret as disgust. Talus grabbed her forcefully by the arm and showed her a seat at the table. He motioned for Captain Alimede to the seat across from her.

Captain Alimede glared at Alessa as she soothed her baby. "You've caused quite a bit of trouble. You sent a guard to the infirmary with swelling of the brain. For that alone you should be hanged. Tell me, where've you been hiding?"

"On the fifth floor of the north tower," Alessa whispered, averting her eyes.

Captain Alimede leaned over the table. "What was that? Speak up, woman."

"I was hiding on the fifth floor of the north tower."

"And, what was your plan? Were you to kill the king?"

"No!" Alessa's eyes snapped to meet her accuser. "All I wanted was to get out of the castle with my daughter."

"Let me see the . . . child."

Alessa pivoted in her seat to show Captain Alimede the baby's face. She chewed on her fist and looked at him with golden irises.

He edged back from the table. "Gods. No wonder the king wants nothing to do with it. I've seen enough. Sir Jochen, a word before you go?"

Talus walked Captain Alimede to the door. "How'd I do?" The captain asked once in the hall.

"A bit heavy handed but convincing."

"I'd appreciate your feedback when you return. I will call off the manhunt and report to the king with our findings first thing in the morning. Good luck with the work ahead. I can't say I envy you."

"We are often called upon to give much of ourselves in service of the crown but never too much."

Captain Alimede saluted and strode down the hallway. Once he was out of sight, Talus returned to Alessa. Her body shook as though she were freezing. Tears streaked her face.

"You did well. I'm sorry if Alimede upset you. He was putting on a bit of a show, himself."

"I'm just glad it's over. When can we leave?"

"Presently."

"Will you hold her while I clean myself up a bit?" she asked, handing Talus the infant before receiving his answer.

Talus held the child with rigid arms, inspecting her tiny grey features, her gold eyes and the dark rings around them. He had never held an infant before. He feared he would hold her too tight and hurt her . . . or too loose and drop her. There wasn't a thing about the experience he enjoyed.

Alessa smiled, retrieved a brush from her cloak, and brushed her hair. She straightened her dress and put her hands on her hips as if she had been waiting for hours. "What you see is what you get," she said, flashing a sheepish smile.

Talus stepped up to Alessa and handed her the swaddled child. He opened the door, grabbed her by the right arm and thrust her into the hallway.

"All for show, I assure you," he whispered, "Cover the child's face if we encounter anyone. We don't need to attract any more attention than necessary. We will stop for provisions once we have some distance between us and Vanyareign."

She nodded—curled the baby into her chest and rounded her shoulders to shield her further.

CHAPTER 9

I have waited too long already. It is time for me to step forward and lead Evelium to war against the wild things.

—*The Collected Letters of Modig Forene*
Letter to Meldrius Schrent dated 8th of Prien, 939 AC. Unearthed from the Ruins of Vanyareign, month of Ocken, 1301 AT.

—▲—

Having ridden at full pace for the better part of the day, Talus slowed his lathered steed to a trot just outside the north gate of Tayrelis and entered the city beside the River Torrent which delivered logs to the timber mills from the Wistful Timberlands. He dismounted and led Maelstrom to a poor section of town.

Drawing near to his childhood home, he hesitated for a moment, thinking of how he had promised himself never to return to this place—at least while his father still lived. They'd given him up. Even after all these years that wound was still raw.

It wasn't until Alessa and, more importantly, her child entered his life just over a week ago that he'd even considered the possibility. Now, despite his parents' willingness to house Alessa while Talus returned to Vanyareign to report to the king of her death, he was unsure if he'd made the right decision.

Potholes pocked the dirt roads, still filled with water from the prior night's rain. Groups of log drivers trudged home from the river, each with a peavey over his shoulder. They were covered in sawdust and grime and spoke among themselves.

Talus guided Maelstrom down a narrow alley, where modest wood-framed buildings on either side were in terrible disrepair—their rooflines wilted from years of rot and neglect, their windows dingy and cracked.

Two-thirds of the way down the alley, which ended at the towering outer wall of the city, Talus stopped and tied Maelstrom to a rusted iron eyelet imbedded in a large stone that jutted out of the street in front of a small hovel. He took a deep breath and rubbed Maelstrom's snout.

From beneath his hood, he peered up the street where a group of men gathered, whispering among themselves. He reached within his cloak and felt the cold handle of his crossbow. The men moved on. Talus knocked and pressed his ear against the door. He heard labored shuffling from within. Someone approached the door from the other side but dared not open it.

"Who's there?" A gruff, uninviting voice asked.

"It's Talus. I've returned."

The door cracked open a few inches. Talus pushed it open the rest of the way and entered the home. He shut the door behind him and welcomed the warmth of a small fire in a modest stone hearth.

The only other light came from a solitary candle sitting upon a warped wood table along the far wall. An older man with one leg hobbled back to its glow, a hand-hewn crutch under his arm for support. His clothes were clean, but well-worn, and he kept his blond beard cropped short to his square jaw. Despite his disability, he kept himself strong by the looks of his barrel chest and formidable arms. He threw his husky frame into a chair too small for him and scratched his neck.

"The girl and baby are in the bedroom napping," said Tronus Jochen. "It's not yours, is it?"

"No father, it's not. She's in trouble and I'm helping her get to safety."

"Good, I wouldn't want you tied up with a cursed child like that little one. It will bring you nothing but trouble."

"Why would you even care?" Talus walked over to the table and sat across from his father, staring at him through the candlelight. "I'm my own man. I'm not asking you for anything."

"Only to harbor a young woman who is on the run with her oddity of a child."

"We'll be out of your hair soon," Talus said. Alessa appeared in the doorway from the bedroom.

"Don't get me wrong, son. I am happy to see you. Your mother and I are proud of what you've become. Of the life we could provide for you."

Talus's eyes narrowed. "You don't know the half of what I've become. Of my transgressions in the king's name. And, you certainly know nothing of the life you chose for me. You weren't there. You walked away from me without thinking twice."

Tronus leaned forward, his forearms flat on the table, and looked his son in the eye. "I have no defense other than there were too many mouths to feed, and I had to choose one of you for service. Your sisters were too young, and you well know what happens to girls that get put into service at the castle. Besides, you turned out better than you would have if you had stayed in Tayrelis, living off the scraps your mother's income provided until you came of age and could work the timberlands or the river."

"I'm glad you returned safely," Alessa said. Her interruption broke the tension. "Are we to be on our way?"

"In the morning," Talus said, shifting his gaze away from his father's. "Maelstrom needs rest. I pushed him fairly hard on my way back here from the capital."

"You look like you could use some rest yourself." Alessa

tilted her head and frowned. Since we are staying the night, should I prepared supper?"

"That won't be necessary, lass. Benna and the girls will be home soon enough and will see to it."

"Nonsense," Alessa said. "The least I can do to repay you and your family for opening your home to me is to prepare a meal. Talus can run out and get anything needed from the market."

Talus shrugged to his father, not about to broker the burgeoning disagreement.

"Very well," Tronus said. "Have at it. But I'm afraid you won't find much to work with."

Alessa rooted around the small kitchen, taking inventory of the ingredients and tools at her disposal. As she rummaged through a small cupboard, selecting root vegetables for her meal, the door swung open.

"Is that Talus's horse?" Benna Jochen asked as she entered, her arms laden with goods. She was thin, with high cheekbones and greying hair. Her dress was covered with stains, and she had dark circles beneath her ocean-blue eyes. There was a time, before the stresses of life got the best of her, when the men of Tayrelis considered her quite beautiful. Even now, that beauty shown through in her smile.

"It is," Talus said. "I'm glad you're home, mother." The words felt awkward but appropriate as he spoke them. Unlike the contempt he still harbored for his father, Talus had softened toward his mother since reconnecting with his family. He could plainly see how she lit up at seeing him—the child her husband had forced her to give to the king's court when he was only seven. Maybe it was unfair of him to hold his father solely accountable for their separation and growing up parentless. Desperation will make a man do things he never dreamed of.

Benna dropped the items she held onto the table and hugged Talus in a firm embrace. "It's so good to see you. Will you be able to stay for a while?"

Talus bit his bottom lip and fought back the tears. "Only for the night. I must take Alessa and her child south in the morning."

Benna frowned. "Well, at least we have you for the night. I'll take what I can get. Your sisters will be home shortly. I brought rabbit home from the market." She noticed Alessa standing in the kitchen cutting some vegetables. "Let me help you, my dear."

▲

Morning broke and Alessa rolled out of bed, careful not to disturb the infant sleeping peacefully beside her. She hadn't slept well, ruminating on the uncertainty of her future and the long trip before her. She peered out of the bedroom to see Talus leaning against the wall in a small chair, staring out into the street through the singular window at the front of the hovel.

"Shall we be getting on our way?" She asked in a whisper, not to wake Tronus who slept with his face buried in the crook of his folded arms on the table.

"Yes. The earlier we set off, the farther away we can get from those who may recognize us. All will be lost if reports of a grey baby get back to Vanyareign."

"I'll gather my things, then."

"Quietly. I would rather avoid any ceremony," Talus said.

Alessa nodded and returned to the room where she had spent the last few days. It was small and drafty but had served its purpose. Benna slept on a small cot across the room, having given up her bed despite Alessa's initial protests. She gathered the few belongings she had brought with her and scooped her baby from the bed.

"You two take care of each other," Benna said from her cot. "I said my goodbyes last night and don't want to scare him off. It's just now that I have him back in my life."

"We will. I promise. Thank you for welcoming us into your home so unexpectedly." Alessa smiled and left the room.

When she returned to the front room, Talus placed a handful of sovereigns on the small table beside him as they left.

The morning air was crisp, and the din of the sawmills already echoed through the city streets. Talus helped Alessa and her baby upon Maelstrom's back and untethered the horse, leading it by the reins out of the alley and through Tayrelis toward the south gate.

Crossing beneath the portcullis, a light fog clung to the surface of the River Torrent. Talus climbed into the saddle behind Alessa and spurred Maelstrom to a trot, heading south along Englen Penn Way. By midday they passed Mirina's Path, and by evening they had made their way to the Lesser Falls.

Talus halted Maelstrom at the top of the cascades, where the road dropped off toward their base at a steep pitch. The waters of the River Torrent rushed over the precipice, crashing into the great azure plunge pool hundreds of feet below.

"This looks like a good place to camp for the night," Talus said.

"Whatever you think best," Alessa said, all too happy at the prospect of dinner and a reasonable night's sleep. "I must admit that I'm tired."

Talus dismounted and took the infant from Alessa's arms and helped Alessa to jump down from Maelstrom's back. They prepared a modest camp for the night, settled in around their fire, and ate some supper as the sun dropped beneath the horizon.

"Have you decided what you will call her?" Talus asked, nodding toward the bundle in Alessa's arms.

"You're the first person that's asked me that. Turin. Her name is Turin." Alessa smiled down at the infant.

"It's a powerful name for a girl. Turin Archedyne was a great warrior during the War of Dominion."

"I'm familiar. I once read about his exploits, and always liked his name. Besides, she will need to be strong." Alessa pulled the blanket back from Turin's face. "Look at her. Society will never accept her. Her own father doesn't accept her."

"Alessa, Turin is the sole heir to Evelium's throne," Talus said. "She is a Forene and destined for greatness. Yes, her path might not be obvious to us now, but she will be every bit as strong and smart and beautiful as her mother."

"If that were the case, then why did the king toss her aside so easily?"

"The king is a complicated man. While forward thinking in many respects, he is beholden to the lore of his ancestors as though it were sacrosanct. This story that a grey queen would break the bloodline of great kings and mark the doom of civilization has been around since the Age of Grace. The king has interpreted Turin's skin color as an omen that she would fulfill the prophecy. He would rather let the throne fall into less trustworthy hands than disgrace his ancestors in such a way. Either way, he loses."

"And what do you make of this?" Alessa asked, sticking a knuckle into Turin's mouth to soothe her.

"If I agreed with the king, we wouldn't be here right now," Talus said. "I intend to see you to safety and then return to Evelium and try to persuade the king to change his mind. Turin is a true Forene and my future queen. I am sworn to protect her and would see her take her rightful place. There are others who already lay claim to the Raptor's Throne but dare not break the Fracture. If the king dies without an heir then his cousin, Vred Ulest, will declare the treaty null and usurp the throne in the name of the reunification of Evelium. I will not be party to creating such a future."

Alessa rubbed her hands together and held them out to the fire, taking in its warmth. "Where shall we find this safety you speak of?"

"I'm going to secure us passage to Shent. I have a friend there that has agreed to look after you and keep your existence quiet."

"Who?"

"A friend who owes me for saving his life. He'll be receptive to this as payment of his debt."

"If you trust him, I suppose that's a good enough endorsement for me."

"It will have to be," Talus said. "I'm not sure we have much choice. For the next few nights we'll take turns on watch. I won't be caught off guard. Why don't you get some rest until Turin wakes you? Then we can switch."

Alessa nodded and pulled her blanket up around her shoulders. She curled up with Turin on her bedroll and feigned sleep. She watched Talus sitting in the fading light of their fire, sharpening his knife on a whetstone. He ran his fingers through his shoulder-length blond hair, his expression stoic, focused. Such a weight he had taken on by offering her and Turin a chance of a new life. Both were such innocent pawns in this game, but with him, she felt safe. She teared up, wondering what motivated him to act so selflessly on her behalf. Had she encountered anyone except him the night of her attempted escape, she and Turin would long since be dead and buried.

With these thoughts running through her mind, she drifted off to sleep.

"Alessa," Talus whispered with a forceful undertone. It was well into the early morning hours. He shook her awake. "We have to move. Something or someone is hunting us."

Alessa rubbed her eyes and nodded that she understood.

"Take Turin into the stand of trees over there." Talus pointed down the path to a densely covered outcropping barely visible along the waterfalls' edge. She jumped to her feet, gathered Turin, and drew her dagger from her cloak. "Stay quiet, I'll meet you there."

Alessa scrambled down the ridge and disappeared into the copse. Talus readied his crossbow and crept into the darkness, hoping whoever was pursuing them was dumb enough to enter the light of their campfire.

"One of 'em ran down the ridge," a voice whispered from

the cover of night.

"I'll find 'em," another said. "You two gather the horse and look for the other rider."

Two men entered the camp, kicking the bedrolls over and searching for anything of value. One turned toward Maelstrom, who stood unphased, tethered to a low-hanging branch of a lone poplar.

"Steady boy," the man said. In the firelight his stark features were exaggerated. His skin was a deep tan and covered in small scars. His hair was black and shaved close on the left side, the rest was bound in a braid by small bones and teeth. He wore studded leathers that had seen better days and held a bow in his left hand and a short sword on his hip.

He untied Maelstrom's lead and tugged. The horse reared up over him and struck him with his front hooves and crushed his skull.

The other man who was rifling through Talus's satchel spun toward the unexpected commotion. Talus saw his opportunity and let a bolt fly. His aim was true and the bolt struck the man in the neck, blood spraying from the wound onto the campfire. The fire hissed.

Talus ran back into the camp. Blood pooled beside the fire, reflecting Talus's image as he stood over the wounded brigand with his sword Aquila now in hand.

"Who sent you?" Talus asked. "Do you work for the king?"

The man's face twisted in confusion. "The king? No."

Without hesitation, Talus plunged his blade into the man's chest, ending him.

▲

Alessa backed up against the base of an ample tree toward the center of the grove. In one arm she held Turin who was awake but quiet despite her mother's panic. In the other hand she gripped her dagger. The canopy overhead snuffed out any light provided by the star-filled sky. She sat in utter darkness, praying the brigands would not discover her.

There was a rustling in the surrounding woods. Turin let out a solitary squeal. A light came towards them, casting long shadows across the underbrush. Alessa placed Turin on the ground at the base of the tree and held the dagger in both hands and waited for her pursuer to come into view.

From the darkness a blade swiped toward her, knocking the dagger from her grip with a clank. A silhouette approached, lit from behind by the light of a floating orb. As the light caught up, it revealed a middle-aged Iminti man wearing ragged leathers. His green eyes glinted in the unnatural light. Turin cried which attracted the man's attention. Alessa lunged at him, but the man knocked her aside with a swipe of his burly arm. Her head rang, a warm stream of blood ran down her face.

Pushing his greasy dark hair out of his face, he charged at her. She shuffled backward, but with one stride he was atop her, and grabbed her by the ankle.

"Where do yah think yer goin, gal?" He dragged her toward him, roots scraping at her back.

He dropped to his knees, straddling her, a wicked smile smeared across his dirty face. His eyes went wide, his jaw dropped as a sword burst through his chest from behind. His blood sprayed across Alessa's gown as she scrambled from beneath her assailant.

Talus appeared behind the man, put his arm around his chest and pushed Aquila through him further. He pulled the sword from the brigand's torso and cast his dead body aside.

"Are you okay?" Talus picked Turin up off the ground and dropped to his knees at Alessa's side.

"Yes. Thanks to you. I tried to defend myself, but he used the dark to his advantage and was much stronger and faster than I."

Alessa's hands trembled as Talus helped her from the ground. He passed Turin over to her, and both found calm in the embrace. Talus gathered Alessa's dagger and the attacker's rapier from the ground.

"Let's clean up camp and get an early start."

"You haven't slept," Alessa said. "You should rest first."

"I'll be fine. There have been times I've had to go for days without sleep in the service of the king. I think it best we keep moving until we reach Hylara."

They walked back up to their camp and gathered their belongings. Alessa frowned at the sight of Maelstrom standing over the body of the man he had trampled, brains and gore splattered beneath him. Talus stamped out the fire and helped Alessa up onto the steed's back and then joined her. He cracked the reins and they rode for Hylara, the slightest of wet moons hanging low on the western horizon.

CHAPTER 10

After two-hundred-ninety-seven years of rule,ᐟ the great Modig Forene passed into the Everlife and met his forefathers on the beaches of Kalmindon.

—*The Gatekeeper's Abridged History of Tyveriel*
Vol. 3, Chapter 26 – Discovered in the Private Library of Solana Marwyn, the month of Vasa, 889 AT

—▲—

The sheer granite cliff face stretched upward until obscured by ominous storm clouds. Umhra stood at the base and craned his neck, squinting to see if he could make out a probable path to the top. The snow was knee deep and showed no sign of letting up. He shook his head and walked back to Splinter who, despite only being a few feet away, was little more than a shadow through the storm.

"You head back to the keep in Anaris, you hear?" He patted the horse on its ice-encrusted neck. "Go on now."

Splinter shook his head but conceded, turning from Umhra and trotting south out of sight. Umhra returned to the task at hand and walked back over to the monolithic stone wall. He clapped his hands together a few times and reached up, taking hold of the cold, unforgiving surface.

He took a moment to find a solid foothold, and hoisted himself off the ground, beginning his ascent to the Bite. He was unsure of what he would do once he reached the frozen plateau of barren tundra. Hopefully, Spara's call would provide some guidance.

The wind-driven snow lashed his face as he climbed, his footing slipping more than once on the slick escarpment. He continued into the dense blanket of clouds, breaking through the blizzard into clear skies.

Exhausted, he reached the clifftop, and hauled himself onto the snow-laden plateau. The pounding of his heart was only outdone by the persistent pulsing in his right ear, which grew stronger with every step he took toward this unforgiving place.

Umhra rolled onto his back, his lungs burned and his muscles ached. He grasped his icon, its soft aura intensifying to a vibrant blue at his touch. Warmth flooded his body, his energy restored. He stood, looking over the desolation that was the Bite. There was nothing but frozen earth for as far as the eye could see.

He set off north, trudging through the snow and ice. He waded through waist high drifts and fought driving winds, with no sign of civilization to give him hope. Yet, his body did not hunger or ache. The growing thrum in his ear willed him onward.

On the fourth day, a great city pierced the horizon, its towers disrupting the monotony of the tundra's landscape. Umhra scrambled onto a rocky outcrop to get a better view. Once he could see the entire city, its enormous scale became clear. There was no outer wall for protection, likely for the lack of any threat.

He had reached Oda Norde, home of the frost giants. Ivory's Nameless Tome contained several vague references to the city but none connected it to Spara's location. If the Mystic was hidden here, he feared her freedom would not easily be attained. The frost giants did not tolerate outsiders, and Hallgeirr, their king, was known for his bloodlust.

Umhra winced and rubbed his ear. The sooner he found Spara, the sooner this damn pulsing would stop. He buried the annoyance and quickened his pace at the prospect of nearing his destination, and the one that could answer all his questions.

At the edge of the great city the snow formed a natural barrier around its perimeter, but left its streets untouched by the elements.

Umhra stepped from the snow onto the smooth stone of a road which ran toward a tower some distance away. The street's breadth rivaled that of the River Torrent. The doorways of each immense tower-like home that lined the lane reached five-times his height. Enormous bonfires raged at each intersection, in preparation for the long, dark night quickly approaching.

Umhra clung to the shadows of a building at the first intersection he came upon and peered down the cross street. Two frost giants loomed nearby, one with a battle axe over his shoulder, the other holding a torch. They had pale-blue skin and wore heavy fur clothing that covered their gargantuan forms. Umhra drew in a deep breath and fortified himself, tucking back against the building wall.

He strained to hear their conversation but did not understand the frost giants' language. Their voices were so deep that little more than a resonant rumble was even audible. With thunderous footsteps, the giants ended their discussion and separated—one walking in Umhra's direction. Umhra stepped out into the street directly in the behemoth's path.

The frost giant took one last step, his foot crashing into the ground just feet away from where Umhra stood. The giant stopped and looked down at the diminutive half-Orc standing before him. Umhra held his ground, and the giant kneeled on one knee to inspect him.

"What do we have here?" The giant spoke in perfect Evenese, its tone like rolling thunder. "What are you doing in Oda Norde, Orc? We do not take kindly to intruders."

"I've come to see King Hallgeirr," Umhra said, shouting to match the volume of the giant's resonant voice.

"And what business do you have with our king?"

"I wish to offer him a trade." Umhra took a brazen step forward. "The Mystic, for his life."

At this, the giant roared with laughter and the ground shook beneath Umhra's feet. "Oh, Hallgeirr will welcome the challenge," he scoffed. "I will bring you to him presently."

The frost giant stood and lumbered toward the northern most region of the city. Umhra followed, running to keep up with the gargantuan's stride. They came to a three-spired tower of considerable enormity constructed of white stone. Beyond it was a cliff face that dropped to the Amarthian Sea below. The doors of the tower were iron and had the image of a mammoth engraved across them. The giant hauled the heavy door open, revealing a central hall that stretched on for the better part of a mile.

Colossal marble statues of Hallgeirr's relatives lined both sides of the hall—the generations that had led Oda Norde and the frost giants of the Bite. Preferring to keep to themselves, the frost giants claimed the Bite as their sacred land and met any intrusion with merciless force. They, however, did not respect the sovereignty of Evelium and often raided villages in northern Windswept.

Umhra continued after his chaperone, the iron doors slammed shut behind them with a resonant crash. There was no turning back. They continued through the pyre-lit hall. The frost giant paid no attention to Umhra. Coming to a large stone staircase that ascended beyond Umhra's field of vision the frost giant continued onward and Umhra struggled up the stairs—each riser his full height.

Atop the landing, an archway led to King Hallgeirr's court. Here, the frost giant pulled his great axe and prodded Umhra forward. At the far end of the room sat the king's throne, a stone chair adorned with mammoth skulls, their tusks jutting out in every direction. The chair was empty. At the very center of the room was a Waystone, like the one Umhra had seen outside the Stoneheart Pass when he traveled with the Barrow's Pact to Meriden to end the resurrection of Naur. But this one's sigil pulsed red and had a series of interlocking circles of various sizes.

Hallgeirr was walking the perimeter of the room, perusing the multitude of iron grates built into its walls. He wore a black fur mantle over heavy leathers etched with runes. Looking up, his ice-blue eyes met the intrusion with curiosity.

"My King," the frost giant accompanying Umhra said, slapping his chest with both arms crossed. "This Orc has come here with a challenge for you. He says he wants the Mystic."

The pulsing in Umhra's ear was deafening. His head spun.

King Hallgeirr laughed under his breath. "My Mystic is not for sale or trade, Orc. She is most prized among my pets, and so she will stay. If you were not so mundane, I would suggest you should be the next addition to my collection. But you are not worthy of such distinction."

Umhra banged the side of his head with an open palm, hoping to drive out the thrumming. "King Hallgeirr, let me leave here with the Mystic and I will leave you with your life." He took a step forward.

Hallgeirr tilted his head, surprised by the absurd challenge. "Kill him." The king gestured to Solveigg with a dismissive flip of his wrist. "I have no interest in such games."

Without hesitation, Solveigg's great axe came arching down toward Umhra, who rolled out of the way. The weapon crashed into the stone floor, sending chunks of rock scattering across the room. Umhra focused on his icon, which swung out from beneath his cloak. Small scales of rhodium armor grew in an intricate overlapping pattern around his body, and Forsetae materialized in his hand.

Azure ether wafting from his form, Umhra leaped from the ground onto Solveigg's knee and then, in a second bound, plunged his sword under the giant's chin and into his throat. Umhra tore the blade free, leaving a gaping wound, blood pouring forth in spurts. Solveigg dropped his axe to a resounding clatter and reached for his hemorrhaging throat, his eyes wide with surprise and terror. Umhra summersaulted off him, landing out of reach of the cascading blood pooling on the ground below. King Hallgeirr strode to his throne and pulled a massive claymore which rested across two mammoth tusks.

"I will make my offer one more time, should you have reconsidered," Umhra said as Hallgeirr approached. Solveigg collapsed lifeless to the ground.

"You may be more than you seemed at first, but I am Hallgeirr the Frostborn, and you shall feel the steel of my blade."

Hallgeirr took one step and swung his claymore, its gleaming blade whirring through the air toward Umhra. Umhra parried, but the force of the impact threw him backward into one of the iron grates lining the room's walls. A manticore jumped at the bars, its claws streaked down Umhra's armor.

Hallgeirr laughed and circled the center of the room, awaiting Umhra's advance with a flourish of his enormous blade. Umhra crept along the perimeter of the room, eyeing the contents of each cell over his shoulder. In the cell left of the manticore resided a dire wolf. Next, a wyvern. Then, a young woman with black hair and soft, bronze skin. She wore a celadon gown, and her feet were bare. Reaching through the bars, she grabbed Umhra's arm. He looked into her smoky grey eyes. She could be no other than Spara.

"Umhra," she said. "Did you bring my icon?"

Umhra nodded, the pulsing dissipated in his ear.

"Give it to me and I will help you get us out of here."

Measuring Hallgeirr from afar, Umhra retrieved a rhodium orb on a simple but unbreakable chain from his belt and passed it through the bars to Spara.

"Come." Hallgeirr spat on the floor. "I grow weary of this folly and shall have your life."

Umhra strode toward the center of the room where Hallgeirr stood at the ready, his blade in both hands. As Hallgeirr hoisted his claymore, Umhra ran between the giant's legs—hastened by his connection with Vaila—and swept his sword against his left ankle, severing the Achilles tendon just above the heel. Blood sprayed across the room and Hallgeirr released a roar of pain as he fell to one knee.

Umhra focused on his icon and the glow from his armor intensified. The wisps of blue smoke emanating from him enveloped Hallgeirr, and trapped him in a cocoon of searing light. The giant fell to his hands and screamed, unable to move. Umhra came before him on the Waystone, deciding whether to spare the frost giant king or end him as promised.

Thunder rumbled from the rooms below . . . Umhra envisioned a veritable army of giants shouting and drawing weapons as they gathered to come to their king's defense.

Spara placed her icon around her neck and flashed a grin two thousand years in the making. She closed her eyes and threads of green ether spiraled from her icon and enveloped her in their radiance.

"I'll leave you with your life, King Hallgeirr. For I have what I came for." Umhra walked to Spara's cage. "With a kindness you weren't willing to extend me, I bid you peace."

As Umhra neared Spara's cell the iron bars of her cage door glowed red. The incandescence shifted to yellow, then white, and the bars melted away.

Spara stepped from the prison. "I cannot allow such restraint, Umhra," she said, beaming with celadon light. "Two millennia of imprisonment deserves some recompense. And it is imperative we destroy his Waystone."

Two frost giants appeared in the throne room's archway; weapons readied. A crowd formed behind them.

"Well, you better hurry," Umhra said. "I won't be able to

hold them off for very long."

Spara nodded and swaggered to the giant king's side. "Alas, we have run out of time, Hallgeirr. I've dreamed of this moment for two thousand years and now my only regret is it must be so rushed. If I were to take another two thousand years to flay the skin from your body, it wouldn't be long enough."

Hallgeirr struggled under Umhra's control through gritted teeth.

"Lady Spara, I suggest we make our exit now," Umhra said. "Give yourself time to heal before deciding who the targets of your revenge should be."

"Under normal circumstances, an admiral position, Umhra. But, in our current circumstance, merely uninformed." Spara waved her hand and the iron grates holding Hallgeirr's collection of beasts crumbled to dust.

Creatures flooded the room, and charged toward the horde of giants funneling through the doorway. Spara stood before Hallgeirr then spread her arms wide and placed a hand on either side of his massive head. For a moment she held them there, rubbing his temples, the pair lit by the glow of the Waystone upon which he kneeled. With the strength of a hundred men, she slammed his face into the floor below, shattering the Waystone.

The Waystone flickered erratically, its essence drifting into the air from the fissure the impact with Hallgeirr's face created. The crimson vapor whirled around Spara and then was absorbed by her body.

Hallgeirr's body slumped to the floor, blood pooling around him. Spara took a graceful step back to avoid the encroaching garnet slick. She then turned to face her former cell and strode toward it, waving for Umhra to follow.

Once inside, with Umhra a few feet behind her, Spara took an imposing stance, causing the thick stone walls to flex around her. The exterior wall shattered under the force, and crumbled away, leaving a yawning hole through which a strong, icy wind drove a blinding snow.

Behind them, the horde of giants waded through Hallgeirr's pets, their immense weapons swatting the beasts from their path. Their leader roared at seeing Hallgeirr and Solveigg lying dead amidst the chaos.

"Kill them," he said, pointing toward Spara and Umhra, who now stood at the edge of the precipice, peering down to the Amarthian Sea miles below.

Umhra turned to face the giants but Spara placed a gentle hand on his shoulder. "There will be no need to fight, Champion of Vaila. Follow me and pray to your god."

She turned and leaped out into the raging storm, disappearing from sight. The giants bore down on Umhra, tearing at the walls of the cell to widen the opening and thrusting their weapons within. There was no time to hesitate. Umhra turned and blindly followed Spara in her plunge.

Umhra plummeted toward the dark sea, the air biting his face. Spara was far below, a mote of emerald light amid the swirling tempest. In a flurry of white feathers, she lifted into the sky on angelic wings.

Umhra fell past her, the angry black waters approaching at an alarming pace. He grabbed his icon and closed his eyes in prayer to Vaila as Spara had instructed. Nothing happened. He opened his eyes to see black waters racing toward him and plunged into their frigid depths.

The initial impact nearly knocked Umhra unconscious, and Forsetae and his armor vanished. He was left in total darkness. The shock of the cold followed. He gasped, salty water burned his throat and lungs. He heaved, expelling the fluid but leaving himself with precious little air. Disoriented, his head pounding, he could not tell in which direction was the surface.

A green light shown overhead and he swam toward it. His heart raced as he realized how deep his dive had taken him, how far he was from the surface. His burning lungs begged for air. There were yards of water overhead. Then, an unseen force gripped his body and tore him from the water.

Umhra choked, spit up what felt like half the sea. Above him, Spara hovered, a halo of green light around her. Her wings spread wide, she held a hand outward and controlled Umhra's descent to a nearby beach.

He came to rest on the icy sand, shaking uncontrollably and gasping for air. Spara landed beside him, kneeled, and placed a hand upon his heaving chest. The halo of celestial light around her intensified and warmth coursed through Umhra's body. His breathing slowed, his muscles relax.

"That was not the outcome I expected," Spara said, leaning over Umhra with a smile on her face. She helped him sit up. "We have a lot of work to do."

"I did exactly as you told me. I prayed for wings like yours and nothing happened."

Spara wrinkled her nose. "Well, anyone can pray for wings. It doesn't mean you're going to get them. For that, you have to believe in yourself. Which, I sense, may not be where your strength comes from. Do you rely on her for everything?"

"Vaila? Yes. Our bond is what gives me power."

"Wrong." Spara shook her head. "You are a demigod now, no longer a man. Your true power comes from within. To be honest, it always has. The gods merely amplify the strength within you. Let's try again. This time, pray to Vaila not for wings, or power, but for guidance to find your own strength."

Umhra climbed to his feet. The frozen sand cracked beneath him in brittle sheets. He prayed to his god that she help him to draw upon the strength within—to find the confidence to believe in himself. His icon alighted with a vigor unlike he had ever seen before and power surged through him. He did not ask his god for wings but, rather, demanded their presence from himself. Grey feathered wings sprouted from his back.

"Much better," Spara said. "Now will yourself to fly and follow my lead." She lifted into the night.

Fly. With three strong beats of his newfound wings, Umhra raced after Spara, skimming the surface of the sea before arching into the air.

CHAPTER 11

Roen aspires to be a great leader. I should see him become a great man, first.

—*Entry from the Diary of Vred Ulest*
Dated 8ᵗʰ of Prien, 903 AF. Unearthed from the Ruins of
Ohteira, month of Lusta, 1399 AT

—▲—

Weary from their restless travel, Talus and Alessa arrived in Hylara slumped upon the saddle they shared. It was late in the afternoon and a steady salted wind blew from the south. At the port, bells rang out, forewarning the approach of inclement weather. Stores and homes battened down their seaward windows in anticipation. Shopkeepers dragged their wears off the street. A nervous energy pervaded the town.

"It doesn't look like anyone will be setting out tonight," Talus said, helping Alessa and Turin down from Maelstrom's back. "I suggest we find an inn and charter a ship first thing in the morning."

"I'm not about to turn down a good night's sleep in an actual bed," Alessa said. "Nor a bath before heading out to sea."

"I can't say I disagree. Let's see if we can find ourselves something suitable."

Similar to Anaris far to the west, Hylara was circular in construction, with its broad southern border abutting the Sea of Widows. What made Hylara unique was that the River Torrent flowed through its center, emptying its contents into the sea. Bridges spanned the broad river at regular intervals throughout the city, unifying it as one, as if holding together a wound with sutures made of stone and wood.

Talus led Maelstrom across the river and into a respectable neighborhood along the Torrent's western bank. Alessa stayed close, clutching Turin to her chest as they walked. Along the side of the street, they saw a well-kept building, three stories high, with a widow's peak at the top looking out over the river delta and beyond to rough seas. The house's cedar shakes were weathered by design rather than neglect and the patinaed copper sign out front read, *The Fulmar's Landing,* with a picture of a gliding seafaring bird above the lettering.

"Storm's comin'," a man said from the expansive porch that spanned the entire front of the structure. "You and the family in need of a room, son?"

"Oh, we're . . . yes," Talus said, feeling a rush of warmth to his cheeks.

"Well, c'mon in, then," the man said. "We have a few rooms still available."

He clapped his hands twice and rose from his chair. He was a portly Zeristar and kept his brown hair short and his face clean-shaven. Middle-aged, he wore a fine blue suit with a green ascot.

A young Iminti man, thin with warm features and pointed ears that jutted out from beneath a tangle of bourbon hair, came running at his call and flashed a broad smile at their new guests at the front steps.

"My stableman will see to your horse. We'll take good care of him during your stay. Quickly now, before the storm comes in."

The young Iminti man ran down the stairs and took the

reins from Talus's hand. He nodded and rushed Maelstrom around the southern side of the building. Talus and Alessa followed the Zeristar man into the inn.

"The name is Folsom Centrian, welcome to my pride and joy, The Fulmar's Landin'," the man said, taking a seat behind a desk at the center of a large lobby decorated with oil paintings of the sea. "The finest you'll find in Hylara, I'll assure you that much."

"I'm sure it will do fine," Talus said. "We're just happy to find a place before the storm hits."

"No doubt. Especially with a child in tow. How old?"

"Just a month old today." Alessa smiled, looking down on Turin.

Folsom leaned forward and took a peek, his broad smile twisting into a grimace. "Congratulations." He snapped his gaze back to his ledger.

"Thank you," Alessa said, not seeming to recognize his reaction.

"Alright, one room for the night. That'll be ten sovereigns."

"And for the horse?" Talus asked. "We sail abroad early tomorrow. Can you board him until my return?"

"I shouldn't think that would be a problem. It'll run about two sovereigns per day for room and board."

Talus reached into his satchel and pushed forty sovereigns across the table, accepting the key in return.

"If I am delayed, I'll settle up upon my return."

"Very well. Third floor, second door on the right," Folsom said.

"Thank you." Talus bowed his head.

Folsom nodded. "Just leave the key on the desk when you depart, if you will."

"Of course. It's been a pleasure meeting you, Lord Centrian."

"And you as well."

Thunder cracked overhead as Talus and Alessa walked up the wide staircase, passing nautical paintings along the way.

They reached the third floor and found their room. Its wood-slat walls were painted sky blue, and a dark blue rug sat beneath an expansive bed dressed in white linens. Alessa spun in a slow circle, her eyes glinting. She laid Turin on the bed and shook her arms.

"Would you mind if I freshened up some?" She asked.

"Not at all, I can wait downstairs," Talus said. "I saw a small tavern toward the back of the lobby."

"I would actually prefer you stay. Maybe you can turn that chair and admire the view out over the river, if you wouldn't mind?"

Talus cleared his throat. "Of course. If it's what you wish." He took the blue and white upholstered chair from beside the window and turned its back to the room. He slumped into the chair, his legs weary from the travel, and looked out over the River Torrent as it emptied into the Sea of Widows to the immediate south. Lightning flashed, followed closely by a crack of thunder. The wind kicked up, and the river churned as a heavy rain buffeted the window, blurring the view. Another flash of lightning and Talus saw the reflection of the room behind him. Alessa was naked, her back turned toward him as she bathed. He admired her form briefly and then shut his eyes, allowing himself to wonder if she would have found him suitable should things have been different.

The storm raged through the night, Alessa and Turin were comfortable in the bed while Talus was somewhat less so in the chair. He woke early and bathed. When he was dressed and ready, he woke Alessa and helped her gather the few belongings she had brought with her.

They departed The Fulmar's Landing, careful not to disturb anyone, and headed toward the wharf. Water dripped from the eaves of the buildings they passed, forming vast puddles along the warped cobblestone streets. The sounds of the city gave way to those of the sea, as boats rocked on their moorings and sails flapped in the persistent wind. Crewmen shooed brazen gulls as they loaded their cargo and prepared their ships for the open water.

Talus approached the dockmaster who was walking the length of the wharf and monitoring the crews' progress. Talus held his hand in the air to get the man's attention. The man nodded in recognition and waved Talus over to him.

"What can I do for yah, fine sir?" The rotund man asked. A large black cap obscured his eyes.

"I'm looking for safe passage to Shent," Talus said. "Have you any ships heading that way today?"

"I do," the man said. "Are yah traveling alone?"

"No. It will be me, my wife, and our infant child."

The man lifted his cap from his chestnut eyes and stared up to meet Talus with an awkward smirk. "Yah aren't in any trouble, boy, are yah?"

"Certainly not," Talus said. "I have family in Shent and we look to restart there with a little help from them."

"I guess it matters not, as long as yah have the funds for the voyage. One-hundred-fifty sovereigns for the lot of yah and no trouble aboard." The man held his hand out and tapped his foot impatiently.

"Fair enough," Talus said, pulling the notes from his satchel and handing them to the dockmaster. "When do we set sail?"

"The Jilted Rose leaves for Port Denarin in two hours. Yah can board in about an hour. I'll let Captain Dunrik know to expect yah."

"Excellent," Talus said. "Thank you for your time."

"No worries and safe travels to yah and the family."

Talus nodded and made his way back toward the wharf's entrance. Alessa waited for him there, swaying from side-to-side with Turin in the crook of her arm.

"We're all set to board a ship called the Jilted Rose in an hour's time," Talus said, greeting her. "Is there anything you need to see to before we depart?"

"No," Alessa said. "I never thought I would say this, but I just want to leave everything behind and start over. Nearly being executed has a way of shifting one's perspective, I suppose."

"The prospect of one's own death certainly crystalizes what's important in life," Talus said.

"You've been in such a situation before?"

"I have escaped death many times," Talus said. "Let's just say it's an occupational hazard."

"Well, twice in two years is plenty enough for me." Alessa sighed. "I should hope for things to settle down once we get to Shent."

"You and Turin will be safe there," Talus said. "That much I promise you. The Shent are a peaceful people. Come, let's walk the city a bit while we wait. It will be quite some time before we can enjoy such freedoms again. We'll be aboard the ship for several weeks."

"If you think that's alright, it sounds nice to me."

They strolled the streets of Hylara's market district. It was early and the shops were yet to open for the day. A rat scurried into a narrow alley. They turned a corner and came upon a bridge that crossed the River Torrent where two soldiers stood in conversation. Alessa flinched, pulled Turin in close.

"Just act normal," Talus whispered. "They have no reason to suspect us of anything."

They crossed the bridge, the guards halting their conversation.

"Oy."

Talus froze.

"May we have a word?" The taller of the two soldiers approached. Talus turned to face him. The other soldier stayed behind at the foot of the bridge.

"Of course. What can we do for you?" Talus sized the soldiers up. The one that approached held himself with a quiet confidence, his shoulders pinned back and his gait steady. The other soldier wheezed with each breath he took.

"I was telling my partner you looked familiar. You remind

me of a soldier of the Raptor's Grasp I met in Vanyareign a couple years ago when I was stationed there. Did you serve in the king's army?"

"I'm afraid not." Talus's stomach was in his throat. "We're from Tayrelis. Spent enough time working the river to move to Shent and try my luck in the mines. I've only been to the capital once for the Sowing Moon Festival a few years back."

The soldier nodded. "Alright, then. Sorry to interrupt your morning."

"Not at all. Be well." Talus turned back to Alessa.

"Congratulations on the child," the soldier said. "Can I take a quick peak?"

Talus clenched his jaw.

"I just got her to sleep," Alessa said. "We were up all night with her colic. I'm not sure I could handle her waking up right now."

"I understand. My little sister was colicky. Pushed my sweet mother to her limits. Best of luck."

Talus and Alessa returned to the wharf to find the Jilted Rose.

"I'm sorry." Talus hung his head. "That should never have happened. I know better than to take unnecessary risks like that. I just thought—"

"Stop it." Alessa took his hand. "It all turned out well. How were you to know you'd be recognized here?"

Talus nodded. Shops gave way to moorings and they located the vessel that would carry Alessa and Turin to Freedom.

The Jilted Rose was a large ship in the traditional Evenese style, with a cobalt blue hull shaped to resemble the fluid form of a whale, and a large, central mast with two booms, one sloping gently upward from the mast's base, and the other rising at a sharp angle a third of the way up the mast's towering length. Once at sea, the mainsail would billow between the booms while a second would catch wind between the upper boom and the mast. At the bow was an ornately decorated bowsprit of a crying woman holding a rose. Here, the traditional oversized jib sail stretched out from the front of the mast.

"Looks suitable." Talus approached the gangplank with Alessa and Turin at his side.

"You must be the family the dockmaster mentioned would be traveling with us to Port Denarin," a man said from the quarterdeck above. He was well-dressed, with a long black leather coat worn over a lush red vest with silver buttons. Alessa wrapped an arm around Talus's and smiled.

"Yes, we are." Talus's voice cracked. He nodded his head. "And you must be Captain Dunrik."

"I am," Captain Dunrik said. "Come aboard. We have a suitable cabin readied for you."

"Of course," Talus said, walking to the gangplank and offering Alessa to board the ship before him and they stepped onto the Jilted Rose.

"I'm Talus Jochen. A pleasure to meet you, Captain. A fine ship you have here." He shook the captain's hand.

"You'll find your quarters sternward, on the main deck. Third room, port side. I would show you there myself, but I must see to a timely departure."

"Of course. Thank you, Captain." Talus nodded and then escorted Alessa down a flight of stairs at the end of the quarter deck. On the main deck, they turned toward the stern of the ship and entered a hallway with three doors on either side, and one at its end with the words *Captain's Quarters* burned into its surface.

"Third room, port side," Alessa said, coming to the end of the hall and raising an eyebrow as if asking Talus for guidance.

Talus opened the door to a small cabin with a bed against the hull wall and a small hutch beside it. An oil lamp hung from a hook in the center of the ceiling, providing the room's only light.

"It'll have to do." Talus said, staring into the cramped cabin. His pulse quickened. It was one thing to harbor Alessa and Turin in his chamber for a night in Castle Forene, or at his family's home where they occupied separate rooms. By far the easiest, were all the nights camping when they took shifts on watch. Even last night at The Fulmar's Landing he was too tired to care. This was going to be entirely different . . . he was used to living alone. The idea of sharing this cabin for the next several weeks gave him thoughts of jumping overboard.

"It will be fun." Alessa smiled. "I've never been on a ship before. We'll make it work."

"I suppose we will," Talus said. "After you."

Alessa stepped into the room and looked around. "I think I'll feed Turin and put her down for a nap."

"Of course," Talus said. "I'll be up on the main deck should you need me."

"Okay, I'll be up as soon as she's asleep. I should like to see Evelium one last time."

Within the hour, The Jilted Rose disembarked and coursed into the open waters of the Sea of Widows. Alessa joined Talus on the deck as the sails caught wind and pulled the ship forward. They watched Evelium fade from sight and then turned their attention forward toward the Shattered Isles which stood between them and Shent.

CHAPTER 12

As I look back over all that I have accomplished, you are, without compare, my finest creation.

—The Collected Letters of Modig Forene
Letter to Prakten Modig dated 2ⁿᵈ of Mela, 201 AF. Unearthed
from the Ruins of Vanyareign, month of Ocken, 1301 AT

—▲—

Spara's bare feet set down on the ground and her wings receded. Umhra crashed down clumsily behind her, landing on his left knee and a palm in the middle of a field buttressed by rolling hills and littered with the ruins of an ancient complex.

He stood, his wings retracting, and walked over to the Mystic. "I had no idea," he said, Spara's gaze still fixed on the remains of her watchtower.

"There is so much more, Umhra," she said, tilting her head and grimacing at the rubble strewn out before her. "You haven't even scratched the surface. To be honest, I wasn't sure I'd be able to fly in my weakened state, but I didn't see any other way out of that mess we made." She walked toward the ruins. Umhra followed, silent, considering the possibilities of his nascent powers.

"This is my watch." Spara said, ambling across the grounds,

tall grasses rising to her fingertips. "Or at least it used to be. It was a glorious place back in its day, I promise you. It's amazing what two thousand years of neglect can do to a place." As she walked, green ether wafted from the rhodium orb around her neck. She raised her hands and gracefully curled her fingers. The toppled stones which once formed the magnificent structure lifted into the air around her and shed the soil and plant matter that had overgrown them through the ages. Umhra froze still and watched as, layer-upon-layer, Spara rebuilt the tower as if new. Spara disappeared through the yawning entry.

The early morning light cast Umhra's shadow across the length of the tower's great hall. "If you take pause and feel the vibrations of the world around you, you'll learn to control those vibrations and flex space to your will," Spara said. Umhra quieted his mind and searched for the vibrations. "It takes time, but you'll get it. Watch."

Spara took a firm stance, as if ready to defend herself, and bore down on the space before her. The floor receded, forming a spiraling staircase leading down below the watchtower. "One of the many things Atalan taught me. Come . . . follow me."

Umhra stepped into the room and inspected the staircase as Spara descended into the darkness below. He followed while small, honey-colored orbs materialized overhead to light the way. The staircase wound deep into the earth, ending as the stone folded away and formed a large octagonal room identical to the one Umhra found below the undercroft of Ember's Watch. More orbs lighted the perimeter as they entered.

"I wish I would have known about the staircase when I was at Ember's Watch. It would have been a lot less messy."

"We all enjoy our little secrets, don't we?" Spara flashed a coy smile over her shoulder. "Each of us had a watch during the Age of Grace and each watch had a hidden room like this to protect our most prized possessions. I suppose they're all in a similar state to mine at this point. Sad, really."

"I've traveled almost the entirety of Evelium and have only

seen Ember's Watch, and only from a distance until my recent visit to acquire your icon. The main tower stands, but little else. I had no idea there were others like it. So, you really lived during the Age of Grace?" Umhra asked, already knowing the answer, but still finding it hard to believe.

The receding wall unveiled a chest made of polished metal. "Of course," Spara said, her tone disappointed. "I'm a Mystic. The last of my kind on this plane. Well, that is until now. Your powers are still growing and your knowledge severely lacking, but you show great promise."

"And the others? They ascended to Kalmindon as the legends read?"

"Yes. And left me here to wallow for all eternity under the control of that brute Hallgeirr. I'm sure your legends mention nothing of the like," Spara said, her tone turning cold and the storms within her eyes flashing with lightning. She kneeled before the chest and opened its lid.

"No. There was no mention of you being left behind. I only learned about it after visiting the spirit king of Antiikin. My book confirmed it and directed me to Ember's Watch to find your orb."

"Book?" Spara turned from the chest to face Umhra.

Umhra retrieved Ivory's Nameless Tome from his satchel and passed it over to Spara. She inspected the cover. "It's radiant. Who gave this to you?" She leafed through its pages.

"My adoptive father. It seems he spent a lifetime studying the Mystics so that one day, should I succeed in my Rhodium Suffusion, I would have something to guide me in understanding my powers."

Spara stopped at a page and stared at Umhra. "This is impressive. Not entirely accurate, it would seem, but your father put great care into curating this for you. He must love you deeply."

"Yes, he did. And I him. He was a wonderful man."

"Experiencing loss is the only way we truly know we are

alive. The only way we know we've connected—had an impact on someone's life and them on ours. Keep this close. You will find it useful, I'm sure."

Spara returned the book to Umhra and swiveled back to the chest in the center of the room. From the chest, she retrieved two hand axes. Made of polished rhodium, their surfaces were so pure it was difficult for Umhra to tell if they were of solid form. They had ancient glyphs in the celestial tongue of the gods etched into their handles and a flawless emerald embedded in base of their grips. Spara spun the axes, one in each hand, reacquainting herself with her weapons of choice—a soft green glow bearing witness to their connection.

"Shatter and Quake," she said, introducing them to Umhra by name. "At least that is their names in the common tongue. They were forged in the heavens, akin to the very swords of Vaila, which I believe you have seen. I cannot summon mine as you do. That is a most rare ability."

"Impressive," Umhra said, dismissing the weapons in favor of their prior conversation. "You were saying, the others left you behind?"

Spara furrowed her brow and gritted her teeth. "Yes. I tracked Naur across Evelium to the Lazarus Woods. It was there I alerted the gods to his presence, and they banished him to Pragarus, ending the War of Rescission and the Age of Grace. For my faith and exemplary service, I had my eyes taken from me and was abandoned here in the material plane, imprisoned by that wretched giant, as the rest ascended to Kalmindon to live among the gods."

"You seem to see just fine."

"Yes, I had to retrain myself. And what I *see* differs from you. As best I can explain it, I see the energy of things. You are nearly blinding to me when in battle. I was immediately enamored, I must admit."

"Why did they leave you behind?" Umhra asked, ignoring the approbation.

"In my weakened state, I wasn't able to make the journey. They were unwilling to wait for me to heal—scared to remain on Tyveriel during the Age of Chaos—without their precious gods to protect them. They stripped me of my icon and hid me away in Oda Norde, locked in that cage for nearly two millennia. And the gods did nothing to stop any of this. They turned their backs on me as well."

"And your ambition now that I have freed you?"

Spara looked up at Umhra from her knees, her face ageless, beautiful. Grey smoke swirled in her eyes—a storm trapped within her. "Ascension, of course. I mean to rejoin the others." She stood, dusting off her celadon gown and securing her axes in her belt. "I believe I deserve as much considering my sacrifice."

"What does that entail?"

Spara smiled and stepped close to Umhra. She put her hands on his chest and gazed up at his face. "You remind me of him. Stronger than you know . . . but naïve."

"Who?" Umhra asked, rigid at the contact. He had not known a woman so bold.

"Someone I knew long ago," Spara said. "I doubt this world would have room for the two of you."

"And your ascension?"

"Oh, yes." Spara did not offer Umhra any quarter. "We will need to destroy all but one of the remaining Waystones. For that, I will need you. Your power. Being held in captivity has left me weak. I'm not sure how long it will take me to recover now that I have my icon back."

"I thought the Waystones were inactive," Umhra said, putting his hands on Spara's wrists and lifting them from his torso. "Even then, aren't they for travel across Tyveriel?"

"One can use them for travel within this plane, but their true purpose was always for travel between Tyveriel and Kalmindon," Spara said, smiling. "And then only for a Mystic. They are inactive, yes, but only because they are fueled by our power. You and I are not strong enough to activate them all, so they will remain inert as long as there are more Waystones than Mystics. If we destroy all but one, I'll be able to ascend."

Spara spun from Umhra's grasp and held her hand out to the wall before them. One after the other, small blue lights illuminated the wall depicting the lands of Tyveriel. Upon the continents grew six red beacons forming the shape of a cross. "The others knew that, by myself, there was no hope for me to ascend. What they didn't count on was you," she said, pointing to one light which flickered irregularly. "Of course, I already fractured the Waystone in Oda Norde with Hallgeirr's face." She grinned. "That leaves one each on Tukdari and Shent, two more in Evelium—the one at the Stoneheart Pass inert—and the last to the east in Malara. Tukdari and Shent are the farthest. We might as well start there."

"Why leave only one?" Umhra asked. "If there are two of us, could we not achieve your goal by leaving two?"

"Normally, yes," Spara said, "but neither of us are at full strength, and you have another matter to attend to here before you may ascend."

"That being?"

"The Grey Queen, of course." Spara turned back to Umhra, letting the lights fade behind her. "She is coming. If you don't stop her, it will mean the end for Tyveriel as you know it. It will mean the end of the races of man."

"That seems to be a possibility every few years," Umhra said. "I thought the Grey Queen was nothing more than a folk tale. A child's story."

"When I lost my sight, Vaila granted me a moment of clarity in which I saw the rise and fall of the Age of Man, the latter coming at the hands of the Grey Queen. She is real, Umhra, and she will be the ruin of this land . . . of humanity."

"And I'm to stop her?"

"Ideally, yes," Spara said. "I'll show you everything I know in order to assist you. While you help me with the Waystones.

Deal?"

Umhra raised an eyebrow, not yet sure what to make of his supposed teacher. "Seems like a fair trade."

"Then, let's be on our way," Spara said, bounding up the stairs. Umhra hurried after her. The room closed in behind him. As they returned to the main chamber of Spara's Watch, the basement was once again hidden, her secrets concealed. "We make for Tukdari to destroy the first Waystone. Along the way we'll make a stop so I may give you another lesson in your abilities."

"Very well," Umhra said. "I look forward to what you have in store for me."

Spara took one more look around and grimaced. "A little more disheveled than I would like, but good enough, I suppose. I have no intention of returning." She walked out into the relative warmth of the afternoon sun, her wings sprouting from her back, and flew into the air. Umhra followed.

CHAPTER 13

The Orcs were the first of the exalted races. Displeased with their blood-thirsty ways, the gods created the Evenese to counter them.

—*The Gatekeeper's Abridged History of Tyveriel*
Vol. 1, Chapter 2 – Unearthed from the Ruins of Meriden, the month of Anar, 1217 AT

—▲—

The channels between the Shattered Isles were narrow but deep enough for a laden vessel to traverse. Talus sat upon a simple wooden stool at the rear of the quarterdeck as a steady light breeze blew, forcing the crew to work feverishly to keep wind in the ship's sails. The water ran from light turquoise in its shallows to near-black beneath the Jilted Rose. A slight current towed the boat forward, maintaining pace in the lackadaisical wind as the ship moved closer to the shore.

Heavy foliage choked the islands' beaches, limiting any view of the path forward as they weaved their way through the maze of channels. Captain Dunrik kept a hand on the helm and squinted as far out on the horizon as the conditions would allow.

"Let's keep a keen eye out through this stretch," he said to his first mate.

"As you wish, Captain," the Farestere man said in a shrill voice. He ran off to convey the message to the rest of the crew.

"Privateers frequent these waters," the captain said. "Sometimes we run into worse. We'll be on the ready."

Talus allowed his mind to wander as the captain returned to his duties.

"Privateers," a crewmember shouted from his perch on the mast high above. "Approaching starboard."

Captain Dunrik passed the helm to an Iminti man and ran to the rail of the ship. "Left full rudder," he said. The Iminti man spun the wheel, sending the ship listing to the left.

"Man the ballistae."

A large black ship came into view as the Jilted Rose crossed between islands. Crew members scrambled across the deck and prepared for battle.

Shots rang out from the other vessel. Elongated projectiles affixed to ropes hurtled through the air toward the starboard side of the Jilted Rose. Three large, barbed tridents slammed into the ship, two penetrating the hull while the third careened into the side of the quarterdeck just beneath where Talus sat.

The impact threw Talus from his stool. Wood splintered in all directions. The ropes groaned, growing taut, and tied the two vessels together.

"Cut the ropes," Captain Dunrik pulled his rapier and pointed to the side of the ship. Crew members lashed ropes around their wastes, climbed over the rail, and rappelled to the tridents below.

Talus clamored to his feet and drew Aquila. Leaning over the side of the ship, he swung at the rope affixed to the trident embedded somewhere within the captain's quarters. The rope was thick and waxed. His first slash frayed only a few threads. He climbed onto the rail to improve his leverage and hacked at the rope several more times until it snapped, falling slack into the sea below.

He jumped down from the rail and ran down to the cabin where he, Alessa, and Turin were staying. He swung the door open to see Alessa sitting up in bed with a start, clutching Turin to her chest.

"What's going on?" She asked, her face pale.

"We're under assault by privateers. Stay close to me. I may need to get you off this ship at any moment." Talus bolted to the main deck, Alessa two steps behind.

By the time they returned to the deck, the pursuing ship had cut the distance between the two vessels in half. Black iron ballistae crowded the ship's main deck, each loaded with a trident. Privateers, dressed in little more than rags, cranked large iron and wood winches, dragging the ships ever closer.

Their captain stood at the helm, shouting to his crew and waiving a rusted machete overhead. "Again," he said, slashing the machete toward the Jilted Rose. The privateers' ship sent another volley. Splinters of wood showered the crew. Two more tridents lodged themselves in the side of the Jilted Rose. The Jilted Rose shot back. The immense bolts of its four starboard ballistae hit the front port side of the privateers' ship low on its hull. Crew members rushed to reload.

The privateer ship drew closer and loosed a volley of arrows upon the deck, sending the crew of the Jilted Rose scattering for cover. The unlucky among them screamed with arrows jutting from their bodies. Blood and seawater mixed in pools on the deck. The privateer ship came alongside the Jilted Rose, the ropes connecting the two ships groaning under the strain. The crew on the Jilted Rose drew their melee weapons, preparing for the privateers to come aboard.

A swell formed behind the assailant's ship, sending it crashing into the Jilted Rose. Crewmen that hung over the side to cut ropes were crushed. Others from both ships fell into the water.

The swell erupted. A monstrosity with a dozen tentacles protruding from a teal whalelike body burst through the sea's turbulent surface. It was covered in white scars, each a testimony to the battles it had survived. The remaining crews on both ships scattered.

The creature lashed out with two of its foremost tentacles, grabbing onto the privateers' ship. It released a furious roar. Hundreds of spear-like teeth filled its mouth, along with a sinuous tongue with countless teeth of its own. Its sputum rained down upon the ship, burning through the wood of the deck and hull.

"Tursas." A deckhand pointed at the creature as he staggered backward past Talus and Alessa.

"If that thing comes for us next, jump ship and swim for that island," Talus said, grabbing Alessa by both shoulders and pulling her close to his face. She nodded, her eyes wide with terror. "I'll meet you there if I can."

The privateers shifted their attention toward the monster. The lines connecting the two ships went slack. The Tursas bore down on the pirate vessel, tightening its grasp by adding two more tentacles to its assault. The crew attacked the beast, slashing into its thick skin and shooting their ballistae at its enormous green eyes, but to no avail.

The Tursas's tongue lashed out across the deck, scooped up several crewmen, and impaled them on its teeth. One of its tentacles coiled around the ship's main mast and snapped it at the base as the monstrosity's toothy mouth tore a giant hole in its sternward hull. The ship listed. The ropes connecting it to the Jilted Rose grew taut again, then snapped under the pressure.

The monster thrust the prow of the privateers' ship into the air. It rent the hull in two and lifted both sides of the ship from the water's boiling surface. The beast dropped the sundered vessel into its open maw.

Privateers swam toward the Jilted Rose. The Tursas plucked them from the sea one at a time and dropped them into its gullet. The Jilted Rose, now freed from the ropes that tethered it, turned due east through a narrow channel between two larger isles where a stronger current hastened its escape.

The Tursas dove beneath the surface in pursuit, a great swell building ahead of its massive form. The wave hit the Jilted Rose, sent it lurching forward. Two tentacles shot out of the water and grappled the ship, and the creature once again rose to the surface and released a terrifying roar.

Talus threw his arm across Alessa's chest to protect her and drew Aquila once more. Much of the crew dove off the port side of the ship and swam for the nearest island. Captain Dunrik pointed his rapier at the beast and held his ground, not willing to cede control of his vessel. Turin cried.

Tentacles whipping overhead, the Tursas grew calm and released the Jilted Rose from its grasp. Its eye, a solid emerald green orb the size of a water wheel, stayed transfixed on the wailing infant.

Alessa noticed the reaction and stepped out from behind Talus's guard. She pulled the blanket down, exposing Turin's face to the monstrosity. Turin's crying continued, the Tursas's tentacles quieted into a synchronized wave. Alessa continued forward, those remaining aboard the Jilted Rose watched with mouths agape, and the Tursas gave quarter and returned to the depths of the Sea of Widows. Turin's crying ceased.

"What was that?" Captain Dunrik asked.

"I don't know," Alessa said. "I'm just happy it worked."

"The child, is she cursed?"

"I've been told she has been touched by the gods, Captain. I must confess, I didn't have any notion of what that meant until this very moment. No doubt, my little one is special, but we wish to keep that hidden as best we can."

The captain leaned in to look at the child. "She saved my life, and that of my crew. Your secret is safe," he said, stone-faced.

"Let's gather the crew that abandoned ship—the worthless bastards—and see you safely to Shent." Captain Dunrik looked to his first mate who was coming back from the bow of the ship where he commanded a ballistae. "Douse the sails and drop anchor."

"Yes, Captain," the Farestere man said.

The Jilted Rose came to a halt off the east-most point of the island to which the crew had swum. The ship sat in the azure sea as the sun set on the western horizon and the waxing Reaping Moon rose into a pastel sky.

The remaining weeks of the journey to Shent saw little more than open water—a veritable desert. Talus worried for Alessa who withdrew to their quarters with Turin since the incident with the Tursas.

"You needn't stay cooped up in this cabin so much," Talus said, sitting on the bed beside them. "The captain gave you his word, and the crew are too scared to even look at Turin.

"I've heard them whisper of the 'cursed child.' Superstitious people act irrationally. Though they owe her their lives, they wouldn't hesitate to throw us into the sea."

"I would never let that happen."

"You would try to not let that happen." Alessa put her hand on Talus's. "You can't take on the entire crew."

Talus considered the challenge. "Have you seen them? I like my odds."

Alessa laughed. "We're lucky to have you as our guardian. So brave . . . and foolhardy."

"Port Denarin off the port bow," a crew member said, his bellow muffled by the deck above.

"Shent is in sight," Talus said, an uncharacteristic playfulness in his tone. "Come with me to the deck. Surely, we can swim to shore if they throw us overboard now. And you must see Shent's coastline."

He grabbed Alessa's hand. It seemed fragile and warm in his. With a gentle tug, he led her out of the cabin and onto the deck. The sun warmed the back of their necks as it grazed the horizon, the sky shading purple. The soft, sandy beaches of Shent were now well within view. From the beaches rose towering black cliffs covered with lush tropical flora.

"I've never seen anything like it. The colors are all so vibrant," Alessa said, "and the air so sweet."

"You and Turin will be happy here," Talus said. "The Shent are a good people."

Fluttering along the beaches and atop the jungle-choked cliffs were small lights with luminous tails, reminiscent of a tiny, haphazard meteor shower.

"Fae Hobs," Talus said. "A true rarity in Evelium, but here in Shent, they thrive."

"I should very much like to see them up close," Alessa said, raising up on tip toes.

"No doubt you will, in time. But I must warn you they are austere creatures with a particular distaste for fools and villains alike."

"Then I will find myself among the like-minded." Alessa grinned. The gentle curve of her lips elicited a shallow smile from Talus. Alessa's eyes connected with his and held his attention. "You don't do that nearly enough," she said.

Talus hid his smile and pointed to an inlet toward which the Jilted Rose headed. "Port Denarin. We will stay there for the night. I'll let Lael know we have arrived and we will secure passage to his home tomorrow."

"Lael," Alessa said. "You trust this man?"

"With my own life," Talus said. "You'll be in good company."

Despite the late hour of their arrival, the wharf at Port Denarin hummed with activity. Men and women alike labored on the docks, the eucalyptus wood beneath their feet silvered with age and wear. A blend of human and Iminti, they hummed in unison as they worked, the culmination of which was a whir that put the most active of beehives to shame.

The crew of the Jilted Rose threw its mooring ropes ashore, the wharfingers securing the ship in place. A thin middle-aged man with chestnut skin and eyes approached the vessel with a welcoming wave. His hair was shaved close on both sides but long on the top and back. He wore a navy-blue vest over a white linen shirt, tan pants drawn tight just below his knee, and no shoes.

"Captain Dunrik," he called, his Evenese fluid, but spoken with a heavy accent. "Wonderful to see the Jilted Rose back in Port Denarin. The Federation of Shent welcomes you, brother."

"Thank you, Mosi," the captain said over the noise of the wharf. "It's wonderful to be back in your fine land. We'll be at port for seven-to-eight days and then returning to Evelium with a load of trade goods. My friends would welcome accommodations ashore for the night if possible."

"Of course, Captain Dunrik," Mosi said. "I shall see to this right away."

"Thank you, my good man."

"Think nothing of it, Captain."

The captain left the helm and joined Alessa and Talus at the gang plank, delaying them from departing the ship. He placed a hand on Talus's shoulder. "It's been a pleasure having you aboard my ship. May you find peace and tranquility here in Shent. I secured you a room for the night. I hope I didn't overstep."

"Much appreciated, Captain," Alessa said from Talus's side. "And thank you for the eventful journey, and all you have done in getting us here safely."

"My very least, Lady Alessa." The captain bowed. "I would expect great things from a child such as yours, but it won't be an easy path, I presume."

Alessa curtsied and took Talus's hand to guide her across the gang plank and toward her new home. Talus did not turn to follow her before placing his free hand on Dunrik's shoulder. "Thank you, Captain. And for your discretion."

"Of course, Sir Jochen," Dunrik said. "All is between us and the sea."

Talus gave in to Alessa's tugging and followed her across

the gang plank and onto dry land. Alessa held Turin close and checked to make sure her swaddling blanket completely covered her, despite the humid heat in the air. Mosi greeted them and led them up the wide carved stone stairway ascending to the cliff tops in a steep, jagged path. Broaching the last steps, they arrived in the city of Port Denarin, its domed buildings painted in bright primary colors welcoming them.

CHAPTER 14

It was Naur who believed differently. He sought dominion by leveraging the exalted races' most base instincts.

—*The Gatekeeper's Abridged History of Tyveriel*
Vol. 1, Chapter 20 – Unearthed from the Ruins of Meriden, the month of Anar, 1217 AT

—▲—

Having flown for two days over open water, an island appeared on the horizon. Umhra flew at Spara's side, wondering what she had in her bag of tricks to teach him next. Spara banked right and began her descent toward the speck of emerald land.

Breaking through a cloud, they neared the island, and the jagged terrain became clear. Immense shards of green glass covered the landscape, forming a haphazard array of razor-sharp spines. Every few moments, another shard would pierce the skyline, shattering the others around it.

"Is' Savon," Spara yelled over the rushing air. "A good place to stop and take a lesson."

"Looks more like a good place to end up dead," Umhra said.

Spara chuckled and dove further toward the island, pointing out a broad, gently angled spike of glass upon which to land. They touched down, another shard exploding through the island's surface nearby.

"This island is a place of great magic." Spara picked a sliver of glass from the ground beside her and looked through it. "Long ago, when wizards still graced Tyveriel, one called Aldresor claimed this land as his own and buried something precious deep below its surface."

"Aldresor . . . I've heard this name before. Something to do with apples. What can you share about him?"

"He was among the most powerful of his kind. He came close to achieving Mysticism without the sponsor of a god. Without suffusing metal. Aldresor's only aspiration was that of achieving immortality. His quest led him to study the lost arts of necromancy. He came to know more about death than most people ever care to learn about life. Ultimately, Aldresor was successful in staving off his mortal end for a time, and then vanished. He was never heard from again. It is thought his passion ultimately consumed him."

"A fanciful tale," Umhra said. "How does it pertain to us?"

"Twofold. Is' Savon regenerates in perpetuity." Another immense shard tore through the surface, scattering emerald slivers into the sea. "Therefore, we can do no lasting damage as you learn the new skill I am going to teach you. Secondarily, there is something within the wizard's lair beneath us that belongs to me. I should hope to retrieve it."

Umhra found Spara's story hard to believe and was torn between his skepticism and his eagerness to learn the extent of his newfound powers. There were few things more precious to Umhra than allowing himself to trust another. He believed trust was something one earned through shared adversity. Yes, Spara rescued him from the frigid depths of the Amarthian Sea, and he owed her a life debt as a result, but it seemed she needed him in order to realize her goals and, thus, her motivations were compromised. For now, he would give her the benefit of the doubt. "Alright. Where do we begin?"

"Remember at my watch how I reassembled the tower stone by stone?"

"Of course."

"A bit of bravado, I admit, but a lesson as well." Spara pointed at a group of spikes to her left and rubbed her palms together. Her icon alit with virescent energy and the protrusions snapped at their bases and lifted into the sky. Each the size of tree, the shards turned end-over-end, and then returned to the island's surface, balancing on their sharp tips. "A Mystic can rearrange matter as they see fit. If you quiet your mind and picture what you want from the material objects around you, the world will bend to your will.

"What I want you to do is picture a stairway leading beneath the island's surface to Aldresor's lair. There is a door somewhere beneath this shell. Find it."

Umhra rubbed his hands together like Spara had and turned to get a better lay of the land. "Okay. I can do this." He closed his eyes, took a deep breath, and searched his mind. The image of a heavy iron door came to him. Hammer blows pocked its surface, giving it a mottled texture. He sensed the door far beneath them—his right ear pulsing toward a new target—and imagined a stairway through the emerald glass leading to it.

Starting at Umhra's feet, the glass cracked, creating a long hairline fracture emanating from his location. The break widened, becoming a fissure. The glass broke away to form a set of steps leading down into untold darkness. Umhra opened his eyes.

"Very impressive." Spara smiled. "You, sir, are a quick study."

"You were right. I could see the door in my mind . . . sense it beneath us. I could feel the path to it forming."

"The secrets of Tyveriel lay themselves bare to a Mystic. Would you mind leading the way?"

Umhra stepped to the edge of the staircase and peered into the darkness. He focused on his icon and summoned Forsetae and his armor.

"Do you think that will be necessary?" Spara asked, coming up behind him.

"I don't know what will be necessary. You said Aldresor was a necromancer, no?"

"Valid point." Spara pulled Shatter and Quake from her belt.

They crept down the stairs, the light of the afternoon sky fading to little more than a grain of sand behind them. The glow of Umhra's armor illuminated the door he had seen in his vision, which now blocked their path forward. The door emanated a faint purple aura that fluttered as though weakened by time.

"I've seen such an enchantment before," Umhra said. "I can't say I know how to dispel it, though."

Spara wedged past him, sliding against the glass wall which, at this depth, appeared black but for the light cast by Umhra and the door. Her icon alit, sending a blinding celadon light through the chasm. She waived her hand, and the door's enchantment dissipated.

"Remind me to show you that when we get a chance. It comes in handy every so often. Looks like it slides open. Would you mind?"

Umhra tugged on the door's handle, but it didn't budge. He put a foot up against the glass wall and strained against ages of disuse. The door groaned, a plume of dust billowing from its path, and slid open.

Spara threw her arms forward and set adrift from her hands six orbs of light into the dark chamber. She stepped into the room and walked to a table at its center. Umhra entered behind her.

"Our friend seems to have had some interesting hobbies," Umhra said, inspecting a jar labeled *Pureblood Fetus*. Numerous lacerations bound with heavy stitching scarred the well-preserved unborn child's body floating within. Umhra's stomach turned.

Oddities cluttered the room so that nary a surface lay uncovered. Umhra walked among the shelves, perusing Aldresor's collection, while Spara rifled through stacks of papers strewn across the table.

"I don't want to be here a moment longer than need be," Spara said. "What we are looking for is a small pink stone. It will look plain enough but is very important to me."

Umhra rolled a metallic sphere the size of a human skull between his hands. Etched upon its surface were geometric shapes inlaid with vibrant yellow paint. "A small pink stone?"

"Yes, the Eye of Eminus. It was a gift given to me ages ago and I should like to leave this world with it in my possession."

"And, this eye . . . how did it fall into the hands of Aldresor?"

"When Pyra turned me over to the giants of Oda Norde, Hallgeirr's great grandfather took it from me and lost it to the wizard in a game of chance."

Umhra returned the sphere to its shelf. "Two thousand years ago?"

"More or less. Why?"

"Only because I heard another story involving Aldresor which put him in Tyveriel a little over nine hundred years ago. It involved a similar bet and some apple seeds. So, either we are talking about different wizards with a common name and predilection for gaming, or he may have been more successful in his quest for immortality than you believe."

Spara paused, rubbed her chin. "Well, as long as he doesn't show up anytime soon, we should be fine." She laughed uneasily.

Umhra finished perusing the shelves. "I don't see what you are looking for in this room. Is there more to this place? Seems like a lot of effort to go through for one strange room."

"There's always more to a wizard's lair. It's just a matter of uncovering its secrets."

Umhra closed his eyes and tried to imagine a small pink stone and ascertain its location. Nothing came to him. No image, no pulsing in his ear. Nothing.

"What are you doing?" Spara asked.

Umhra opened his eyes, frustrated. "I was trying to sense the eye's location. Like I was able to do with the door?"

"I've been trying since we arrived." Spara left the desk and went to a shadowed corner of the room. "Aldresor has safeguards in place against such magic. Come here. I've found something."

Umhra joined Spara in the corner where she crouched over a mote of amber light the shadows had obscured. "What is it?"

"A portal. My guess is it will lead us to Aldresor's vault."

"Or our deaths."

Together, they reached out and touched the bead of light. The light enveloped them, its radiance growing until the details of the room washed away and they stood in a vacuous expanse of pure amber. A force dragged them backward at tremendous speed, the light streaking past them and shifting color to gold, and then white. They came to rest, and the light closed in on itself, revealing a windowless room constructed of lead and lit throughout despite the lack of any corresponding fixtures.

The walls, floor, and ceiling were smooth, with no noticeable joints as though the room was cast from a single mold. Along the far wall was an immense lead door, its surface unadorned other than with a small triangle which glowed blue on the side opposite its heavy iron hinge.

"Aldresor's vault," Spara said. An impish smile crept across her face.

She walked over to the door, crouched before the triangle inset, and cocked her head. Something slammed into the door from the other side, the crash of the collision reverberated through the chamber. Spara jumped backward with a start and looked back at Umhra, her eyes wide.

There was a second impact, this one followed by the muted sound of metal scraping against metal. Umhra approached the door.

"This eye of yours must be quite dear for the wizard to go through such lengths to protect it. Is it worth opening this door and unleashing whatever is on the other side protecting it?"

"It is," Spara said. "I wouldn't bother if it didn't mean the world to me."

"Somehow, this recess matches my icon . . . almost as though this is planned. Remind me, what happened when the other Mystics took your icon?"

"I was rendered powerless for eternity."

"And, you think I should risk the same fate by placing my icon in this clasp and welcoming some undead horror upon us for a sentimental trinket you want to take with you to heaven?"

Spara pursed her lips. "Fine. It's more than a sentimental trinket. It's a sending stone. With it, I can speak with the person who holds its compliment."

"May I ask who holds the other?"

"You're going to think I'm ridiculous." Spara stared at the floor and kicked at it with the ball of a bare foot."

"Try me."

Spara looked into Umhra's eyes, tears streaking her face. "My mother died holding the other while we used it. I never found out what happened to her and I hoped it would help me find her when I reach Kalmindon." She buried her face in her hands.

Umhra thought of his mother, Joslin, who had been torn from his life when he was only four by a Tukdari horde. He thought of how he missed her and what trouble he would go through for the chance to see her again. He stepped closer and placed his hands on Spara's shoulders.

"Very well. This is a worthy cause. I would do the same."

Spara sniffled, offered Umhra a shallow smile. "Thank you."

Umhra pulled his pyramid from around his neck, allowing his armor and Forsetae to dissipate. He sized it up against the triangular recess. A third collision rang out, and Umhra stepped closer and pushed the icon into the recess, snuffing out the light it emanated.

Metal clasps grabbed the icon, locking it in place, and the door lurched inward, scraping against the metal floor. Umhra pulled on his icon's chain, trying to wrest it free from the recess's grasp, but to no avail. He drew a dagger from his belt and forced its edge into the gap between his icon and the recess. He wrenched the blade back and forth in an effort to pry the icon free. The blade bent but the clasps held fast.

"Dammit!" Panic set in, and an enormous form bound past him into the room.

Spara pulled Shatter and Quake from her belt and broadened her stance.

The creature crashed into her. It had been human at one point, or at least parts of it had been. Now it was a misshapen brute standing ten feet tall and held together by braided copper wire that was frayed and patinaed with age. Grafted to each arm from elbow to wrist were rusted blades with six large, serrated teeth ending in sharp points. They were terrible looking things.

The force of the first blow sent Spara careening into the lead wall behind her and down onto one knee. The abomination pursued her, thundering across the room in a matter of strides. Spara shook her head and scrambled to her feet. A saw-toothed arm swung at her. She rolled out of the path of the attack into the corner of the room.

Umhra gave one more pull at the chain attached to his icon and then dropped it. He scanned the room, found nothing. Unarmed, he charged at Aldresor's sentinel.

The creature whipped around from Spara and lumbered toward Umhra, groaning with each swing of its bladed forearms over Umhra's head. Umhra thrust the bent dagger at the monstrosity's abdomen, just above the waste of its tattered and soiled pants. The blade broke upon its skin as though the monster was itself made of hardened metal.

With a stiff backhand, the creature slashed through Umhra's leathers and sent him hurtling across the room.

Umhra tumbled, came to his knees, his momentum halted by the cold, unforgiving wall. He glared at his adversary through strands of tussled hair and climbed to his feet.

Spara clapped Shatter and Quake together, and they set aflame. The action garnered the creature's attention, sending it staggering back at the sight of the vibrant green flames licking from the weapons.

"Umhra," she said, angling around the behemoth to force it away from the vault door, "would you mind retrieving the eye while I hold our friend at bay?"

Umhra nodded and made for the vault. The creature protested with a grunt and a swipe of its arm, then once again recoiled as Spara waived Shatter in its face.

Like the outer room, the vault too was lit by a dim ethereal light, the source of which was indeterminable. The vault was empty but for a small pink stone floating at its very center, where the room's light shone brightest.

Umhra inspected the Eye of Eminus. It was oval and polished smooth. The stone's color was that of the apple blossoms he was so fond of when visiting Xavier Pell at his orchard and seemed to have an inner glow all its own. He plucked the stone from the air, surprised by its innate warmth, and turned for the exit.

The spell that fueled it now broken, the light flickered, and the vault went black. The door lurched and scraped against the floor. By the flickering green light of Spara's weapons, Umhra found his way back to the vault door and wedged his way through the narrowing gap.

"You get it?" Spara asked, jabbing at the monster with her axes.

Umhra plucked his icon from the recess in the door and threw the chain around his neck. He summoned Forsetae to his hand and his armor grew around him. "Yes, let's get out of here."

He strode across the room and raised Forsetae, intent on striking down Aldresor's monstrosity.

"I don't think that will be necessary," Spara said, halting Umhra with a stiff palm. "If we leave it here, it can't harm anyone. I doubt it can figure out how to use the portal."

"So, we just leave it here . . . forever?"

"Well, Aldresor saw fit to. I don't think we are doing it any harm. At least, no more than running it through with your sword."

The flame of her weapons fluttered—emboldening Aldresor's monster momentarily.

It lunged at Spara, swatting her weapons aside with one hand and lashing out at her with the other. Its jagged blade was inches from her face, then the creature froze.

Umhra held the monster in place with an outstretched hand. "May I suggest we leave? I can't hold him for long."

"Let's." Spara crossed the room to the mote of light through which they had arrived.

Umhra backed away from the monster he held in place until he was at her side. Spara took his hand and, together, they touched the portal and an unknown force tore them from Aldresor's vault.

They raced through time and space, the white light shifting to gold, and then amber as it sped past them. The light faded and they tumbled back into the antechamber beneath Is' Savon.

The room was dark—Spara's lights having faded—other than the light from the surface illuminating the doorway.

"We have all we came here for," Spara said, leading Umhra across the room to the door. "Let's be on our way to Tukdari and the first of the Waystones. You've done well here today."

"Well, I have an experienced teacher." Umhra turned and took another look at the mote of light that connected the room to Aldresor's vault.

"It won't escape," Spara said.

"I'm not worried about it escaping. For some reason, it bothers me we left it there forever."

"Your compassion knows no end. An admirable but

dangerous trait. Let's go, we have much to do."

Umhra nodded and stepped aside to allow Spara through the doorway and then followed. He slid the door closed behind him and bound up the emerald glass stairs.

CHAPTER 15

Of the more curious inhabitants of its jungles are the Fae Hobbs. These mischievous beings gave our caravan no quarter as we explored the interior of Shent.

—*A Traveler's Guide to the Odd and Obscure by Sentina Vake* Chapter 18 – Unearthed from the Homestead in Maryk's Cay, month of Riet, 1407 AT

—▲—

Fae Hobbs darted through the humid air, fluttering about the wagon as it rattled over the pockmarked earthen road. Alessa sat, Turin swaddled in her arms, and followed their every move with awe. Every so often one would hover before her, inspecting Turin with the same wonder Alessa held for them, and then dash back into the jungle that encroached upon the road from either side.

"Lael lives in a town toward the center of Shent known as Gelarra," Talus said, turning over his shoulder from the front of the wagon.

"And how do you know and trust this Lael you seem to think so highly of?" Alessa asked, trying to coax a Hobb into landing on her finger.

"We served together under the king," Talus said. A smile

broke across his face as Alessa and the Hobb played their little game. "He's been among my closest of friends since I joined the king's army."

"And how did he end up in Shent?" Alessa held her breath as the Hobb came within inches of landing at her request.

Up close, the creature's skin looked as if made of pure porcelain, its eyes too large for its face. It had no nose or mouth, and its ears were exceedingly long and came to a point. The Hobb's body was lithe to a point of being almost skeletal and gave no evidence as to age or sex.

The Hobb darted away. Alessa exhaled sharply and turned her attention back to Turin.

"A group of fellow soldiers accused him of a crime he didn't commit. When it became obvious the trial was not going his way, I busted him out of prison and brought him here. That was three years ago. He loves living here and will welcome your company until you get your own footing."

Alessa raised an eyebrow. "Accused, you say?"

"Yes. He was innocent. I promise, you'll warm to him immediately."

Turin fussed, which sent the Hobbs into a state of frenzy, some of which circled the wagon until a halo of light formed from the trail in their wake. Alessa soothed the child, and the Hobbs returned to their regular activities.

"How long will you be staying, then?" Alessa asked.

"Only a few days," Talus said. "I spoke with Captain Dunrik this morning. I mean to return to Evelium on the Jilted Rose as to not raise any suspicion."

Alessa's stomach sank at the prospect of being alone in a foreign land. "How can you go back to serving the king, knowing what he's done? He asks too much of you. Besides, I was hoping you would stay with us for a while."

"Things between the king and I will never be as they were," Talus said. "I will never feel the same way about him again. I plan to return to Anaris. I was quite happy serving Evelium alongside the Barrow's Pact. The king will approve of such an arrangement and continue to think you and Turin no longer pose a risk to him. It's best that way."

Alessa nodded, tears welling in her eyes. "Best for who?"

"When I brought Lael here, I gave him a sending stone. I possess its counterpart. With their use, we can talk whenever you like. Not that I'm such a skilled conversationalist."

"Definitely not your strong suit, I must agree."

Talus laughed.

"I'm glad you aren't going back to Vanyareign. I would hate to think of you around the king and all his paranoia."

"It isn't quite paranoia if your confidante runs off with the mother of your child against your wishes," Talus said.

"I suppose not." Alessa considered all Talus had done for her and Turin—all the risks he had taken. "I'm glad you did, though."

"The day we saved you from the Morion Swamp and put an end to the aid Varina the Decayer provided the Brothers of Resurrection, the ancient witch said something that stuck with me."

"What was that?" A shiver ran down Alessa's spine remembering that day.

"She said that position determines perspective, as though insinuating her actions were just. At the time, I didn't appreciate her meaning. Everything was black and white for me before I joined the Barrow's Pact on their journey to Meriden. She was evil . . . we were good. It was that simple. Now all I see is shades of grey."

"Both are sad ways to go through life, Talus. There are so many colors to brighten each day." A Hobb landed on Alessa's shoulder, just above Turin's head. It sat, hunched over, and rubbed its hands over its ears. Alessa marveled at it.

"We've led two very different lives," Talus said. "I hope you continue to see those colors here in Shent. Gelarra is just ahead."

The wagon hit a pothole and sent the Hobb darting off into the underbrush. "Me too," Alessa said, once again tasting the bitterness of disappointment.

They emerged from the jungle and crested over a ridge. The better vantage point revealed a large settlement in an immense caldera below. An acrid scent gripped the breeze. Alessa recoiled, burying her nose in the crook of her arm.

"You must be kidding," she said, laying bare her entitlement. She'd only lived in Vanyareign, whether at her parents' manor or Castle Forene, and hadn't truly considered that her new life might not offer any of the comforts she was accustomed to.

Talus pointed out over the caldera. Before them, a wide path wound down its perimeter until reaching the town, from which the sounds of heavy labor billowed. Its center held a lake of teal waters, surrounded by farmland.

"I'll admit it looks better than it smells," Alessa said, unconvinced.

"Gelarra is predominantly a mining town," Talus pulled the wagon to a halt. "The volcano is dormant and it left behind a vast deposit of gold and copper deep within its core. The people here work hard and have amassed great wealth for Gelarra and Shent. They don't flaunt this wealth, as is so common in Evelium, preferring to live modestly and well within their means. Here, the dirtier you are, the richer you are. And, I assure you, the air below is quite pleasant."

"I see. I'm not sure how I can contribute here. I know nothing of mining."

"Don't worry about your contribution. For a time, Lael will introduce you as his guest. Take that time to get comfortable with the town and its people. You'll figure out how to contribute once you settle in."

Alessa nodded, biting her bottom lip. Just weeks ago, she was lounging about Castle Forene expecting to become the next Queen of Evelium and today she found herself in a foreign land with little more than the clothes on her back. It was all quite shocking.

The wagon lurched forward, and they began their descent toward Gelarra. They dropped within the caldera, the air growing lighter and cooler as they progressed—a respite from the tropical heat they had so far experienced since they arrived in Port Denarin.

They neared the end of the path, closing in on the town below. Gelarra came to life, with miners dumping ore from large holes in the base of the crater's perimeter and transporting it by yak-drawn wagon to the many refineries dotting the landscape. They passed a large smelting complex where piles of copper discs lay stacked, ready for transport to market. Beyond the industrial ring lay the miners' homes and then businesses. The inner-most ring, abutting the shores of Lake Gelarra, was comprised of farmland.

"Lael's farmstead is just to the west," Talus said, pointing right at an intersection just in front of an extensive field teeming with cattle. A copper sign at the property's entrance read *Crater's Crest Ranch*. He nudged the horse, pulling their cart along the intersecting path, farms to their left and modest, but well-maintained homes and small businesses to their right.

They rode for another twenty minutes when Talus turned the cart into another property whose sign read *Eagle's Nest Farm*. The property was larger than Alessa had imagined, with an ample farmhouse close to the edge of the lake and several outbuildings scattered about. The architecture was quite unlike anything she had seen before. Houses of stone construction were topped with flat copper roofs and trim, all green with patina. Large, open-air windows spanned the façade, made possible by both the predictability of the climate and the city's inhabitants.

From here Alessa could see beyond the shores of the lake. Four stone bridges with copper trussed arches stretched out to a central island covered in buildings. "What's out there?" she asked, shielding her eyes from the sun with her free hand.

"Gelarra Island houses the town's civic buildings and the homes of the wealthier business owners and politicians," an unfamiliar voice said. Emerging from an outbuilding they were passing on the way to the farmhouse was a tall, strong-looking human man dressed in tan pants which came down to the middle of his calf, a white linen shirt opened past his sternum, and a sky blue vest. His hair was dark but had greyed with age at the temples. His well-groomed beard faded to stark white at his chin "Well, if it isn't Talus Jochen, himself. You look no worse for the wear, boy."

"I wish I could say the same for you, old man." Talus laughed, jumping down from the wagon and embracing his friend. "Wonderful to see you, Lael. Please let me introduce Alessa Elmont and her daughter, Turin—the mother and child I spoke with you about."

"You didn't do her beauty justice, Talus," Lael said, walking around the front of the wagon and extending a dirty hand up toward Alessa to help her down from her seat. "You've always been a horrendous conversationalist."

"We were actually just talking about that," Talus said. "I'm glad we're all in agreement on my social shortcomings."

Alessa gathered Turin and took Lael's hand. She stepped onto the gravel path and curtsied. "A pleasure to meet you Lord . . ."

"Azrina. But please, call me Lael. We're all friends here, and there is no need for formality. Not that I ever earned such title, anyway."

"Thank you, Lael. And thank you for welcoming Turin and me into your home."

"Anything for Talus. Besides, we could use a little youth to liven this place up a bit. Come, let's get you settled in and introduced to Dorin."

"Dorin?" Talus asked. "You made no mention of a Dorin in our talks. It seems I'm not the only one lacking in my communication skills."

Lael smiled. "You'll both like him. He's made my life here on Shent complete in a way I would have unlikely ever realized in Evelium."

"Glad to hear," Talus said. "I'll take the wagon up to the house and unpack Alessa's belongings. Why don't you two get to know each other?"

"Perfect," Alessa said, accepting Lael's outstretched arm and turning toward the house.

Like old friends, the two left Talus to the labor at hand. They paused just outside the house, Lael pointing to two points of light in the evening sky. "That's odd," he said. "It's early for stars to be shining so brightly."

"I don't think those are stars," Alessa said. "It seems they are moving."

The lights streaked across the sky in a southward direction.

"We occasionally get meteor showers, but rarely do they make it through the atmosphere like that."

"It must be a good omen for my stay here in Gelarra," Alessa said. "Pay it no mind. Let's go inside so I can meet Dorin."

CHAPTER 16

*I have successfully bound the subject's soul. How to retrieve it
is the mystery that remains.*

—*Entry from Aldresor's Journal*
Undated. Discovered in the Tower of Is' Savon, month of Riet,
1444 AT

—▲—

Umhra marveled at the Tukdari landscape as the expansive
steppe came into view and took over from the vast ocean
they had flown over for days without rest. A sea of sage colored
grass soon dominated, only broken by the occasional tree or
scattered clump of shrubs. The ferocious waves of Tukdari's
northern shores crashed against tall cliffs of blue marble
which, over the eons, had eroded into a twisted labyrinth from
the sea's relentless pursuit.

Spara and Umhra flew to the southern shore of the
continent, passing several barbarian encampments, their
leather and thatched-roof huts well camouflaged against the
arid landscape. Here, the sea was calm, beaches of blue sand
lazed in the sun. Several ports dotted the shoreline, each held
barbarian warships ready and willing to wreak havoc across
Tyveriel.

"So, where's the Waystone?" Umhra asked. "I thought it would be more obvious from this vantage?"

"Ember was always one for dramatic flair," Spara said. "He hid his Waystone in a sunken cave off the southern shore." She pointed to a dark patch beneath the sea's boiling surface. "Down there."

Spara dove out of the sky and plunged into the warm ocean waters. Umhra hesitated for a moment, took a deep breath, and then followed after her.

They swam through azure waters that teemed with life of all colors and located a fissure in the sea floor. Spara turned to Umhra and laughed at him as he held his breath.

You can breathe underwater, Umhra. Her voice resonated in his head, reminding him of Forsetae. *It can be uncomfortable at first, but I promise you'll be okay.*

Umhra closed his eyes for a moment, a bed of kelp swaying around him. He gave in and let the saltwater fill his lungs. His chest burned as though filled with lava, reminding him of his plunge into the Amarthian Sea. This time was different, though. When he opened his eyes, the burning abated, and he breathed easily.

Spara smiled. *The Waystone is within the fissure. It is guarded by Siasha, Mistress of Tides. Keep a sharp eye out.*

Umhra nodded and followed Spara through the chasm and into the depths below. They dove further, navigating a narrow passageway in complete darkness. The passage leveled off and ascended at a gentle angle. They swam until they came to an enormous cavern of blue marble identical to the cliffs they saw on their approach. The room was mostly submerged, with large stalactites hanging from the ceiling high above, and was lit by a solitary source that pulsed at its center.

The floor of the cavern tapered upward from each side toward a pedestal which rested in shallow water and from which the soft-white light emanated. Spara and Umhra breached the surface, coughing up water in favor of the stale air the cavern offered. They swam for the pedestal.

Umhra clambered onto the pedestal's edge, the cavern's course floor scraping at his hands and knees. Spara collapsed in the shallows along the edge of the Waystone's platform. She turned onto her backside and sat up, her hair hanging in doused strands across her face, her soaked dress clung to her body.

"I'm still so weak," she said, her chest heaving. "I was hoping my power would be replenished by now."

"The effects of two millennia of imprisonment can't possibly reverse in a week." Umhra said, "Give yourself time."

From the shadows behind Spara, two tentacles lashed out of the water. One grappled Umhra and the other tore Spara from their perch. Siasha, Mistress of Tides broke through the surface. The giant octopus held them in the air and inspected them with black oblong pupils, then slipped back into the depths.

Umhra crashed back into the water. As he was pulled deeper, he glimpsed Siasha dragging Spara closer. The creature was cobalt blue, with irregular grey striations which camouflaged her perfectly against the stone of the cavern. They must have swum right over her when they entered the cavern and not noticed her hiding in plain sight.

Umhra summoned his sword, accepting water back into his lungs, and hacked at the tentacle wrapped around his legs that pulled him toward the cavern floor. Siasha's flesh resisted the damage—Umhra's strike left only a superficial wound which healed immediately.

You must find another way. Forsetae said. *The creature is invulnerable to my blade.*

Below, Spara struggled to free Shatter and Quake from her belt, her arms bound in place. Siasha dragged her close and exposed her beak-like maw, snapping at the anticipation of an unexpected meal.

Umhra thought of Spara and spoke to her like he had so many times with Forsetae. *Forget the weapons. They're of no use against it.*

Spara closed her eyes. Her hand slid up through the coiled tentacle and grasped her pendant. As she neared Siasha's mouth, Spara opened her eyes. Instead of grey swirling orbs, her eyes shone with green radiance. She placed her hands on Siasha's flesh and from her fingertips, a black necrosis crept forward and caused the tentacle that gripped her to wither.

Siasha released Spara and clouded the water with opaque ink. Unable to see through the murk, Umhra was ripped through the water. Siasha lifted him into the air, thrashed him against the cavern wall, and threw him across the expanse of the room.

He summoned his armor moments before he crashed into the cavern wall and fractured its surface, sending chips of blue marble showering to the water. Wings sprouting from his back, he hovered among the stalactites, surveying the room. From here he could see the Waystone pulsing from its pedestal.

Spara burst from the sea, a cascade of water falling from her shimmering form.

"Quick, to the Waystone," Umhra said. "I'll hold Siasha off."

"If only it were that easy," Spara said, "In order for the Waystone to break, we must dispel the Guardian from this plane. We must destroy Siasha. If I can get my hands on her one more time, I might be able to do so."

Umhra sighed, frustrated with his lack of effectiveness against their foe. With Forsetae of no use, he was unsure what he could do to sway the battle in their favor. He scanned the cavern for any sign of Siasha. As the cloud of ink dissipated, the submerged floor became visible through the clearing waters, but gave no indication of Siasha's presence. With a flash of color, Siasha dropped her camouflage and lashed out with two tentacles at Umhra , and plucked him from the air.

With one tentacle wrapped around his throat and face, and the other around his abdomen, Siasha dragged Umhra back beneath the water's roiling surface. He resisted Siasha's oppressive grip, remembering Spara's lesson, and bore down on the surrounding space.

Spara dove back into the water, and chased the tangled pair into the depths of the cavern. She grabbed Siasha's trailing tentacle and, again, necrosis pervaded the tissue and spread along the appendage.

Another tentacle dying, Umhra envisioned Siasha torn to pieces just as he did the emerald glass shattering to form the staircase to Aldresor's lair. He drew energy from the space around him and unleashed his strength outward. The explosion tore Siasha apart. The cave shook, shards of rock splashed into the water and joined the cloud of blue blood and gore that spread throughout the cavern's pool as the great cephalopod's dismantled body slowly sunk into the depths.

Spara treaded water as Umhra swam to her side through the murk of ichor and pulp. He burst through the surface, expelling the water from his lungs, and they swam for the pedestal that held Ember's Waystone. Spara climbed into the shallows. Umhra rose out of water behind her and stood over the pulsing stone.

"That was a little more difficult than I had expected," she said as Umhra approached her flank. "You did well. It took me months to learn how to control my powers like that, and here you've done it in a matter of days. And, with such force I can see why Vaila favors you."

"Beginner's luck, I suppose," Umhra said. "I didn't know what else to do. Are all the Waystones guarded in such a manner?"

"All but the one in Oda Norde. For some reason, Pyra favored the giants as her last line of defense. Of the Guardians, there is one I hope to reason with. The others are ruthless killing machines. I'm afraid we will have to kill them. Each is formidable in their own way. I'll tell you more of their nature on our journey to Shent. For now, let's concern ourselves with the matter at hand.

"Each Waystone carries within it a modicum of divine power—much like our icons. Once we defeat the Guardian, shattering the stone releases that essence, which we will then absorb, bestowing upon us the associated power. When we at least equal the number of Waystones remaining intact, there will be enough power between us to ascend to Kalmindon and take our rightful place among the gods. That is, should you choose."

"And, this is what you want?"

Spara walked the perimeter of the Waystone, the water lapping at her ankles. "Of course, it's what I want. Ascension is our destiny, our birthright. You can't possibly prefer to stay here among all of this filth and impurity. Not when you've given up so much to achieve Mysticism."

"Is that how you view Tyveriel? As filth?"

"You've lived what, thirty years? I have lived for millennia, the last two of which I spent locked in a cage as a prize, abandoned by my family who swore to love and protect me. I believe I've earned the right to my petty criticisms. Wouldn't you agree?"

"Thirty-two years. And yes, I understand your point of view, but if the purpose of gods and Mystics is not for the betterment of Tyveriel and its creatures, what's the point?"

"It's a big game, Umhra. This whole experiment, the mortal plane. Vaila won, and the Mystics left so she could consolidate her power. The gods don't care about Tyveriel. They don't care about you and me or the common folk. They only care about themselves and their petty squabbles. You should have seen them when they walked Tyveriel among us. Your history books would have you believe they were flawless. I assure you the truth is quite a disappointment. But, enough of these things for now."

Spara pulled Shatter and Quake from the belt of her soaked gown. She dropped to her knees at the center of the Waystone. She held both axes in one hand and ran her other over the smooth, warm surface of the submerged stone. Then, she again took an axe in each hand and struck down on the stone's surface, sending a spray of water into the air. She smashed the axes upon the stone several more times until it cracked. With one more strike, she shattered the stone.

"Come, quickly."

Umhra stepped closer as an ethereal energy escaped from the fracture and drifted into the air like wisps of smoke from a dying fire. It hung for a moment, as if deciding whom to favor, and then split equally in two distinct clouds and emulated Umhra's and Spara's forms and entered their bodies.

A surge of power coursed through Umhra, his senses heightened. The weariness from the battle with Siasha was gone. He felt lighter but sturdier, faster but steadier, stronger but also clear of mind. In that moment, the image of a glass tower flashed in his mind. A great plume of smoke rose from its riven façade—a streak of black against a coral sky.

"That has a bit of a kick, doesn't it?" Umhra extended a hand to help Spara to her feet. For now, he decided to keep the vision to himself as its meaning was unclear to him.

"It does. I wasn't sure what to expect when I broke the stone in Oda Norde, but it was everything and then some."

"And we head for Shent next?"

"Yes, but may I suggest we spend the night here?"

"There isn't a dry spot in the cavern. Not the most hospitable sleeping environment. Surely, we can do better on Tukdari if you need rest."

"I think I can provide a suitable space, if you don't mind sleeping in close quarters."

Umhra furrowed his brow and shot Spara a wary glare, eliciting a giggle.

"I had no idea you had such a healthy ego. I promise I'll do my best to not make you uncomfortable."

"It has nothing to do with ego, but the recent behavior of the company I keep." Umhra said, less than assured. "What do you have in mind?"

"All in good fun, I assure you," Spara said. "There is another lesson for you in terms of your powers, if you will allow me."

"By all means."

"While we cannot yet travel to Kalmindon," Spara said, "we can tear a small hole between the planes which will allow us both safe and comfortable accommodations for a time."

"Go on."

"It's been a while since I've done this, so bear with me." Spara sounded unsure of herself for the first time since they had met.

She stared at the space between them, focused on something imperceptibly small. Her icon alit and she tilted her head and picked at the air. She pinched something between her fingers, pulled downward, and tore a rift in the space between them.

From within the rift, a soft, welcoming light glowed. Spara pushed two hands into the tear and pulled it apart to make room to pass through.

"Come on. Let's get some rest. I'm exhausted."

Umhra stood dumbfounded at what he had just seen.

"How did you—what did you—"

"I'll explain it to you once we are inside. I can't hold it open for very long."

Umhra inspected the edge of the tear where sparks danced. He reached a hand in and quickly withdrew it.

"It's not going to hurt you," Spara said. "See, I'm fine."

Umhra stepped through the rift into a small garden. Surrounded by a white stone wall that reached up into a coral sky speckled with billowing white clouds, the garden was perfect. The manicured grounds teemed with plantings unknown to Tyveriel. The air warmed Umhra's soaked body and a lazy path of glass beads lead to a small patch of grass at its center. Spara joined him, allowing the rift to close.

"So, we are in Kalmindon?" Umhra asked.

"Technically, yes," Spara said, walking over the glass beads to the central lawn. "We're in a tear between realms. A pocket in reality. It will provide us safety and comfort when needed, but we cannot go beyond the garden. For that we would need to ascend."

Umhra crossed the path of beads, a soothing warmth crept up his legs from the soles of his feet. He joined Spara on the grass. "Why are they so warm, the beads?"

"Each one is a soul from the mortal plane. Their combined energy is the source of the gods' powers . . . and, by extension, ours."

Umhra plucked a bead from the edge of the path. It warmed his fingertips, the sensation traveled up his arm. No bigger than a bean, the soul was oval and clear with a small orb of honeyed light at its center. "Amazing."

"Yes, the energy of every living creature ever to have walked Tyveriel finds its way to the gardens of Kalmindon, of which we are in but a small annex. Well, those the gods favor. You've seen where the others end up."

"I must say, I prefer it here."

Umhra placed the bead back on the path and together he and Spara sat as the sun set in their garden and they prepared for an undisturbed night's rest.

CHAPTER 17

*I chose to be a beacon of light in the darkness. Now the weight
of the world rests on my shoulders.*

—*The Collected Letters of Modig Forene*
Letter to Prakten Modig dated 2nd of Ocken, 1 AF. Unearthed
from the Ruins of Vanyareign, month of Ocken, 1301 AT

—▲—

"You may enter," King Shale Arving said from within his
private quarters.

The guard opened the door and stepped into the room.
Ornate rugs covered the floor, and tapestries and fine art lined
the walls. Since his most recent failure to sire a suitable heir,
the king had spent more and more time alone in the confines
of his chambers. He no longer cared to socialize and held court
only when absolutely necessary.

It wasn't that he regretted his decision to recognize the infant
as his own, or even that he ordered her and Alessa executed.
Rather, he felt the weight of his forefathers' expectations
crushing him. His inadequacies meant the end of his family's
bloodline which placed Evelium in great peril.

"My Lord," the guard said, bowing when addressing his
sovereign. "Most sorry for the interruption, but Sir Talus

Jochen requests a moment of your time. He says that he carries a message of utmost import."

"Very well," King Arving said, rising from the purple velvet lounge upon which he lazed beneath a sunlit window. He left the book he was reading face-down in his place. He smoothed his red robes and unkept hair, having cast aside his circlet along with the formality of the day. "See him in and then leave us in peace."

"As you wish, my Lord." The guard stepped back and out of the doorway, allowing Talus into the room. The guard closed the door behind Talus, leaving the two men alone.

"It has been some time, Talus," the king said. "I was beginning to think that you soured toward me after Lady Elmont."

"Not at all, My King." Talus said, bowing his head in reverence. "A triviality, I assure you. I have just been preoccupied with my duties."

King Arving nodded. "Well, what brings you to me?" He walked over to Talus and put a caring arm around his shoulders. "I am told you have something pressing to discuss."

Talus flinched at the embrace. King Arving's heart sank. The two were once closer than brothers, now a gulf roiled between them. "My King, I have heard whispers of an infiltrator here within the castle walls who means you harm. I am trying to figure out who it could be but, so far, I have come up empty-handed."

King Arving released Talus and walked over to the window. It was midday, and the sun strained to break through the grey winter sky. "Talus, do you remember when you first came to the castle? How old were you, fourteen?"

"Yes, My King, but this is not the time to reminisce. There is something foul afoot."

King Arving turned to face Talus, his gaze falling to the sheathed sword resting on the table next to his circlet. "And, Aquila . . . may I see my ancestral blade?"

Talus sneered.

King Arving lurched for his sword, but Talus stepped around the table before he could reach it and plunged a dagger deep within the king's stomach. A bolt of pain started in the king's abdomen and quickly spread through his chest. He tried to call out for help, but Talus covered his mouth with his hand and pushed him back to the chaise.

Guiding the king onto his lounge, Talus's doppelganger dropped its disguise and showed its natural form. Its skin resembled blue clay, and its pupilless eyes glowed with a soft opalescence. The doppelganger dragged the dagger upward to the king's sternum and flashed a fiendish grin. It removed a clammy hand from the king's mouth.

"Who are you?" King Arving coughed. Hot blood pooled at the back of his throat.

"Garrus come of Winterashe with greetings of your cousin," the creature said, its Evenese now broken and plagued by a thick accent. "Garrus make it so you know your killer. A man must to die with peace in the mind."

Garrus twisted the blade and the king's hands went cold. He felt no pain, just his own blood running from the side of his mouth.

"So, ends your House of Forene. The Fracture." The doppelganger tore the blade from the now exaggerated wound and wiped it clean on the side of the lounge. With a flip of its wrist, the door across the room locked. The fiend went to the window and threw it open, careful to re-assume Talus's form and then tossed the table holding the king's items on its side. The thunderous crash alerted the guards outside, who banged on the door.

King Arving felt his body wrench one last time. His vision faded.

"Is everything alright, King Arving?" There was no response. The guard waiting in the hall rattled the door. It shouldn't have been locked. He put his shoulder to it, but the door did not budge. He took a few steps back and charged the door. This time the lock broke and the door swung wide.

He burst into the king's chambers to see King Arving's body draped limply across the lounge, the fabric stained deep crimson, a pool of blood on the floor beneath him. The guard's gaze flashed to the windowsill where Talus Jochen stood, his face plain as day.

"Halt," the guard said, pulling his sword.

The guard lunged for the doppelganger in Talus's form. Garrus smirked and then leaped from the window and plummeted from the tower toward the distant courtyard below. Before he crashed to his doom, a great winged reptile swooped beneath him, breaking his fall. The creature reeled, narrowly avoiding the parapet of Castle Forene's outer battlement, and then turned to the south and lifted into the air.

The guard searched the allures below. He located a patrol within earshot. "Don't let that wyvern escape," he yelled, "It carries Talus Jochen, the king's assassin."

Two of the men rushed into a nearby tower and sounded a high-pitched horn that commanded two eagle riders into the air.

The guard turned from the window ran to the door. "Help. Get the cleric. Talus Jochen has murdered King Arving."

Doors burst open, and a frenzy filled the hall. Two more guards came rushing into the room, followed by Cleric Dynava, who ran to the king's side and fell to her knees, ignoring the pool of blood. She gripped the gold talisman hanging around her neck with one hand and placed the other over the king's wound. She closed her eyes and a white glow appeared within the wound but quickly dissipated.

"No, this can't be," she said, baring down on the wound once more but to no effect. She paused and hung her head. "The king is dead." She looked up over her shoulder at the guards who stood over her expectantly. "Which of you was witness to this?"

"I was, Cleric Dynava," the guard said. "That is to say, I

broke down the door when I heard the table thrown over. When I stepped into the room, the king was lying on the lounge soaked in his royal blood and Talus Jochen stood in the window."

Cleric Dynava raised a brow. "And what came of Sir Jochen?"

"He dove out the window and a wyvern caught him. They flew off to the south. I alerted the eagle riders."

"My son, surely you could have come up with something more plausible than that," Dynava said.

"It's the truth," the guard said. "Every word."

Dynava once again grabbed her talisman in her right hand. "Bend forth."

The guard agreed, and the cleric placed the holy symbol against his forehead. It was warm against his skin. Inviting. He stood tall.

"What is your name, soldier?" she asked.

The guard's mind was clouded, dull. He could not have resisted Dynava's question if he had tried. Luckily, he had nothing to hide. He gave in to the cleric's will. "Dellon Marthwait, Captain of the King's Guard."

"Well, Captain Marthwait, can you tell me again what happened here today?"

Captain Marthwait was transfixed by the glow of Dynava's talisman. "Sir Talus Jochen arrived to see the king. He said that he had urgent news to relay. I enquired with the king, and he accepted Sir Jochen into his quarters for a private conversation." He told everything to the cleric.

"Bend forth, Captain Marthwait," Dynava said. The captain obliged, and the cleric placed her hand against his forehead. The cleric's hand was cool to the touch as though the captain had been running a high fever. A blinding light emanated from beneath her hands. As the light dissipated into wafts of ether, the captain's forehead no longer burned and his mind cleared.

"Thank you for telling the truth and for your faithful service to the king," Cleric Dynava said. "Your valor shall be noted with the Elders Syndicate. When we are done here, I need you to contact Lady Jenta Avrette in Anaris. As the king had no heir to his throne, she will assume his responsibilities in his stead."

"I will see to it immediately."

"You two, the Raptor's Grasp has been compromised," Dynava said. "Bring them all in for questioning and begin a search for Talus Jochen. Let every city in Evelium know he is to be given no quarter."

"Yes, Cleric Dynava," the other men said and hurried from the chamber.

Cleric Dynava walked back over to Shale Arving's body and sat beside it on the lounge.

"Captain, come."

Captain Marthwait joined her as she pulled back the king's shirt and exposed the full length of the wound which ran from naval to sternum. Beside the gash, on the left side of his torso just beneath his chest, a birthmark in the shape of an eagle's claw was revealed. Dynava ran her finger over the mark. "He was the last to hold the mark of the House of Forene," she said, looking at Captain Marthwait. "The Age of Forene has ended. May he find peace among his forefathers. I will contact the grave clerics. Please stay with him until he is collected."

"As you wish."

Dynava stood and turned from the body, a crimson smear of blood covered her gown at the knees. Taking a quick look out the window, she left the room.

Captain Marthwait stood vigil, faithfully guarding the king in death as he had in life.

▲

Vigilant eyes trained on the wyvern that skirted the treetops below, the eagle riders dove out of the clouds in pursuit. The wyvern attempted to roll from their path, but the giant eagles caught it in a tangle of outstretched claws.

The raptors' talons pierced the wyvern's leathery hide. The

beast screeched in agony and sent Garrus plummeting into the canopy below.

The wyvern lashed out with its stinger—a last attempt at survival—and punctured an eagle's wing, impaling its rider. The wyvern ripped its tail free and jerked the eagle rider from his mount just as the eagles tore it asunder and cast its bisected body to the earth.

The remaining eagle rider circled the area, the injured eagle of her fallen partner laboring to keep up. Finding a narrow opening in the dense canopy, she commanded the eagle down into the Wistful Timberlands.

She dismounted in a cramped clearing, drew her sword, and waded into the forest in the direction she believed her partner and Garrus had fallen. Slashing through undergrowth, she came upon a trail of blood which she followed. Her partner lay slain at the base of a large hemlock. She rushed to his side.

As she dropped to her knees and checked his shallow breathing, his form shifted, and a blade ran her through.

"Garrus must get to home now. Your games have been fun." Garrus pulled the blade from her chest and rolled her onto the forest floor.

He stood, his skin still flowing into its natural state—a clay-like mockery of the human form—and walked to a fallen tree hollowed by rot. A soft, purple glow emanated from within—a portal to Wethryn. Garrus crawled on hand and knee toward the portal as the eagle rider watched. The gate crackled erratically on his approach, and then Garrus slipped out of Tyveriel.

The eagle rider choked—spitting up blood—and closed her eyes.

CHAPTER 18

With this knowledge, one could travel vast distances in the blink of an eye. I'm only beginning to fathom the possibilities.

—*Entry from Aldresor's Journal*
Undated. Discovered in the Tower of Is' Savon, month of Riet,
1444 AT

—▲—

Laudin crouched at the trunk of a hornbeam, his gaze fixed on a red stag. The beast scratched at the earth, and huffed, its antlers draped with creeping myrtle. The ranger drew his bow and fixed his aim on the stag. The limbs flexed, and the bow string groaned as though begging for release.

Laudin loosed his arrow. The stag startled, dipped its shoulder, and the arrow struck true. The stag jumped and bound off through the woods.

Throwing his bow over his shoulder, Laudin followed the trail of blood down a ridge and found the lifeless stag lying in the undergrowth. He kneeled beside it and put his hand on its chest.

"Thank you for your sacrifice. May your soul find its way to Kalmindon."

Taivaron landed on a branch overhead and ruffled his

feathers.

"No luck for you, huh?"

The harrier chirped.

Laudin pulled a short-bladed knife from his belt. The wooden handle was smooth from wear and the blade tarnished but kept sharp. He recalled the day his father gave it to him. A gift for a nine-year-old son to remember his father by while he was away at war. It worked.

He rolled the stag onto its back and inserted the blade at the base of the deer's ribcage, carving an incision along the length of its belly. He reached his hands into the chest cavity and severed the esophagus. Rolling the stag back to its side, Laudin pulled, and the organs spilled onto the forest floor.

He looped a length of twine from his satchel around the stag's front legs and antlers, and wound the other end of the rope around a stick. Holding the stick behind him, he hoisted the front of the stag off the ground and hauled it from the woods.

Laudin's legs burned as he approached Peacebreaker Keep. Crossing the gardens with his buck in tow, he heard the iron gates at the front of the property swing open. He watched as Nicholas entered the property on Tipper's back, followed by four white horses bearing guards who wore green tunics, the golden lion of Anaris adorning their chests.

Nicholas guided Tipper over to meet Laudin. "I was on my way to see my brother this morning, and I ran into these guards who bring word from Lady Avrette. They requested I return with them at once."

Laudin dropped the stick supporting his stag and offered Nicholas a hand down from his saddle. "Well, let's welcome them into the keep and see what this is all about."

"Agreed."

Miara came from the stables and took Tipper's reins. "Should I see to our visitors' horses as well, my Lord?"

"Please, Miara. And, if you could find someone to tend to

my friend here, I'd appreciate it."

"He's a beauty. Perfect morning for a hunt."

"Yes. Thank you."

Miara led Tipper to the stables as Laudin and Nicholas turned to the soldiers who had dismounted and waited beside their horses.

"Good morning, gentleman," Laudin said, a hand extended to the highest ranked among them. "Nicholas tells me you bring word from Lady Avrette."

The lead soldier shook Laudin's hand. "Aye. We were ordered to come to Peacebreaker Keep and deliver a message by word directly to the Barrow's Pact and no other."

"Very well. Come inside. Miara will see to your mounts. I will fetch the rest of our party while Nicholas sees you to the game room. We can speak privately there."

"Our mounts will be fine. We shall not be staying long."

Laudin and Nicholas strode to the front door of the keep which was made of pewter and bore a relief of Umhra's pyramid icon on its surface. Laudin held the door open for Nicholas and the guards, then bound up the stairs to find Naivara, Gromley, and Shadow.

He found Naivara curled up on their bed napping, having taken the form of a weasel with a red coat and white belly. Of late, her sleep was plagued with recurring nightmares of a dark forest spreading across the land like a cancer, destroying anything that stood in its path with relentless dispassion. She could not shake the dread and sought solace in a simpler mind. At the moment, it seemed to be working. He hated the idea of waking her, and watched the slow rise and fall of her diaphragm, the occasional twitch of her whiskers.

Laudin stroked the curve of her back. Her tiny black eye flitted open. She yawned, baring elongated canine teeth, and transformed back to her Reshinta form.

"I'm sorry to wake you. We have visitors who bring word from Jenta. It seems urgent."

"It's alright," Naivara said, her voice dry. "It was time for me to wake up anyway. I don't want to sleep the day away."

Laudin kissed her forehead. "I'm glad you got some rest. I'll get Gromley and Shadow. Take a moment for yourself and meet us in the game room."

He left Naivara and gathered Shadow and Gromley from the library. The Barrow's Pact converged on the game room.

"Is this all of you?" The lead guard asked. He stood before the crackling fire staring at the large bearskin that hung above it.

"Yes," Laudin said.

The guard turned to face his hosts. "What of the half-Orc and Talus Jochen?"

"The half-Orc has a name. You should address him as Umhra the Peacebreaker, the man for whom the king named this keep. He is away on personal business. As for Talus, the last we heard from him, he was in Vanyareign in service of the crown."

The guard frowned, folded his hands behind his back. "Lady Avrette urgently requests your presence at the lord's manor."

"Of course," Laudin said. "We are always available to the Lord and Lady. May I ask what she requires of us?"

"I think it best the Lady deliver this news, personally. We will accompany you back to Anaris and see you to the lord's manor. The Lady is anxious for your arrival and requested we provide you escort. Please bring with you what you deem necessary for a lengthy stay. I know not what lies ahead."

"Then, I will have our horses readied and we can be on our way."

The guard nodded and saw himself out of the keep, his subordinates in lock-step behind him.

"This sounds important," Gromley said. "We can be in Anaris by late afternoon if we ride with purpose."

"No sense in keeping Jenta waiting. I can be ready to go in a few moments." Shadow sprang up the stairs.

With their horses readied, the Barrow's Pact reconvened with the guards and rode for Anaris. They kept pace for as long as Tipper's short stride would allow. When the pony tired, they slowed to a trot, eventually passing Pell's Orchard and entering Anaris. They continued past the Kormaic Temple where the statue of their fallen friend, Balris Silentread, loomed in the courtyard. They crossed a bridge over one of the city's concentric canals. The city hall and lord's manor came into view, their bluestone towers near black as the sun flirted with the tree line.

They entered the compound, guards posted in twice the number they were accustom to seeing. Archers, with readied bows, loomed overhead upon the parapets.

"I don't like the look of this," Laudin said, leaning over to Naivara as a guard took his reins.

"Yes. Something terrible has happened. I hope Jenta is alright."

They dropped from their horses and followed the guards who had come to Peacebreaker Keep into the lord's manor. Within, guards lined the main hall, each with a pike in hand.

"Lord Morrow and Lady Avrette have retreated to their private chambers. They will meet you there."

They filed up the stairs and along a hallway to a door guarded by four soldiers. One of the guards knocked on the door, the others stepped aside to allow entry.

The door cracked open.

"My Lord," the guard who knocked said, "the Barrow's Pact has arrived."

The door opened wide, faint candlelight flickering within the chambers.

Laudin entered the room and was greeted by Lord Espen Morrow. The Lord of Anaris was an Evenese half-blood, his ears pointed but less so than a pureblood, his dark skin and features softer. He wore robes the color of goldenrod and the bags under his eyes betrayed his exhaustion.

Lord Morrow closed the door behind the Barrow's Pact.

"Thank you for coming. Jenta has been anxious for your arrival. She knew not who else to turn to. We both appreciate your cooperation."

"Of course," Laudin said. "We are, forever, at your service."

Lord Morrow nodded. "Let me get Jenta. She wants to speak with you directly." He opened a door to another room and poked his head inside. He held the door open and Lady Jenta Avrette entered the room.

Lady Avrette wore a heavy, white fur cape of winter wolf—Laudin admired the flawless pelt. Her hair was up in a tight bun, with small crystals reminiscent of frozen teardrops placed throughout. She was radiant but for a redness in her eyes that her fair skin accentuated.

Laudin held out his hand, which she took, feigning a smile. "As always, it is a pleasure to see you, Lady Avrette."

"You as well, Laudin," Lady Avrette said. "Unfortunately, I beckoned you here to deliver grave news. Are Umhra and Talus not with you?"

"No, my Lady. Umhra travels alone in discovery of his new abilities. He now walks a path separate from ours."

"A worthy path, it is. And what of Talus—do you know where he is?"

"Last I had heard, he was back with the king, but I must confess that was months ago."

"I feared as much."

Naivara walked to Lady Avrette and hugged her. Lady Avrette reciprocated the embrace. "So nice to see each of you," Lady Avrette said. "Unfortunately, my heart breaks. Last night, news came to me from Vanyareign that our king, my brother, Shale Arving, has been murdered."

Naivara gasped.

Lady Avrette's lips quivered as she uttered the words, otherwise she maintained her stoic veneer. Naivara hugged her again. Lady Avrette's eyes welled with tears. The others stared in astonishment. Nicholas buried his face in his hands.

Laudin's heart sank. Not for the loss of the king, as he'd not warmed to him the few times they'd met. He found Shale Arving to be a petty man, more concerned with the image of things than the welfare of those he sought to govern. No, the sorrow he felt was for Jenta, whose judgement and generosity he learned to trust and admire. He saw the pain in her face and wished he could help carry the burden. Alas, one does not carry the burden of another's loss. That grief was solitary, indivisible. All anyone could do for her was be there in whatever capacity Jenta needed.

"How could this be?" asked Gromley, breaking the heavy silence.

Naivara released Lady Avrette, who swallowed the pain and continued. "I know this will come as harsh news, but all reports claim it was Talus, in a fit of rage. One of the King's Guard found him standing over the body before he jumped out of the window of the king's chambers, landed on the back of a wyvern, and flew off toward Tayrelis. There is a search underway as we speak."

"Never," Shadow said, throwing his hands into the air. "He's the most loyal person I've ever met. To the point of annoyance. He loves you and the king as if you were blood."

"I find it hard to believe as well, Shadow," Lady Avrette said. "But the facts are what they are. I called you here today as my faith in each of you is implicit. With no heir to the throne, I am to be named queen. My coronation ceremony is to take place as soon as I arrive in Vanyareign. Espen and I leave in the morning. I would like you to accompany me as my personal advisors and guards. I apologize for the short notice. I expect the news of my brother's demise and my crowning will reach Winterashe, and my cousin may very well contest my claim to the throne and seek dissolution of the Fracture under his rule. I may well need your skills. And those of Umhra in particular."

"We are honored," Laudin said, "and shall ready ourselves for travel and an extended stay in the capital."

"Thank you." Lady Avrette's head sunk. "I can never repay your friendship and loyalty. I assure you, becoming queen is not among my wishes. Espen and I came to Anaris to escape the political circus of Vanyareign. But what is duty other than stepping forth when called upon?"

"Your sense of honor knows no bounds, my Lady." Gromley bowed. "Your reticence is what will make you a great queen."

"Thank you, Gromley. Thank you, all. For now, I will take some rest. We will see you in the courtyard at first light. Until then, I bid you peace. We have taken the liberty of preparing you rooms for the night."

Naivara rose from her seat beside Lady Avrette. "Thank you. If you need anything, please don't hesitate to ask. We are here for you."

The Barrow's Pact left Lord Morrow and Lady Avrette alone, and followed the guards who had escorted them from Peacebreaker Keep to a spacious suite on the other side of the manor.

Once they were alone, Shadow's eyes alit with rage. "I do not believe for a moment that Talus assassinated the king. He loved that man like a brother. And even if he didn't, the fool was so blinded by duty, he would never harm a hair on the king's head."

"Settle down, Shadow," Gromley said. "There isn't a believer among us that Talus would commit such a heinous crime. The only question is, what do we do about it?"

"We travel, as promised, with Lady Avrette to Vanyareign," Laudin said, "and see to her coronation before King Ulest can contest. While there, we'll try to determine the truth behind the king's assassination."

CHAPTER 19

On this twenty-fifth anniversary of our victory over darkness,
I invite you to visit our fine capital and witness for yourself
how Evelium thrives.

—*The Collected Letters of Modig Forene*
Letter to Ailene Pirragle dated 7th of Anar, 25 AF. Unearthed
from the Ruins of Vanyareign, month of Ocken, 1301 AT

—▲—

U mhra landed a few feet behind Spara at the edge of a dense
tropical jungle in the heart of Shent. A tangled canopy of
rubber trees and immense strangler fig covered in epiphytes
choked out most of the light. An endless sea of vibrant green
fern and other shrubs covered the ground. Sweat poured from
Umhra's brow, the air thick with an oppressive humidity.

"How do we locate the Waystone now that we are here?"
Umhra came to Spara's side as she peered into the thick
undergrowth. "Or do you recall the exact location like the last?"

"Can't you feel it?" Spara asked, wading into the jungle.
"It is a little different for everyone but should be like how you
tracked me down in Oda Norde. For me, the call resembles a
chirping bird."

Umhra stopped and closed his eyes. "For me, it is the

pulsing of blood flow in my right ear. Quite a nuisance, to be honest. The first time it happened, I thought I was about to die."

"You will grow accustomed to it . . . learn to let it guide you."

"And this Waystone will also be protected by a Guardian," Umhra said, following Spara into the morass. "May I ask, before running headlong into battle with this fiend, what exactly it is that we will face this time? A giant octopus seems unlikely."

"Well," Spara forced a large, leafy shrub to the side, "this Waystone was the responsibility of Warda, and so, San, King of Serpents is its Guardian."

"Sounds pleasant. Anything else I should know before we find this King of Serpents?"

"San is quite poisonous and can read minds. It wouldn't surprise me if he already knew we were here. If we kill him, he will revive within a few days in his natural plane of existence. This happened to the Guardian you and your friends bested on the way to Meriden and will happen to Siasha as well."

"You speak of the beast we fought in the Stoneheart Pass. That was the Guardian of the Waystone at the pass's entrance?"

"Yes, that was Ballan, Master of Darkness, Torrent's Guardian. When you killed him, you rendered the Waystone he guarded inert. Had you broken the stone would have absorbed its essence—assuming you were found worthy. I'm sure only a modicum of its energy remains at this point."

Umhra paused and remembered the battle he and the Barrow's Pact fought with the giant myriapede. That battle seemed like a lifetime ago. "He wasn't all that impressive, to be honest."

Spara rolled her eyes and cut away a last wall of brush, revealing the base of an ancient structure constructed of the black volcanic stone ubiquitous throughout Shent. The tiered façade rose from the jungle floor, disappearing into the canopy high above.

"The Waystone is atop this temple." Spara sighed. "I wish

we could fly up there, but this jungle is just too dense, and I still have not regained all my power."

"It'll be a bit of a climb, but nothing we can't manage."

"Remember, San will be close and will not welcome our presence. Stay alert."

Umhra nodded, and they began their climb up the side of the temple, their path choked by twisted vines and thick foliage. They clambered over roots and crumbled stone, continuing upward into the treetops.

"Warda said you would one day come to challenge me, Spara," the deep, resonant voice of San hummed from somewhere unseen in the blanket of leaves. "I did not expect that it would have taken you this long. And you bring a friend . . . it has been so very long since I have eaten man-flesh. I appreciate the offering."

"I've waited nearly two thousand years for this, San," Spara said, peering into the canopy which seemed to close in around them. "I don't intend on letting you stop me from reaching Kalmindon." She climbed another step.

"And, so angry," San said. "You have such hate in your heart. Such sinister thoughts in your mind. This will be your undoing."

"I don't need a lecture like I'm some impudent child."

A green blur swept across the tangled branches between them and the temple's peak. Umhra spun to follow its path—too fast. San lunged out of the jungle, fangs exposed, eyes black as the darkest of nights.

Umhra willed his armor to coalesce around his body as the gargantuan serpent-like Guardian struck. The blow was deflected. He summoned Forsetae, slashing the blade downward in an invitation to battle, as Spara drew her axes. San once again disappeared into the treetops.

"You have so much more to lose than I." San slithered lithely around the Mystics. "One bite and you fall for an eternity. Should I lose, I shall return in a matter of days and live out my life in the Fae, no longer burdened by this responsibility."

"That is exactly why we will succeed," Umhra shouted into the trees.

"Insular mortal," San said. "You have no right to approach my Waystone . . . and no idea what you contend with."

The Guardian struck out at Umhra again, sending him rolling down several steps. He regained his balance and readied himself with his sword in both hands, taking a wide stance.

Spara, run for high ground. Umhra said, again relying on psionics. *We are at a distinct disadvantage down here.*

Spara nodded and turned back toward the top of the ruin. Just as she took her first step, San's tail whipped out of the jungle and sent her plummeting into the undergrowth below.

"Fool. You're not worthy of my attention. Do you suppose that I cannot hear your every thought?"

"That's enough, you coward," Umhra said. "Show yourself and fight. No more of your games."

At that, San lashed out with another attack. His green sinuous body hurtled toward Umhra with fangs the length of daggers. Umhra dodged the attack and countered with a swipe of his ancient Evenese blade, cleaving one of San's fangs from his mouth as he passed.

The Guardian spun and coiled, releasing an angry hiss. He raised up, venom dripped from his broken fang, and loomed over Umhra. Trees overhead snapped from the force of his presence.

"How dare you question the will of the Ascended," San said. "I shall swallow you whole." He came down upon Umhra with his mouth agape and ingested him.

____ in San's esophagus constricted Umhra so
                    ____reath. He was upside down within the
                    ___is arms bound to his sides. A wave of
                    ___ him further within. Covered in digestive
                    ___osed skin tingled.
                    ___rsetae and his armor to dissipate, worked

an arm up across his chest, and drew in as deep a breath as he could muster. The air was acrid and stifling. The muscles around him closed in on his smaller form. Without his armor, the totality of their strength bore down on him. Air wheezed from his lungs. Umhra would not be able to suck in another breath.

In total darkness, Umhra closed his eyes and thought of his god, Vaila. Another contraction of San's esophagus squeezed him and Umhra screamed. He summoned Forsetae to his hand, the sword's pommel buried in his sternum. He felt San shudder as the blade pierced his flesh. What little daylight the jungle offered streamed in through the wound and gave Umhra hope he would escape.

Umhra wrenched Forsetae toward the ground and exacerbated the wound. The Guardian hissed and writhed. Completely disoriented, Umhra threw all the strength behind his blade and split San open.

Umhra forced his arm through the gash, then his shoulder and head. He gasped for air. The great serpent twisted around itself in spasmatic knots and Umhra slipped onto the temple steps.

San writhing in pain, Umhra climbed to his feet and dealt a deathblow through San's lower jaw and up into his skull. The Guardian fell to the ground. Its lithe body jerked as life escaped it. Umhra raised Forsetae overhead and brought it down. The one blow severed San's head, ensuring the Guardian's demise.

"You continue to impress, Umhra," Spara said as she pulled quake from San's side

"I have seen hubris be the downfall of so many." Umhra wiped the gore from his face and his sword vanished. "Shall we see to what we came here for?"

"Yes," Spara said, her smoke-filled eyes fixated on Umh·

Together, they climbed the rest of the structure, culminated in a square plateau amidst the treetops. At´ was a polished stone similar to those Umhra had e first at the Stoneheart Pass and, more recently, in Oda Norde and Shent. Its surface was etched with glyphs from another time, an intricate pattern of intersecting ovals. The etchings still emitted a green light from within, which strengthened as Spara and Umhra approached.

"You were just eaten by a giant snake." Spara rubbed her chin as she observed the Waystone.

"Swallowed . . . not eaten," Umhra said. "Eaten implies failure."

"Fair enough. A novel strategy, nonetheless."

"Well, you were busy lounging in the bushes."

"I would have you know, I fought for your life. Alas, my recovery is slow and I spent nearly all the energy I had just getting here."

"Maybe we should wait until you are fully recovered."

"No. With every Waystone, I grow stronger. After this, there are only two Guardians left. I will be ready for them." Spara shot Umhra a sideways glance and stepped into the very center of the Waystone. The sigil pulsed at her presence. She pressed Shatter and Quake together in her hands. Spara held the axes out before her, and closed her eyes. A vibrant light grew from them as they merged to form a great axe of unmatched elegance.

The leading blade of the weapon was thrice that of the trailing edge. Smooth arcs connected the two blades, forming a perfect circle that met seamlessly with the rhodium haft. Engraved wildflowers stretched up the haft toward the head of the axe, as though it were the sun itself.

Spara lifted the axe high and imposed herself upon the Waystone, the material plane flexed around her—bent to her will. She brought the axe down upon the surface of the stone and sent a shockwave bursting past Umhra and out over the jungles of Shent.

When the dust settled, Spara stood upon the shattered Waystone, its energy wafted around her in green plumes of ether. Fae Hobbs darted from the surrounding canopy, and gathered what they could of the essence. Umhra joined her on the shattered stone, and the energy enveloped them and merged with their bodies.

Spara separated her hands, one axe in each, and space collapsed back in on itself. "Two down, two to go," she said, turning to Umhra as an immense power surged within them. "I have no doubt the others will be just as challenging but I feel my power returning."

She held her hands up overhead and raised her gaze toward the canopy. Pulling her hands apart, the dense canopy parted at her whim, and a stream of sunlight flooded their position.

"Much better," she said. "I will be back to form in no time."

Her wings sprouted from her back, and she flew through the treetops and burst into the open air. Umhra followed suit, and they made north toward the next Waystone.

CHAPTER 20

I hope to draw the beast from his lair and lay waste upon him
before he seizes the opportunity to take flight.

—*Telsidor's Missives*
Diary entry dated 17ᵗʰ of Mela, 999 AC. Unearthed from the
Ruins of Anaris, month of Emin, 1156 AT

King Vred Ulest looked out over Ohteira, an oversized
window protecting him from the howling wind buffeting
his crimson tower with a driven snow. The spire rose out of
the barren, ice-covered landscape below, its smooth, rounded
façade in stark contrast to its jagged glacial surroundings.

It was midday despite the darkened sky, and the city
bustled below paying no matter to the weather. People hurried
about from building to building, dark flecks against an endless
blanket of white.

King Ulest clasped his hands behind his back and shook his
head. He turned from the window and sat beside his wife, who
watched their two children play before a large stone hearth that
warmed the room with a raging fire.

He removed the gold circlet from his head and ran it
between his fingers, paying special attention to the inset rubies.

"My father commissioned this circlet just before the Fracture," he said, staring at the crown. "When it became obvious Evelium would be divided between the houses of Forene, he promised the people of Winterashe a better future than my uncle could from Vanyareign. I fear we've failed them. It pains me to see how they toil to make it through the winter. They worry for their children's lives, while ours play without a care beside a warm hearth. I must do better for them." He sighed. How unfair it was for the son to bear the burdens of his father's failures. Such was the life of a king, to always be held responsible for the past no matter how forward looking they were.

His wife was well into her third trimester with what would have been their fourth child if their first had not been stillborn. She lazed upon the supple couch beside her husband, covered in a heavy green blanket. She had flawless brown skin and wore her plait of chestnut hair draped over her right shoulder. "Vred," she said, putting a hand on the wolf hair trim of his coat, "you work tirelessly on their behalf. Yes, life in Winterashe is hard, but people have a sense of hope under your leadership. They know your love."

A knock on the heavy wooden door of their chamber interrupted their conversation.

"Enter," King Ulest said.

The door opened and a young woman—no more than sixteen—peered inside. "I'm sorry to bother you, My King, but your nephew has arrived from Amnesty as per your request. I thought you should like to know without delay."

"By all means. See him to the throne room immediately and summon Baron Jemivere. I will be there to greet them presently.".

"Right away, My King." The young woman bowed and pulled the door closed behind her as she left.

"How do you think Roen will take the news?" Avanla asked, pushing herself upright on the sofa. "I'm sure he is anxious to hear why you called him to Ohteira this time of year. I suspect he will be rash in his counsel."

"We will find out soon enough, my dear," King Ulest said. "But don't trouble yourself with these matters. You don't need the stress that often accompanies Roen's visits."

She smiled. Her eyes glimmered in the firelight when she looked at him. King Ulest kissed her forehead. "I will be back soon. The children are playing together so nicely. Get some rest. Children, please behave for your mother. I will be back in time for dinner."

The two children, both boys, turned from the warmth of the fire, their faces flushed. "Yes, father. Our battle is far from over. We should be here for some time."

King Ulest chuckled. "Well, don't forget to protect your mages with a strong cavalry and support from your archers."

"Of course, father," the younger of the two said with a lisp.

King Ulest left the room and walked out into a long hallway lit by oil sconces along the right wall. No longer warmed by the fire, he wrapped his leather coat around him and walked the length of the hallway. Coming to a staircase that widened as it fell away from him, he strode down the stairs to the antechamber of his throne room. Two guards greeted him as they opened the heavy oaken doors.

King Ulest entered the throne room, the garnet walls and floor contrasting with the stark white of the blizzard that raged just outside. He walked to the immense oval window that, under better conditions, allowed him an unbroken view of Ohteira and the plains of Winterashe beyond. He ran his hands through his black hair as if something troubled him deeply.

The Three were already present, his twin nieces, Myka and Veien, wore gowns as white as a new-fallen snow. They were slim, with a gaunt-like appearance and porcelain white skin and platinum blonde hair. In silence, the sisters sat close to one another on a settee along the far wall.

Their brother, Roen, paced the room before them, his face twisted with concern. He, by all measures, was a contradiction of his sisters. Where they were pallid, he had a fair but healthy complexion with dark eyes and hair. He was dressed entirely in ebony leathers and bore the concern of being called to Ohteira with a furrowed brow and stern scowl.

King Ulest welcomed the Three to join him before his marble throne. "Beloved children of my brother. Please embrace your uncle."

The Three approached—Myka and Veien at Roen's back—and stood upon the great seal of a snake twisted around a saber with a gently sweeping blade which graced the floor before their uncle's throne. Roen bowed.

King Ulest bound forward, passing the formality of his throne, and gave Roen a firm hug. "It is wonderful to see you, nephew," he said. "And girls, as always, when I set my eyes upon you, I see my sister's beauty . . . how I miss her so."

"Uncle," Roen said, "it is wonderful to see you as well, but what troubles you so that you call us here from the west in the depths of winter? The journey was harsh, even for the mammoths."

"Yes. I must apologize for calling upon you in such inhospitable times, but my news is of such import, I dare not convey it by any other means than in person."

The door to the throne room swung wide and Baron Rennik Jemivere entered the room. His flowing brown hair brushed against the shoulders of his tailored magenta frock coat. He was slim, and held his nose in the air as though he were perpetually offended by a foul odor. Baron Jemivere came to Roen's side and bowed to King Ulest with a grand sweep of his arm.

"How may I be of service, My King?"

"Thank you for coming, Jemivere. As the two of you are my most trusted advisors, I was hopeful I would be afforded the opportunity to speak of this matter but once." King Ulest paused, fought a lump in his throat. Roen's face twisted in anticipation.

"I have word from Vanyareign. Shale Arving is dead."

At this, Myka and Veien craned their necks, suddenly more intent on listening to the conversation. Roen's expression slackened, the news coming as no apparent shock. Baron Jemivere hung his head.

"Dead, you say?" Roen asked. "How?"

"I only received a brief message from Garrus saying that Talus Jochen, one of the intruders who passed through Retribution two years ago on his way to Meriden, murdered my cousin. It turns out he was a member of the Raptor's Grasp and held great resentment for Shale."

"It was wise of you to install Garrus among Arving's court after the intrusion," Roen said. "Not only did he prove useful in connecting the travelers to Vanyareign and the nature of their journey, but now this. He has bought us time to prepare."

"Prepare for what?" Baron Jemivere asked.

"Prepare for our response to the end of the Forene bloodline. Have you considered an appropriate course of action, uncle?

"In accordance with Treaty of the Fracture as signed by both Shale's father and mine, if there is no heir to either kingdom at the time of a sovereign's death, the surviving sovereign shall reunify Evelium," King Ulest threw himself down on his grey marble throne. "I intend to exercise that right. I call upon you to gather my army. Every able body from the farthest reaches of Winterashe. We shall ride for Vanyareign as soon as possible."

"As you wish, uncle." Roen bowed and a smirk grew across his face. "I will get started right away. It will take some time given the weather, but everything will be as you command. While I mourn the loss of your cousin, I revel in the prospect of reunification. Long have I wished for Evelium to be one again."

"As have I. The accounts of Winterashe and Windswept have long been imbalanced. I aim to see the end of these days and bring our people a new age of prosperity with new trade routes to the south. Jemivere, I will need you to begin laying the groundwork for reunification. I would like an account of the Elders Syndicate as well as the nobles of Winterashe."

"Sire, are you certain your claim to the Raptor's Throne will require such a show of force? Dare I suggest we exhaust channels of diplomacy first? You may well be greeted with open arms in Evelium's time of need."

Roen sneered. "I would contend these channels of diplomacy you are so fond of were exhausted ages ago. I shall gather your army for a march on Vanyareign, uncle. You will be recognized as one of the great kings of the Forene bloodline. I celebrate he who knits a kingdom long riven."

"Thank you, Roen. I would only trust you with such a great responsibility. There is much to do . . . I beg you leave me to my work. Jemivere, may I count on you to execute what your king asks?"

"Of course, my Lord. I will begin presently." Jemivere bowed and hurried from the room.

"He is weak and foolish, uncle. I beg you not to consider his misguided counsel."

"Jemivere is a good man, Roen. What we aim to accomplish—unifying a nation long since divided—will require a man with his silver tongue. He will have the Elders Syndicate eating from our hands within a week."

Roen nodded and backed away from the throne. He motioned to his sisters for them to follow. "We shall leave you to your work. Myka, Veien, we have our orders from the true king of Evelium. We shall set to them at once."

The twins glanced at one another and then curtsied to their uncle. Roen joined them with a bow. "Rest at ease, uncle," he said. "I will amass an army the likes of which Tyveriel has never seen. I shall rally the races of men to your cause in numbers that dwarf even the great army of Modig Forene, himself. Vanyareign will have no choice but to yield to your will."

King Ulest nodded.

Roen turned for the door, his sisters fell in behind him.

"Roen, one more thing," King Ulest said. "Should I find out you were in any way involved in assassinating my cousin, I shall see you disemboweled. And, you two . . . well, I don't know what I will do with the likes of you, but it will be something dreadful."

Roen didn't flinch at the threat. How calculating he had become since his own father's death. "Of course, uncle. I assure you we had nothing to do with this tragedy." He continued to the door without looking back upon the king. "We bid you well and will not squander your trust."

King Ulest returned to his quarters where Avanla napped on the plush couch where he left her. Toy soldiers were scattered across the floor in front of the hearth, and the boys obviously had been taken by the nursemaid to wash before dinner. He sat beside his wife, his body as exhausted as his mind. She stirred and greeted him with a weary smile. "How did it go?".

"I have no doubt as to his involvement," King Ulest said. "I don't know what to do with him. He did not even flinch when I shared the news of Shale's murder. It would seem Garrus was not acting under my orders while in Vanyareign but, rather, Roen's. I know how passionate Roen is about reunification, but I find his methods deplorable. I thought I had done better in guiding him. How does one teach if not by example?"

"You were aggressive . . . sometimes rash at his age. One learns temperance with experience. You know this better than any."

"That I do," King Ulest said. "I suppose it's possible I expect too much. But this . . . this is a step too far. I can't condone regicide among my ranks. Especially from my most trusted."

"I agree. If Roen's involvement in Shale's death comes to light, you risk emboldening others who would challenge your rule. It would be wise of you to keep Roen's transgression within the family and use it as a teaching moment. Besides, there is no proof he was involved, only your astute observation."

King Ulest nodded. Avanla was right, which she was more often than not. He had always found her unflappable faith in reason a most attractive quality. "Thank you for your counsel.

As always, you guide me to being a better man . . . a better ruler." King Ulest kissed Avanla's forehead. "Shall we meet the children for dinner?"

"Yes, I would like that."

▲

The Three walked down the long, lamp-lit corridor away from the throne room. At the top of a great, spiraling staircase, Roen stopped, his sisters coming to rest just behind him.

"Do you question my judgement, sisters?" He shot a sideways glance over his left shoulder.

Myka and Veien stared back placidly.

"Then, we agree that it is our uncle's destiny to reunify the throne of Evelium," he said. "And that he needed this gentle nudge in that direction."

The statement drew no discernable response from the sisters.

"All is now in motion. There is no time to waste. We must mobilize the armies of Winterashe at once. If our uncle is to be the face of unification, we shall be its heart."

Myka and Veien grinned in unison, their eyes meeting. Roen ran down the stairs, his sisters followed.

CHAPTER 21

All but one perished. The lone survivor hid itself in the deepest recesses of the Wistful Timberlands and awaited opportunity.

—*The Gatekeeper's Abridged History of Tyveriel*
Vol. 1, Chapter 2 – Unearthed from the Ruins of Meriden,
the month of Anar, 1217 AT

—▲—

It was well into the night when the Jilted Rose arrived at port in Hylara, a waxing half-moon centered in a starry sky. The worst of winter's fury held a tight grasp over the land. Talus's breath hung in the air as he pulled his cloak around him and prepared to disembark.

Two crewmen secured the gangplank in place, and Talus hurried off the ship and into the city in the most direct path to The Fulmar's Landing, fighting the wind-driven snow. It was quiet—nobody would have been outdoors in these conditions but for necessity. The only sound he heard was the snow crunching under his boots, and his only thought was getting to a warm place for the night before leaving for Peacebreaker Keep tomorrow at dawn. It had been some time since he had last seen the Barrow's Pact and he was eager to be among friends.

He braced himself against the cold as he approached The

Fulmar's Landing, the light of a single candle in the main parlor a welcoming beacon against the darkened windows he had been passing throughout the city. He strode up the steps onto the porch and tapped at the door. He could hear someone shuffling within. The candlelight warmed the door as it cracked open.

"Come in, come in," a bleary-eyed Folsom Centrian said. "Before the weather gets the best of you."

Talus pushed his way into the lobby and Folsom forced the door shut behind them. The snow and ice encrusting Talus's cloak recoiled at the warmth of the inn and dripped to the fine wood floors.

"Don't mind the mess," Folsom said. "You must be mad to be out on a night like tonight."

"Not much of a choice, I'm afraid," Talus said, throwing the hood back from his head. "The Jilted Rose just returned from Shent."

"Oh, dear boy," Folsom said, his face twisting with concern. "I was wondering if you were ever coming back for your horse or if you aimed to stay hidden, what with the charges levied against you."

"Charges?" Talus asked, removing his cloak and following Folsom into the rear parlor where a fire fought the late hour.

"You don't know?" Folsom grimaced. "Boy, the king has been murdered and the only witness claims it was at your hand."

Talus fought back the urge to vomit. "What?"

"You are Talus Jochen, aye?"

"As I told you when we met, yes."

"Boy, your face is on posters all over Hylara, and no doubt in every other town south of Winterashe, I would assume." Folsom sat in one of two high-backed chairs in front of the fire. He leaned forward and urged the hearth back to life with a fire iron that was leaning against the wall beside him. Embers flew up the chimney as he prodded.

"King Arving is dead?" Talus asked, refusing the other chair's invitation.

"Yes. Run through, from what I hear. The Elders Syndicate has named Lady Avrette as his surrogate. The bloodline has been broken."

Talus's heart sank at the news of the king's death. Despite the strain put on their relationship by the king's desire to see Alessa and Turin put to death, he still found a place within him that loved Shale as a brother. The kind of unconditional love one reserves only for a sibling or child.

"The Raptor's Grasp came here looking for you," Folsom said. "They took your horse from the stable about a week ago. I tried to convince them you had been gone for some time, but it fell on deaf ears. You, of course, are welcome to stay the night, but I'm afraid you aren't safe here. I may be the only one in Evelium who believes in your innocence."

"No, thank you, Lord Centrian. I will go at once. Do you have a horse I could buy from you, though?"

"Take any you choose from the stable," Folsom tossed a log from beside his chair onto the fire. "I have no affinity for the beasts, nor am I in need of compensation."

"I will repay this kindness." Talus bowed. "I must first clear my name."

"May the god's watch over you, boy," Folsom said, rising from his chair and taking Talus's hand in his. "You don't deserve what is coming to you. You can leave through the back door."

Talus made for the blue door at the rear of the room. Pulling it closed behind him, he found himself along a roofed passage that connected the inn to the stable. Someone had swept the snow to one side, forming a notable drift which broke at least a portion of the wind coming from the north. More than once, his footing gave way on the slick surface in his effort to reach the darkened stable.

The door resisted his shove, as if protecting the beasts within, but begrudgingly scraped against the icy ground as

Talus insisted. The door slammed closed behind him and he lit a small oil lamp that hung beside the entrance. There were a dozen stalls, ten of them in use. Talus walked the length, eyeing his options as he made for the saddles and bridles hanging along the far wall.

A paint horse, brown and white and of good size and condition, would suit him just fine. He opened the stall gate and held out his hand. The horse pushed his nose into Talus's palm and snorted. Talus slipped the bridle over its head, the horse accepting the bit without hesitation. He led the horse out of its stall and hung the reins on a hook beside the stall gate. Beneath the hook was a small brass placard with the name "Swizzle" engraved on it.

"Who would do such a thing?" Talus asked Swizzle as he walked over to grab a blanket and saddle. "Such a fine, powerful horse . . . and they named you Swizzle? How does Swizz work for you?"

The horse tossed his mane and nickered.

"Okay, then. Swizz it is."

Talus placed the blanket upon Swizz's back and saddled him. "I'm not going to pretend this is going to be a fun ride, Swizz, but I have to get to Vanyareign as quickly as possible and while attracting no attention. We will ride along the Torrent and stay off the major roads."

He grabbed the reins and led Swizz to the stable door. Putting his shoulder into the door, he forced it open, letting a rush of frigid air and snow into the room. Swizz objected, pulling at the reins–his hind hooves scraping against the straw-covered stone floor.

"C'mon you wisp," Talus said. "It won't be that bad."

With a firm tug on the reins, Swizz followed Talus out into the blizzard, his hooves crunching on the newly fallen snow. Talus closed the door behind them and climbed into the saddle. He secured his hood overhead and nudged Swizz forward. As he rode out from behind Fulmar's Landing, he noticed Folsom

Centrian standing at the window of the sitting room bidding the pair a safe journey with a sincere nod. He returned the gesture and rode for Vanyareign.

▲

Chandeliered ice gave way under Swizz's hooves as he carried Talus along the rocky eastern bank of the River Torrent. Steam lifted from the rushing waters and danced with a light snowfall. It was early yet, and a solitary mink frolicked in a slow pool along the far shore.

Ice encrusted Talus's cloak, and he sat rigid in the saddle. Every muscle in his body ached for the warmth of a campfire, but he pressed on toward Vanyareign–anxious to learn what felled his king and to clear his own good name.

As he neared a bridge where Englen Penn Way crossed over the river, he tugged Swizz to the east, heading into the woods to avoid detection this close to the capital.

"You there," a voice said from the bridge above.

Talus looked over his shoulder, continuing toward the tree line. He saw two mounted Eagle Guards peering down at him.

"Yes, you," the guard said. "We need a word."

Talus considered running, after all, the woods were so very close. He doubted Swizz could best two steeds belonging to the king's army and knew if he were captured in such a way, his perceived guilt would all but be set in stone.

He turned Swizz with a tug of the reins and urged him up the embankment and onto Englen Penn Way. The horse's hooves clattered on the cobblestone road, as though it sensed Talus's nervousness at the encounter.

"How may I be of service to the king?" Talus asked, hanging his head so that his hood obscured his face.

One guard split off to his right–Talus tracked him with shadowed eyes.

"Off the horse," the guard who had called him up onto the road said.

Oblige. Run. Kill. Talus weighed his options.

"Dismount." The guard's tone hardened.

Another tense moment and Talus freed his left foot from its stirrup, swung his leg over the saddle, and dropped from Swizz's back.

"The hood," The first guard said, while the second swung around behind Swizz so they blocked both directions along the road. Swizz stomped and whinnied.

"We are looking for the one known as Talus Jochen. Murderer of the king. Traitor. Now show yourself." The guard dismounted from his burly brown steed. Talus could hear the other guard behind him do the same. Their blades made a familiar scraping sound as they drew them from their scabbards.

Talus's hand reached for Aquila and gripped its frigid hilt as the guards approached. He would not shed the blood of those loyal to King Arving, despite the cost. He released the sword, threw his hood back, and dropped to his knees.

The guard gasped as Talus folded his hands behind his head. He pointed his sword at Talus's chest.

"Quickly," he said to the second guard, his voice faltering. "Secure him."

The second guard, who was shorter in stature than the first, sheathed his sword and pulled a set of iron manacles from beneath his sky blue winter cloak. He cleared his throat and approached Talus from behind. He clamped the manacles to one of Talus's wrists and the cold metal burned his skin. The guard pulled Talus's arms behind his back and bound the second wrist to the first. Each of the guards put a hand under one of Talus's arms and hoisted him into a standing position.

With a sigh of relief, the senior guard sheathed his sword and made to remove Aquila from its scabbard. "I wouldn't, if I were you," Talus said. "That is Aquila, Modig Forene's own sword. Only the chosen may wield it."

"Are you refusing to turn over your weapon, traitor?"

"No," Talus said. "I am asking you to take the entire belt

and not handle the sword in order to save you an immense amount of pain."

The guard glanced at his partner and then unfastened the belt from around Talus's waste, careful not to grip Aquila directly. Thrusting the scabbard into the lashings at the rear of his saddle, he turned back toward Talus. "Anything else you care to share with us?"

"I have a dagger bound to my left forearm and another within my boot," Talus said. "They won't electrocute you as Aquila would."

The guard removed the two daggers and slipped them into his belt as his partner lashed Swizz's reins to the horn of his saddle. Talus studied his captor as the guard spun him around and forced him backward against the flank of his steed. The guard's eyes were green, his skin weathered. Tufts of grey hair poked out from beneath his battle-scarred helm.

The guard retrieved a length of rigid rope strapped to the rear of his saddle. Without a word, he tied the rope around Talus's waist and then the other end to horn of his own saddle. He checked the knots at either end twice before giving a nod of approval.

"If you resist, I'll drag you back to Vanyareign on your face."

Talus nodded—he would have done the same if the roles were reversed.

The junior guard mounted his horse and spurred him forward with a nudge of his heals. Swizz tugged at his reins but fell in line. The more-senior guard followed. The rope tightened and yanked Talus forward. He fell to one knee, the cobblestone cut into him.

"Curse the gods," he said under his breath.

The senior guard stopped his horse which gave Talus a chance to catch his footing. "Next time, I'll just drag you. Consider this a courtesy between soldiers."

Talus struggled to his feet, and the senior guard nudged his horse forward. Again, the rope yanked Talus forward. This time, he settled into an awkward cadence, trying his best to keep the rope from dragging him again to the cobblestone paving.

People recognized Talus as they neared the capital. Some praised the guards, while others jeered at the king's killer. More than once, the crowd struck Talus with rocks and showered him with rotting bits of food. They coursed through the Burning Wood where the red fern met the snow in combat, brighter than ever against the ubiquity of white. The birch trees were now hollow vestiges of themselves just a month earlier.

It was late in the day when they crossed the portcullis and entered Vanyareign. Here the guards sat tall in their saddles, parading Talus through the busiest parts of town as they made way for Castle Forene. The crowds swelled around them to get a peek at the now-famed assassin. They choked off their path forward. Guards from within the city pushed back against the onslaught of gawkers, some of whom reached out to grab Talus in the hope they would get a small piece of him for posterity.

They proceeded around the Grand Bazaar, gathering guards as they went. "Hang him here for us all to bear witness," a man said from the crowd to a round of applause. "Draw and quarter him," another said. Some just leaned over toward the procession for a chance to spit in Talus's face.

They reached the north gate of Vanyareign and made their way up the side of Mount Orys, the crowd jeering behind them. Talus's mind wandered along the march. How many times had he ascended King's Walk, triumphant in the name of his king? How many times had he ridden high in his saddle upon the back of Maelstrom with some despicable miscreant in tow to the cheers of the crowd? He lifted his eyes from his feet and stood tall.

CHAPTER 22

Atalan led the Paladins of Mela in battle against Naur's army. They proved valiant, despite suffering heavy losses. In the end, the day was won.

—*The Tome of Mystics*
Unknown Origin. Unearthed from the Ruins of
Oda Norde, month of Bracken, 1320 AT

—▲—

"What are you so scared of?" Naivara asked as she followed Laudin through the underbrush of the Wistful Timberlands.

"Scared? Who said anything about being scared? I just don't see why I have to go first. Besides, we are scouting the area for potential threats to Jenta, not out for a walk. I'm not sure it's the right time."

"You said the same thing on the way back from Ember's Watch. Not to mention the times you've avoided the matter since. And, what makes you think our current forms are the best for scouting? You've never perceived the world through the senses of another."

Laudin turned to face Naivara and sighed. "I have questions, first."

"Of course."

Laudin rubbed his hands together. "Okay. Do I keep my faculties?"

Naivara laughed. "Your faculties? Yes. You will continue to reason as you do now. However flawed that may be."

Laudin smiled and looked at the ground. "And, you can turn it off?"

"Certainly. Whenever you wish."

"And, I will keep all my things? My clothes?"

"Do I end up naked every time I shape change?"

"Unfortunately, no."

Naivara shoved Laudin.

"Alright," Laudin said begrudgingly "As long as it stays between you and me."

Butterflies fluttered in Naivara's stomach. "I promise."

She focused on her circlet and thought of Laudin taking the form of a wolf. Green mist enveloped Laudin and his form shifted to that in Naivara's mind. He made for a handsome beast, with a thick coat of black fur, ice-blue eyes, and a scar that ran the length of his left cheek.

Naivara squealed. "I can't wait to tell Nicholas about this."

Laudin growled.

"I mean, of my ability to shape change others. Not this, specifically, of course."

Naivara joined Laudin, assuming the form of a wolf, her fur a vibrant red that faded to white at her belly. She padded over to Laudin and rubbed her cheek against his. She then stretched her front legs out, raised her hind quarters in the air in a playful bow, and dashed off into the dark woods. Laudin gave chase.

Winding through a narrow deer path, Laudin came to an abrupt halt and raised his nose to the air. Naivara followed suit. A strong odor of peat hung heavy in the air and irritated her sensitive nostrils. From the forest ahead, she heard a resonant rumble that rose in both volume and intonation until it became a shrill screech.

Laudin shook his head and spun in a circle. With a whimper, he fell to the ground, unconscious, and reverted to his natural form.

The caterwaul ceased. Naivara crouched at Laudin's side and licked his face in an attempt to wake him.

Trees creaked and the canopy swayed to heavy footfalls. Naivara froze as a towering entity ducked beneath the branches of a hemlock and squatted before her. It resembled an ancient tree with long appendages that each ended in a tangle of roots. From its head protruded three branch-like horns, and its mouthless face was covered in lenticles, two of which bore small forest green eyes.

Naivara transformed back to her Reshinta form. "Tayre. To what do I owe this great honor?"

She dropped to her knees and bowed so her forehead touched the forest floor.

"Rise, my child." The God of Forests' ancient voice rumbled like rolling thunder. "Look upon me."

Naivara complied.

"I come to you in recognition of your faith and devotion. You call to me in your dreams."

"Yes. I've been plagued by nightmares of a terrible evil originating from these woods. Can you tell me the meaning behind what I see?"

Tayre's eyes flared with celestial energy. "There is a corruption spreading throughout this land that could once again be the downfall of the mortal races. My attempts to maintain balance have failed. These were not nightmares, but premonitions. You see a potential future should this burgeoning force go unchecked."

"What can I do to stop it?"

"The source remains unseen to me. Masked by a power older than my own. It bides its time. Until it makes itself known, there is little one can do. I offer you some solace, however."

Roots grew forth from one of Tayre's hands. They unfurled

before Naivara and revealed a gobbet of platinum enough for her next Suffusion. The precious metal glinted in the light emanating from Tayre's eyes.

Naivara reached out for the platinum, hesitated. "Are you certain I'm ready? I'm still learning much about my Gold Suffusion."

"One does not always have the luxury of being ready. I bestow upon you the material necessary for Suffusion and offer you another piece of my essence. Your path is yours to choose. Do with my gifts what you will."

Naivara plucked the platinum from Tayre's tangled mass of roots and stared into her god's eyes. "I will not disappoint you."

Tayre stood, his joints creaking like branches in a raging gale. "By Vaila's grace, I have been allowed to remain in this world after the Rescission. Now, she calls me home to Kalmindon. I shall ascend and await your call."

"Thank you." Naivara climbed to her feet and embraced one of Tayre's trunk-like legs. "You've always been there for me. Even during my darkest hours, I have felt your presence. Because of you, I've never truly felt loneliness."

Naivara released Tayre. He trudged back into the forest and vanished from sight. Laudin, stirred in the leaf litter, and she dropped to her knees beside him. She brushed the hair from his face as his eyes fluttered open.

"I think you need to work on your new skill," Laudin said, his voice unsteady.

Naivara kissed his forehead. "It wasn't me. That sound we heard that rendered you unconscious was Tayre. He confirmed my dreams are premonitions and gave me this."

Naivara produced the gobbet of platinum in the palm of her hand.

"That's enough . . ."

"For my Platinum Suffusion," Naivara said. "There is an ancient corruption growing somewhere in the Wistful Timberlands. Tayre wants me ready should it spread further."

"He couldn't have chosen anyone better. We should return to the convoy. They'll be wondering what became of us."

Naivara helped Laudin to his feet and they pressed on through the Wistful Timberlands.

▲

Vanyareign was even more frenetic than usual when the caravan arrived at the south gate. Naivara rode tall in her saddle and watched with intrigue as people lined the streets to get a look at Lady Avrette's carriage and wish her a long reign as their queen. Others offered their condolences on the death of King Arving and their hopefulness that the capture and pending execution of his killer—the treasonous Talus Jochen—would bring closure.

As the convoy circled the Grand Bazaar, Shadow handed Gromley his reins and hopped down from Ramoth's back, disappearing into the crowd. Among the chaos, nobody was the wiser, and the caravan circled the bazaar and continued to King's Way and, ultimately, Castle Forene.

The castle's banners, lifted by the steady wind atop Mount Orys, muted the rumble of the caravan as two Eagle Guards greeted them at the portcullis. The guards waved them forward across the expansive bailey to the gold doors which marked the keep's entrance.

Four more Eagle Guards held the doors open as the caravan arrived—two on each side of the entry—in accordance with the custom of never greeting a sovereign with the entry closed. They stood at attention as Lady Avrette's carriage came to a halt in front of them. Lady Avrette's porter, a small Iminti man who wore a green velvet suit matching the adornments of Castle Forene, came rushing up to the carriage's side and opened the door.

Lord Espen Morrow stuck his head out of the carriage and looked up to the conical spires overhead. Smoothing his dark hair back with one hand, he stepped down from the carriage and turned, extending a hand to his beloved wife. A delicate hand, pale against that of her husband, obliged and Lady Avrette emerged from the carriage. The guards genuflected, their heads bowed in respect for their new queen. She chewed her bottom lip, uncomfortable with the adoration, and then righted herself and lifted her chin regally. She stepped onto the castle grounds.

Her ice-blue gown was hidden beneath a heavy fur cape. She passed the Eagle Guards, who stood—still as statues—as she entered the keep, and paused in the doorway. She waived Naivara up from the rear of the procession.

"Yes, my Lady?" Naivara asked, coming to her side.

"My dear," Lady Avrette whispered, "I've never felt at ease within these walls. It was my reason for seeing Espen appointed to his station in Anaris. Now, seeing the bust of my brother among those of my ancestors, I'm not sure how I am going to get through this in a manner befitting a queen."

"I always felt that way in my homeland, my Lady. I ran away because it was the easier path. For me, it also turned out to be the right path, as I've found happiness and purpose in the life I have chosen. While you may not feel as though you have a choice, you most definitely do. There is the path where you run from duty . . . and there is the path where you step forth and lead Evelium to new glory as only you can. I don't doubt for a moment you will make the right choice. For you, and Evelium."

Lady Avrette nodded and cleared her throat. She walked the hall lined with busts of her ancestors and stepped before the bust of Modig Forene. She kneeled and fixed her gaze at the ground. "Father of Evelium, in your honor, I approach the king's court, and to his command, I promise myself." She rose and stepped aside and waited for the others to finish the ritual before the Great King of Evelium. When they had finished, she continued through another set of open doors to what would be her court.

A throng of nobles crowded the throne room, giving it the same oppressive feel as the city streets outside. They left only a narrow aisle for her to ascend to the throne. The Elders

Syndicate, those who would lead her immediate coronation, stood at either side of the Raptor's Throne, and awaited their duties in their traditional yellow doublets.

The crowd bowed as Lady Avrette passed, flanked on both sides by the Eagle Guard, and followed by her husband and most of the Barrow's Pact. She ascended the stairs to the throne and turned to face her audience of subjects.

The Elders Syndicate came before her and bowed. Lord Tybus Cillian turned and faced the crowd. He held in his hands an emerald green pillow upon which sat the simple gold circlet of the Forene dynasty—the Circlet of Everlife. His braided beard was as red as the robin's breast, and he wore a green sash around his neck that hung nearly to the ground because of his slight stature, identifying him as the leader of the sovereign's advisors.

"Today, we crown our queen, Lady Jenta Avrette, sister of our fallen king." His deep, Zeristar voice boomed with confidence and resolution. "Her ascension is one of right by blood and ensures the continued sovereignty of Evelium under the House of Forene. Long may she reign."

Another member of the Syndicate, a woman of Reshinta blood, stepped forward and put her hands beneath the pillow. Lord Cillian took the circlet in his hands. "By the power vested in me as Speaker of the Elders Syndicate, I take this sacred crown, once worn by Modig Forene himself, and bestow it upon his scion, Lady Jenta Avrette. When she rises, let it be known she rises as our queen."

Lady Avrette kneeled on both knees before the throne, still facing the crowd. Lord Cillian lifted the circlet high, turned, and placed it upon her head. Once in its rightful place, the circlet shrunk to fit Lady Avrette as though made for her that morning. The Elders Syndicate backed away from the kneeling queen, the circlet upon her head beamed with an impossible luster. After a moment, she rose. As she did, the room bowed and held their positions.

"Please rise," she said. "It is with great reluctance that I assume the position of your queen. This is not for lack of love for our kingdom, but for the loss of my dear brother. While villainy cut his time short, it shall not shorten the reign of the Forene family. As your queen, my first act will be to see the king's killer brought to justice and his death avenged. Talus Jochen will be drawn and quartered in the morning."

The crowd cheered for the coming spectacle. Gromley took a brazen step toward the throne, but Jenta glared at him and he froze. Laudin put a hand on his shoulder and whispered in his ear. Gromley stepped back into place.

"I promise you, as your queen, I will always hold what is best for Evelium closest to my heart, and I will be steadfast in my devotion to the security and prosperity of our people."

The crowd, again, roared with support.

Lord Cillian held both his hands in the air to quiet the crowd. "Queen Avrette will begin holding court tomorrow at high sun. She has traveled from Anaris and, with no respite, was brought directly to the coronation. You are all welcome to stay and celebrate the occasion, but the queen will now take her leave."

Queen Avrette smiled, and extended her hand to Lord Cillian, who ushered her out a door at the back of the throne room. Lord Morrow and the Barrow's Pact followed. As soon as the door closed behind them, they could hear the crowd return to a state of revelry.

"Drawn and quartered?" Gromley asked, his face reddening as he bounded up the stairs after the queen.

The candlelight cast long shadows across the stairwell, relegating some to darkness as they made their way to the royal living quarters.

Lord Morrow turned on his heal. "You are talking to your queen, Lord Strongforge,"

"Espen, it's fine." Queen Avrette stopped at the next landing and allowed for everyone to stand face-to-face. "Gromley, you shall never have to suffer such formality with me. Without each of you, we would not be here in the first place. Yes, I am now queen, but I owe you a debt that I can never repay. That being said, Evelium needs to put Shale's death behind it. I need to put Shale's death behind me. So, whatever Shadow snuck off to do better work by tomorrow morning, or I will sacrifice Talus to that end."

"My Queen, you just sentence an innocent man to death . . . and a gruesome death at that. One of the very people you say you owe an incalculable debt to. I beg you reconsider."

"Maybe I am naïve, Gromley, but it seems that I have more faith in each of you than you have in yourselves. I have much to think about. I beg your pardon for the night. Thank you all for seeing me here safely and remaining such good counsel."

Gromley stood firm as the queen climbed the last flight of stairs and left the Barrow's Pact alone in the stairwell. Naivara stepped up next to him and took his hand.

"Come, Gromley. We're all tired from the trip."

"Yes. You are right. Go on ahead. I need but a moment."

The rest agreed and proceeded up the stairs and out the same door that the queen and Lord Morrow had left through.

Gromley stood alone in the stairwell. After a moment, he closed his eyes and grabbed the talisman that hung around his neck. A soft light emanated from his hands.

"You have until tomorrow morning," he said. "You better move fast."

Already in position. Shadow's voice resonated in the cleric's head. *See you tomorrow at the rendezvous spot as planned.*

Gromley snorted, as he did when pleased, and made his way to his quarters.

CHAPTER 23

What remained of mankind lived in the Ruari Caves west of Farathyr. Here they built great cities that rivaled those of the surface.

—The Gatekeeper's Abridged History of Tyveriel
Vol. 2, Chapter 7 – Unearthed from the Ruins of Meriden, the month of Ocken, 1240 AT

—▲—

The delicate pink grasses of the Malaran plains reached up past Umhra's waist, their wispy awns tingling his outstretched palms. Miatherum roamed the surrounding grasslands. The giant sloth-like creatures had dark violet coats, with the younger among them well camouflaged among the rosy grasslands. They grazed in large groups and took turns keeping watch on the intruders, rearing up on their hind legs and grunting to one another.

Spara glanced over her shoulder—the towering black monolith in the distance framing her form. She bit her bottom lip.

"I haven't seen you nervous like this before," Umhra said. "Even when facing San."

"Atalan always loved this place." Spara's voice fluttered in the persistent cross wind. "I never understood it myself. It is a land of barbarism, controlled by monstrosities that have been warring since the beginning of time. He would tell me to look for the simplicity in it all. That civilization was far too complex . . . far too narcissistic."

"I can see his point," Umhra said. "You've been here before, then?"

"Only once. I bound myself to Atalan. Like you, my ascension into Mysticism was . . . well . . . unexpected. The gods meant for there to be only six, as there is a limit to the power shared between us. When I achieved my Rhodium Suffusion, I took an equal portion of that power away from each of the others, assuring they could never become gods unless one of us were destroyed. For this they resented me—all but Atalan, that is. He took me in, taught me the ways of the Mystics, as I teach you now, and I gave myself to him fully. For centuries, we were inseparable . . . I would have followed him into the hells of Pragarus."

Umhra wondered if that resentment would now extend to him. "Trust me, it's not a place you would care to visit."

Spara smiled for the first time since arriving in Malara and then turned back toward the monolith.

"So how did the six of them manage to ascend if they didn't possess the power necessary to power the six Waystones?" Umhra asked.

"When they stripped me of my icon and locked me away in Hallgeirr's throne room, my fall from grace was final. There was no chance for me to reclaim my power. No way for me to connect to the gods. As a result, my power reverted to the remaining Mystics. It wasn't until you achieved your Rhodium Suffusion that my icon called to me. You were the anomaly no one saw coming. Other than Vaila perhaps."

"There has to be more to this story than you are letting on. What aren't you telling me? Or are we really doing all of this for vengeance of a bygone love?"

Spara spun and grabbed Umhra by the throat, unleashing a force he had never experienced before. The storm trapped within her eyes raged and the sky darkened around them. "Don't chastise me, Champion of Vaila. Only I know what terrible fate awaits this world. So be it if I get something out of this as well. I share with you my power, my knowledge, so you can save Tyveriel from the Grey Queen and you dare question my right to ascend to Kalmindon and seek justice for the wrongs done to me?"

Umhra stepped into her grasp and envisioned Spara's vise-like grip broken, her body thrown from his proximity. He imposed his power into the space between them, and a shock wave blew Spara backwards. She landed prone in the tall grasses. With one great leap, Umhra was upon her, his left knee pinning her chest to the ground. The rage faded from Spara's face, and she flashed a prideful smile.

"You are an exceptionally quick study, Umhra," she said, her breathing labored. "It took me years to learn how to control my powers like that."

Umhra released her and sat back amongst the grass. "And, you have an exceptionally volatile temper. It very well could be your undoing."

"You may be right," Spara said, sitting up beside him. "I was out of line. I let my emotions get the best of me." She rolled to her knees in front of him and put her hands gently on his face. She leaned in and kissed him.

"What would Atalan say?" A deep, unsympathetic voice asked from the anonymity of the surrounding field.

Spara's lips released Umhra's but stayed close. "Bettle has found us," she whispered. "I was hoping to fight him on our terms. It would seem my foolishness has stolen from us the element of surprise."

"I have been tracking you since you landed on my shores," Bettle said. "The Orc, I could smell from miles away. You were much more subtle. Are you simple enough to think approaching on foot would give you cover?"

"No," Spara said. "I did that out of respect, as Atalan taught me."

"So, you learned something, then. But not enough to keep you from coming here to challenge me."

Umhra pushed Spara aside and stood. His armor coalesced around him. He summoned Forsetae to his hand and surveyed his surroundings. The grass rustled in the wind, unbroken by man or beast alike.

"Show yourself, Bettle," he said. "Face me directly, not like that coward San."

"A new Mystic," Bettle said. Umhra tried to track Bettle's voice, but it seemed to come from all directions at once. "How interesting. The Orc is quite aberrant."

"In more ways than one, I assure you," Umhra said. "Prove yourself worthy of your station."

Spara screamed. Umhra spun, seeing a disturbance in the field now twenty feet behind him—the beast was on her and yet still hidden. He closed his eyes and murmured a prayer to Vaila.

Let this arid land taste my blade.

Umhra thrust Forsetae into the earth. Glowing cinders swirled around the blade and set the dry grasses aflame in each direction.

The grasses incinerated instantly, revealing Spara on her back, Shatter & Quake in hand, fighting an invisible form that pinned her to the ground. The shape plucked her from the earth and ran for the monolith. Umhra gave chase.

Running at full speed but still losing ground on his quarry, Umhra's wings sprouted from his back and lifted him into the air. He circled the monolith once, its black granite smooth and dull as it tapered to a rounded peak. Keeping his eyes trained on Spara, he dove toward her from the side, Forsetae ready to strike.

He hit Bettle just behind where he held Spara. The three

of them tumbled through the fields, burning a path like a meteorite that survived the journey through Tyveriel's dense atmosphere.

Rock and earth scattered everywhere and smoke choked the air. Bettle's invisibility spell dissipated as he scrambled to his feet, bleeding profusely from a gaping wound in his neck just above his left shoulder. His white fur was singed and soiled. The immense wolf bared his teeth, each the length of a dagger, and turned toward Umhra, who now stood over Spara's limp body.

"You are powerful, Mystic," the beast said with a snarl. "I have seen nothing like it, not even Atalan. You shall be a worthy challenger."

In a single leap he was upon Umhra, his jaws snapping just shy of a deathblow. Umhra slashed at Bettle's right canine, but Forsetae caromed off the tooth and left only a superficial mark. He drew Bettle away from Spara and in front of the monolith. Foam dripped from the guardian's mouth as his snout tensed with rage.

Bettle ran at Umhra. The Guardian grabbed Umhra by the leg as he tried to dodge the assault. Bettle careened into the side of the monolith, shattering a sizeable chunk of the base as Umhra's body crashed into it. The wolf slammed Umhra into the ground and pinned him with his giant paw. Umhra thrust his blade up through the center of the paw and slashed sideways, taking a toe.

The wolf howled, spitting lathered saliva which burned the grasses it came into contact with. Umhra rolled from under him and regained his footing. Bettle took a few lame steps away. Umhra bore down on the beast, but Bettle spun and released another howl. Acid spewed from his mouth and showered Umhra.

Blinded in searing pain, Umhra swung his sword wide and stumbled into the unforgiving stone of the monolith. He turned, held Forsetae out before him, and took a defensive stance. Bettle laughed.

This one is unseen to me. Forsetae's voice resonated in Umhra's mind.

The wolf's snarl grew closer. Umhra swung Forsetae in a sweeping arc, desperate to connect with Bettle's hide. Instead, the sword was knocked from his hands, and clattered to the earth. Umhra scrambled along the wall of the monolith, searching for cover and wiping the acid from his eyes. His vision blurred. Bettle limped beside him, a fiendish grin on his face. He opened his jaws wide, the earth hissed with each drip of blood from his neck and paw.

As he struck at Umhra, a great stone spike shot out of the ground, and impaled Bettle through the bottom of his chest and out through the top of his back. Acidic gore sprayed across the monolith's surface and the spike lifted Bettle's quivering body from the earth. Spara stood behind the Guardian, a hand thrust up to the heavens.

She ran to Umhra's side and covered his eyes with her hands. "The gods took my sight . . . I will not let the same happen to you."

Umhra closed his eyes against the vibrant light that grew beneath her hands. Warmth surged through his body and his pain receded. Spara slid her hands from Umhra's eyes, down the length of his face, and held them on his cheeks.

Umhra opened his eyes to the sight of Spara's pleasant smile before the lifeless body of Bettle, his torso held high on the stone spike.

"You aren't going to kiss me again, are you?" Umhra asked.

Spara frowned and then laughed. "You should learn to enjoy life, Umhra. There is little of worth in the world other than love." She stood and helped Umhra to his feet. "Let's go break a Waystone. I feel as though this will be the last of our physical trials. The Stoneheart Pass lay spoiled and Vendarithe will not fight us."

"Vendarithe? A dragon?"

"Yes. The last Guardian. The most wise and powerful of all. She protects Mirina's Waystone beneath the Ilathril Mountains."

"But dragons no longer exist in Tyveriel."

"Neither do Paladins, but yet you plainly stand before me."

"And why won't she fight us?" Umhra asked.

"Because she would kill us both far too easily. She wouldn't find it very sporting. Besides, she always believed that I deserved to be a Mystic every bit as much as the rest. She will have no interest in keeping me from Kalmindon."

Spara led Umhra around to the other side of the monolith. There, she walked up to the wall and pressed her hands against the smooth surface. An enchantment faded, revealing an enormous cave opening through which she entered the spire.

"This is Bettle's lair," she said, her voice echoing in the expansive antechamber. "The Waystone lies within."

They navigated through the piles of bones strewn across the room, and continued down a wide path, the air growing cool and musty as they went. The passage leveled out and opened into a cavern with a bed of dried grass on the far side. The room was lit by the subtle yellow pulse of the Waystone at its very center.

"You shatter this one," Spara said. "Take as much of its essence as it will allow and grow strong."

Umhra nodded and once again summoned Forsetae, which materialized in his hand. He walked to the center of the stone. Its irregular light caused his shadow to dance across the uneven roof of the lair. He raised his sword high overhead and plunged it deep into the center of the stone. Cracks spidered out from the wound and the Waystone's yellow essence drifted into the air and spread between him and Spara.

"I suppose the Waystone deems us equals," Spara said as she absorbed half the Waystone's energy.

Umhra welcomed the flood of power. He once again felt renewed. "Was this our final battle, then?"

"I hope so," Spara said. "I grow weary of resorting to such base physical combat. Vendarithe takes pride in her civility. I expect she will rally to our cause. Would you like to stay here tonight? You look tired."

"No. I'm fine and see no point in delaying our return to Evelium."

"As you wish. What does your father's book tell you of dragons?"

"Only that the Mystics ascended to Kalmindon in part to avoid confrontation with them."

Spara nodded. "That is true. I will fill in the details on the way."

CHAPTER 24

I don't aspire to be king of all Evelium, but I should see the
kingdom reunified as my forefathers intended.

—*Entry from the Diary of Vred Ulest*
Dated 17th of Mela, 905 AF. Unearthed from the Ruins of
Ohteira, month of Lusta, 1399 AT

—▲—

"You have truly outdone yourself, Roen," King Ulest
said. Troops had begun to arrive from Amnesty and
Retribution, with others promised from points farther west. A
sea of bonfires now stretched from the base of Castle Ohteira
for as far as the eye could see. "Jemivere, you must admit, it's
an impressive sight."

"Indeed, my Lord." Baron Jemivere sat at the oval giltwood
table along the far wall with a sullen expression on his face.

A horn bellowed in the distance and a herd of mammoths in
full armor came into view through the relentless snow. Behind
them, another thousand men trudged.

"Our forces from Meriden should arrive within the week,"
Roen said from a comfortable chair between sips of a steaming
cup of cider, "and just this morning, I received confirmation
from as far as Travesty that the legions in the east will be

ready to meet us just north of the Ilathril for the march on Vanyareign."

King Ulest folded his arms behind his back, gripping each of his wrists with the opposing hand. He took one more look at the army below and turned from the window. He walked across the room to join his nephew and nieces at the raging mouth of the glowing hearth. The heat lapped at his face as he stared into the roaring fire. "We shall march the morning after the forces from Meriden arrive. I will not waste another moment when Evelium sits on the precipice of reunification. My forefathers would expect no less of me."

"And what do you have planned, Uncle?" Roen asked. "Surely, Jenta will not simply take a knee upon your arrival."

King Ulest turned to face his nephew. "Bring in the Fate. I wish to know what she foresees."

Roen bowed his head, allowing the deflection. "As you wish, Uncle." He walked to the door and poked his head out into the hallway for a moment. He left the door ajar and returned to his uncle's side.

A guard entered behind Roen, ushering in an old woman— her pace hobbled by gout. Her faded blonde hair hung in oily clumps down the length of her back. Her paper-thin skin was covered with liver spots. Innumerable trinkets adorned her soiled yellow robes, clattering with every uneven step. Her hunched posture gave her a frail appearance as though, after seven hundred years, Tyveriel was finally winning their well-fought battle.

She shuffled across the room, the guard gesturing from afar to a chair on the far side of the table where Baron Jemivere sat, seemingly afraid of coming too close. As King Ulest and Roen came to greet her, she fell back into the chair—her legs giving way. The chair groaned at the impact.

King Ulest dismissed the guard with a wave and sat at the head of the table beside the Fate. "Kob'Anni, thank you for coming to me today. I know it is most inconvenient in this weather."

"The weather is of no concern to me, child," Kob'Anni said, her voice weathered and coarse. She watched Roen as he sat across from her and folded his hands on the table. "I should say that your soldiers lack my constitution, however. The castle grounds wreak of discontent."

"We have a long march ahead. I believe in my soul that it is justified, but I was hoping you could provide some insight as to the future of it all."

Kob'Anni craned her neck to make eye contact with him. A cataract clouded one of her eyes—the other was black and discerning. She retrieved a modest leather bag from her robes, amid the clutter of tangled trinkets. She untied the chord that cinched it and turned it upside down on the table.

Tiny vertebrae skittered across the table's smooth surface, like dice cast in a game of chance. She turned her functioning eye toward them as they came to rest. She studied the bones, her crooked fingers gliding over them one at a time, careful not to touch.

"Shale Arving lays slain," she said. "Your heart is pure in its desire to unify this land once more. I see your father on his death bed. He speaks to you, a young man with little hope of fulfilling a father's dream. Your love for him was absolute. Your love for this land, even more so. Give me your hand."

King Ulest reached across the table and laid his open hand before the Fate. She took it in both of hers and pierced his palm with the long, sharpened nail of her left thumb. The wound stung more than the king expected. Kob'Anni turned his hand over and allowed the king's blood to run down his fingers onto the vertebrae and table below.

Myka and Veien joined and watched from over their brother's shoulder.

Kob'Anni released King Ulest's hand and turned her attention back to the scattered bones. For this, she favored her clouded eye.

"There is another claim to the Raptor's Throne, my Lord." Kob'Anni tipped one of the vertebrae over with a fingernail. It left a bloody imprint of its form behind.

"Jenta has no claim. She will fold to my challenge."

"Not the Lady Avrette . . . another."

"Arving has an heir?" Roen asked of his uncle in surprise.

"Not to my knowledge," King Ulest said, "but if this is what the Seeing Spine shows us, then it must be true."

"I do not see an heir specifically, my Lord," Kob'Anni said, her voice cracking. "I only see a claim to the throne that will contest your own. The Grey Queen is coming."

King Ulest stood from his chair, sending it screeching across the stone floor. "Now I have had enough. Am I honestly to believe the Grey Queen has arisen from my cousin's untimely demise? That is nothing more than a child's tale from a bygone age."

"What else is a child's tale, my Lord, other than cautionary advice adults have come to ignore?" Kob'Anni collected the bones with a sweep of her arm and dropped them back into their bag. She struggled to rise from the table and limped over to King Ulest. "Should you ride on Vanyareign, let it be known that your advance will not go uncontested. That is all I have seen. The Seeing Spine did not foresee your victory, nor did it see your defeat. It only told me you choose a difficult path."

King Ulest contemplated the information as Kob'Anni turned and left without another word. It was not what he had wanted to hear, but he knew in his heart that if there was ever a time to reunite Evelium, it was now. How could he face his ancestors in the Everlife if he did not seize this opportunity? Better to die a failure than to live as a coward.

Baron Jemivere stood. "I beg you to reconsider your course of action, my Lord. The Fate has warned your quest will not be an easy one. If you would just let me contact the Elders Syndicate—"

"Nothing worthwhile is ever achieved with ease, Jemivere."

"Uncle, what would you have me do?" Roen asked, still seated.

"We continue with our plan," King Ulest said. "As soon as the forces are amassed, we head east to meet the others and then we march on Vanyareign."

▲

Roen knocked on the heavy oak door, a bottle of Revel Redemption and two glasses in his other hand. He peered down the hallway to either side as he waited, tapping his foot on the smooth stone flooring.

The latch clicked from within and the door creaked ajar, Baron Jemivere's face appeared in the gap. He opened the door wider. "Roen, to what do I owe this honor?" His tone dripped with sarcasm.

Roen raised the bottle of wine and stemware. "A peace offering."

Jemivere eyed the hand-painted label on the wine bottle depicting a phoenix rising into the night sky from a nest of ash. He nodded. "By all means, come in." Jemivere swung the door wide and stepped aside so Roen could enter.

Roen entered the room and placed the wine bottle and glasses on the table before a warm fire. He drew his dagger.

Baron Jemivere stepped back, searched his hip for a dagger that was not there.

Roen deftly cut the wax seal from the bottle and cast it onto the table. He sheathed his dagger and pried the cork loose. "If I did not deserve such a response, I would be offended." Roen poured two glasses of wine and passed one to Baron Jemivere, whose posture slackened. "I know I must seem like a warmonger. You and I simply have different methods of achieving the same end. We share a vision. One of a unified Evelium under my uncle. I salute your loyalty."

Roen raised his glass, the garnet wine swirling within.

Baron Jemivere met Roen's glass with a clink. "Thank you.

I want nothing more than your uncle's success and the lands that will come along with it." Jemivere pursed his lips. "In all seriousness, I hope for a long, amicable working relationship with you."

Roen held his nose to the rim of his glass and drew in the wine's bouquet. Dark plum, exotic spices, rich soil. He took a sip and swirled it in his mouth, allowing the wine to coat his tongue. Jemivere followed suit.

"Please, sit." Jemivere offered Roen a seat by the fire. "Tell me, what makes you think marching an army on Vanyareign will meet with success rather than war?"

Roen sat, took another sip of his wine, and allowed himself a moment to savor the full experience. "It is my experience that the best way to prevent war is to prove your absolute, unquestionable dominance. To prove you will go to any length to achieve your desired outcome. There is no room for diplomacy. It wreaks of weakness."

Baron Jemivere took another sip of wine and tilted his head in curiosity. "And, now?"

"Now?" Roen snickered. "Now, you share my wine from a glass rimmed with lypranthium gel. You have no more than ten seconds until paralysis sets in."

"Surely, you—" The baron dropped his glass on the rug. He pulled at the collar of his shirt, then froze, his eyes wide.

Roen finished his wine, placed his glass on the table beside him, and pushed himself up from his chair. "Worry not, Baron. The paralysis only lasts a moment. It doesn't take long for the poison to reach your lungs. Make peace with the gods for you join them this evening. We shall march on Vanyareign in your absence."

Roen retrieved a letter sealed with green wax with the image of an eagle embossed into its surface and slipped it into Baron Jemivere's pocket. "To assure the blame for your death falls upon our enemy," he said as he collected the glasses and the half-empty bottle of wine.

He observed Jemivere as the color left the baron's face and his fingernails blackened. Quietly, he left the sitting room.

CHAPTER 25

Of all my failures, losing track of the wizard is perhaps my greatest. I fear that his survival poses a threat to my kin and the world I have built.

—*The Collected Letters of Modig Forene*
Letter to Stryke Modig dated 22nd of Anar, 199 AF. Unearthed from the Ruins of Vanyareign, month of Ocken, 1301 AT

Talus sat in the corner of his cell, his back against the unforgiving stone wall of Castle Forene's dungeon. There were no windows nor means to circulate airflow—just the stagnant sights, smells, and sounds of despair. He maintained a rough sense of time only by the rhythmic drip of dank water that fell from the ceiling into a puddle at the center of his cell every thirty seconds.

Drip.

He had, so many times, been on the other side of these bars, deep beneath the surface of Mount Orys—deriding a petty thief for the error of his ways or sometimes interrogating enemies of the king. No matter your crime, if you crossed the Eagle Guard, you ended up in this gods-forsaken place until the magistrate determined whether you be set free or sent to the gallows.

Drip.

Surmising it was late at night by how the guards so shamelessly shirked their duties, he had been trying to sleep for hours but could not find peace on the cold, damp floor.

Drip.

Then, the sounds of a heavy door scraping open and closed, followed by muffled voices tinged with frustration. Footsteps came down the hall, pausing every so often to the sound of a struggle. The voices grew louder and angrier.

"Come on, you lousy drunk," a guard said, forcing a slouching figure into the room from a doorway on the far side. "You've gotten yourself into enough trouble for one night. Broke the captain's nose, you damned fool. And spit in my face one more time and I'll beat you sober."

Talus squinted, but the light was too dim to make out the details and he was too tired to care enough to stand and walk to the front of his cell. He'd seen dozens like this poor soul come and go since he'd been here. None of them ever learned their lesson, either. You'd think a stretch in a place like this would have you reevaluating your life. At least, it was having that effect on Talus.

"My advice would be to sleep it off, and plead for grace in the morning," the guard said, shoving the figure into an empty cell across the way. The drunkard slumped to the floor with a thud. Talus shuddered at the sound of the door slamming and the nauseating click of the lock tumbling closed. It was all so helpless.

Drip.

The guard grunted and straightened his uniform. "Pain in the ass," he said, and made his way out of the room. With a loud click, he secured the heavy door behind him.

Talus closed his eyes and curled up as if covering himself with a blanket that didn't exist.

Drip.

Scrape.

Click.

"Hey, King Killer," a voice whispered from closer than Talus thought possible. He looked up to see Shadow's face peering through the bars of his cell. "You aren't supposed to answer to that, you idiot."

Talus scrambled to his knees and crawled to the to the front of the cell. "What? How?"

Shadow held a finger up to his pursed lips. "Doesn't matter. Only one thing does. Did you do it?"

"Of course not." Talus tried to whisper, but the thought that it was popular opinion he was King Arving's murderer made his blood boil.

Shadow hushed him again. "Then come on, let's go. Gromley is waiting for us."

Talus shook his head to clear the fog that had sat with him for days. He watched as Shadow stepped over to the door of his cell and toyed with the lock.

Drip.

Scratch.

Click.

The door swung open, prompting Talus to his feet—a surge of energy drove his despair away. In two strides, he met Shadow in the hallway and grabbed him by both shoulders. "Never has it been so good to see you, my friend."

"You look absolutely horrendous," Shadow said. "Not to mention you smell. But now is not the time for friendly salutations. We must get out of this dungeon."

"How? The only way in and out is through the entrance at the base of King's Way."

Shadow chuckled. "I've been in and out of here many times, and only once have I used the door to leave. Let's go, before the guards make their rounds."

Talus was eager to leave the dungeon behind him and see what Shadow knew about it that even he did not. Together, they made their way across the room, sticking to the dimness along the walls, passing another inmate who either slept or no longer cared enough to stir. Talus followed as Shadow moved effortlessly and without sound.

They skulked down a long hallway to a cast iron door. Shadow retrieved a set of picks hidden in his beltline and sprung the lock with ease. The door cracked open, allowing them vantage into the adjacent room.

The interrogation chamber was empty at this time of night, but the ferrous smell of dried blood clung to its every surface. It had never bothered Talus, that he remembered. Not until now.

Shadow opened the door just wide enough for them to slip through one shoulder at a time. Once they were both inside, Shadow closed the door, careful to hold the handle down until the door was flush with the wall. Only then did he release his pressure on the handle, allowing the lock to click into place.

He turned to Talus. "Lovely things you Raptor's Grasp do in here." He shook his head as he looked around the room.

"All in the name of king and country, I assure you. I never took pleasure or pride in this part of the job. This room is also a dead end. Designed so that one may only exit if granted by the guards outside."

A stone table with a smooth surface that sloped away from its center to either side acted as the room's centerpiece. Manacles were affixed where the head, hands, and feet would be of whatever poor soul should find themselves upon it. Around the base was a drain that collected liquids used in the interrogation process and released bodily fluids.

Against the wall across from them was another table upon which sat an array of iron torture implements splayed out on a leather mat. Shadow went to this table and picked up a short, curved blade. He inspected the blade—turning it in his hand— and then went to the central table and kneeled in its stained basin.

Curious, Talus came around behind him and looked over his shoulder as Shadow wedged the blade in a narrow gap between the base of the table and the slick floor of the basin. Torquing the blade, he pulled on the stone. It gave way, grinding against the floor as he drew it out from the base.

"I'd better go first," Shadow said, looking up at Talus, who now peered past him into the dark interior of the hollow base.

"In there?" Talus pointed.

"Aye. It won't be pleasant and can be treacherous your first time. Keep your feet beneath you and be careful as you exit. The fall would surely make this the least satisfying jail break in history. Now, do me a favor and replace the blade."

Shadow handed Talus the blade he had used to pry the stone free. It was now somewhat chewed up, but they would be long gone by the time anyone would figure out they used the tool in their escape.

Talus returned the blade to its spot among the other implements. He turned back to an empty room; Shadow having begun his descent.

Talus sat and draped his feet into the narrow drain that faded away from him at a steep angle. He slid forward, turned onto his stomach, and drew in a deep breath. He wedged the stone Shadow had removed back into place, and sealed them into the dank passage.

Talus shimmied downward, keeping his feet wide beneath him to control his descent. The smell was sickening—he gagged on more than one occasion.

After several minutes, Talus's feet swung free. He slipped forward, remembering Shadow's warning. His hips emerged from the drain, the sharp stone edge its mouth created cut through the simple clothing he wore and sliced into his torso. The stone wall was slick with residue from ages of torture performed high above. Talus's grip slipped free.

A hand reached out from the darkness and locked with his, arresting his fall. He slammed into a sheer obsidian facing, but Shadow's grip on him held fast. He scrambled to find footing to support his weight.

"You okay down there?" Shadow asked. "I told you the exit could be problematic."

"I can't see a thing," Talus said as he peered into the darkness of what he presumed to be a natural cavern within Mount Orys.

"You are about fifty feet above ground with jagged shards of obsidian beneath you. Down climb heading to your right and you should be fine. I swear, you humans are inferior in so many ways. It's a wonder you've become such a dominant race."

"Only by unfettered debauchery, I assure you." Talus stretched his right foot out and down until he found sufficient footing. He released Shadow's hand and climbed as Shadow had instructed until he found the base of the cavern. Releasing the wall, his hands bleeding, he found Shadow somehow waiting for him at the edge of a pond of putrid water. Large mushrooms that grew in clusters cast an eerie, purple light across the cavern.

"I never knew how that worked," Talus said, holding an arm up over his nose and mouth. "Where do we go from here?"

"I was about to ask you the same thing," Shadow said. "How do we go about clearing your name?"

"I don't know. I wasn't even in Vanyareign when Shale was killed. Or Evelium, for that matter. I was returning from Shent."

"What were you doing in Shent?" Shadow asked. "Stay close, there won't be adequate light for some time."

Shadow leaped across a series of rocks from one side of the fetid pool to the other, helping Talus as they went. On the last rock Talus slipped and his bare foot tapped the water's surface, sending a ripple into the darkness.

He tried to wrest his foot clear, but the water clung to it, small black tendrils climbed up his ankle.

"Something's got me." Talus held a hand out for Shadow.

"Got you?" Shadow jumped back onto the rock upon which Talus struggled. "Let me see."

Shadow dropped to his knees at the edge of the rock and

inspected Talus's foot. Black sludge had now enveloped his heal and toes.

"It's burning," Talus said, pulling at his calf against the ooze's grasp. "Get it off me."

Shadow pulled a dagger from within his leathers and plunged it into the puddle beneath Talus's foot. Ice crystalized where the blade broke the surface. The ooze recoiled, releasing Talus, and reared up into a great pseudopod.

"Go," Shadow said as the ooze loomed over them. "I'll be right behind you."

Talus clambered back from the rock's edge, the skin of his foot stung from the ooze's acidic grip. He jumped to the shore, the pain shot up his leg and sent him tumbling to the jagged cavern floor. He scrambled backward, his gaze fixated on Shadow and the ooze.

Shadow thrust his dagger into the ooze once more, ice spreading across its oily black surface. The ooze quivered, sending frozen shards scattering across the cavern, and then lashed out at Shadow with another pseudopod.

Shadow flipped backward, just out of the ooze's reach and narrowly cleared the other pseudopods it sent shooting into the air after him. He landed on solid ground a few feet from Talus.

The ooze reached out from its pool with elongated tendrils, searching for its prey. Shadow motioned for Talus to remain still. The tendrils stretched forth, tapping the cavern floor as they crept within inches of Shadow's boots and then retracted back into the pool.

Shadow pointed toward an opening in the wall from which a dim light emanated, and both men slipped out of the cavern into the tunnel.

"Thank you," Talus said, his chest heaving. "I was transporting Alessa Elmont and her newborn daughter to safety."

"What?" Shadow asked.

"You asked where I was when the king was murdered. I was

in Shent with Alessa Elmont."

"Why would the king call upon his most trusted soldier to take a rich girl and her baby . . ." Shadow's voice trailed off in the darkness. "It was his and something was wrong."

"Yes. Please don't take offense, but the child's skin is grey, and she has black rings around her eyes. Her eyes, themselves, are pupilless, and golden.

"It was not the first time Shale's seed had produced such offspring. Several of the mothers and their children died in childbirth. Those few that survived, the king had murdered. Shale asked that I take care of the matter, but I hadn't the heart, so I took them away—where I knew they would be safe. The child is the rightful heir to the throne I serve, after all. How could I bring death to one bearing the Mark of Forene?"

"Look where your chivalry has gotten you. You really should think these things through before you act."

Shadow led Talus through the tunnel to a fork in the path. To the left, light beckoned them forward, while the right fell into darkness. Shadow kept to the left, entering another tunnel big enough for the friends to walk side-by-side. "This tunnel empties at the east fork of the Torrent," Shadow said, "Gromley will meet us there. What do you want to do about all of this?"

"First, I need to get a message to Shent and have Alessa return with the child so Turin can claim the throne. Then I need to speak with Lady Avrette," Talus said. "She will assume the throne, not knowing the child lives. I will clear my name with her and bring the king's actual killer to justice."

"Queen Avrette. The Elders Syndicate coronated Jenta earlier today. If we get you back to Laudin, I'm certain he will offer that Taivaron deliver your message. As for the queen, I'm not sure how she'll take all of this. Power has a natural way of solidifying itself quickly. How is it a guard saw you in the king's bedchamber standing over his dead body?"

"I'm not sure. Either the guard lied to cover for the killer, or some kind of magic deceived him." Talus placed his hand on

Shadow's shoulder. "Thank you for coming for me."

"I didn't really have much of a choice." Shadow grimaced. "The queen scheduled your execution for the morning. There will be a certain unwillingness for her to change her mind. Staying your execution would make her look weak and threaten the strength of her tenuous mandate."

In the distance, a horn blared through Vanyareign.

"Word must already spread that the king's killer has escaped," Shadow said. "We must get you to safety."

CHAPTER 26

By the grace of the gods, their power may be suffused and harnessed by the pure of heart.

—*The Tome of Mystics*
Unknown Origin. Unearthed from the Ruins of Oda Norde,
month of Bracken, 1320 AT

—▲—

Roen crossed the war camp, the first signs of thaw welcoming the armies of Winterashe as they converged in the east and readied their march on Vanyareign. With the change in the weather, so came a change in demeanor. What was once discontent with the long journey through bitter cold and relentless snow had become a frenetic anticipation of crossing into Windswept to reunite Evelium under the rule of their king, Vred Ulest.

A tent of scarlet canvas dominated the center of the massive war camp. Innumerable legions of Winterashe soldiers surrounded it, along with their beasts of the north. Saddled and armored mammoths, dire bear, and winter wolves pulled at heavy chains, trying to free themselves from the burdens imposed upon them. Wyverns and manticore circled overhead, their riders keeping close watch on the border for any spies that might unveil their plans prematurely.

"Uncle, the last of the legions will arrive shortly," Roen said, throwing open the heavy fur-covered tarp that covered the tent's entrance, and letting in a bitter wind. "Nine thousand Orc mercenaries from Orrat Skag with two thousand ogres among them."

"Excellent work, Roen," King Ulest said. He leaned over a broad wooden table, his hands spread wide to support his weight. A polished orb held the map in place at each corner, each emitting a vibrant light. His crimson leathers, complete with the serpentine emblem of his house emblazoned on his chest, made it look as though blood seeped from the stark white furs that covered his shoulders. "You have assembled the most impressive army Tyveriel has ever borne witness to. Jemivere will be avenged. I could not be more proud."

"Your praise is too much." Roen extended his arms and King Ulest embraced him. "They come to honor you, and your promise of unification. I too share your added desire to see those who brought about Jemivere's demise brought to justice."

"They see a better future than I can offer them isolated in Winterashe. A future the Fracture has robbed them of. It is time Evelium was one kingdom again."

A horn bellowed in the distance, announcing the Orc parties Roen had spoken of. The thunderous foot falls of the ogres they commanded shook the earth as they approached camp. "Vanyareign will have no answer for this show of force." Roen smiled.

"Then the decision shall fall to Jenta."

"Certainly, she will not face you in single combat."

"Never underestimate of woman of her resolve, nephew. The mother wolf is most unpredictable when defending her pups. And Jenta will wear the crown of Modig Forene. It alone can bring ruin to any man if she knows how to harness its power."

"And you have Tedarrin."

"Yes." King Ulest placed his hand on the leather-wrapped pommel of the sword he wore at his hip. "The Blade Unmet. It has been years since I have wielded it in battle."

"Then it will be hungry," Roen said, his gaze cut to the sword.

"I shall not yield, Roen." King Ulest drew the sword from its sheath and admired the soft amber glow of its blade. "I mean to see this through to the very end. Whether that end is my ascension to the Raptor's Throne or my death."

"Uncle. It is your time. My sisters assure me."

"And what do your sisters see that Kob'Anni has not? They are not fates."

"They are . . . well, they are what they are." Roen poured himself a glass of wine from a decanter hanging from one of the tent's sturdy pine poles. "And their sight is as gifted as their voices are faint. They see a unified Evelium . . . an end to the Fracture."

King Ulest sheathed Tedarrin. "When the last of the Orc party arrives, I will address my army."

"I will see to the arrangements. Shall we say this evening, after they rest and eat?"

King Ulest accepted Roen's suggestion, and turned back toward the table at the center of his tent. He placed both hands down on the rough wooden surface and stared at the map of Evelium resting upon it. It was not the map of a land broken by political conflict or a long-held family impasse. It was that of a land unified and whole, as his forefathers always intended it to be.

He placed a copper token with an axe on it—representing the Orc mercenaries that had just now joined their ranks—next to those amassed on the map north of Requiem. The tokens sat upon a convergence of arrows originating from across the far reaches of Winterashe. A thick black arrow marked their path forward, traversing the eastern foothills of the Ilathril Mountains, along the outskirts of the Morion Swamp, and ending at Vanyareign.

▲

King Ulest stepped into the crisp air; guards trailed close behind him dressed in red armor. He led his escorts toward the southern edge of camp where the army had gathered and awaited his formal address. This very evening, with the late-winter sun hanging low in the sky, he would rally them to his cause and charge them to make their final preparations for the march on Vanyareign. If everything went according to plan, a new age would dawn by the Sowing Moon.

At the edge of camp, he came to a procession of mammoths, the first of which wore thick red leather armor adorned with gold plates and outfitted with jagged blades on its tusks. A wooden ladder led up to an empty carriage high upon its back. The beast's master was wrapped in heavy furs and awaited his passengers. Behind the mammoth was another similarly impressive beast, armored in black. In its carriage sat the Three, awaiting their uncle's arrival.

King Ulest climbed into the carriage of the lead mammoth. He acknowledged Roen and then peered beyond his nephew at the trail of mammoths behind him. An awe-inspiring sight. Gripping the front rail of the carriage, King Ulest directed the driver to set his mammoth in motion.

With a tap of the drivers' pole, the mammoth lurched forward, each footfall its own earthquake. The other creatures followed, descending an embankment toward an open plain where the assembled armies of Winterashe stood in formation—a dark sea of metal and leather.

The roar was deafening on the king's approach—the thunder of tens-of-thousands of troops crashing their weapons against the firm earth and heavy armor. King Ulest drew in a deep breath and closed his eyes. His gut twisted as the army stared at him. As his mammoth came to a halt before the throng, the King of Winterashe opened his eyes and raised his hands. Silence reigned.

"My loyal friends," he said, his voice echoing over the open grasslands, "You have left the safety of your homes, the comfort of your families, the routine of your daily lives to be here at my side as we march to change history. For this, I thank you from the bottom of my heart. We do not march to take power, nor to claim fame and fortune. We march instead to right a wrong that has plagued our land for too long. We are an army of the benevolent. It is my solemn goal that our vast numbers allow us to avoid bloodshed and bring peace to our land. Just as you are here to fight for me, I am here to deliver to you a better future. A better future for those of us from the north and the rest of our brethren throughout Evelium. For, together, we are stronger than we are apart."

A cacophony of support swelled up from the ranks before him as a light late-winter snow fell upon the land.

"Tomorrow, we march for Vanyareign, where I will lay my rightful claim to the Raptor's Throne and reunify Evelium. Our numbers cannot be deterred, our movement cannot be quelled. Together, we will build a new world. The people of Winterashe shall go unheard no longer."

"Ulest. Ulest. Ulest." The army's chant sent a cloud of steam into the air.

King Ulest held up his hands in a request for silence. The crowd obliged. "There is much we must do to prepare. A long, tiresome road lies ahead of us. I ask you worry not of these things tonight, but rather to feast to your hearts' content. I have provisioned camp for your indulgence to celebrate the history we create together."

As another round of cheers shook the surrounding earth, King Ulest motioned to his driver who gave the mammoth a firm tap on the right cheek with his pole, setting the beast into motion. The procession followed, taking an arching path around the amassed army back toward camp.

By the time King Ulest returned to camp, the revelry had begun. Music blared from around the countless bonfires.

Tables piled high with delicacies were picked clean, and barrels of fine wine and ale were emptied and toppled. He greeted a few soldiers along the way but made for his tent without delay. There was too much on his mind to partake in the celebration. Instead, he went to his map, the orbs that held it in place illumed as he approached.

"A rousing speech," a guttural voice said from behind.

King Ulest turned, surprised to see an enormous Orc sitting in a chair across the room, picking at his teeth with a splinter of wood. "Most obliged. And you are?"

"Yardish the Violator, Chieftain of the Wolfsbane clan of Orrat Skag. Your nephew summoned us to your cause. His plea was compelling enough for me to come and see what this was all about."

Yardish stood. He was imposing, standing over seven feet tall, his shoulders broad and muscular. He wore his greying hair in dreadlocks and a steel hoop through each of the tusks that protruded from his lower jaw. A patchwork of leather and furs covered his jungle green skin, and he wore two human skulls on his left shoulder as a symbol of his station.

"Tell me, Vred Ulest, King of Winterashe, do you mean what you say? That you intend to deliver to us a better life? Do these intentions include the Orcs?"

"I always mean what I say, Chief Yardish. I can assure you of that. And, yes, I include your people in my sentiment."

Yardish pointed to Orrat Skag on King Ulest's map, "Evelium has forsaken *my* people. The gods tossed us aside as mistakes. The Forenes thought of us as inferior to the Purebloods. For ages the establishment has left us in a wasteland while the other races thrive. We seek a place in your new order . . . not your sentiment."

"And you shall have one of honor," King Ulest said, "You show great faith in bringing such a formidable army to my aid. I will not forget this faith once I reunite Evelium. I see a future where all the races thrive. Where everyone has equal opportunity."

"Your words are silken, but silk tears easily. To the Orcish, a promise is an unbreakable oath sealed with blood and ale."

Yardish pulled a tarnished dagger from his belt and cut his own hand, squeezing his fist closed and passing King Ulest the blade. King Ulest maintained eye contact with the Orc and sliced his own hand. The men pressed their palms together and were bound by blood.

"Now, we drink." Yardish grabbed two mammoth tusk tankards and slammed them down on the table. He fetched a barrel from across the room on one shoulder. King Ulest pulled the stopper and Yardish filled the tankards. He slammed the barrel on the floor beside him. The men each took a cup, now overflowing with a lazy foam, and drank.

"Brothers?" King Ulest asked, banging his empty tankard down on the table.

Yardish laughed. "It will take several more of these for that," he said, "but friends is a good start."

King Ulest motioned to the tankards, "Well, you better pour another then."

Yardish smiled, his tusks fully exposed. He hoisted the cask in the crook of his arm and poured another round. Ale splashed from the cask.

"I like you Vred Ulest. I am proud to call you my king."

CHAPTER 27

By the end of the battle, only the great tower of Antiikin remained. The rest of the ancient city lay in ruin along with its people.

—The Tome of Mystics
Unknown Origin. Unearthed from the Ruins of Oda Norde, month of Bracken, 1320 AT

—▲—

Among the depths of the abyssal trenches of the Sea of Widows, a cavern of impenetrable ice kept safe one of Tyveriel's great secrets. The interior of the cavern was in complete darkness except for a soft glow emanating from a single egg of green obsidian-like glass that sat nestled in the crook of an immense arm, undisturbed for over a millennium. Its guardian, a flawless dragon of pure white, lay motionless in a dormant state, waiting for her offspring to come forth and bring glory to her house once more. One would have assumed the noble creature long since dead, if not for the rhythmic cloud of luminescent blue frost escaping her toothy mouth.

Within the translucent egg, her progeny stirred. At first the motion was all but imperceptible—little more than a twitch— but over time it grew into a violent thrashing. For months, the hatchling within waged war against the hardened shell with no ground given on either side. Finally, an occlusion grew within the egg's flawless surface. The imperfection first appeared near the center of the egg, where the hatchling's efforts brought damage to the wall that imprisoned it. From there it spread, spiraling its way around the orb toward the surface, the resonant cracking of glass under immense pressure accompanying it.

One flake of glass after another fell from the egg's surface, as though chiseled away by an unseen force, until only the thick amnion at its core was left. Now able to expand its form, the hatchling sliced through the membrane and forced its head out into the world with a screech that echoed throughout the chamber.

The small, grey dragon climbed from the sac, stretched its limbs, and shook the gelatinous coating from its scales. It turned once to get a sense for its surroundings and roared—a definitive announcement of its arrival.

Trapped in her slumber, the ancient white dragon didn't stir.

Investigating her mother by the fading glow of her shattered egg, the hatchling bit into the white dragon's immense chest. A giant eye blinked open, the hatchling's serrated teeth scraped off her mother's armored torso.

The white dragon huffed, pushed herself onto her forearms, and reared her head up to the roof of the cavern to get a better look at her child. She yawned, frost billowing from her agape mouth. The hatchling paced in circles following after her own tail in the gargantuan beast's presence.

"Welcome, my beautiful terror," the white dragon said. Her voice was as resonant as waves lashing the shore. "I am so very pleased that you have chosen your time."

"There is a weakness in the world of men," the hatchling said, "a divide."

"I have sensed this as well. The great king's bloodline withers. Soon, their factions will fight to lay claim to Evelium.

You will be their reckoning."

"Avarice will be their undoing. But where am I to start? I am too small."

"You need time, child, but you already know the answer. You need only one thing from me. For you are the daughter of the great Mesorith and Zalinrithe. The unity of the darkness and the light. You are born with all the knowledge and experience of those before you, but are the only of your kind. You shall devour the races of man, cauterize the lesions they build upon the land, and cleanse Tyveriel of their memory. Search within the recesses of your mind and all the answers you seek shall reveal themselves to you."

The hatchling blinked. "I possess memories that are not my own?"

"Yes. We are all born with the memories of those who came before us," Zalinrithe said, "Our greatest strength lies in each of us having lived a thousand lives."

"And there has never been one like me before. There has never been a grey dragon."

"No. You are unique. A product of a unity so powerful it could only happen once and at significant cost. You are the prophecy that will unleash us from the bondage of man. The prophecy our kind has been waiting ages for. I give you the name Silyarithe, but those that fear you shall know you as the Grey Queen."

"I must feed first. I must grow strong, so I am unmatched by all who would challenge my rule."

"Indeed, you must," Zalinrithe said, "And this shall be my last gift to you, my beloved child. My time has come to an end, my purpose fulfilled, and I tire of this world. I shall sustain you here until you are strong enough to go out into the world of men and fulfill your destiny. Through you, I shall live on . . . Zalinrithe the White Death."

Zalinrithe inspected one of her fore-talons. It was as sharp, even after her long slumber, as it was on the day she helped

Mesorith take Mount Anvil.

"You were with him when he reigned over man and beast alike," Silyarithe said.

"For a time, yes," Zalinrithe said. "I was beautiful and terrifying in my prime. Not the shell I am today. Time ravages even perfection."

"I shall make the world know your fury again," Silyarithe said.

Zalinrithe grinned and then turned the talon she was admiring on herself and pierced her scaled torso just below the base of her neck. Bright green blood, matching the color of the egg from which Silyarithe had hatched, poured from the nascent puncture. She dragged the claw down the length of her abdomen, welcoming her end.

A ravenous hunger overcame Silyarithe at the sight of the exposed flesh. She drew in the ferrous smell now pervading the room and licked her lips. For one last moment, there was nothing in the world but her and her mother.

Zalinrithe pulled the wound open, exposing her immense green heart to Silyarithe. "Come, My Queen. Sate yourself upon my flesh. I am of no other use to you."

Without hesitation, Silyarithe lunged at the much larger dragon and plunged her head into the wound. She grabbed a hold of Zalinrithe's heart and thrashed wildly, tearing a sizeable chunk from it and gulping it down into her gullet.

Zalinrithe reared back in pain—her heart ruptured—and then fell to the floor of the cavern. The crash sent a shower of rock cascading across the room. Silyarithe dove back into her mother's cavernous form, devouring Zalinrithe's heart before the life had faded from her eyes. Silyarithe didn't waste a moment to even recognize the sacrifice her mother had made, nor did she feel any remorse. She just ate—swallowing as much meat as she could muster with every gulp, according to her nature. Her appetite was voracious, and knew no end until she had fully consumed Zalinrithe's heart.

When Silyarithe finished her meal, she wobbled away from her mother's corpse as if in a drunken stupor. Her mind whirred as a rush of power inherited from the feast coursed through her body.

She collapsed in the corner and curled her tail over her eyes. Ancestral memories raced through her head, a menagerie of triumphs and failures that were their legacy. It was her turn to wage a great war against mankind. A war Mesorith and the ally he found in the blights of the Wistful Timberlands had failed to win. She would not make the same mistakes. Comforted, she slept.

▲

What seemed like such ample space just a few months ago, was now oppressive in its confines. Silyarithe yearned to stretch her wings and soar amongst the clouds. The cavern held nothing for her now but the skeletal remains of her mother and the dank odor of excrement. What kind of life was this for a queen?

During the process of consuming all Zalinrithe could offer, the young dragon had recovered a peculiar shard of semi-translucent crystal lodged deep within her mother's body.

The moment she tore it free in a greedy mouthful of meat, she saw a vision from long ago. A diminutive Farestere man, dressed in yellow robes, sat over the shard and traced a sigil with his pale, boney fingers. As he finished his incantation, a bead of darkness formed at the center of the shard, growing into an undulating mass that, to this day, swirled discontentedly within its core. The soul of her father bound to a phylactery.

Her questions regarding the path forward had been answered. Silyarithe turned the crystal in her claw, and contemplated her next move. She had outgrown the need for safety, the need to be tucked away from the world of men. It was time for her to set her plan into motion.

Her impatience grew with her strength. She tore at the thick ice of the lair's walls, the natural warmth of her form aiding in their retreat. The exposed stone—now marred with claw marks—glowed with dark violet glyphs that formed a ward against the outside world.

She cleared the ice and paced the perimeter of the cavern, looking for a point of egress. At first, the cavern seemed inescapable—solid rock in every direction. She continued her search and found an area that was smoother than the rest of the cavern walls. The rock had been melted under great heat.

Silyarithe tore into the unnatural surface and the rock crumbled away. Her suspicions confirmed, she increased her efforts, furiously burrowing into the cavern wall without rest. With one final gouge, the rock gave way and ice-cold water flooded her tunnel and the cavern behind her.

She strained against the deluge, her claws holding fast to the edge of the tunnel opening. As the cavern filled and the inflow subsided, Silyarithe squeezed through the fissure she had created and swam out into open water and made for the surface—a glimmer of light an impossible distance away.

Her arms held flush against her sides, she snaked through the depths with purpose, her lithe tail propelling her forward. She emerged from the darkness, the pressure lifting from her body, and sped up toward the surface. The light above her intensified. Then she burst through the chop and caught the wind in her wings and lifted into the sky. With two strong beats, she orientated toward the Isle of the Twelve Mines.

CHAPTER 28

The Tursas attacked from behind, tearing the rear ships of the fleet asunder. It was only the flagship that managed to escape into a narrow channel.

—*A Traveler's Guide to the Odd and Obscure by Sentina Vake* Chapter 6 – Unearthed from the Homestead in Maryk's Cay, month of Riet, 1407 AT

—▲—

Umhra crouched and peered into the small, dark hole at the base of a rocky outcrop nestled amongst the lush foliage of the Wistful Timberlands. It was not much wider than his shoulders and seemed an unlikely place for the last Waystone. He looked up at Spara, who stood behind him leaning against a sturdy hemlock—her arms crossed as if impatient with his investigation.

"There's a dragon . . . down there?" he asked, raising an eyebrow.

"Yes," Spara said. "Way down. Mirina is maybe half your size, if she's lucky. I'm sure the tunnel seemed ample to her, and she was always quite overprotective of this location. She only visited it, herself, when necessary."

Umhra looked back down the hole. The air was stale, damp.

He opened Ivory's Nameless Tome to a page he had dogeared that discussed dragons.

"Ivory's research suggests Mystics and dragons are adversaries . . . opposite sides of the same coin."

"I wouldn't characterize it that way. It's more like dragons are nearly impervious to a Mystic's magic. They are the perfect check to our power."

Umhra considered the disparity between the two accounts. He had no interest in finding out which was correct.

Spara pushed forward and cracked her knuckles. "Feels good to be back to form. Shall I lead the way? Vendarithe might take more-kindly to seeing me show up in her lair first. I'm certain we will find her sleeping, but she is not known for tolerating strangers. And, whatever you do, please don't compare her to the chromatic dragons of old. She despises them to no end."

"By all means. I wouldn't want to upset her."

"Agreed," Spara said, "she is a beauty—scales the color of rose gold, eyes red as rubies—but it's best we keep her as placid as possible. Disturbing her rest for too long could end in disaster. The gods gave Mystics many gifts, but fighting such beasts was not one of them."

Spara winked and plunged into the hole, starting the descent toward Vendarithe's lair. Umhra drew in a deep breath—as if it might be his last of fresh air—and wedged his broad shoulders into the opening in pursuit.

The interior of the tunnel was even tighter than it had appeared. Umhra's leathers scraped the sides, dislodging earth and stone as he progressed. Unencumbered, Spara pulled ahead until she was out of sight. For several hours, Umhra labored on his stomach, with nothing but the stale air and the smell of his own musk to accompany him.

As the tunnel's composition shifted to lavender stone, he could see a dim, warm light in the distance. Umhra paused for a moment, his chest heaving, and pondered the power necessary to establish the tunnel's path through the coarse limestone. He wiped his brow and continued.

With each elbow Umhra dug into its rough-hewn surface, he drew closer to the light. When he got to the end of the tunnel, he found Spara standing in a cavern of surprising enormity, waiting for him. A loud wooshing sound—as though a subterranean river coursed along the cavern's far side—echoed throughout the cave.

Umhra crawled out of the tunnel and stood beside Spara. He kicked a pile of bones aside to gain comfortable footing. Dusting himself off, his eyes drew to the room's only light source, a gargantuan dragon whose slightly agape mouth glowed like a forge in the center of her lair. The heat came in waves with every breath the beast took, causing the air to ripple between them and searing the exposed skin of his face and hands. He raised an arm and squinted against the blistering heat.

The dragon trained its massive ruby eyes on the intruders, but she otherwise looked quite at peace, obviously not ascertaining any threat. She tilted her scaled head toward Spara.

"And this is the Paladin you claim has ascended?" Vendarithe asked in a baritone voice.

"It is," Spara said, "May I introduce Umhra the Peacebreaker, Champion of Vaila, and Savior of Tyveriel. Among other things, I'm sure. Umhra, this is Vendarithe the Gilded Death."

With no advance warning, the great serpent spat a ball of fire at Umhra. His dragon scale armor formed around him, the tiny plates clicked into place in rapid succession. He summoned his sword to prepare for battle. Umhra dodged the attack, somersaulting across the floor of the lair. Bones scattered and broke in his wake. The fire hit the wall behind him and melted the rock, partially blocking the path through which he had arrived.

"You speak the truth," Vendarithe said. "Paladin, you may put your sword away for now. There is no need for our meeting to come to blows."

Umhra looked at Spara for assurance—she gave him none. He looked back at the immense beast and allowed Forsetae to vanish into wisps of blue ether. Umhra's armor peeled back from his body.

Vendarithe pushed herself into a seated position. Her presence loomed over the Mystics. Her rose gold scales glimmered in the light she emanated as though a million polished sovereigns clung to her form. "Does the hero speak?"

"He does," Umhra said. "What do you ask of me?"

Vendarithe picked at the floor of the cavern with a curved talon which was as long as Umhra was tall. "There is much I would like to know about you. Paladin. Mystic. Champion of Vaila. Savior of Tyveriel. There are none I can recall who have achieved such lauded titles. Tell me, what does one such as yourself desire?"

"Desire? All I've ever desired is to protect the ones I love. The land I love."

"No fortune? No fame?"

"I have everything I need."

Vendarithe exhaled which sent a plume of smoke to the cavern's ceiling. She turned to Spara. "And, you? What is it you seek, Spara? Vengeance? Recompense?"

"I merely seek to rejoin my family and fulfill my destiny as they did so many years ago. Haven't I that right?"

"And you come to me for this, having dispatched the others of my kind?"

"A regrettable necessity, I assure you. Unfortunately, you are the only Guardian that will listen to reason. The others were but blunt instruments."

"Very true. My siblings were most irrational at times. I think they should find it pleasant, returning to the Fae—no longer beholden to this tedious responsibility. I long for it myself at times." Vendarithe scraped one of her talons across the floor of her lair, putting a deep gouge in its stone. "And what do you bring as compensation for my breach of contract? My allegiance toward Mirina runs deep."

"Is it not obvious? Why, the Paladin, of course."

Umhra snarled at the betrayal. How could he have not seen it until now? All her impish games and minor seductions. She played him for the fool he was. He summoned Forsetae to his hand, ready to strike her down. Vendarithe snorted, commanding him to reconsider.

"A fair trade," Vendarithe said, leaning in close to Umhra. "He is most special. I have eaten many with Orcish blood, but none like him." She drew in a deep breath, taking in Umhra's stench. "Tell me, Peacebreaker, did you not consider what she asked of you? Did you not concern yourself with her motivations when you slew my brothers and sisters? Were you so blinded by what she could give you that you did not think about what you took from others?"

Vendarithe was right. Umhra hadn't consider the justness of his actions in following Spara's lead. He had been consumed by the knowledge she proffered. Now, with her plan laid bare, everything came into focus.

The rose gold dragon shifted its glare to Spara. "Who am I to stop you? I shall not keep you any longer. You may pass to the Waystone and ascend to Kalmindon."

"Sorry, Umhra." Spara flashed a wry smile. "I appreciate all you have done for me. I couldn't have gotten here without you, but I now have greater matters to attend to. Surely, you understand."

"Another regrettable necessity," Umhra said through gritted teeth.

Spara nodded, and slipped past Vendarithe who lifted her majestic head so Umhra could, for the first time, see the purple glow of the Waystone she protected. He watched, transfixed, as Spara stepped onto the center of the stone, her form lit from beneath by its radiance. Umhra stepped forward, tempted to stop her, but Vendarithe placed a claw in his way as an overt warning that he should reconsider.

The Waystone's light intensified until its glow was so vibrant it forced Umhra to shield his eyes. As he did, the portal released a blinding flash of pure-white light and a shock wave of equal strength. Umhra strained against the force, the soles of his boots abrading against the rough stone flooring.

The aura of the Waystone receded to a slow, rhythmic pulsing. Spara was gone, and Umhra was left standing alone beside his captor.

CHAPTER 29

The fool of a beast believes he coerced me into granting him lichdom. After failing on lesser creatures, I lured him in as the perfect subject.

—*Entry from Aldresor's Journal*
Undated. Discovered in the Tower of Is' Savon, month of Riet,
1444 AT

—▲—

Queen Avrette entered the throne room and sat on the Raptor's Throne, still uncomfortable with her new station. She shifted in her seat. The wings of the eagle that wrapped around the throne back enveloped her, making her feel cut off from the rest of the room. The Elders Syndicate turned from their argument over who was at fault for the escape of Talus Jochen the night prior and bowed to their sovereign. Their discourse had been going on for hours and, despite the queen having just returned to the room, was already growing tedious. The moment of silence was most welcomed.

"Thank you, all," Queen Avrette said, putting her hands in the air to hold the Syndicate's attention.

The elders stood with blank expressions on their faces while their new queen took a moment to gather her thoughts.

The queen took a deep breath and improved her posture—she clasped her hands in her lap.

"There is nothing more pressing a matter to the court or myself, than bringing my brother's killer to justice. This being said—no amount of bickering is going to put Talus Jochen back in our dungeon. It doesn't matter how he escaped, or who is at fault. All that matters, is we find him. The longer he is on the run, the less likely our chance of apprehending him. We will have plenty of time to point fingers at one another after justice has been served."

"I could not agree more, My Queen," Lord Cillian said. He stepped forward from the mass of yellow robes. "And, until then, I would like you to agree to take on extra security measures. After all, Jochen slew the king in his own quarters. I fear he could return to finish the job, and I refuse to fail in protecting another of your family."

"Very well, Lord Cillian. See to whatever measures you deem appropriate. I leave the details of my safety in your capable hands."

"I will see to it at once, My Queen," Lord Cillian said, bowing at the praise.

"As for the matter of Talus Jochen, where do we stand on our search?"

Lord Cillian stood tall, even as the other members of the Elders Syndicate cowered at the question. "My Queen, we have no leads on the whereabouts of the accused. Every available soldier we have has been sweeping the city and its surrounding areas. We have searched the dungeon and there is no sign of Jochen or evidence of his escape. The only thing we know for certain, is that he was not alone. The guards we interviewed reported bringing an intoxicated Ryzarin man to the inner ward just a short time before Jochen's escape. That man's cell was open and empty as well. They consider the unidentified Ryzarin a fugitive and have provided a description of him in our search."

"A Ryzarin, you say?" Queen Avrette asked.

"Yes, My Queen."

"Rare, wouldn't you agree?"

"Yes, My Queen. There are only a few in the capital. It should help narrow the search."

"It should, indeed. Thank you, Lord Cillian. I appreciate your efforts and the thoroughness of your update. That will be all for now."

"Thank you, My Queen," Lord Cillian said, "Please let us know if you require anything. I will double your personal guard until we bring this matter to fruition. And I request that you remain within the confines of the castle for the time being."

"Very well," the queen said, nodding to Lord Cillian and the rest of the Elders Syndicate.

The elders hurried out of the throne room. Lord Cillian trailed behind. With the others out of the room, the queen called to him. "Lord Cillian?"

"Yes, My Queen?" He turned to face his sovereign.

"Could you please locate Lord Strongforge for me? I would like to have a word with him in private."

"As you wish, My Queen. I shall see to it right away."

"Thank you. And thank you for your sound counsel. While everyone else stares at me like I am out of my depth, you have proven a most trustworthy advisor."

"Anything for the crown, My Queen." Lord Cillian gave the queen a reverent bow and left her alone on her throne.

▲

Gromley arrived at the throne room early in the evening, escorted by Lord Cillian. The two Zeristar men waited at one of the banquet tables along the side of the expansive room.

The queen sat on the throne; her eyes ringed with dark circles. She spoke with two Iminti women, both of whom wore lavish silk gowns. The women shared a friendly farewell and the immense doors slammed shut, leaving Gromley and Lord

Cillian alone with the queen and her detail of guards.

Queen Avrette turned her head and hid a yawn. "I would like to have a moment alone with Sir Strongforge."

The guards left their station at the back of the throne and held the door open for Lord Cillian to leave with them. Gromley stepped before the throne and bowed.

"There is no need for formality with me, Gromley," the queen said, walking down the steps from the throne, "At least not when we are alone. Walk with me, I'm tired of sitting in that chair."

"I can think of countless men who would kill to have that problem, My Queen."

"Formality, Gromley. Address me by my name. And you well know, I do not desire the power that comes with my appointment . . . nor the attention."

Gromley nodded and held out his arm as the queen approached. She smiled and took his arm.

"Lord Cillian seemed to think that your request to see me was of an urgent matter."

"I would much prefer to have this conversation out in the gardens of the bailey where we may breathe the fresh air. My favorite part of growing up here was the scent of honeysuckle that graced the breeze. Today, however, my ridiculous cadre of guards insist on following me if I leave this room, what with Talus on the loose again. It is all quite stifling, to be honest, and I hope to be beyond this matter in short order."

"Of course. I hope I may help with that."

"I found it quite curious when Lord Cillian informed me of a Ryzarin man, a drunkard I believe, who went missing with Talus. I do not have a mind for crime, but I would think if anyone had planned such a bold escape, they would prefer the perpetrator to be a little less . . . shall we say . . . distinctive."

"As you well know, Jenta, I don't have much of a mind for crime myself, so I couldn't say what the nefarious mind would prefer. I may, however, know a thing or two about a Ryzarin capable of such things."

"I suspected as much. Please speak freely so you do not force my hand in declaring all this treason. I am having trouble reconciling how those I brought with me to Vanyareign as my most trusted council could go behind my back and free my brother's killer. Their king's killer."

Gromley paused for a second, staring at a large elaborate tapestry of Modig Forene's army colliding with a horde of blights at the edge of the Wistful Timberlands. Modig Forene, himself led the charge, Aquila held overhead preparing to dispatch the first of his enemies. "You grew up with Talus, didn't you?"

"You know I did."

"So, you recall why your brother gave the sword in this very tapestry to him, making him the first without Forene blood to wield it?"

"Talus came to us as a child before my father died. My brother was thirty-five and was unknowingly about to ascend to the throne. My mother saw fit to have Talus entrusted to my brother as his ward. At first, Shale thought this arrangement nothing but a bother, but the boy grew on him, and soon they were inseparable. Shale treated Talus more like a brother than a poor child thrust into his care. And Talus loved and admired him for it.

"As Talus grew into adulthood, he showed a certain adeptness for swordplay, whereas my brother was much more capable at pursuits of the mind. When Shale named him head of the king's personal guard and, ultimately, the Raptor's Grasp, he gave Talus Aquila despite objections from my mother and the Elders Syndicate."

"To do such a thing, your brother must have trusted Talus implicitly."

"Yes. And I dare say Talus earned it many times over. He would have done anything for Shale. There was a bond between them that seemed unbreakable."

"And he stands ready to do so still, Jenta. Talus remains

loyal to the Forene bloodline, and his account of what happened was told within my zone of truth. I am quite certain of his innocence. He aims to clear his name and share with you his story, as it carries a certain sensitivity. Of course, it was Shadow who abetted . . . no, orchestrated Talus's escape. That is no surprise to you. He did not act in deceit, but out of loyalty to Talus, to you, and to the throne. Your brother trusted Talus, giving him one of your family's most powerful relics. All we ask is you give him the opportunity to convince you of his innocence and bring the king's true killer to justice."

Queen Avrette maintained eye contact with Gromley as she considered the plea. "I have no interest in seeing the wrong man put to death and you've never been anything other than trustworthy—almost to a fault. What do you propose? I'm willing to listen, but you can't just march him into the castle."

"I propose a meeting at a neutral location . . . say the Marwyn Homestead. Join the Barrow's Pact for dinner tomorrow night. I'm sure you could find the need for a quiet moment in the main library."

"Lord Cillian will take a little convincing, but I can do that. My one condition is that Espen will join me. I will not be alone with Talus until his name is cleared. And I will hold you and the Barrow's Pact accountable for his actions. For your sakes, I hope you are right about all of this."

"Whatever makes you most comfortable. Talus assured me he would agree to any terms you put on the meeting."

"I should hope so. The alternative is him being hunted down and drawn and quartered. Thank you for your candor here today. It is good to have honest friends. I am accustomed to everyone lying to me to gain my favor, but it has never been worse since claiming the throne."

"Jenta, we have known each other for some time now, and I believe we have grown quite close. Close enough that you came to us when the king was slain and asked us to accompany you here as your guard and council. I can't believe our taking it upon ourselves to investigate the king's murder in our own way comes as a surprise to you, especially when considering Talus's life hangs in the balance. In fact, I dare say you may have wanted our help in this matter. Unless I read you wrong."

"I suppose you could be right. I take no pride in ordering a man's death. Not to mention one with such a vaunted history with my family. The evidence is overwhelmingly against him. It causes me great consternation . . . as though I have lost two brothers."

"Meet us tomorrow night. I'm certain we will put your concerns to rest," Gromley said, "as there is much you don't yet know."

"Very well. Tomorrow night. I will not call off the manhunt, though."

"No need. You will never find them."

Queen Avrette pursed her lips and nodded. "I believe I will turn in for the night, Gromley. I look forward to putting this behind us. I bid you well until tomorrow evening."

"Good night, Jenta." Gromley kissed the queen's hand. "Please don't lose faith in us. You have asked us here as your council and we act in good faith. We have not failed you yet, and we have no designs on starting now."

Gromley released the queen's hand and left her to her thoughts in the throne room.

CHAPTER 30

*The surviving primordial gods still wander Tyveriel. Their
numbers are few, but they yet possess remnants
of their wild magic.*

—*The Gatekeeper's Abridged History of Tyveriel*
Vol. 2, Chapter 25 – Discovered in the Private Library of Solana
Marwyn, the month of Vasa, 889 AT

—▲—

As evening arrived, the Marwyn Homestead came to life,
welcoming the customary deluge of Vanyareign's elite. The
endless parade of evening gowns and tailored suits streamed
past Hurston Marwyn, who acknowledged each of his patrons
with a nod and a smile. On a normal night, he would engage in
small talk with those gracing his establishment, but this was no
normal night and he concerned himself with a more pressing
matter.

Earlier in the day, he had set the table in the private
dining room himself, with his finest linens and accoutrement.
In less than an hour, the queen would arrive for dinner with
the Barrow's Pact. Her first public appearance since being
coronated, and he wasn't able to tell a single soul. His stomach
fluttered at the thought.

Lord Marwyn walked across the main parlor dressed in a fine green suit that accentuated his thin frame. He checked every flower and assured himself each was in the exact right location and that every picture frame was level.

Gromley strode across the room, passing the porter who held the door wide. Laudin, Naivara, and Nicholas followed close behind, all of them dressed in their finest. Lord Marwyn rushed to them.

"Welcome friends," he said. "It is such a pleasure to have you and your party dining with us this evening. I trust things have been well with each of you?"

Nicholas smiled. "My dear, Lord Marwyn." The child-sized Farestere wore a blue suit with gold embroidery over an open-collar silk shirt and a pink cravat. "Wonderful to see you again. We are so happy to return to your wonderful establishment despite the current circumstances."

"Yes, yes. Terrible news about the king. Evelium will never be the same for his loss. I thought his reign would have outlasted me. He was still so young." Lord Marwyn sniffed.

"It is terrible, my Lord. He has left us far too soon." Nicholas said, "I'm sure you have gone beyond the call of duty to prepare the Marwyn Homestead to host our guest of honor tonight."

"I have had the staff hard at work all day. They are wondering what all the fuss is about, but I have let no one know. Despite the temptation. It is a rare honor."

"We appreciate the discretion. More than you know hangs in the balance of this night going well. If you don't mind, we'll go straight to the table."

Lord Marwyn nodded, greeting Laudin and Gromley, and then extended his arm for Naivara. "My Lady."

She accepted, smiling, and allowed Lord Marwyn to escort her to the dining room. Together, they weaved through the well-dressed masses that awaited their reservations. Talk of murder and the end of the Forene Dynasty consumed the crowd.

"Pardon the question, Lady Naivara, but I simply must

know if what I have heard of your friend Talus being the killer and having escaped the dungeon at Mount Orys is true?" Lord Marwyn asked in a whisper, despite nobody other than Naivara being able to hear him over the myriad conversations in the main parlor.

"For now, Lord Marwyn, we simply aren't certain who killed the king. There are those of us that believe in Talus's innocence, but the evidence against him is convincing on the surface. With no other explanation for what happened . . . no other suspect in the king's murder . . . many find it easy to blame the one they have in hand."

"I see." Lord Marwyn shook his head. "Would be a shame. He seems like such a fine young man."

"Agreed, my Lord."

Reaching the private banquet room, the parlor hushed behind them as a half-dozen Queen's Guard entered the homestead and cleared a path through the crowd. They drew their swords in a show of intolerance. The last two guards assumed the porter's role and held the doors open as the royal carriage arrived, circled by warhorses in full regale, each boasting a soldier in heavy armor and a flail slung over their shoulder. A great eagle landed on a rooftop across the street, the rider on its back pulling on the reins as it screeched.

Lord Marwyn hurried back into the parlor just in time to witness the queen's arrival on Lord Morrow's arm. The crowd watched in awe as the queen ascended the stairs to the Marwyn Homestead, her sky blue silk taffeta gown with floral embroidery flowed behind her—her gold circlet glimmered in the candlelight.

The entire room bowed as she breeched the threshold. Lord Morrow walked two steps behind, his hands clasped at his back. Queen Avrette rushed by the throng who rose to watch as she approached Lord Marwyn, who bowed low.

"Lord Marwyn, it is a pleasure to see you in good health. It has been too long. Please, rise and greet me as a friend."

Lord Marwyn stood tall, a hand on the lapel of his coat. "My Queen . . ." His voice cracked. "The pleasure is all mine. In all my years of running this establishment, a sovereign has never paid me such an honor. Your table, and party await you."

"Thank you. I shall meet with them presently and let you get back to the rest of your guests."

"As you wish. Please, this way."

Lord Marwyn led Queen Avrette to the private dining room where her party waited—each stood as the queen appeared in the doorway. The guards swept the room and, finding nothing out of the ordinary, shut the doors behind the queen, giving the group privacy. As they took their positions on either side of the door, the Marwyn Homestead erupted with excitement over the unexpected guest.

▲

Queen Avrette noted the perfection of the dining room, while Lord Morrow held the queen's chair for her. She sat at the head of the table with Naivara and Laudin flanking her. Espen then sat at the other end of the table between Gromley and Nicholas.

Jenta folded her hands in her lap. "You asked me to meet you here tonight to hear Talus's side of this wicked story. As Espen and I have known none of the Barrow's Pact to be the least bit nefarious, and our trust in each of you is implicit, I have obliged. Let's not delay any further."

"Thank you both for your trust," Gromley said, nodding, "I'm certain that, by the end of this evening, you will have a very different view of the circumstances pertaining to the king's murder. What you are going to hear tonight from Talus, he told me and the others around this table within a zone of truth. My magic bound every word he uttered. Not to boast, but I dare say it impossible for him to lie. If you like, I will provide the same assurance here this evening."

"I think that best." Queen Avrette cast a hand forward. "Please."

Gromley shut his eyes—his star-shaped talisman illuminated—then the visages of Naivara and Laudin faded—revealing Shadow and Talus in their stead.

Queen Avrette pushed away from the table at the surprise.

"Most sorry for the illusion, My Queen," Talus said, "There was no other way to get me to you unnoticed. It would seem you have the entire Eagle Guard canvasing the capital for me."

"In all fairness, Talus, you are accused—with testimony from one of your own men—of murdering the king, my brother. Would you have the matter treated any other way?"

"Indeed not, but you must know, deep in your heart, I would never have seen any harm brought to Shale. Besides, I have testimony to provide tonight that puts me elsewhere when the crime was committed . . . a crew full, if I'm to be honest."

"Then, explain how one of your own men saw you standing over Shale's butchered body, knife in hand, before diving out the window to escape by wyvern?"

"Wyvern?" Talus asked, his brow furrowed, and he scratched the side of his head. "Jenta, I have never in my life flown such a beast. I cannot explain my visage being present at Shale's murder—some kind of magic, I suspect—but I can tell you I wasn't even in Evelium at the time."

"And, why is that, exactly?" Jenta was skeptical but willing. "Where were you?"

"I was in Shent."

"This I must hear," the queen said.

Talus cleared his throat. "Just before his death, Shale bore a child with a young lady from Vanyareign named Alessa Elmont. The child was flawed in Shale's eyes and—"

"Shale had a child?".

"Flawed how?" Lord Morrow asked.

"Her skin is grey, her eyes are gold with black rings around them as if she were night incarnate."

Queen Avrette gasped. "Touched by the gods— the Grey

Queen."

"Shale surmised as much and ordered me to murder the child and her mother to avoid him being responsible for fulfilling the prophecy. By his own words, this was not the first time he'd had such an order carried out."

"Ghastly." Queen Avrette frowned. "And you followed through on this order?"

"No. I hadn't the heart. I assured Shale that I would see to the matter, but I was incapable of turning against the woman and her innocent child. Instead, I took them to Shent, where they are staying with a close friend. Jenta, the child bares the Mark of Forene. I've seen it with my own eyes."

"So, there is a true heir to the Raptor's Throne. The bloodline remains intact."

"Yes. But there is more. The child shows signs of wielding a power I don't completely understand. When our ship, the Jilted Rose, was under siege by a Tursas, the monster refused to attack in her presence and it retreated when Alessa presented the child to it. Without her aboard, I am certain the Tursas would have destroyed us all."

Jenta sat back in her chair. "If all of this is true, we must send for the child at once, despite the risk."

"My love." Lord Morrow threw his chair back and stepped away from the table. "Surely you are not considering abdicating your rule in favor of a bastard infant."

"Espen, I will not sit upon the throne of my ancestors under false pretenses. Look what damage such selfishness has done to our land already. If the bloodline remains unbroken, I shall see that child in her rightful place. No matter what superstitions my brother and the Forene kings before him clung to." Jenta turned back to Talus. "But first, I should like to verify your story. If what you say is the truth, then there is also the matter of bringing my brother's true killer to justice."

"This is where I may be of use to the crown," Shadow said, "If the intent of the killer was to end the House of Forene, very well by order of Vred Ulest, your coronation and meteoric rise in popularity among the people renders their mission a complete failure. Any professional assassin would make an attempt on your life before you solidify your rule. I would contend that, with Talus having escaped, there is a unique opportunity for the killer to reinsert themselves into the milieu of Castle Forene and complete his charge."

"What, exactly, are you suggesting, Shadow?" Lord Morrow asked, returning to his seat.

"My Lord, I believe our queen is already likely being targeted by the killer, and that no matter the increased presence of common guard, which is laudable, she is in grave peril. If the assassin can disguise themselves as I have done for Talus and myself tonight, they could be among your guard already."

"And, you have a plan to assure my safety?" Jenta asked, unphased by the notion she was in harm's way.

"I do, My Queen," Shadow said, "but it will require some good faith on your part."

"That, I can offer you if I can prove Talus's version of the events. I would like to verify what I've heard here tonight by my own means. Send for the Captain of the Jilted Rose and have Shale's child and her mother return from Shent at once. The crown shall provide them with all necessary protection. I should like to meet my niece."

"I think it best we leave Talus out of this process until proven innocent," Gromley said. "I shall see your orders carried out. We will bring the true killer to justice and bring closure to this harrowed chapter in Evelium's history. Thank you for your continued trust."

"You're welcome. While I would love to stay and dine with all of you, it doesn't quite feel right given the circumstances. I will see you all soon enough . . . and I hope on only the best of terms."

Lord Morrow came to her side and ushered her from the

room. The guards snapped to attention, lining a safe path back to the royal carriage. They hurried through the crowded parlor and out into the crisp evening air.

CHAPTER 31

When finally face-to-face, I must admit I shuddered at the dead glare in his eyes. In all my vast conquests, I had never seen anything like it.

—Telsidor's Missives
Diary entry dated 4th of Bracken, 1 AF. Unearthed from the Ruins of Anaris, month of Emin, 1156 AT

Vibrant ribbons wrapped the lamp posts and fluttered from the eaves of nearly every building in Vanyareign in preparation for the Sowing Moon Festival. Amidst the frenzy of color, six members of the King's Guard approached the Raptor's Memorial. They were dressed in ceremonial blackened steel armor and violet cloaks and their faces were veiled in black chain mail. They removed King Arving's body from upon the memorial where it had been lying in repose since his death.

They brought the fallen king's body to the Kormaic Temple where it was to be cleansed, blessed, and readied for final viewing. The funeral procession would follow the traditional tour through the capital's streets before the body was interred in the Bed of Kings beneath Castle Forene.

Ushered in by his most trusted soldiers, four grave clerics

met the king's sallow and withered form. The clerics had gathered from disparate parts of Evelium for this great honor, and stood around the preparation table, heads covered by the hoods of their chestnut-brown cloaks—they were never to reveal their identities to anyone other than those of their chosen path and, occasionally, the immediate family of the dead for which they were performing their sacred rite.

The soldiers placed the king upon the table and retreated from the room, leaving a bouquet of herbs on the stone pedestal as an offering to the grave clerics who would one day care for them. Alone, the clerics set to work, removing the king's white robes and inspecting his body thoroughly. The desiccated corpse was now ready for the final ritual.

They meticulously washed the body and then allowed it to dry for several hours. They then wrapped the body in a burial shroud made of three layers of fine linen, each layer separated by symbols of the king's reign. Against his body were the feathers of a giant golden eagle representing his direct descendance from Modig Forene. Next was his sword, a testament to his power, and then, a gold sovereign coin that paid honor to the prosperity he brought to his subjects.

Once they secured the shroud, the grave clerics painted it in the tradition of his forefathers. Unlike the myriad colorful lanterns being hung from the tree branches in anticipation of the great festival, the clerics painted the king's shroud with ochre, signifying his return to the clay-laden soils of Evelium. His head and torso were made to resemble that of an eagle and his legs became that of a lion—the majestic griffin was a symbol of dominance over the heavens and earth. Finally, they placed a replica of the Circlet of Everlife upon his head.

The following morning, the grave clerics carried the king's remains from the temple to the courtyard and placed him in a glass carriage upon a bed of foxglove. Two guards, dressed in blackened steel armor, sat upon the driver's box awaiting the procession's start.

A horn blew in the distance and the march began—the footfalls of thousands of soldiers thundered down King's Way, their ceremonial pitons clanking in unison against the stone between each step.

The procession marched into the city and to the temple grounds where they came to a halt, allowing the carriage to pull out onto the road in front of them. Resuming, they made for the Grand Bazaar, spectators lining their path, and circled the park four times before spiraling out through the city to assure even the poorest neighborhoods would have an opportunity to pay their final respects.

Admirers filled the streets. Those who could afford the extravagance threw bouquets of foxglove upon the carriage. The procession exited the city through the south gate and circled the outer wall before returning to King's Way and ascending Mount Orys.

▲

The procession thundered into the bailey of Castle Forene and filled the space in formation, coming to complete quiet. Four guards opened the castle's gilded doors and stepped to either side of the staircase. Queen Avrette emerged from the castle; her head held high. She wore an ochre high-collared dress with a silver griffin embroidered on the bodice—her shoulders covered by a matching cape. She followed the guards across the courtyard to the carriage, where the grave clerics removed the body and presented it to the queen.

"He will forever be welcome in the Bed of Kings. Thank you for your care of his transition," the queen said.

The hooded grave clerics bowed their heads in acknowledgment. Without a word, they proceeded into the castle and stood in the great hall. There, Cleric Dynava waited beside the bust of Shale Arving which had joined those of the former kings of Evelium. Candlelight danced across the walls as six guards lifted a thick slab of the stone from the floor and slid it away on iron casters.

A staircase descended into darkness. Cleric Dynava stepped forward, took a torch from one soldier, and lit the path forward. She led the group below.

Queen Avrette followed, the staircase widening as they descended. They stepped into an expansive room where four sarcophagi made of carved green marble lay. Among them was a chair fashioned of the same stone and iconography which was flanked by two iron braziers.

Cleric Dynava set the braziers aflame, which threw a soft glow across the tomb while the queen walked to the sarcophagi. At their very center rested Modig Forene, a griffin carved into the surface of his sarcophagus, of which King Arving's burial shroud was a likeness. The two other sealed sarcophagi contained the remains of Prakten Modig, Modig Forene's first-born son, and Arving Stryke, Shale and Jenta's father. She ran her fingers over each surface and lingered over her father's grave which she hadn't seen since he was placed here.

The final sarcophagus remained open and welcomed King Arving to his final resting place. The grave clerics carried the body around the perimeter of the tomb four times and then lowered it into the awaiting sarcophagus. They each retrieved a tightly bound bundle of dried herbs from within their robes and lit them on the braziers' flames.

Smoke rose to the tomb's ceiling and danced into the darkness. In unison, the clerics chanted a prayer to Gurtha, the god of death, and waved the smoking herbs over the king's body, drawing in deep breaths to infuse their own bodies with the smoke. When they finished the ritual, they brought the stone lid from the shadows and sealed the sarcophagus.

Queen Avrette stepped forward, looked down upon the graves of her father and brother, and cried freely for a moment.

"He has joined his forefather's, My Queen," one of the grave clerics said, her voice creaking. "Your loss is transient, like the passing of the seasons. As, in the depths of winter, one longs for spring, death eventually blooms for us all and we once more long for the frigid sting of life. You will one day join your brother in the Bed of Kings and miss him no longer, but dare I suggest you not be in a hurry."

Queen Avrette tilted her head, surprised, and stared into the shadow that hid the cleric's face. For a moment, she considered probing their logic, but thought better of it and nodded. "Thank you, your Holiness. I shall begin my vigil if the rite is complete."

The grave clerics bowed and retreated to the stairway. Dynava followed, pausing at each of the sarcophagi to pay her respects. As the torchlight disappeared beyond the stairs, the queen took a seat among her ancestors in the Bed of Kings and began the Concatenation—a ritual she never imagined nor desired to preside over.

▲

"My Love," Lord Morrow said, reaching the bottom of the staircase, "How are you managing? Is there anything I can do?" A soft smile came over his face at seeing his wife sitting dutifully in the chair. He had been down to visit her twice over the last two days and she had barely moved a muscle.

"I'm fine, Espen. Thank you for your concern, but you need not worry about me. I am up to the task. The solitude gives one a lot of time for self-reflection. I suppose that is the point of a new sovereign sitting in a crypt among those who passed before them."

"Then, will you at least walk with me? The Concatenation allows you to do so."

"I would be happy to." The queen gestured to the large tomb around them. Its walls were of rough-hewn stone and barren. "Unfortunately, there is little to occupy the mind down here other than the very one-sided conversations I have been having with my deceased relatives."

Lord Morrow extended his hand and helped Queen Avrette to her feet. She took his arm and walked with him between the sarcophagi.

"Did you know my father never desired to be king?" the queen asked. She ran a finger over a rose carved into the corner of the sarcophagi's lid.

"I can imagine that he never planned for it," Lord Morrow said, "But are you certain he never wanted it? You don't think he envied his cousin who was treated with such favor during their youth?"

"I remember he called me into the great hall once. I must have been twelve or thirteen. He bid me sit with him at the banquet table and began reflecting on his one hundred plus years of rule. He told me of the Fracture and his bastard cousin. He told me how his uncle hid the fact that the child wasn't his so his lineage would keep the throne. Father never understood the pettiness of it all."

"Could you so easily give up your reign in a similar situation?" Lord Morrow asked.

"You know I would . . . I have. Unless—"

Each drew a dagger from their robes and struck out at the other as if they read each other's minds. Sparks flew as the blades clashed and locked in place.

"Let's drop this charade and get on with it then," Queen Avrette said.

Teeth gritted, Lord Morrow pushed the queen backward. The two circled each other, attempting to ascertain some modicum of advantage. With the staircase to his back, he transformed his visage of Lord Morrow into his real appearance—that of a creature with opalescent eyes and slate blue skin.

"I thought as much," the queen said, her voice dropping. Her image shimmered and Shadow stood in her place. Without hesitation, he swept in upon the doppelganger, his blade whirring on approach. The doppelganger parried each advance, more than willing to cede ground toward the stairwell.

The doppelganger countered, its agility and adeptness with a dagger nearly equal to Shadow's.

Shadow slashed at the monstrosity, his blade missing its target and scraping against the stone of the narrowing pathway. The doppelganger took an opportunity to lunge at the momentary opening in Shadow's defenses as his momentum carried him too far.

The doppelganger knocked Shadow to the ground and dove atop him, their blades locked together just inches from Shadow's face. The blade inched closer to Shadow as the doppelganger bore down with gritted, sharpened teeth. It wanted the satisfaction of killing the famed member of the Barrow's Pact with its own two hands.

Shadow rolled, using the doppelganger's force against itself, and threw the creature from his chest. Both jumped to their feet and leaped toward each other, locking their blades once more. Each struggled for the upper hand, when Shadow pulled a second dagger from within his cloak and buried it in the doppelganger's stomach. Pain sheared through its belly and it dropped its dagger to the floor with a clatter. Shadow kept his dagger buried and a stream of blue-black blood poured from the wound. The doppelganger peered over its shoulder at its only salvation.

"Turn to run, and I'll sever you in two," Shadow said. "And I'll take my time with it."

The doppelganger faced Shadow, who buried the delicate point of his first blade beneath the creature's chin. It held its hands up in resignation and stared Shadow in the eyes.

"More than one can play your mendacious games, fiend. Now, on your knees before I show my blade the roof of your skull."

The doppelganger complied, folding its hands behind its head. Shadow stepped closer and leaned in as if to whisper. With a quick thrust of his forearm, he bashed the butt of his dagger into the doppelganger's temple.

▲

"I wouldn't believe it, if I weren't seeing it with my own eyes," Lord Morrow said, pacing before the holding cell, his gaze locked on the doppelganger who lay unconscious, bound to an iron table in the center of the cell. "And you say this creature disguised itself as me coming to pay Jenta a visit during her Concatenation?"

"Yes," Shadow said, "Whereas I expected magic to be at play, this is quite exciting. I've never encountered such a creature. I grew up to cautionary tales of such shape shifters living deep below the Ilathril Mountains. I always discounted them as harmless lies Ryzarin parents told their children to keep them from wandering beyond the colony."

"You mean, you've never encountered a doppelganger to the best of your knowledge." Naivara smiled.

Gromley stepped forward and peered into the cell, surveying the creature. He rubbed his beard. "No doubt this explains the confusion over Talus's involvement in the king's murder."

"I would think so," Lord Morrow said, "But Jenta insists we fully vet the fiend before passing judgement."

"Well . . . let's give it a stir, shall we?" Gromley asked. He motioned to the guard standing watch at the doorway to open the cell.

The guard pulled a key chain from around his neck and walked to the cell door, springing it open.

The guard locked the door behind Shadow and Gromley. Gromley placed one hand upon the doppelganger's head and his other on the golden star-shaped talisman hanging around his neck. He closed his eyes and took a deep breath. A soft, white glow spread from beneath his palms and their prisoner stirred.

The light faded and the doppelganger's eyes flitted open. Its gaze darted wildly about the room and it tensed against the manacles that bound it to the table at his wrists, waiste, and ankles. Its eyes came to rest on Gromley and Shadow.

"You will torture now. It matters not. You will learn of

nothing. You will send to the gallows never knowing the truth of it."

"Torture?" Gromley asked. "Do I strike you as one that suffers such base means of getting what I want? Friend, I won't harm you a bit and you're going to tell me everything."

The doppelganger spit in Gromley's face. "Curse you."

Gromley wiped his face with his sleeve. He placed both hands on his talisman and shut his eyes. A vibrant white light grew from the talisman and spread across the cell in every direction. Shadow stepped backward as the light encroached, careful to avoid the spell's area.

Gromley leaned forward and bathed the doppelganger in his divine light, eliciting a hiss. "Now, shall we start at the beginning? Who are you and from where do you hail?"

The doppelganger writhed, trying to resist the spell's effect. "Those on the surface have given the name Garrus. In the beautiful depths of Sepyltyr, where I call home, they called Ris'perat."

"Did you kill King Shale Arving?"

"Garrus flayed the man you called king, yes. But he was no king to Garrus."

"Who do you work for?"

"The king true of Evelium, Vred Ulest, by the authority of the Three. The act to kill was a permission given Garrus by Roen Anstand. No orders had they gave me, but permission if I saw fit. I saw the king disgusting and decide myself to take the life of him."

Lord Morrow gasped at the horror of it all.

"What was the intended nature of your mission here in Vanyareign?"

"To learn of the intruders Arving sent to Meriden two years ago and learn of Arving's plans for insurrection."

"And you took it upon yourself to assassinate the king?

"Ulest talks much of ending the Fracture, Garrus take action to do so as gift to Ulest with blessing of Roen. Now Ulest's army will prepare for march on Vanyareign. Ulest will claim the Raptor's Throne. He will sit the seat owed to his bloodline."

"I must go," Lord Morrow said, "The queen must know of this at once. We must prepare for potential war."

Gromley nodded and Lord Morrow made for the castle. Having gotten everything he needed from his prisoner, Gromley turned and faced Shadow.

"Don't you dare, you louse." Gromley stepped forward, cornering Shadow against the cell's wrought iron bars. The light that encircled him enveloping Shadow. "So, what exactly was the nature of your relationship with Ampeleia Tilk?"

CHAPTER 32

We landed on the shores of Malara, its pink grasses fluttering against the persistent breeze. My party insisted on heading south, having been warned by the natives that the north offered nothing but death.

—*A Traveler's Guide to the Odd and Obscure by Sentina Vake* Chapter 3 – Unearthed from the Homestead in Maryk's Cay, month of Riet, 1407 AT

Silyarithe soared in expanding concentric circles over the Isle of the Twelve Mines, searching the dark sea below. She resisted her father's memories that drove her to crash into the gates of Mount Anvil and have her way with the Zeristar who so shamelessly stole his lair from him so many years ago. There would be plenty of time for that. Tonight, she served a higher purpose than vengeance.

Even without the aid of light, she could make out the faint but enormous abnormality resting beneath the silt in the frigid depths just a few miles from shore. She hovered in place for a moment, verifying her quarry, and then collapsed her wings and went into a dive.

She plunged into the water at tremendous speed and

swam. Her tail propelled her into the deep, the temperature plummeted to near freezing. Silyarithe fought through the cold and reached the powdery white sea floor. Before her, an immense mound rose from the otherwise featureless expanse. She paused, inspecting the formation. It teemed with life, an ecosystem unto itself. Innumerable crustaceans and fish swam through the purple sea whip coral that called the structure home.

She tore into the side of the mound with her claws, throwing a cloud of silt into the water around her as she worked. It took the better part of an hour until one of her talons scraped across the unyielding surface of what she had come here for. She expanded her hole, revealing the massive face of what was once an ancient black dragon.

It had been almost one-thousand years since Telsidor slew the giant within. Decay had taken its toll. Bone and rotten flesh protruded in patches from beneath its armored black hide. Its eyes were sunken beneath closed lids, and many of its teeth were exposed in a macabre smile. Silyarithe grimaced. Though unsure of her plan's viability, she continued.

She had grown quickly since gorging herself on her mother's flesh, but still she was only a quarter of Mesorith's size. She reached within her scales and pulled out the phylactery containing his soul. The sentient force at its core swirled, anticipating its reunion with Mesorith's corporeal form.

She rested it upon her father's form and retreated. Nothing happened. The sea life swirled around her, unphased by her presence. She considered whether it had been too long since her sire's demise to resurrect him. Rearing back, she exhaled with all the force she had left in her lungs and sent a stream of purple plasma blasting into her father's decrepit face. The water boiled around them as the plasma arced across Mesorith's corpse, entering him through the gaps in his flesh until absorbed.

Darkness encroached once more, with only the sporadic

flash of energy from within Silyarithe's maw holding it at bay. She watched as the black center of the shard dissipated and a nascent purple glow grew within her father's body. It began in his eyes and spread down his face and torso, toward his tail. The mound glowed from within, revealing his hidden form.

Mesorith's corpse shuddered, silt and coral cascaded from the mound that covered him. His exposed eye opened, the empty socket now filled with a swirling purple orb. His jaw snapped closed, and he thrashed, breaking free from his grave in an enormous plume of sediment.

Silyarithe took up the phylactery in her mouth and shot upward toward the surface. Her reanimated patriarch tracked her ascent and bounded from the sea floor. Together, they burst through the swells into the night sky toward the quiet shores of Lertmor.

Landing on the island's jagged, rocky southern shore, Mesorith roared—putrescence and sea water cascaded from his decayed body. Silyarithe answered in kind, unwilling to cower before the newly-made lich.

The dragons came nose to nose, inspecting one another.

"You followed my instructions." Mesorith wretched awkwardly, turning his attention to his own form. "How long has it been since I fell?"

"It has been nearly a millennium since man took Tyveriel back. I restored you to help me reclaim our place at its helm."

Mesorith's lips curled into a snarl. "Their civilization shall burn to the ground, its ashes will be the foundation of your reign."

"And, my gift to you, father. Tonight, we begin by retaking Mount Anvil."

Mesorith looked to the west. "My lair." His malformed lips curled into a jagged grin. "That would be most pleasing."

"Then let us not delay any longer. I have yet to taste the flesh of men and, for you, it has been far too long."

Silyarithe lifted into the air. Mesorith roared and, with

three beats of his tattered wings, followed. They soared side-by-side into the starlit sky, the soft glow of the watchtowers surrounding Mount Anvil coming into view.

Mesorith crashed through the first of the watchtowers, casting the stout building into a shower of dark stone and aged wood. Zeristar guards scattered like rats, the undead dragon doused them with his acid breath. Some dissolved on contact, those on the periphery of the dragon's ire suffering a far worse fate—and fell to the ground, their skin sloughing from their bodies.

"Dragon," a scream rang out in the dark. Mesorith lunged forward, treading on the informant and several others around him, as one would ants they hadn't noticed, and turned toward the next tower as a volley of arrows scattered off his armored hide. Only a few found their marks within his decay. He roared, inviting their assault, and strode toward the archers.

Silyarithe circled wide of the fray, preferring to reconnoiter as opposed to her father's brazen onslaught. She veered around Mount Anvil, a horn blared from below. Four immense iron doors rumbled open and a legion of Zeristar warriors poured forth, followed by trebuchets and heavy ballistae.

The soldiers wore golden armor, each with a red sun emblazoned on their cuirass. Some charged forward with long, serrated blades glowing amber against the night sky. Others held back and readied long bows nocked with sturdy arrows tipped with obsidian.

Amidst the burgeoning chaos below, the agape doors drew Silyarithe's gaze. Where they let the Zeristar soldiers pour out of their stronghold, they also invited her in. She dove forward, ensnaring a ballista in her talons as she swept inside the Zeristar's main armory.

Men scattered, screaming as the second dragon crashed into the center of the enormous cavern and released a torrent of corrosive plasma upon them. Her tail slashed at those daring enough to stand their ground, and threw a dozen men into the dark stone walls of the armory.

The Zeristar attempted to reassemble, rushing to their weapon racks and grabbing javelins and heavy crossbows. A ballista just outside the nearest door turned and fired an enormous bolas at Silyarithe. The chain that connected the projectile's two hooked iron weights wrapped around her front legs, the hooks digging into her armored skin. Despite all the time that has lapsed since the last of her kind had been spotted in Tyveriel, the Zeristar had not been caught completely unprepared.

Silyarithe screeched in pain and lashed out at the heavy chain that held the door open. She bit down on the chain, severing it, and brought the door down in a thunderous crash.

A barrage of javelins and spiked balls from the heavy crossbows rained down upon her. She thrashed indignantly, crouched to absorb the impact, then lunged forward, breaking their ranks and tearing several of the Zeristar apart with her talons and consuming a dozen others in a single gulp.

She came to the next door and roared to Mesorith below as he swept through the Zeristar ranks on his way up the side of the mountain to meet her—hundreds of soldiers falling from the mountain path in his wake.

The trebuchets fired, but Mesorith—even in his decayed state—was far too lithe to succumb to such crude weaponry. The rocks shattered against the ground where he stood only a moment earlier and cascaded down to the fires below.

The archers and heavy artillery attempted to retreat, but Silyarithe loomed behind them, leaving them nowhere to go. Mesorith closed in, trampling everything in his path, and released a spray of acid that cut down the majority of the terrified soldiers. Casting the rest aside, he met up with Silyarithe and entered Mount Anvil once more. Together, they descended into the fortress's depths, crashing through carved stone pillars and laying waste to the Zeristar that got in their way. Their rage was indiscriminate, their sense of justice, dispassionate. A bell sounded three times from deeper still within the fortress.

▲

"Fardrom, the dragons have breached our defenses, the fortress has fallen. We must get you to safety," Bekah Cepryn said.

Fardrom Cepryn sat in a great chair sculpted from a single piece of red hematite, covered in ancient Zeristar glyphs, which boasted a war hammer carved into the crest of its back. For nine generations his family had sat upon this throne, leading the Zeristar people since they reclaimed the Isle of the Twelve Mines from Mesorith's clutches. And now it was crumbling in a single night to an enemy long thought extinct. Dragons? It had been a millennium since one flew the skies of Tyveriel, and here there were two within his fortress, laying waste to his people.

"I will certainly not get to safety, Bekah. Not until every man, woman, and child is out of harm's way."

"My love." Bekah stepped closer and took Fardrom's hand. Her dark eyes had never looked so sincere, so defeated. "If we were to mount an evacuation now, we could get to the wharf undetected and escape by ship under cover of darkness. Our chance of salvation dies with the rising sun."

Fardrom considered the advice. Bekah was not one prone to panic. "Very well, as always, your counsel is sound." He turned to the head of his personal guard. "The keep is lost, we shall evacuate. Ring the bell thrice. If the beasts are within the mountain, we shall exit through the secondary passages at the base. It will take us longer, but a dragon cannot fit in those tunnels. We make for the wharf and pray the gods are with those of us that remain."

The guard nodded and ran from the great hall. Moments later a great bell tolled three times and Fardrom stood. "We shall hesitate no longer. We shall seek asylum in Evelium and live to fight again. Never did I think we would see this day."

"None of us did," Bekah said. "But a reckoning is upon us and we have but one chance for survival."

Fardrom and Bekah left the great hall. As the guards closed the door behind them, Fardrom took one last look at his legacy coming to its knees. The immense stone pillars were shattering and set to topple as the dragons neared.

The tunnel narrowed and descended to the mountain's base. A group of guards stood before an unadorned iron door, expecting their king's arrival. From fifteen other identical doors, the remaining Zeristar streamed out into the dark of night and toward the wharf at the Bay of Tailings.

The path lay in waste—death and destruction ruled. The bodies of the Zeristar's fallen—many of them torn asunder, others excoriated—littered the landscape. Fires raged uncontrollably, throwing a dense pall of smoke and embers into the air. It was too much to bear.

Men, women, and children descended upon the wharf, scrambling to get aboard and ready all available vessels. Ships pushed out into the Bay of Tailings; the narrow inlet was choked by the fleet's mass exodus. In the dark of night, ships careened into one another, leaving some smaller vessels capsized—the fleet behind them running them over in their frantic escape.

As sails unfurled, the ships lurched into open waters and left the Isle of the Twelve Mines behind. Reticence prevailed, only the creaking of the ships cresting through the rolling waves broke the silence.

Fardrom walked from the stern of his ship to sit with Bekah, his body numb. He placed a gentle palm on his wife's pallid cheek. Her expression was as stern and determined as ever.

"We have lost so many. How am I to look our people in the eyes? How am I to lead after such a complete failure to protect them?"

"You will lead because you must. You will lead because you are a Cepryn and that is what Cepryns do. We must get to Gromley. Surely, our nephew will be able to rally Evelium against this threat. Only then may we look forward, may we rebuild our lives."

Fardrom nodded and embraced his wife. Standing to return to his duties, he held Bekah's hands for a moment and thanked the gods for her wonderful mind and steady heart. He let her hands drop as a streak of purple light lit up the night sky around them. The ships to their west burst into flames, some of them exploding, as a grey dragon strafed them with a stream of plasma.

The burgeoning hope Bekah had instilled in Fardrom vanished as he tracked the dragon through the sky. The beast took a wide turn and made a second pass over the fleet, with Fardrom's ship in its path.

Many of the Zeristar jumped from their ships in a vain attempt at preservation. Fardrom sat next to Bekah and held her face in his hands as the dragon's blast obliterated their ship. The explosion threw them into the boiling water, the force of the impact tearing them from one another.

Fardrom's vision faded as he watched Bekah drift away through the wreckage. Overhead, the sky flashed a vibrant purple as the dragon ensured Fardrom's failure.

CHAPTER 33

I threw the phylactery into the Sea of Widows. Nothing good can come from resurrecting such a vile creature. My experiment, however, was a resounding success.

—*Entry from Aldresor's Journal*
Undated. Discovered in the Tower of Is' Savon, month of Riet, 1444 AT

—▲—

Alessa stood at the gilded rail of the Tides' Fortune as it entered the calm waters of Hylara. She bit her bottom lip, not knowing what awaited her upon her return to Evelium. The idea of never again returning to her homeland had just set in when Talus and Gromley arrived in Gelarra seeking her return. Now, as she approached her native soil, she grew excited at the prospect of introducing her parents to their grandchild. She hadn't so much as written them since her abrupt departure. No doubt the king had made some excuse for her absence—maybe they thought she was dead—and Talus had warned her against making her whereabouts known to anyone.

Within the warmth of her heavy cloak, she cradled Turin, protecting the infant from the elements and the prying eyes of the ship's crew who whispered to one another since leaving port about the cursed child they transported and how relieved they would be to have her disembark. Even the promise that Turin would be named Queen of Evelium, with Queen Avrette as her regent and mentor, didn't assuage the fears Alessa had of others judging the child because of the grey of her skin. If someone was so quick to assassinate King Arving, what would stop another from attacking a defenseless child?

Talus came to Alessa's side as the crew threw their lines ashore. Unlike the ragtag group aboard the Jilted Rose, the crew of the Tides' Fortune wore green and blue uniforms identifying them as members of the royal navy. They fulfilled their duties with efficiency and pride.

A company of guards awaited them, lining the dock to assure the precious passenger aboard would come ashore without incident. Behind them, a carriage awaited, stewards at the ready, and a procession of cavalry both to the fore and aft.

"Is this all for her?" Alessa asked, glancing down at Turin.

"Yes. I'm guessing life will be quite different for the two of you going forward," Talus said. "When we come ashore, we are to head directly to the carriage. You will climb aboard and draw the curtains closed. Gromley and I will be on horseback, flanking you on either side. If you need anything along the way, ring the bell within and one of us will answer your call. We will restrain and incarcerate anyone who approaches the carriage."

Alessa nodded, swallowed a lump in her throat. "I suppose I didn't quite take you as seriously as I should have when you arrived in Gelarra. I've seen nothing like this."

"With the king's murder, and the attempt on Jenta's life, we are not taking any chances bringing the rightful heir to the Raptor's Throne back into Evelium. Things will be a little less stressful once you get settled at Castle Forene."

The crew set the gangplank against the dock and a soldier of high station, given the epaulettes on his uniform, waved Talus ashore as the others formed a narrow pathway to the carriage.

Alessa took a deep breath and flashed Talus as convincing a

smile as she could muster. Talus put a comforting hand on her shoulder and escorted her across the gangplank and through the throng of guards to the green and gold lacquered carriage. Gromley followed closely behind and mounted Swizz, who waited for him on the far side of the carriage. Beyond him, Alessa caught a quick glimpse of yet more soldiers holding the gawking public at a distance.

A steward opened the carriage door as Alessa approached and bowed gracefully. Talus ushered her and Turin inside to a plush green velvet bench. To her surprise, Queen Avrette sat opposite with her hands folded in her lap.

The carriage jerked into motion, hooves clopping on the cobblestone path.

Alessa bowed her head, not knowing what to say.

"Welcome home," the queen said, a friendly smile bloomed on her lips.

"Thank you, Your Grace, I am sorry not to have greeted you properly. Your presence took me by surprise."

"No need for apologies, Alessa. I didn't want to make a spectacle of my presence, but wanted to be here to greet the future Queen of Evelium in person. May I see her?"

Alessa nodded. "Of course. I don't have her dressed in a proper gown, though."

"It is no matter, my dear. We are family, are we not?"

Alessa placed Turin on the bench and unwrapped the blanket that swaddled her. Turin fussed for a moment but calmed quickly as her mother picked her up and rocked her.

"You have excellent instincts as a mother," the queen said. "I am afraid I have not had the opportunity to test my own."

Alessa placed Turin in Queen Avrette's arms. The queen cradled her niece, staring into her eyes for some time. When she looked up at Alessa, a tear ran down her cheek.

"I'm sorry." The queen wiped the tear from her face.

"I know," Alessa said, "She's not normal. The Grey Queen."

"No. That's not it. I actually find her to be quite beautiful.

Striking and unique. It's just that seeing Turin in person somehow makes me feel my brother's death even more."

"I'm sorry for your loss. I wish I could mourn him as well, but his last acts toward me and our child were so deplorable. He promised, if I bore him a healthy child, I would be his queen. There was a time I thought I would grow to love him, and he, me. The last I remember of him was the scowl on his face when he laid eyes upon her. How could one hate one's own child? And for the color of her skin?"

Queen Avrette glanced again toward Turin and played with her tiny grey hands which grasped at the queen's necklace.

"This was a side of my brother I had never seen, and I apologize for what he put you both through, for whatever that's worth. I am ashamed of his careless and wicked behavior, and for how beholden he was to the lore of a bygone age. I hope you and I can start anew and that you will grow to love me as a sister and as Turin's aunt. May I check her birthmark?"

"Of course," Alessa said, answering both requests at once.

Queen Avrette rolled Turin onto her side and pulled her gown down at the back of her neck, exposing a talon-shaped birthmark. She nodded and rolled Turin back, so she cradled the baby's head at her knees, letting Turin's feet kick at her stomach.

"Her birthmark matches that of my brother's and the great kings of the Forene line before him. I have no doubt Turin is the rightful heir to the Raptor's Throne. Thank you for bringing her back to us. I fear all hope is lost without her."

"The prophecy doesn't concern you?"

"No. She is a Forene, and she is beautiful. I have never subscribed to my family's interpretation of that tale. How is it that, from a line of men, a woman shall be our undoing? I believe she will be our salvation."

Alessa smiled at the notion. "And you will step down as queen for her and act as her regent until she comes of age?" She found it hard to believe that anyone could be so selfless.

"Yes. When we return to Vanyareign, we will introduce Turin to the Elders Syndicate and have her coronated without delay. Together, you and I will raise the greatest ruler Evelium has ever seen."

"I believe I am already in her presence," Alessa said. "Thank you."

"It is my duty and my honor. Now, being that we are to live as sisters, let's get to know one another so we may be friends as well. For the rest of our journey, I am an open book."

"May I come and sit beside you?" Alessa asked.

The queen slid over and patted the cushion beside her. "It would be my pleasure."

Alessa sat beside Queen Avrette. "Sisters and friends. I like the sound of that."

▲

The doors leading from the royal residence opened and four guards led Queen Avrette, Lord Morrow, and the Barrow's Pact into the throne room.

The Elders Syndicate gathered, degrees of puzzlement on their faces. They wore their formal yellow doublets and whispered among themselves, their chatter echoed unintelligibly throughout the chamber.

The queen sat upon the Raptor's Throne and the others gathered around her. She waved to Lord Cillian for the Elders Syndicate to join them.

The members of the Elders Syndicate approached the throne, each taking a turn bowing before their sovereign.

"Thank you all for gathering at my request," Queen Avrette said. "I have some very important news to share with you. News that will change our kingdom's direction."

"You have our attention, My Queen," Lord Cillian said.

Queen Avrette nodded to a guard standing by the door through which she had entered the room. He opened the door, and Talus entered the room with Alessa, who held Turin in her arms. They came to the queen's side before the Elders Syndicate.

"It has come to my attention that, before his death, my brother sired an heir with this young woman, Alessa Elmont. Despite being lost to us initially, Sir Talus Jochen has recently located Lady Elmont and her daughter, Turin, and brought them forth."

The Elders Syndicate gasped in surprise and began whispering again among themselves.

"Quiet," Lord Cillian said, his tone stern. "I believe the queen has more to share."

The Syndicate hushed.

"Thank you, Lord Cillian," Queen Avrette said, "I have spent some time with Alessa and Turin and have seen the Mark of Forene at the nape of the child's neck. It is authentic and Alessa has agreed to allow each of you to see for yourselves."

The queen urged Alessa to step forward. She complied, her new lavender gown cascading the steps as she approached where the Elders Syndicate stood, their shocked eyes affixed on her. Lord Cillian took a step toward her, a warm smile playing on his bearded face.

"Lady Elmont, a pleasure to make your acquaintance. Thank you for making your child available to us. I am sure this moment's importance is not lost upon you."

"It certainly is not, my Lord." Alessa presented Turin to Lord Cillian, unwrapping her from a white satin blanket.

"Oh," Lord Cillian said, biting his lip, "She is most distinctive."

Alessa frowned.

"No, my dear, I mean nothing by it. I simply have never seen a child who the gods had so touched before. Only have I heard of such a miracle."

The rest of the Elders Syndicate crowded around Lord Cillian so they too could lay their eyes upon the child.

"The Grey Queen," one of them whispered.

"I will have none of that," Queen Avrette said. "That toxic story has hung over my family for too long."

The elder that had made the claim, an Iminti man with short, black hair, and narrow eyes, slinked back into the mass of yellow outfits.

Lord Cillian turned Turin over and revealed the Mark of Forene to the rest of the elders. They each took a turn inspecting the mark, some running their fingers over it. At the end, none dissented.

"Your Highness." Lord Cillian turned back to his queen and returned Turin to her mother. "What would you have us do?"

"With the king's true assassin now incarcerated and nearing his execution, I would have Turin named Queen of Evelium. I will abdicate the throne and assume the position of Regent until she comes of age and no longer requires my guidance. We will hold a proper coronation ceremony and all shall celebrate her reign."

"If that is your will, we shall see it done."

"It is not just my will, but my duty, and the law of the land, Lord Cillian. This is a most glorious day, as the Forene bloodline lives when we thought it lost. Through this child's body runs the blood of Modig Forene and all the great kings of Evelium. History shall see her name among their ranks. There is no other path forward."

"And what shall be her full name?" Lord Cillian asked.

"I thought it fitting," Alessa said, "to call her Turin Forene, for my name is common and she is the future of the Great King's bloodline."

"And the queen finds this agreeable?"

"I do, Lord Cillian."

"Your position is clear, My Queen. The Elders Syndicate will set to making the necessary arrangements."

"Thank you, Lord Cillian, that will be all."

The Elders Syndicate bowed and turned to depart as the main doors to the throne room scraped open. Two soldiers, each in sky blue tunics, trimmed in silver with the image of an eagle embroidered on their chests entered the room. They approached the queen, bowing in haste as to not waste any time in delivering their message.

"My Queen," the older of the two said. He was human and taller than average, with sandy hair and a clean-shaven face that boasted a scar at the center of his top lip. "We have urgent and grave news from the Isle of the Twelve Mines."

"Tell me," Queen Avrette said. Gromley took a step forward from behind the throne, and Lord Cillian turned back to the room.

"A number of Zeristar ships washed ashore just north of Anaris. The survivors claim dragons have attacked Mount Anvil. The assault caught the Zeristar ill prepared and they suffered a great number of losses. The beasts have claimed the mountain, with many of the Zeristar ships destroyed during their evacuation. We are not sure what to make of this hysteria, but they were quite consistent in their reporting of the events."

"Dragons?" Queen Avrette asked. "How can this be? There haven't been dragons in Tyveriel in over nine hundred years. Send a scouting party to the Isle of the Twelve Mines. Have them report back to me with immediacy. Prepare a fleet for rescue and aid, but do not approach the island unless it appears safe. And only then, with great caution."

"As you wish, My Queen. Lords Cillian, Strongforge, I am sorry to deliver such news in your midst. It bereaves me that you have lost so many of your kin." The soldiers bowed and left.

"Jenta," Gromley started, forgetting their company, "My apologies, I mean, My Queen. I should like to accompany this expedition."

"No, Gromley, I will not risk further harm to your people . . . not until we know what exactly we are dealing with here."

"You cannot expect me to stand by—"

Shadow put a hand on his friend's shoulder, eliciting a glare that warned him against interfering. Shadow held fast but remained silent.

"I expect you to obey your queen," Queen Avrette said, "which I believe I still am for the moment. I can only imagine your pain in hearing this news. And that of Lord Cillian. I promise you both that, whatever happened on the Isle of the Twelve Mines, we will avenge your loss with the totality of our resources. That does not mean we run blindly into confrontation with a force we do not yet understand."

Lord Cillian approached Gromley, holding out a hand in friendship. "Brother, the queen's wisdom guides you justly. Today, our hearts break beyond repair— I can feel the loss, as I can tell you do as well. There will be a time for revenge, but now is not that time. Join me, so we may mourn our people according to our customs. For I need a cleric's guidance as much as you need to be among one of your own kind."

Gromley stared back at Lord Cillian, his eyes tearing. He took Lord Cillian's hand in both of his. "Thank you, Tybus. My Queen. If you will excuse us."

"Of course, Gromley. My heart goes out to both of you and all your people. I will keep you informed as soon as I receive further news. If you should need anything in the meantime, don't hesitate to ask it of me."

Gromley and Lord Cillian left the throne room. Queen Avrette's brief reign would end as it began—with murder and despair.

CHAPTER 34

Ulest Prakten chose the hamlet of Ohteira as the capital of his kingdom. There he built a great tower of red stone which rivals Castle Forene in its enormity and beauty.

—The Gatekeeper's Abridged History of Tyveriel
Vol. 3, Chapter 37 – Discovered in the Private Library of Solana Marwyn, the month of Vasa, 889 AT

—▲—

Silyarithe landed on a rocky outcrop in the middle of a large clearing amidst the Wistful Timberlands. On the ground, surrounded by the muted greens of the forest, she felt out of place and clumsy as loose rock shifted underfoot. Peering into the ominous forest, foreign memories of this place flooded her mind. Memories belonging to great dragons that had come here before her . . . each drawn to this location by a force older than time.

She turned around several times, much like a dog deciding on a suitable place to sleep. Her concern, however, was not with finding comfort, but to assure herself she would not be ambushed. She was hopeful the Aged One would honor the pact they had formed with the dragons during the Age of Chaos, but she well knew this territory was not her own.

The timberlands were cold and quiet, the normal chatter of woodland creatures had ceased at the grey dragon's arrival. Steam wafted from Silyarithe's form as an unquenchable inferno raged inside her. She roared, making her presence known to any too witless to have not already noticed, or too cunning to emerge from the shadowed and twisted protection of the woods.

A strange clicking sound came from the edge of the clearing where the undergrowth grew thick. The notes began sharp and fast, gradually elongating and slowing to a brief pause. Others answered in kind from the forest to Silyarithe's rear. It slowly spread, this cacophony, until a unified chorus of wood clacking against wood surrounded the grey dragon.

Silyarithe scanned her surroundings, looking for any sign of those with whom she kept company. It wasn't until the chorus subsided that she saw motion. A small, unassuming shrub seemed to twist and contort until it took on a humanoid form, its roots pulling free from the earth. The yearling blight, no bigger than a cat, bobbed up and down and chattered as it approached the enormous dragon. Its eyes glowed a vibrant green, as did a small orb of energy swirling at the core of its tangled body. With each footfall, growth bloomed beneath it.

"I seek an audience with the Aged One," Silyarithe said.

The blight ratcheted its head at the intruder's request. It again began clicking, beckoning its siblings to its side.

From all around, blights formed from the smallest twig to the most gnarled of old-growth trees. Their organic, twisted forms shambled forward, gathering around Silyarithe. She held her ground as the blights assembled and then reiterated her demand.

"I seek an audience with the Aged One."

The blights that came from the depths of the Wistful Timberlands parted, forming a path into the darkness. Deep within the ancient forest, a dim light grew.

Silyarithe crouched, her shoulder blades rising to meet high on her back. She leaped down from her rocky perch and crept into the forest, scanning the blights on either side of her.

Branches cracked and trees splintered as the massive dragon followed the beacon into the woods. The life-energy of the blights gathered around her came to light like a procession of lanterns. Green, yellow, orange, red.

Beneath the dense canopy she was at a distinct disadvantage to the blights as she could not lift into flight. Her mind raced through her options should the Aged One find her presence unwelcomed. She would prefer not to set the forest ablaze, but it very well could be her only means of escape.

Purple streaks of light crackled along the jagged ridges of Silyarithe's maw as she approached a smooth black monolith covered in pale green lichens. It stood nearly as tall as her and had done so in this spot since the end of the Age of Chaos. Will-O'-Wisps floated about the stone, changing color as they danced. The wisps' glow bounced off the monolith's worn surface, casting the surrounding woods in an eerie light.

Silyarithe circled the monolith, weaving between the trees as nimbly as she could. She completed her circle and crouched before the stone. The Will-O'-Wisps drifted up into the canopy overhead and faded from sight. In the darkness, with only the glow of the surrounding blights lighting the area, the monolith broke apart.

Crack by crack, thick legs and arms became distinguishable, followed by an ovoid face on a head set slightly below broad, rounded shoulders. Nearly as wide as it was tall, the entity pulled its feet from the earth that had built up around them over the ages and turned toward its guest.

"A Child of Fire summons the Aged One?" Its voice was resonant, ancient. "Many ages have passed since the dragons have called upon the Aged One."

Silyarithe bowed so the crown of her head touched the forest floor. "A long time ago my ancestors had a great alliance with you and your kind. They revered you until the very end of our bloodline. With my birth, I have restored that bloodline and, as their progeny, I seek to renew our alliance and once again free Tyveriel from the scourge of mankind."

"The Aged One has walked this realm since time began—a primordial god. Ages have come and gone but the Aged One endures. Mankind is impermanent, a cancer upon this world that will see its day pass as quickly as it has arrived. While they fight each other, we grow to untold numbers, awaiting the day Tyveriel returns to us. There was a time the blights roamed freely—shared the land with the gods and their creations. The one they called Modig Forene saw an end to that, slaughtering countless of our kind with his armies. The scales shall one day be rebalanced."

The Aged One lumbered over to Silyarithe—the forest floor springing to life beneath its feet—and looked the dragon over with dull black eyes.

"And here the Grey Queen is in the Aged One's forest, new to this world but talking of old alliances. The Aged One once thought better of your kind."

Silyarithe seethed at the insult, watching the blights multiplying around her out of the corner of her eye. They now surrounded her and the Aged One, crowding the forest floor for as far as she could see. The smaller among them climbed upon their larger siblings and up into the trees, perched upon crooked branches. Their eyes glowed like countless stars in the night sky.

"As well you still should," Silyarithe said, "I do not seek you out on my own accord but at the advice of my father."

"Mesorith lay slain at the bottom of the sea," the Aged One said, "I felt his soul pass beyond the veil of life."

"It would seem even gods are fallible." Silyarithe sighed. "Telsidor did not take Mesorith's soul, but freed it from its mortal prison. Before meeting Telsidor in battle, Mesorith bound his soul to a phylactery which he hid far from humanity's reach. For he envisioned the Age of Man's arrival and embraced temporary death so I could one day resurrect him. He flies once more. Together, we reclaimed Mount Anvil and ravaged the Isle of the Twelve Mines. We already set our plan in motion."

The Aged One bent down and allowed a small blight, no larger than a sprout, to climb aboard his rough-hewn hand. It placed the creature on its shoulder upon a sage green lichen.

"If what you say is true . . . that the great Mesorith has attained lichdom and will join us in the alliance you speak of, perhaps the time has come for a new age without man. A new age for the wild things to rule Tyveriel once more."

"It is my destiny," Silyarithe said. "What must I do to convince you to take up arms with me as you did with my ancestors all those ages ago? Alone, we are formidable, but together, we are an unstoppable force."

The Aged One tapped a small stone on the forest floor with the tip of its foot, sending it scurrying out of the way. "When we last came together, it was hubris that destroyed our union. That of the great Mesorith and the others of your kind. They viewed themselves as superior to the blights and were unwilling to share equally the realm with us. The Aged One would be a fool to enter a pact expecting a different outcome."

Silyarithe snarled and light crackled between her teeth. She thought better of such a base reaction. Instead, she curled her right claw beneath herself and touched her forehead again to the earth. She remained there prone before the Aged One as a sign of trust and admiration.

"It is true, you have graced Tyveriel since the dawn of time, and I but for a season," Silyarithe said, rising to look upon the Aged One once more, her expression repentant. "I do not know all of what transpired ages ago, for I see only glimpses, while these transgressions are still fresh in your mind. I understand your reticence and respect your decision. Before I leave you in peace, biding your time until the world is delivered to you, I would have you know that my motivation is not that of self-gain but one of self-fulfillment. I have no interest in ruling over Tyveriel, for the prophecy states that I must only bring about the end of man, not that I must rule afterward. That responsibility I leave to you."

"And what of Mesorith?" The Aged One asked. "What are his desires? Surely, he seeks to restore the power he once had."

"Do not concern yourself with the lich that was once my father." Silyarithe slid a talon beneath one scale on her chest and retrieved the crystal shard that had contained Mesorith's soul. Its glow was now dim and inconsistent compared to when she had found it within Zalinrithe's corpse. "He entrusted his phylactery to my care until we secure Mount Anvil and destroy Evelium's navy. With it in my possession, he is incapable of determining his own course of action. For the moment, he is agreeable to this arrangement, and has assured me he supports our union with the blights of the Wistful Timberlands on the terms I have proffered."

The Aged One trained its gaze on the phylactery as though Silyarithe had faded away and it was all that was left in the world. "Your terms are acceptable to the Aged One, but the decision is not alone the Aged One's to make." The primordial god raised its hands in the air, its fingertips barely reaching the top of its shoulders. The primordial god turned slowly in a complete circle, addressing the myriad blights surrounding them.

"The Aged One is immortal. Each of you, from the smallest twig to the great titans that still slumber, risk much more by agreeing to walk the path of war with man. Therefore, it shall be your decision as to the course of the future of Tyveriel. The Grey Queen has called for a new union between the last of her kind and our vast numbers. Do we rise to that call, reignite the flame, and raze the world of men?"

The forest fell silent. One of the blight elders, its bark misshapen and knotted, and its life force a deep, autumnal orange, stepped out from the masses. It hunched over, its back bristled with branch-like appendages, and clicked. The clicking was slow and guttural—laden with experience and wisdom. The blight elder stood tall, its monologue echoed through the forest, inciting the others to join in its conviction.

One after another, the blights joined the elder, until they all clicked in unison. The blight war cry spread throughout the Wistful Timberlands—a war cry that hadn't been heard on Tyveriel for a millennium. Their life forces grew in strength, forcing Silyarithe to shield her eyes against the glare.

The Aged One focused its attention back on Silyarithe. "The blights have answered. They will join you in your cause and wrench this land back from the sullied hands of mankind. Tyveriel shall once again be ours."

Silyarithe grinned at the notion. "Very well," she said, "we have an accord. No doubt news of our offensive against the Isle of the Twelve Mines will spread to the mainland and man will begin preparing for war. I will require your aid before long. Until then, share no sign of yourselves with the enemy, for surprise is our greatest ally."

The Aged One turned back toward its resting place. "The Aged One will hold the Grey Queen accountable for her actions and those of the lich. The Aged One will weigh any blight life given in vain against your own."

The blights parted, creating a path back to the clearing where Silyarithe had landed, their life forces lighting the way. Silyarithe crawled back through the nearly impregnable swath of trees as the Aged One closed its eyes and reverted to its monolithic form.

As Silyarithe reached the clearing, she turned and watched the lights that animated the blights fade, starting with those next to the monolith and spreading throughout the forest, as the blights returned to their rest.

Welcoming the warm sun on her face, she looked into the open skies above and leaped into the air.

CHAPTER 35

It has been far too long since I've felt the exhilaration of taking a truly daring risk. Immortality has become mundane. I aim to reintegrate myself with society.

—*Telsidor's Missives*
Diary entry dated 16th of Anar, 750 AF. Unearthed from the
Ruins of Anaris, month of Emin, 1156 AT

A plume of dust billowed in the lone horseman's wake as he galloped south from Requiem along Spara's Trail at full speed. With patrols spanning the border from the Ilathril Mountains to Wicked Pass, inevitably, the Requiem Brigade would spot an army of this size as it crossed into Windswept, and that they would send word to Vanyareign. A lone rider at least signified the city's surprise, and that Queen Avrette had yet to assemble an army to halt their progress. At least not this far north.

King Ulest was perched upon his mammoth at the edge of a ridge overlooking the outpost city. Requiem loomed on the open plains below, surrounded by an impenetrable black granite wall that arched outward from the city and stood three hundred feet tall and nearly one hundred feet thick. A black iron door lay locked beyond four portcullises—an image of a wolf engraved upon its surface.

"Send two manticore riders to run him down," he said, shielding his eyes against the sun.

"Yes, sir." The guard at his side accepted her orders and unlashed a polished bison horn from the belt that bound her red leather jerkin.

The horn bellowed twice, calling to the riders that weaved in and out of the clouds overhead, maintaining a vigil over King Ulest's army. Two of the riders peeled off from their patrol and darted out over Requiem and toward the horseman who raced to reach the tree cover where Spara's Trail fell away from the Ilathril Mountains toward the northern edge of the Morion Swamp.

"It is impressive," King Ulest said of the city as the manticores gave chase.

"Indeed, my Lord," the guard answered.

"My greatest concern while preparing for this march was that Windswept would hear of our approach and have the time to amass an army to fight us here. We would break upon those walls."

The guard nodded. "You were wise to keep your plans hidden. Are we to go around the city?"

"Yes, to the west. I know it will delay our arrival in Vanyareign, but I have no intention of marching an army of this size through that wretched swamp."

▲

The pair of manticores rolled into a dive, closing on the horseman at tremendous speed. As the horseman neared the woods, the first of the two manticores swooped in behind him, its dragon-like wings unfurling to arrest its descent, a feline claw swatting his steed's hindquarters. The horse spun, throwing the horseman along the roadside as it tumbled into a gully, blood spraying from the fresh wound.

The second manticore landed at the edge of the forest and blocked the path forward in case their initial attack failed. It snapped at the horseman with a toothy mouth that made its face resemble that of a grotesquely deformed man with a wild mane of red hair.

A decorated member of the Requiem Brigade as witnessed by the forest green cape affixed to his tan leather armor by a golden eagle claw clasp, the horseman brushed sandy bangs from his face and drew his sword, taking a defensive stance.

The first manticore pounced upon the horseman's steed, tearing the flesh of its neck open with a mouthful of razor-sharp teeth. The horse screamed, but the manticore quickly silenced the beast. The manticore then circled around behind their quarry to block any chance at escape, not that the horseman would get far on foot. The riders that sat upon the manticores' backs climbed down and drew heavy crossbows on the horseman.

"There is no need for this to end poorly for you, brother," the rider standing before the horseman said. He wore red leather, the uniform of the enlisted Winterashe army and a matching helmet with wings which swept back from his temples. A long tail of brown horse hair hung between his shoulders from the helms exaggerated comb. His blue eyes peered out from behind the spiraling gold-inlay of his facemask. "We simply cannot allow you to continue on to Vanyareign. We would be happy to escort you there, though, if you will come with us peacefully."

"My allegiance is to the queen and the true Forene bloodline. There is nothing you can say that would convince me to go with you. I'd rather take my chances against the two of you and your rancid beasts."

"King Ulest seeks nothing more than to claim his rightful place upon the Raptor's Throne. He wants nothing of war with the southerners, just your recognition."

"I assure you he will get no such treatment." The horseman ran at the manticore rider that blocked his path forward, sword hoisted overhead.

The rider fired a bolt, the horseman deflecting it wide with a deft swipe of his blade. The other rider followed suit, burying a bolt in the horseman's back. Injured, but undeterred, the horseman lunged at the first rider who scrambled to pull his blade from its sheath and defend himself.

As the horseman brought his sword down upon his adversary, the rider's manticore thrust his spine-covered tail forward and released several long, serrated spikes into the horseman's chest, knocking him through the air and backward onto the dirt path.

The horseman lay, run through by the spines. The two manticore riders approached and stood over him, watching the blood overflow his mouth and join the darkened pool saturating the earth beneath him.

"King Ulest will want us to account for this," the blue-eyed rider said to his partner, "It will not please him that this ended in bloodshed."

"He will understand. Besides, what is the life of one southerner worth?"

The blue-eyed rider nodded, grabbed the horseman's hands, and dragged him back to his manticore. "You get the horse. We bring everything back to King Ulest should he want proof."

The second rider returned to his manticore and climbed atop his saddle, nudging the beast toward the horse's carcass. Grabbing the carcass in its mouth and between its massive front claws, the manticore thrust its wings, struggling to lift into the air with the added burden.

The blue-eyed rider heaved the horseman's body across the front of his own saddle, climbed upon his manticore, cracked his reins, and lifted into the air. He circled once, waiting for his partner's mount to catch the wind.

▲

"And how, exactly, did it come to be that you killed this soldier of the Forene Army? And so brutally?" Roen asked of the two manticore riders standing outside his uncle's tent.

The body of the horseman lay before him in a wagon beside the corpse of his steed. The horseman's body was pale. There was an empty expression on his face, and manticore spines jutted from his blood-soaked chest. The manticore riders stared at their boots as Roen shook his head, displeased.

"Well?" Roen asked while his sisters, Myka and Veien, circled behind the rider, their stares fixed on the dead horseman.

"How is it that two highly trained soldiers of Winterashe, both with manticores, can't subdue a single soldier of the Forene Army without resorting to exsanguination? Frankly, it's embarrassing. And King Ulest does not take kindly to being embarrassed. You both well know we were to accomplish the march on Vanyareign without blood on our hands."

"We understand, my Lord."

"Back to your duties. I'll decide what to do with the two of you in due course."

The manticore riders bowed and climbed back aboard the wagon to transport the horseman's body to a funeral pyre.

"Actually, leave the body with me. He may yet be of use."

"My Lord?"

"Bring him into my tent. Then, you can be on your way."

The riders nodded and walked around to the back of the cart. The blue-eyed rider grabbed the horseman under his armpits and pulled him from the cart, the second rider grabbing him by the ankles.

The riders laid the corpse on the floor of the tent as instructed. "Anything else, Lord Roen?"

"No. Go. Think on the lack of judgement that led to this man's death."

The riders bowed to Roen and then to his sisters and left the Three to their business, no matter how macabre.

"May I speak with him, Myka?" Roen asked once they were alone.

Myka and Veien lifted their eyes from the corpse for the first time since it had arrived and smiled at their brother. Myka walked to the horseman and dropped to her knees at his side. She pushed her platinum blonde hair behind her shoulders so it draped down the back of her white dress and leaned in close to the horseman's ear, whispering but making no audible sound.

She kneeled upright and placed her hands upon her lap. Roen and Veien peered over her shoulder in anticipation. She looked up at her siblings. The corpse of the horseman twitched on the floor. Then it drew in a feeble breath, air wheezing and blood bubbling from the wounds in its chest.

The horseman, a reanimated shell of his former self, jerked his head upward to look with blackened eyes upon those who summoned him from his slumber.

"Brother of Evelium, I am sorry for your misfortune," Roen said. "Your fierce loyalty was your undoing. This is something for which no soldier deserves punishment."

The horseman's jaw dropped open, and he released a portion of the air within him, his words escaping as part of his preternatural exhale. "It matters not," the corpse said with a raspy tone, "my soul has crossed to Kalmindon and is at peace among its endless gardens. Why do you disturb this fetid husk?"

"In life, you were an honored soldier of the Requiem Brigade. We are interested in knowing what forces your queen has at her ready between your fine city and Vanyareign."

"Your words drip with honey," the corpse said, "Requiem has only a small force charged with alerting Vanyareign to any intrusion from the north. The capital has a vast army. My commander dispatched me to warn them to arms."

"Were you the only one sent with such instructions?"

The corpse adjusted its stiffening neck, rigid muscles and joints cracked from the unnatural movement. "I was, but they will try again after my failure. They will send word under cover of darkness. You shall not go unnoticed. Requiem will not fail the queen."

With that, the rest of the air within the horseman's chest escaped and his head fell back to the floor. The corpse shuddered as the semblance of life Myka had imbued it with faded.

"Sister, as always, you amaze me."

Myka smiled at Roen, obviously pleased with herself. Veien extended a pale hand and helped Myka to her feet.

"We must inform our uncle that news of our approach will reach Vanyareign and we are likely to meet significant resistance," Roen said, "Then we can make proper arrangements for our friend."

The sisters nodded and followed their brother from the tent.

▲

In the early morning hours, the air still crisp as spring struggled to wrest Evelium from winter's harsh grasp and the moon waxed toward its annual apex, a wolf slinked through the north gate of Vanyareign and up along King's Way. She trotted up the path until she came to the castle grounds. She paced at the open mouth of the portcullis, her gold collar catching the moonlight when she turned.

Laudin drew his bowstring and let an arrow fly, striking the bullseye on his target across the open green of the bailey. A glint caught his eye, and he turned to see the wolf stuck in her stride.

He threw his bow over his shoulder and kneeled on one knee, welcoming the intrusion. With a pat on his thigh and an airy whistle, he called the she-wolf over to him.

At first the wolf hesitated, unsure of approaching an armed man not in uniform, but gave in to the need to deliver her message. She trotted through the portcullis and approached the Iminti ranger, her tail curled under.

"C'mon girl," Laudin said, coaxing her to a scrap of dried meat he pulled from a pouch on his belt. "You're safe with me."

She padded up to him, her nose held high, sniffing for a

sense of threat. Finding none, she came to his hand and took the scrap of meat. Circling away from him, she gulped it down eagerly.

She returned to Laudin and pushed her forehead into his hand. He scratched her behind her ear and took notice of the cylinder hanging from her collar.

"What do we have here?" He asked her. She tilted her head at the inflection in his voice.

He slid a small button on the cylinder to the side and depressed it. The end of the cylinder popped open, revealing a roll of parchment. He pulled the scroll from its case and unraveled it, reading its every word.

Laudin stood, and the wolf jumped back, startled. The ranger took one more look at the scroll and ran for the castle doors.

CHAPTER 36

Tayre created the Wistful Timberlands and placed a primordial god as its steward so the aspirations of man would always be held in measure.

—*The Tome of Mystics*
Unknown Origin. Unearthed from the Ruins of Oda Norde, month of Bracken, 1320 AT

—▲—

The Waystone continued to flicker, its power seemingly drained from Spara's ascent. The enormous cavern sat in silence but for the rushing water of the underground river at its rear and the rhythmic rumble of Vendarithe's breathing. The rose gold dragon arched her back like a stretching cat and yawned. "You may go, Umhra the Peacebreaker."

Umhra looked up at the dragon in surprise. "Go?"

"Yes, I have no use for you at the present moment. If I ever do, I will make myself known to you. I doubt you will find this arrangement burdensome. Besides, a Mystic is of little interest to me. You are ill-equipped to put up any semblance of a struggle."

"Spara alluded to as much."

"It is why she brought you here last. She knew I was the

only of the Guardians that could contain you. Quite clever, that one. She never told you that a dragon is the only creature a Mystic's powers are useless against.

"There was a reason the Mystics rushed to ascend when the Age of Chaos took hold. They feared for their lives. Without the gods to maintain order, they knew the dragons would rise up and claim Tyveriel for themselves. There was nothing else for them to do but flee."

"She seemed to have neglected that among her lessons. I must ask, however, why did you agree to me as payment for her passage?"

"Spara had every right to ascend along with the others. As do you, it would seem, as you are obviously no longer just a Paladin, but now a Mystic. I thought it educational for you to see Spara for what she truly is before she left. She has always been one to leverage the emotions of others for her own benefit. Truly detestable, if my opinion matters. Regardless, it is important to know who your true allies are, is it not?"

"Most important. I appreciate the clarity you have given me."

"Now, leave me be. You and the deceiver have interrupted my Long Sleep too much already, and I shall grow hungry if I do not return to it soon. I assure you it is in everyone's best interest that you disturb me no longer. You might find the river an easier means of exit."

Umhra nodded. He walked across the lair, watching the light of the Waystone flutter erratically. Beyond it he found a shallow river that ran in a smooth channel carving its way beneath the mountains. He followed the flow of water, only hesitating for a moment to look upon Vendarithe once more as he left the lair. The great dragon had already curled herself up into a tight ball, her tail covering her eyes, her mouth a waning fury.

"She will wreak havoc in the heavens, Umhra the Peacebreaker. They have no idea what comes for them. I'm afraid there may be no salvation from her rage."

Vendarithe's warning swirled in his mind. Umhra stepped into the darkness, and waded through the knee-high waters. How could he have been so blind to Spara's deception? What could he have done if he had been wise enough to recognize her ruse? And what should he do now that he was aware of her true intentions for Kalmindon?

The more he thought of her betrayal and its implications, the faster he splashed through the water looking for a way out from beneath the mountains. The river widened and slowed as it opened into an expansive cave with crystalline walls. High above, the sun peaked through a small hole in the roof and light danced across the cavern.

Umhra leaped for the opening. Wings sprouted from his back, and he lifted into the sky. He gained speed during the ascent and burst from the hole into the fresh air of a lush valley among the Ilathril Mountains.

He flew toward Vanyareign, steeped in self-pity but somehow aware that his friends were there. As he flew south, the mountains faded into the distance behind him. He noticed a familiar thrumming in his right ear. Curious, and piqued by Spara's lies, he banked westward. The pulsing grew along with a smile on Umhra's face. Not all hope was lost.

Shades of orange stained the sky as the sun dipped below the horizon when Umhra touched down beside the Waystone. The entrance to the Stoneheart Pass incited memories of his journey to Meriden and his descent into Pragarus all those years ago. The memories were raw, jagged, as if it all happened yesterday. He rubbed the scar on his side where Evron Alabaster's dagger had cut through his leathers—a twinge of pain greeted him, as was often the case when he thought of that time.

For a moment, he stood and stared into the chasm's inhospitable depths, and thought of Balris and the Barrow's Pact. He welcomed any distraction from the self-flagellation that had consumed him since the surprise of Spara's betrayal.

He went over in his mind the entirety of his time with Spara, from their first meeting in Oda Norde, to their bitter parting in Vendarithe's lair. Whereas he was blind to her deception until it was too late, now, it was clear. All of Spara's promises, all of her instruction, it was just enough to give her exactly what she wanted and to keep him from being able to follow her to Kalmindon. She had toyed with him as a cat toys with an injured mouse before dealing a death blow—patting with gentle paws only to run him through when she tired of her game.

Umhra returned to the present and looked down upon the Waystone. Its blue glow remained as vibrant as he remembered when he was here last, despite the Barrow's Pact having defeated Ballan and Spara's claims that their victory rendered the stone inert. She had miscalculated, after all.

Ready to shatter the Waystone and absorb its power, Umhra stepped upon it and summoned Forsetae to his hand. He twirled the blade as he contemplated the moment, and then hoisted the sword overhead and struck down on the Waystone with all his might. Whereas in his prior experience the unguarded Waystones fractured under such a blow, to his surprise, his blade careened off the stone's surface, creating a spray of sparks but inflicted no discernable damage. His hands stung.

It was then that it struck him. The Barrow's Pact hadn't defeated Ballan, they only temporarily returned him to the Fae. Only a Mystic can defeat a Guardian and leave the Waystone vulnerable. Inevitably, Ballan would return as long as the Waystone beckoned him. Another lie from Spara's lips. What a web she had woven.

The myriapede comes to confront you, Forsetae said, the sword's warning resonating in Umhra's mind.

Umhra turned just as Ballan burst from the ground. Rocks and earth rained down on Umhra as his armor coalesced around his body and deflected chunks of cascading stone to the earth. The gargantuan myriapede raised its torso into the air on countless rust-colored legs, its mandibles snapped together in a fit of unbridled rage.

"Aren't you going to say something clever like your siblings?" Umhra asked.

Ballan roared, yellow sputum streamed from his mouth.

"Nice to see you again as well."

Ballan lunged forward to attack. Umhra spun from his path, slashing his sword across the myriapede's sinuous body as he passed. Forsetae's blade scraped against the Guardian's armored segments until finding purchase toward the rear of his trunk just before two elongated back legs.

Ballan leaped over the Waystone and burrowed back into the earth at an amazing speed. Umhra tried to free his blade from the Guardian's side, but Ballan dragged him beneath the surface despite his struggles. Into the darkness they dove. Umhra held fast to Ballan's trunk as the rough earthen walls of the burgeoning tunnel raked against his armor.

Ballan continued down, cutting through rock and dirt. The tunnel collapsed behind them and they dropped from the ceiling of an expansive cavern, crashing into the soft, muddy floor below.

Ballan threw Umhra from his side and Forsetae dissipated. The impact knocked the wind from Umhra's chest and sent his head spinning. He climbed to his feet, covered in muck, and wiped his eyes clean. In all but utter darkness, Umhra welcomed the light cast by the ether wafting from his armor.

The cavern smelled of peat and decay, the soft flooring rising to Umhra's mid-calf. Water dripped from the cavern ceiling into dank pools scattered across the floor. The persistent dripping of water accompanied a chittering sound that surrounded him.

Ballan spun into a coil and glared at Umhra, emboldened in the safety of his nest. He shrieked and another myriapede came forth from the darkness to join him. Umhra could tell she was larger based on the size of her legs. She snapped her mandibles in response to Ballan's call and screeched.

Umhra closed his eyes and grabbed the rhodium pyramid that hung around his neck. The feel of its cold surface and sharp edges comforted him. He ran his thumb over the ridges of the wind currents etched onto its sides.

He opened his eyes and raised a hand overhead. From the palm of his outstretched hand, he cast daylight throughout the cavern, causing Ballan and his companion to recoil. On every surface of the cave, the spell illuminated hundreds of smaller myriapedes that skittered about, each the size of an adult alligator.

"I see you've been busy since we last met and we sent you back to the Fae, your mortal body claimed by my friend's sword. This time, I return as a Mystic, and I aim to rid you of your duty as Guardian of Torrent's Waystone. I leave the choice to you, Ballan, Master of Darkness—submit to my will or see your progeny perish."

Ballan and his companion shrieked in unison, stirring their brood to action. Umhra, having received his answer, again summoned Forsetae and cast the first few creatures that came for him to the ground upon his blade. The attack was relentless, with wave after wave of myriapede wearing him down until they overcame him with their vast numbers, smothering him in a writhing pile of countless legs and snapping jaws.

Umhra allowed the swarm to take him to the ground, their pincers too weak to breach his rhodium armor. His face was buried in decaying matter. He focused on his icon. When the weight became too much to bear, Umhra envisioned the mass of myriapedes thrown from his body and torn asunder across the cavern. He imposed himself into the space around him and forced his will outward.

The force hurled the myriapedes from him, tearing most to pieces and crushing others against the cavern walls. Umhra stood, the muck and gore sloughed off and his armor gleamed anew.

Ballan roared in abject rage and charged. Umhra countered,

running at the Guardian and throwing Forsetae into its open mandibles and then leaping into the air. Narrowly clearing Ballan's lurching maw, Umhra landed on the monstrosity's back just as Forsetae burst through its chitinous form.

Umhra caught the sword and spun. He slashed at the exit wound and released a spray of ichor across the cavern. Ballan writhed wildly, throwing Umhra from his back and twisting about his own body to protect the grave injury.

Umhra landed and slid through an acrid pool of waste and decay. He arrested his momentum and charged at Ballan, who recoiled from the onslaught.

Ballan's partner came between them and sprayed venom across the cavern. Umhra slid between her legs coming to Ballan's fore and drove Forsetae beneath his poison gland to the cross guard.

Umhra tore Forsetae clear. Blood and venom spurted from the wound and formed a pool beneath him. Ballan writhed, knotting his body about itself and then he collapsed to the cave floor. He tried to right himself but failed, crashing lifeless to the ground.

Ballan's mate hissed, recoiling from the Mystic, venom streaming from the corners of her mouth. She skittered to the far end of the cavern.

"Come forth and I will send you back peacefully to the Fae so you may live out your days with Ballan and your brood," Umhra said. "This world is no place for your kind. I cannot permit you to remain here. Go home and be among your own."

The sole remaining myriapede turned in a circle, as if indecisive, and then slinked forward, staying low to the ground like a repentant dog. She chortled as she neared her superior, laying down before him accepting her sentence.

Umhra leaped into the air, bringing Forsetae down upon her and drove the blade deep into her head. With little more than a quiver, life faded from her eyes.

Surveying the surrounding carnage, Umhra allowed

Forsetae and his armor to dissipate. He searched the roof of the cavern for the tunnel through which he fell as a hopeful means of escape but could not discern an obvious choice along its pockmarked surface.

He burst into the air—wings sprouting from his back—and crashed into the roof, imagining a pathway to the surface. The cave collapsed inward on itself. Umhra flew upward through the deluge of rock and soil. Reaching the surface, he shot into the air, a great sinkhole forming beneath him, the final Waystone teetering on its edge.

As the earth fell away into the abyss, Umhra landed beside the Waystone and summoned Forsetae to his hand.

Your power shall be unmatched and yourself worthy of ascension with but one swing of my blade. I am honored to be a part of this moment. You have delivered me from darkness and brought me forth as a beacon of light.

Umhra tilted his head and looked at the sword. "The feeling is mutual, my friend," he said, as he stepped upon the Waystone. "I wouldn't be here without you." He raised Forsetae overhead, and drove the blade into the heart of the luminous stone, sending a fracture across its smooth surface.

The Waystone's inner light intensified within the crack and then drifted into the air and circled Umhra. It drew back for a moment and then permeated his body, lifting him from the ground in exaltation. Hovering in place, a surge of power flowed through Umhra's body—different from that which he felt at the other Waystones. Here, he received the power to ascend to Kalmindon as a true Mystic worthy to walk among the gods. It coursed through him, like nothing he had ever felt before.

He settled back to the earth, and the light faded. He walked to the edge of the sinkhole and peered into its depths. He raised a hand to the heavens, the earth that had collapsed below regathering at the surface. Any sign of the damage he had caused on his escape from Ballan's lair was erased. Satisfied, he leaped into the air.

CHAPTER 37

The sisters are a great oddity, indeed. Another corruption of the Forene line. They are, however, not without great value.

—Entry from the Diary of Vred Ulest
Dated 8ᵗʰ of Prien, 903 AF. Unearthed from the Ruins of
Ohteira, month of Lusta, 1399 AT

—▲—

Laudin burst into the throne room. Two guards sat at the Elders Syndicate's table rolling dice for sovereigns. They looked up from their game and snapped to attention, a sheepish expression on each of their faces.

"Sorry, Lord Laudin," one of the guards said. "We had no expectation anyone would come to court at such an hour."

"Never mind." Laudin gave a dismissive wave, caring little about their game. "I need to speak with the regent at once. Please summon her, the Elders Syndicate, and the rest of the Barrow's Pact. Let them know I said it was a matter of utmost importance."

"Right away, my Lord." The guards hurried from the throne room.

Laudin waited, pacing the room. Talus was the first to arrive, followed by Nicholas a few moments later.

"What could be so important to drag me out of bed at this hour?" Shadow asked, entering the room with Gromley and Naivara.

"A moment of patience while we wait for the regent," Laudin said, "She needs to be the one I share this with first."

"Share what?" Regent Avrette asked, entering the room with the entire Elders Syndicate trailing close behind. Despite the early hour, she was bright eyed and dressed for her daily duties.

"Regent," Laudin said, "we've received an urgent message from Requiem. As we feared, the army of Vred Ulest marches on Vanyareign. It crossed over from Winterashe, passing Requiem three days ago. There was only one casualty as they ran down a scout to stop him from warning us. The letter refers to an army so vast the earth quaked with every stride. We have, at most, a week before the army arrives."

At this, the Elders Syndicate broke into an uproar. Laudin pulled the note he had retrieved from the wolf's collar and thrust it into the regent's hands. She read it, frowned, and then passed it to Lord Cillian to share amongst the members of the Syndicate.

"I was afraid, once news of my brother's death reached Ohteira, Vred would resort to such a base response. But we have been preparing for this eventuality since the doppelganger's warning. Already, as many fighting men as our other cities can spare have come from across the kingdom to our aid. Every city has answered our call except those in the west. I dare not risk exposing them to what happened on the Isle of the Twelve Mines."

"Regent," Lord Cillian said, stepping forward from the sea of yellow gathered around him, "the King of Winterashe will challenge you for the throne under the Rite of Reunification. He does not yet know of the child."

"Well then, I will meet him in the northern fields. If I cannot convince him of Turin's right to the throne, and of the greater threat, I will fight for her claim as is my duty as regent."

"Surely, there is another way," Laudin said.

Regent Avrette sat on the Raptor's Throne. "It is how the law is written, Laudin, and I intend to adhere to its every word. Let's hope reason prevails. It will be my intention to not risk stoking the flames of war on two fronts. Send word north that my preference is for parley."

"As you wish," Laudin said. "I will send Taivaron to your cousin to relay your wish to talk."

"Thank you," Regent Avrette said.

▲

King Ulest stood at his wash basin as the early morning sun shone through the open doorway of his pavilion. While most would say his pureblood features remained flawless, he could see the wear on the face that looked back at him in the mirror. He was tired and bore the substantial strain of reunifying Evelium under his rule. All he could think about, however, was returning to Ohteira and the warmth of his wife's embrace.

As he patted his face dry with a linen towel, Taivaron darted through the doorway and landed on the high-back of a chair that sat neatly tucked under an oversized table. The harrier whistled to announce his arrival.

Bare chested, King Ulest walked over to greet the bird.

"What have we here?" he asked, noticing the small vial attached to Taivaron's leg. "May I, my friend?"

Taivaron bobbed his head up and down and ruffled his feathers.

King Ulest took hold of the vial and retrieved the parchment from within. He unfurled the document and read.

"Thank you," he said, his voice cracking, "You may return to your master."

Taivaron tilted his head, squawked.

"A free spirit, are you? My apologies. You may be on your way, then."

Taivaron hopped from the chair back and flew from the tent, leaving King Ulest to ponder the confusing note. He walked back to the wash basin and plucked a shirt from a nearby chest, pulled it on, and walked out of the tent.

Next to his pavilion was another of similar construct but colored black and white. He pulled the door flap aside and entered unannounced.

More austere than the warmth of his own quarters, with little more than a bed and lounge, Myka and Veien stood in the middle of the room as though lost, blank stares on their faces.

King Ulest cocked an eyebrow. "Where is Roen?"

The sisters looked at each other and then at King Ulest. They gave no answer.

"Never mind, I'll wait. I have something important to discuss with you all."

He walked over to the lounge and sat, rolling the parchment he just received between his fingers with nervous energy. Myka and Veien stayed where he had found them, content to not engage each other or their uncle as they awaited Roen's return.

"Sorry to keep you waiting, Uncle," Roen said as he entered the tent.

Myka and Veien waited for him to pass and then followed behind him.

"No need to apologize," King Ulest said, "My visit was unexpected, even to me."

"What is on your mind?"

"I received word from my cousin." King Ulest passed the parchment to Roen. "She would like to parley. Pay notice to her given title."

"Regent?" Roen asked. "What do you think she's planning? Kob'Anni warned your claim to the throne would not go uncontested."

"Either there is an heir we are unaware of, or she has made some other arrangement in secrecy. We won't know until I speak with her."

"And, if that is the case, what are you to do?"

"I will hear Jenta out. Should she have a legitimate heir, I will abide by the Fracture. If it is anything less than that, the throne shall be mine whether by her admission or by force."

"What of Kob'Anni's vision of the Grey Queen?"

"Roen, the myth of the Grey Queen arose to explain why the Forene bloodline never successfully birthed a viable female child. That is until Jenta, but even she has proven barren to my knowledge. It was a way of making the mothers of stillborn children with terrible malformations feel better. It had nothing to do with predicting the end of the Age of Forene."

At this, Myka and Veien turned away from their uncle, apparently stung by his careless words. King Ulest stood to apologize to the sisters, but they left before he could, leaving him alone with Roen.

"This conversation has cost us too much time, already," he said, putting his hand on Roen's shoulder, "I must prepare for the day's march. We are less than three days from Vanyareign and I have much to think about. Please let your sisters know I regret my words in their presence when they return. It was crass of me and I will make it up to them."

"Of course, Uncle. I will see you along the way. And, please don't worry yourself with my sisters. They will be fine. They know your words had no ill intent."

"Intent is no excuse. A father, an uncle, a king ... each of these should know better and I fall short of my own expectations."

▲

Naivara watched from her seat upon a nearby window sill as Regent Avrette stood before a full-length mirror, its frame made of solid platinum engraved with images of Fae Hobbs frolicking in the wilderness. She wore white armor with a cape of sheer ice-blue that her attendants affixed at each pauldron with a clasp shaped as an eagle. Upon her head, they placed the Circlet of Everlife, which Modig Forene himself wore into battle.

An attendant handed her two rapiers, hilt and blade alike of unadorned steel, polished to perfection. She inspected the blades and slid them into their sheaths on each of her hips. The weapons secure, she stood tall, and looked herself over, a picture of radiance. She frowned. "And the Barrow's Pact will be at my side?" She asked, peering over her shoulder at Naivara.

"Yes, Jenta. You have my word that you will not leave our sight for a moment. And, you look every part the queen you are. King Ulest will have his hands full."

"Regent, you mean. I am but the voice of our true queen until she comes of age. That's what this is all about. Giving her what she needs to flourish and lead us into a new age. And, what she needs most is time."

Naivara approached Regent Avrette, taking her hands. "You challenge Umhra in your selflessness. How many would yield such power if they were in your position? Evelium would have you as its queen for as long as you choose and yet, you willingly turn it over to its rightful sovereign. For that, we would follow you to our end."

Regent Avrette smiled. "Let's just hope my cousin is of like stock and makes the right choice."

Naivara nodded, returning the smile in kind.

"Shall we, then?" the regent asked. "Our forces await me in the fields, and the army of Winterashe is only a day off. We have already spotted their manticore scouts from the watch towers."

"We shall," Naivara said, "May the gods look over you and Evelium."

Regent Avrette drew in a deep breath and turned for the door. One of her attendants opened the door as she approached, revealing a cadre of soldiers who awaited to escort their regent out to the battlefield. They all bowed as she approached, allowing her to lead the way. At the back of the procession, Naivara found Gromley, Laudin, Nicholas, and Shadow and joined them.

"How is she?" Gromley asked as they descended the stairs

from the regent's personal quarters.

"Well . . . I think," Naivara said, "Nervous, but strong in her convictions. She will see this through."

"That is all we can ask. Much of the queen's army still marches toward Vanyareign. The Winterashe army will vastly outnumber us."

"And, still no news of Umhra?" Naivara asked.

"I'm afraid not," Laudin said, "Not even Taivaron has been able to locate him. I'm afraid we can't count on him interceding."

"I still feel as though he is close and will show himself," Nicholas said, "He has never failed us, and I believe in my heart that, while his own path has diverged from ours, he will hold his oath to always stand with us as paramount."

"No doubt he will be here if he can be," Laudin said. "If he knows where to find us."

The party descended to the stables where their horses awaited them. Lined up five-wide, those belonging to the Barrow's Pact were second in line behind those of the regent and the four generals of her army. Talus, the newest of their rank.

An attendant helped Regent Avrette upon a white stallion and then draped her cape over the horse's hind quarters. As the generals joined her, she nudged her horse through the stable doors and out into the bailey of Castle Forene. The Barrow's Pact followed, trailed by row after row of the Queen's Guard.

By now, the word of Vred Ulest's march on Vanyareign had spread throughout the capital with great fervor and its citizens lined King's Walk to wish their regent luck in her parley for peace and the sanctity of the Fracture. Multiple times during the procession, Regent Avrette trotted ahead of her generals to accept a sprig of foxglove from a small child perched high on their parent's shoulders. She waved and smiled as though she did not have a care in the world, and her charisma ignited the crowd into chants of support. *Jenta. Jenta. Jenta.*

As the procession neared the north gate, preparing to leave

Vanyareign and join the army waiting in formation in the fields on either side of Spara's Trail just outside the capital, a group of commoners armed with pitchforks and makeshift pikes blocked the path ahead.

"My Regent," a middle-aged man with a balding head and a tanned and wrinkled face said, stepping forward from the group, "We are but humble farmers and lay folk of the capital, but we request temporary enlistment with your army. We are prepared to lay down our lives in your name."

Regent Avrette pulled forward to address the group. "My dear friends. I thank you for your allegiance. I ride out to meet my cousin in the spirit of peace and reason. While I may call upon you to serve the crown yet, today I ask you return to your homesteads, keep your families safe and warm, and pray to the gods that our parley be a success. There is no victory in war, only loss. While I am prepared to see this to whatever end the fates have in store for us, I will meet my cousin in good faith as I hope he intends to meet me."

"As you wish, Regent," the man said, looking back at his band of would-be warriors, "We shall abide by your wishes and disperse. Should you need what little support we can provide, we ask that the heralds blow their horns thrice."

"As all here are my witness, I promise you this out of respect for your bravery and love of the crown."

The man bowed, turned to his fellow commoners. "Head to your homes as the regent commands. Stay vigilant and listen for the heralds' call. We regroup here once beckoned. Until then, pray to the gods for peace."

Some in the group scowled, while others sighed in relief. The crowd dispersed, clearing the path for the regent's procession to continue through the north gate and out to the fields.

Cries of support yielded to the riotous sounds of the queen's army as the procession crested a ridge and the troops received their regent. Weapon to shield, they applauded their regent, sister of their fallen king.

Regent Avrette left her procession behind and rode up onto a berm along Spara's Trail that provided her the best view of the entire field. She held her hand in the air and the army fell silent, a cloud of fog thrown to the air with every breath.

"We gather here today, not as a show of force, but as a sign of our commitment to our kingdom and its sovereign ruler, the king's heir, Queen Turin Forene. We shall turn the army of Winterashe back with reason, rather than blade. Their numbers may be vast, but it pales in comparison to our resolve. May the gods look over us all."

The army roared as the regent spun her horse and motioned her procession to the front of their ranks.

"Impassioned, Regent Avrette," one of her generals said, falling in behind her.

"Thank you, General," the regent said. "Let's hope that passion is enough."

CHAPTER 38

I did not possess the will to let the poor fool leave empty-handed. As a parting gift, I gave a clue too easy and bequeathed a handful of apple seeds.

—*Entry from Aldresor's Journal*
Undated. Discovered in the Tower of Is' Savon, month of Riet,
1444 AT

Regent Avrette felt the army of Winterashe before its front line broke the horizon. The earth trembled outside Vanyareign's gates as they approached from the northwest. She sat upon her white stallion, her cape flapping in the persistent breeze, running over in her mind what she would say to her cousin should he agree to meet her for discussion.

It wasn't until she saw the opposing force that she felt the pang of nerves wash over her. Their masses were so vast; they stretched back for as far as the eye could see and just as wide. Led by a procession of war mammoths, some of their ranks rode bears, while others still favored winter wolves. Behind them, countless soldiers came to a halt, sending an eerie quiet through the afternoon air. The regent's horse whinnied.

"By the gods, how did he amass such a force?" She asked

Talus, staring ahead, her hands gripping her reins as though they were her tether to the earth, her knees clattering against the sides of her horse. "Safe to say, Tyveriel has seen nothing like it."

"Have faith, Jenta," Talus said, "At least there are no giants among them."

She turned to Talus and smiled, finding his sarcasm disarming. "Gather the other generals, you will ride at my back to the meeting point. Give us some space, though, I want to appeal to him on an individual level. As equal members of the Forene bloodline."

"As you wish."

Talus spun Maelstrom around and fell in line with his peers. Regent Avrette prodded her stallion forward, taking a cursory glance at the Barrow's Pact.

She led her generals to neutral ground, monitoring King Ulest as he climbed down from his mammoth and motioned to the Three and the Orc chieftain, Yardish the Violator, to join him. They gathered at four steeds adorned with red saddles and matching cruppers, and rode toward the regent and her generals in the open field between their two armies.

Talus and the other generals stopped short of the meeting point, giving their regent the freedom she had requested. Roen, Myka, Veien, and Yardish did the same. King Ulest and Regent Avrette slowly approached each other. Roen nodded to Talus, put his horse into a trot, veering around the convening monarchs, and approached the group of generals. Regent Avrette's gaze followed his path, and she paused to listen.

"Travelers from Travesty, was it?" Roen asked Talus sardonically as he neared. His breath hung in the air.

Talus smiled. "Lord Roen, how nice to see you again. I must apologize for our lack of candor when we last met. You must understand we thought it ill-conceived to tell you we had come from Windswept. Would you have believed we were not, at that time, in the king's employ? The same king that now lays interred beside his forefathers at the hands of one of your thugs. Garrus, I believe its name was."

Roen curled his lip. "It seems apologies are in order on both sides, Sir?"

"Jochen. Talus Jochen."

"Yes, Sir Jochen. I assure you, I deployed Garrus to Castle Forene only to ferret out what we correctly suspected was yet another breech of Winterashe's sovereignty at the hands of King Arving. He had no orders to harm the king or anyone for that matter."

"That isn't what the doppelganger told us after its subsequent attempt on Regent Avrette."

"Coercion, I'm sure. I knew nothing of his daily activities, but it doesn't surprise me he would try to finish a job he considered incomplete. Garrus was thorough in everything he set his minds to. The last we heard from him was when he notified us of King Arving's death before escaping to Wethryn."

"Well," Talus said, "should this meeting have a successful outcome, I hope we may find good stead with one another."

"Yes, and if it doesn't, I hope we may find each other on the battlefield."

"Roen," King Ulest said. "Fall in line."

"As you wish, uncle." Roen pulled his horse into a spin, a bleat of steam billowing from its nostrils, and returned to his sisters and Yardish to await the outcome of the parley.

Regent Avrette continued forward and halted her steed ten feet from King Ulest.

"You have traveled a long way, cousin," the regent said, dismounting her stallion, "and have amassed quite the formidable army. Thank you for agreeing to meet with me as I proposed. I hope we may find common ground."

King Ulest sat upon his horse for a moment and then climbed down. "I intend to abide by the Fracture, Jenta. While I am sorry for the loss of your brother, and hold you in high regard, I have a legitimate claim to the Raptor's Throne, and I intend to make good on that claim."

"And I would honor that claim with no resistance were it not for Shale having sired an heir just weeks before your monster so brutally murdered him."

"What do you mean, my monster? Was it not your own general?" King Ulest nodded toward Talus. "The one known as Talus Jochen?"

"So it was meant to look. We uncovered the truth, however, when a doppelganger named Garrus was caught in the act in an attempt on my own life."

King Ulest gritted his teeth. "Jenta, I had nothing to do with any of that. I would never sanction violence against another Forene. You must believe me."

"I do. I cannot, however, say I hold the same faith in your nephew. The doppelganger told us he followed Roen's explicit orders."

King Ulest glared over his shoulder at Roen. When he turned back to Jenta his eyes were balls of fire. He exhaled as though the breath pained him. He smiled. "I have no justification for his actions. I shall personally hold him accountable. It would seem his generation only sees the distance between us. Not our close bond of history. Now, what of this heir?"

"It came as a surprise to me, but she bares the Mark of Forene. The Elders Syndicate has named her queen, and I am to be her regent until she is old enough to assume her rightful station."

King Ulest bit his bottom lip and stared to the ground. "A daughter? That is most unexpected. How does it feel to no longer be the only female child in our bloodline to live longer than a month?"

"I don't concern myself with such petty things, Vred. I am pleased the Forene bloodline holds strong. I will always serve Evelium any way the gods see fit."

"I will need to see the child if I am to verify the validity of your claim. If I am satisfied that she is Shale's rightful heir, you have my word that my army will return to Winterashe."

"I welcome you to meet her. Just as I assume you would not find comfort in accompanying me to Castle Forene, I surely will not bring a helpless child out into a field between two armies. I have arranged for her mother to bring her to the Kormaic Temple this evening at sunset. I invite you there with a small entourage to inspect the child with clergy and the Elders Syndicate as witness. I assure the safety of you and your companions while within the city. Unfortunately, I cannot extend the invitation to the Three."

"I can only agree to these terms if you allow my security detail safe passage and access to the temple before I am to arrive."

"Of course," Regent Avrette said, "Until tonight then."

King Ulest nodded and climbed back upon his horse, turning it toward his army.

"Jenta," he said, looking back over his shoulder, "should this be some kind of ruse, I shall take the Raptor's Throne by any means necessary. You will not deny me my right."

"Understood," the regent said, "I'm certain it won't come to that."

She mounted her stallion and returned to her generals, her stomach churning inside her. She did not take pause at their side but continued past them toward her assembled forces. All was silent as they awaited her address. She gave none, only to stop at Naivara's side to speak with the Barrow's Pact as she rode from the open field.

"He accepted an introduction to Turin at the temple tonight at sundown. Please make all the necessary arrangements. I would like the Barrow's Pact to guarantee the safety of both my cousin's security detail and that of my cousin and his entourage this evening. Our sovereignty depends on this all going well. Talus and the generals will inform the ranks where we currently stand."

"As you wish," Gromley said. "We'll make certain everything

goes as planned."

Regent Avrette nodded and set her stallion into a gallop toward Castle Forene.

▲

"By the grace of Mela, we pray for a peaceful resolution to the conflict at hand. May those from Winterashe who now seek to wage war at our doorstep find the courage to welcome amity between us and return to their loved ones in the north. May our regent's words and actions guide them toward pacifism. Divided, we are all but grains of soil, while together we build Kalmindon's gardens."

"Thank you, your holiness" Regent Avrette said to the priest beside her. She sat rigidly in the first pew of the temple, awaiting King Ulest's arrival. The regent stared at the large gold triangle hanging from the rafters, wanting nothing more than for this evening to be over with her cousin convinced of Turin's claim to the throne. Only then could she turn her attention to the reported dragon attacks in the west.

Across the width of the transept, the rest of the temple's clergy stood dutifully in their midnight-blue robes, each holding a candle in folded hands before them. They moved so little, from afar, one could confuse them for statues. The Elders Syndicate sat toward the back of the nave, whispering to one another, likely deciding how to best shift their allegiance should the evening's events not satisfy Vred Ulest, and he nullified the Fracture.

As the setting sun lit the western windows of the temple ablaze, the oversized copper doors—patinaed with age—swung open. Everyone but Regent Avrette turned their attention from their disparate activities to the moment at hand.

King Ulest was the first to enter, followed by Yardish, Kob'Anni and a bevy of guards who wore heavy blackened armor covered with red tunics with a winter wolf's head on the chest. Behind them came the Barrow's Pact, Talus, and the other three generals of the queen's army.

The doors closed and they approached the chancel, coming to a halt beside Regent Avrette and the priest.

"I see we are all here but the child. What of her?" King Ulest's tone was cold, impatient.

"I shall call for her now that all are present," Regent Avrette said, standing to face her cousin in the central aisle, before the symbol of the creator gods. "I am glad to see you brought your Fate to verify her authenticity. I am looking forward to having this behind us."

She nodded to a monk standing at the far side of the transept, who walked into the shadows of the chapel and opened a door within. Candlelight flooded the dark recesses of the side aisle. When he returned, Alessa followed him, and cradled Turin in her arms. They walked up to the chancel and stood behind the altar.

The rest of the clergy members spanning the transept divided into two groups and turned to create a pathway up to the altar.

"Shall we?" Regent Avrette asked, motioning toward the altar.

"Indeed," King Ulest said, as Regent Avrette led him up the stairs. Kob'Anni and Yardish followed close behind.

The rest of the attendants followed suit, until the Elders Syndicate, the Barrows Pact, and a smattering of clergy, and Winterashe guards all surrounded the altar.

Alessa held Turin close to her chest, soothing the child with delicate whispers and bouncing her gently. Turin cooed.

"King Vred Ulest of Winterashe, may I present Queen Turin Forene of Evelium," Regent Avrette said, breaking the silence.

"Forene," King Ulest said, "We have come full circle. It is a powerful name. One I hope she can live up to."

Alessa hesitated for a moment, placed Turin on the center of the altar, unwrapped her blanket, and rolled her over to present the Mark of Forene. The moment King Ulest laid eyes on her, he stepped back, his eyes narrowing at the unexpected sight.

"The Grey Queen," a guard said, "The legend is true."

"Don't be a fool," Kob'Anni said with a croak, stepping in for a closer look. She reached out with a gnarled finger and ran a yellowed nail over the birthmark. "Yes, this child's skin is grey, and she is most definitely a queen, but she is not the Grey Queen. She has been touched by the gods. Most rare and beautiful."

Alessa smiled at the atypical compliment.

"My King," Kob'Anni said, "she has Modig Forene's blood in her. She is the rightful heir to the Raptor's Throne. She will grow up to be the greatest leader Evelium has ever seen. I saw her long reign unfold before me when I touched the mark."

"Very well," King Ulest said, "The Fracture remains intact."

He took another step back, still looking at Turin laying on the altar, helpless.

"I did not come here just to turn around and walk home," Yardish said. The Orc chieftain's lips curled and he pulled a kukri knife from his belt. He swung the curved blade down upon Turin.

"Yardish, no!" King Ulest lunged for the Orc chieftain, but Kob'Anni stood between them and was slow to react. King Ulest knocked the witch from his path, sending her faltering backward into one of his guards, but too late.

Gromley tackled Yardish and both tumbled over a stone chair at the side of the chancel into the shadows, Yardish's tarnished blade stuck in space an inch from Turin's chest.

Everyone drew their weapons. Talus came to Alessa's side and knocked the knife away so she could scoop Turin from the altar. The infant's eyes glowed gold in the candle light. Clergy scattered for cover as the two sides squared off, Shadow running to Gromley's aid.

"Nicholas," he said as he came upon Yardish. The Orc's eyes were red with rage as he kneeled over Gromley's body and plunged a second kukri into his chest with wild abandon.

Hearing Shadow's approach, Yardish rolled from Gromley and jumped to his feet. The first of Shadow's daggers buried itself in Yardish's torso. Yardish deflected the second dagger with a deft swipe of his blade, sending it to the floor.

Nicholas dove to Gromley's side as Shadow maintained Yardish's attention. Shadow's daggers returned to his hands just as Yardish slashed at him, parrying the strike and countering. As another dagger found Yardish's abdomen, a blade burst through the Orc chieftain's chest from behind. Amber light poured forth as blood ran from Yardish's mouth. The fire in his eyes faded with his life and he fell to the ground. King Ulest tore Tedarrin free of Yardish's body.

King Ulest sheathed his sword. "Jenta," he said, motioning for his escorts to follow his lead and cover their blades, "the Orc took that despicable action of his own accord. We have no interest in harming Queen Turin. I would hope my actions here prove that point."

"Take the queen back to Castle Forene," the regent said to Talus, "Alessa, please stay in your quarters until our visitors have left the city."

Talus took Alessa's hand and led her back through the door through which she had entered the sanctuary. As the door closed behind them, Regent Avrette turned to her cousin and returned her rapiers to their scabbards. "How dare you bring that beast before the Queen of Evelium," she said through gritted teeth, "You should choose your bedfellows more carefully, cousin. Consider yourself lucky the gods favor her and the weapons of man pose her no threat. I hope you pray to the gods for saving her life and yours."

It wasn't until the tensions eased that Queen Avrette heard Nicholas weeping from the shadows. The Barrow's Pact ran to where Nicholas sat beside Gromley's lifeless body, Nicholas's hands on Gromley's forehead. The ruby ring on Nicholas's right hand pulsed. Shadow stood behind him, his face buried in his hands, shaking at the sight of his closest friend dead on the cold stone floor. He dropped to his knees. Laudin ran over to him.

Naivara turned to the priest who had been sitting beside the regent before the contingent from Winterashe had arrived. Tears ran down her freckled face. "Is there not a more powerful healer among you? And what of you, witch?"

"He's gone, Naivara," Nicholas said between sobs, "There is no healer that could bring him back to us now."

Naivara's eyes lit aflame, her hands turned red as glowing coals. "See what you have all done with your petty politics?" She lashed out at the room. "You are all guilty of taking from this world one of its truly good men. An angel among devils. And when he may very well be among the last of the Zeristar. May you all rot in Pragarus for this transgression."

The circlet she wore glowed a vibrant green. A fiery aura grew around her and then a thunderous crash shook the temple. Naivara's burgeoning spell faded, and the temple shook again as rocks crashed to the ground in the distance. Silence reigned for a moment. The gathering looked at each other wide-eyed. Then there was a blood-curdling roar.

The group ran out of the temple into the streets of Vanyareign. The city was in a state of frenzy as people clambered in all directions. Castle Forene loomed against a dusky sky, one of its towers destroyed, fires ablaze. Two enormous dragons circled above the fallen tower and took turns strafing the castle.

Vanyareign was under attack.

CHAPTER 39

The lesser gods followed Vaila in her retreat to Kalmindon. They left with their disciples the gift of Suffusion. It remains unknown if Vaila did the same.

—*The Gatekeeper's Abridged History of Tyveriel*
Vol. 1, Chapter 50 – Unearthed from the Ruins of Meriden, the month of Anar, 1217 AT

—▲—

Nicholas joined the others out in the street. Smoke billowed from Castle Forene into the night sky.

"Are those—"

"Dragons," Regent Avrette said. "We had heard reports of an attack on the Isle of the Twelve Mines, but with your army marching on Vanyareign, I had no time to give the matter the attention it deserved. Not in my wildest dreams did I suspect they would come directly to the capital."

"The armies are exposed, and ill-equipped for such an onslaught," King Ulest said. "I will call on my Wyvern Riders to rally against them. With your Eagle's Wing at their side, there is a possibility we can stave off the attack. At least until we can mount a proper defense."

"It might be the best chance we have," Regent Avrette said.

"Then, we will return to our camp and organize the counterattack."

"I'll go with you," Laudin said, "You don't know this city as I do. It may be the difference between you getting your riders in the air or not."

"The rest of us will get to the castle and do the same, although, I fear it will not hold up to a direct assault for much longer." Regent Avrette said as a spire crumbled behind the outer battlement.

"Where's Shadow?" Nicholas asked, his stomach an empty pit. He weighed the horrors of Gromley lying dead in the temple behind him and the dragons' attack on Castle Forene overhead. He was unsure how much more he could bear.

"He must still be inside with Gromley," Laudin said. "We will need him, Nicholas— go find him."

"And the queen?" Naivara asked.

"Talus will get her to safety," Regent Avrette said, "He is trained for these moments and holds her well-being as paramount. Trying to find them amid this mayhem would waste precious time. We must hurry."

Nicholas nodded, ran back into the temple.

Shadow sat near Gromley's body, his feet splayed wide, his back propped against a stone pillar. His face shrouded by the shadow cast from the hood of his cloak, he held a dagger by the blade in clasped hands.

"Shadow?" Nicholas approached cautiously. "We need to go. Dragons are attacking the capital. We will need you to help get the regent to safety."

Shadow hung his head.

"I know you feel this loss more than any of us. I can only imagine what it would be like if I were to lose Nathaniel. But there is nothing we can do for Gromley and he would want us to protect Jenta and to fight these dragons that razed his homeland. He will be in excellent hands with the temple clergy until we may return to him."

"You're right. I know you're right." Shadow sheathed his dagger, pushed his hood back, and smoothed his hair with shaking hands. "Don't let them leave him here on the floor with that animal, though. He deserves better."

"Of course." Nicholas extended a hand and helped Shadow to his feet.

Nicholas took a moment with the clergy and requested they see to Gromley's proper care. He then returned to Shadow who stood transfixed on the body of their fallen friend. Together, they left the temple and rejoined the others.

The group proceeded to the north gates where they parted ways with Laudin leading the team from Winterashe back out into the fields, while the rest rode up King's Way toward Castle Forene and into the dragons' attack.

Rocks cascaded down from the crumbling spires above as the dragons continued their assault on the castle's ballista positions. The burgeoning night sky was lit aflame in a display of green and purple salvos that flickered between clouds of smoke. The ballistae returned fire, hurling huge bolts into the air in rapid succession which forced the dragons back from the castle and out over the city. With the dragons distracted, giant eagles took flight and chased Silyarithe above the cloud line.

Regent Avrette led the charge up King's Way, winding around Mount Orys while dodging debris strewn across the road from above. The party nearing the castle, Mesorith dropped into a dive and headed toward them.

"We're exposed out here," Shadow said, pointing to the approaching dracolich.

Naivara stood on her mount's back, dove off the side of Mount Orys, and polymorphed into a gold dragon. She lifted into the air to intercept the massive undead dragon. She met him claw-to-claw and they spiraled through the sky like eagles sparring in mid-flight. Thrown off course, Mesorith snapped at the unexpected adversary, sinking his moldered fangs into Naivara's brilliant gold scales. Reeling, Naivara countered, and took a chunk of putrescent flesh from Mesorith's side. Mesorith lifted Naivara's smaller dragon form into the air, the two locked in a bloody embrace.

Naivara raked at Mesorith's chest with her knife-like claws, tearing away his physical form. As their arc crested amongst the clouds, she exhaled a noxious cloud of gas into Mesorith's face. For a moment, he faltered but shrugged off its effects, and held Naivara in his grasp. The lich roared in anger and bit Naivara on the neck. He reared back, a grim sneer on his face, and bit into her neck again, delivering her dragon form a mortal blow. She returned to her Reshinta form, slipped from his claws, and tumbled toward the castle courtyard below, destined to break upon the inner battlements.

The rest of the party reached the bailey as the guards hurried to close the portcullis gate behind them. Nicholas and Shadow stared to the heavens, trained on the events above. They watched as Naivara's gold dragon form disappeared.

"Get the regent into the castle," Nicholas said, "I'll get Naivara and meet you in the throne room."

Shadow nodded, jumped from his horse, and grabbed Regent Avrette by the hand. They dashed to the castle entrance and Shadow banged furiously on the gilded doors which someone had barricaded against the assault. "Let us in, you fools. I am with the regent."

Two guards opened the doors and allowed them entrance.

"Nicholas and Naivara will be right behind us," Shadow said, pointing to Nicholas, who watched from beside the horses. "Stay ready to let them in." The doors slammed shut behind Shadow, who was staring back at Nicholas.

Nicholas craned his neck, noticing Naivara's decent had hastened. His friend's unconscious body tumbled head over foot to the earth. Nicholas held out his ring and waited, watching her fall. As soon as she was within his range, he murmured a few words to himself and a portal opened before him. He jumped within the swirling black gate, appearing at an identical gate just below Naivara. He grabbed her by the arm as she plummeted past him, her momentum ripping him from the portal toward the battlement below. He pulled her close, cast the spell again, and a new gate appeared beneath them. They fell into the gate and seconds later tumbled out of a last gate into the courtyard.

They slid across the bailey and crashed against the stone façade of the castle wall. Nicholas scrambled to his feet and ran to Naivara's side. "I will not lose two of you tonight," he said, dropping to his knees and laying his hands upon Naivara's forehead. His ring pulsed, a light grew beneath his hands, and he willed Naivara back to consciousness.

She startled awake, pushed herself up and against the wall. "You're okay, but we have to get inside," Nicholas said, placing his hands on her bloodied face. "We aren't safe out here. Can you walk?"

"I think so." Naivara grimaced, rolled to her knees. "The dragon I intercepted is undead and far too strong for me to counter."

Red-hot rocks rained down upon them from above. The age-old bristlecone pine at the center of the great lawn burst into flames as Nicholas helped Naivara to her feet and led their run for the castle door. The guards opened the doors for them as Shadow had instructed. Nicholas gave one last look at the dragons overhead. Ushering Naivara to the relative safety of the castle, he helped the guards close and barricade the doors behind them.

▲

Laudin wove his way through the intertwined armies, who were no longer concerned with one another, but instead prepared for the inevitable onslaught from the skies overhead. King Ulest, his guards trailing close behind, pushed through the morass toward the remnants of the Winterashe camp.

They came upon Roen, who shouted at the top of his lungs

for the army to maintain its formation. Myka and Veien stood amid the chaos with blank expressions on their faces as if unaffected by the threat.

King Ulest waved for the Three to join him and charged into the center of camp. They passed empty tents and approached a group of soldiers tending to manticores. The beasts paced back and forth, caterwauling and testing the thick iron chains that bound them each to a large boulder.

The head of the manticore brigade ran to King Ulest, his troops standing at attention beside their mounts. The spent spines of his beast covered his helmet, he carried a crossbow slung across his shoulder. "My Lord," he said, "We await your orders."

"Muster your troops. You are to join up with the Eagle's Wing to draw the dragons away from the capital—at least until we can prepare a reasonable ground defense."

"Join the Eagle's Wing, my Lord?"

"Yes, we are to work together against the dragons. I have no interest in seeing Vanyareign razed to the ground. We are all one people, after all."

"As you wish." The manticore rider ran to his beast and unhooked its collar from the chain that restrained it. "Manticore Riders, to the skies," he said, raising his crossbow into the air, "We ride to the defense of Vanyareign and fight alongside our brothers of the Eagle's Wing."

The men each unleashed their manticores and climbed upon their backs. The leader spurred his manticore, eliciting a fierce roar and setting it into motion. In three unrestrained bounds the manticore was at full speed—the others close behind—and lifted into the air. In formation, they spiraled upward into the smoke-choked evening sky.

From the ground, Laudin, King Ulest, and Roen watched as Mesorith noticed the assault and barrel rolled toward them, Silyarithe preoccupied with the final ballista tower. As the dracolich swept in on the squadron, a streak of light arced across the sky and collided with him with such force the shock wave it released rattled buildings across the capital. The impact sent Mesorith careening into the side of Castle Forene, destroying a section of the inner battlement and falling from the sky.

"What, in the name of the gods, was that?" Roen asked. "I've never seen anything deliver such a forceful blow."

Laudin shook his head. "I'm not sure. And, it doesn't matter as long as it's attacking the dragons."

Freed from Mesorith's advance, the Wyvern Riders joined with the Eagle's Wing, who swarmed Silyarithe, diverting her attention from the castle. They circled her immense form, like gnats too small to swat. She lifted into the air and dropped chunks of the castle's façade from her claws upon Mount Orys below. Out of the ballistae's reach, she beat the annoyance back with her wings and breathed searing plasma into their ranks.

With a resounding roar, she flew into the night sky and abandoned their siege. Manticore and eagle alike orbited the castle in unexpected victory, both armies below cheering them on in celebration.

The blights came from the Wistful Timberlands to the west and the Morion Swamp to the north under cover of darkness while the armies' attention was focused on the burning spires of Castle Forene. The first volley came without notice and thousands of rough-hewn spears rained out of the night sky upon unsuspecting soldiers. Droves of those donning leathers were impaled while the spears shattered on impact upon those more heavily armored.

Screams rang out across the battlefield. As a second volley approached, soldiers turned to meet the new aggressors and deflected many of the inbound spears with their shields.

The glow of the blights' inner lights became visible as they traversed the fields, a sea of hundreds of thousands. Some carried Will-O'-Wisps in woven soul cages upon their shoulders. The clamber of their numbers drowned out the screams of the injured and dying as they drove toward the armies of man in unbridled pursuit.

"Turn the siege engines," King Ulest said, trying to bring order to the surrounding chaos, "Douse the payloads in oil and light them afire."

Laudin dodged a spear from yet another volley. To his astonishment, another passed through Veien and inflicted no damage.

"We have our secrets as well," Roen said.

Laudin drew his bow and pulled a red-shafted arrow from his quiver. He loosed the arrow into the first throng of blights to cross the River Torrent. Mid-flight, the arrow turned to flame and struck a bulky knotted blight in its torso. Consumed by fire, the blight stumbled into those next to it, their dry bodies ignited like tinder.

A second wave trampled the fallen and snuffed out the fire as the blights continued their charge.

"Laudin." Roen grabbed the ranger by the shoulder as he nocked another arrow. "We must fall back. There are too many of them."

Laudin let one more arrow fly and he ran after the others.

CHAPTER 40

On that night, watching the sky burn, all I could think about was surviving to see Avanla and the children once more. Without them, there would be no point to any of this.

—Entry from the Diary of Vred Ulest
Dated 8th of Prien, 903 AF. Unearthed from the Ruins of Ohteira, month of Lusta, 1399 AT

—▲—

Umhra landed in Castle Forene's courtyard and allowed his wings to recede. He summoned Forsetae to his hand. Mesorith flailed, trying to right himself among the rubble his impact with the inner battlement had strewn across the grounds. He shook his head and came to focus on the half-Orc who brazenly stood before him. Mesorith hissed and released a torrent of acid at his foe.

The ground was scorched around him, the green fumes a shock of color in the night, Umhra emerged from the miasma unscathed. His rhodium armor had coalesced around him one diamond-shaped scale at a time.

Mesorith snarled and slunk sideways, taking on a feline quality as he assessed this flying half-Orc in gleaming armor. He inhaled, drawing Umhra's scent within.

I know this one. Forsetae said. *I have tasted his blood. In life, he was known as the mighty Mesorith, Liege of Chaos. Now he stands before us undead.*

Umhra smiled. Dragons might be a Mystics weakness, but the undead were a Paladin's strength.

"You are not mortal," Mesorith said, choking on his words. "But you are no god. A Mystic . . . how quaint."

"It would seem you are trapped between the realms of the living and the dead as well, Mesorith."

"Perceptive, at least. More than I can say for the rest of your kind." Mesorith whipped his tail out. Umhra ducked beneath the attack and raked Forsetae across the spiny scales that narrowly missed him. Mesorith hissed, a deep black ichor erupted from the wound.

"Your blade, champion. I have felt its sting before, although it looks different in your hand than it did in Telsidor's when I allowed him to believe he slayed me."

"I am happy to give you a closer look," Umhra said. He charged forward with enhanced speed.

Mesorith swatted with his fore claws. Umhra jumped over the first and slid beneath the second. He leaped at Mesorith's chest and plunged Forsetae deep within his torso. The dracolich reared up, beat its tattered wings. The gale that ensued threw Umhra from his perch. Forsetae dissipated. He slid across the ground and crashed into the castle's façade. Mesorith lifted into the air to escape.

Umhra climbed to his feet and ran after the mighty undead dragon. Wings sprouted from his back and he soared upward to place himself above the decrepit beast. Clearing the castle grounds, he calmed his mind and imposed himself into the surrounding space. He released a thunderous force from within.

The concussion from the blast hit Mesorith and sent him tumbling to the Burning Wood below. Mesorith crashed, throwing dirt, rock, and splintered trees into the air. The collision left a gouge in the terrain. Umhra touched down beside the impact crater and surveyed the destruction.

The trench ran deep and wide through the middle of the Burning Wood, the white birch trees and red foliage that once reigned with ubiquity were now a broken, tangled landscape. From the cloud of dust hanging in the air came a blast of acid. Umhra dove backward among the scattered debris, just out of reach.

"You are a fool," Mesorith said, his lips curling. "No Mystic has ever survived combat with a dragon, let alone the great Mesorith. It is only a matter of time until I devour you and get on with my imperative."

He brushed a stand of shattered trees aside with a swat of his claw and charged into the pile of debris behind which Umhra had dove. The dragon tore into the mound, throwing debris from his mouth in a frenzy. "Come out and face me, Mystic."

Umhra slipped along the back side of the wreckage, keeping a watchful eye on Mesorith through the uprooted trees and twisted undergrowth. He emerged behind the dracolich, Forsetae once again in hand and blue ether wafting from the gaps in his armor. "You are right, oh Liege of Chaos," he said, "No Mystic has ever survived an encounter with a dragon. But you are no dragon—just the undead shell of one—and I not only a Mystic but a Paladin of Vaila."

Mesorith spun to face him and roared. Umhra held out his hand. The air rippled between them and held Mesorith in place.

Unable to move, Mesorith struggled to free himself from the spell, and thrashed violently within its confines.

"My daughter will peel the skin from your body and savor every moment as she devours you. This death, too, is only temporary. Nothing will stop me from ridding this world of the plague that is mankind."

End him now. Forsetae said. *The daughter he speaks of returns.*

Umhra bound toward Mesorith and leaped into the air,

landing on the crest of Mesorith's head. He thrust Forsetae into his skull and pierced his putrid brain. A second strike elicited a shrill, mournful wail and sent the ancient dracolich to the ground, its physical form shuddering.

Umhra braced himself against the screech. He dropped to one knee as he jumped down from the monster and landed beside it. Calling upon his god, he summoned a pure-white light from the heavens and focused it on Mesorith. The flesh sloughed away, the bones beneath turned to ash, and a mote of purple energy drifted into the air.

Umhra sat back, exhausted and allowed his armor and Forsetae to fade. His focus broadened from the scourge he had just dispatched, allowing the sounds of war coming from the northern side of the city to garner his attention. He stood, his chest heaving, and readied himself to return to battle but an unnatural breeze picked up around him. The swirl of air gathered leaves and other remnants of the Burning Wood and took the familiar shape of his god.

"Umhra, my champion," Vaila said, her voice wavering. "You shall find him upon my altar. He needs you more than the others. Go to him now and he will be your most loyal disciple."

"Of whom do you speak?" Umhra asked as he approached the tempest. "I don't seek nor want followers."

"He is upon my altar. You will need him before long. He will act as your conduit as you act as mine. He needs you, now. Go to him and bring him under your wing."

"People are dying—I can help them first."

"No, he is running out of time. He is your priority, your responsibility. You made that promise to each of them."

"Who?" Umhra's voice faltered, betraying his concern.

"He is upon my altar," Vaila said. The leaves fell to the ground and left the woods in silence.

A nascent thrumming returned to Umhra's right ear and drew him back toward the capital to the altar Vaila spoke of. He crouched, one knee nearly touching the ground. His wings sprouted from his back and he leaped into the air. He followed the growing rhythm in his head back over Vanyareign until he reached the Kormaic Temple where the pulse grew so loud, he landed in the city streets out of fear he might lose consciousness.

The streets were empty, a light rain wetting the cobblestone but posing no threat to the fires that raged throughout the embattled capital. Umhra looked toward the north gate beyond which the cacophony of a great battle called to him. He turned to the temple doors before him. The clergy had left the doors unlocked, having neglected to secure them in their rush to get to the undercroft.

Inside, candles still flickered, although most of them neared the end of their lives. Otherwise, the nave was empty. Umhra walked the length of the center aisle toward the altar where a body laid, wrapped in an ochre shroud which the clergy had bound with gold rope. Each candle he passed fluttered in his presence. He ascended the four stairs. A hollowness filled him as he wondered to whom the body belonged.

The rhythm in his ear abruptly stopped. He untied the rope. He drew the shroud back to reveal a pallid face. He clenched his jaw as a great anger welled up inside him. His lips and nose quivered into a grimace. He inhaled and centered himself, calming his rageful mind.

"Gromley," he whispered. A hot tear ran down his cheek. He grabbed Gromley's cold hand in his and pressed his forehead against the fallen cleric's chest. Cold metal. Gold, to be precise. His amulet, imbued with Anar's essence, had not withered as Balris's had when the devils struck him down in Meriden two years ago. Indiscernible though it may be, there was life in Gromley yet.

Umhra wiped the tears from his face and gripped Gromley's amulet in one hand and his own in the other. He closed his eyes and focused on his own life force. He connected with the power that had grown within him with each Waystone's strength he inherited. A nascent warmth spread from his hand up through his arm and flooded his entire body.

The walls of the temple drew in upon them, flexing to Umhra's will. He allowed his life force to flow between them, the two icons glowing in his hands. The warmth grew into a searing heat, almost unbearable.

Releasing his grip, he stepped back from Gromley and the walls of the temple pushed outward and returned to their natural shape. The immense stained glass windows that lined the nave shattered into the streets of Vanyareign. He turned, reaching out his hands and grabbed the colorful shards in his mind and held them in place. He envisioned them coming back together, reforming the beauty that had graced the temple's walls. The shards followed his vision and found their rightful place within their leaded frames. The heat coursing through Umhra's body faded.

"I had the strangest dream," Gromley said, his voice dry and weak.

Umhra returned to his side, smiled as the color bloomed in his friend's face, and helped Gromley sit upon the altar.

"I crossed over. Stood before Vaila, herself. She said you were coming for me to fulfill your promise. That there was more for me left on Tyveriel."

"It was no dream, my friend."

"Then, you brought me back? Only a god can do such things, Umhra. How did you?"

"Ivory's book referred to instances where a Mystic was capable of revivifying a worthy soul by sharing their own life force. I noticed your amulet still intact and willed you back to life by giving you a piece of my life force."

Gromley looked down at the sun-shaped amulet around his neck. Where it had been gold, it was now platinum, a pyramid relief at its center. He shut his eyes.

"I've changed," he said, "I am more than what I once was and yet somehow less."

"I am yet to understand how things like this work," Umhra

said, "I can only imagine there must be some cost to cheating death. Possibly, a little of you was left behind when you returned. Regardless, it seems preferable to the alternative."

Gromley nodded and got to his feet. "So, what comes next?" He faltered, but caught himself on the edge of the altar.

"Earlier tonight, Vanyareign came under attack by a grey dragon and the lich of Mesorith. I dispatched the lich—at least for now. North of the city, I heard what sounded like a great battle. Vaila compelled me to come to you first before I could find out more. I know not what awaits us in the fields."

"The armies of Vanyareign and Winterashe gather there. The last I remember, King Ulest approved of the new queen. I hope something didn't lead the two sides toward battle in my absence."

"The new queen?"

"That's right—you've missed much. King Arving was murdered, and the Elders Syndicate has named his infant heir queen with Jenta as her regent. It's a long story."

"Another time, then. We must head to the fields and put an end to this madness."

Gromley agreed and stood without support from the altar. He crossed the room, slowly at first, and walked to the dark recesses beyond the chancel. Umhra followed closely, not yet convinced Gromley's strength had returned in full. In a small chapel they found a pool of blood. Beside it lay Gromley's war hammer, and in the recess's corner, the body of Yardish.

"He got what he deserved, it seems," Gromley said, staring at the pool of blood. He felt for the puncture wounds in his stomach. He picked up his hammer and tested its weight in his hands. Where he gripped the weapon's shaft, the wood transformed into platinum. The precious metal spread up the shaft and over the hammer's head, refashioning itself into a weapon worthy of his new station.

"We must be on our way," Umhra said. "We have much to do."

Gromley nodded—his gaze returned to the stained floor for a moment—and then he followed Umhra out of the temple, toward the north gate, the sounds of warfare pervading the night sky.

CHAPTER 41

To my surprise, the gem turned out to be an Eketar egg. Quite likely the only of its kind, it has garnered a special place in my collection.

—*Entry from Aldresor's Journal*
Undated. Discovered in the Tower of Is' Savon, month of Riet, 1444 AT

The soldiers of Winterashe heaved boulders into place within the slings of their trebuchets. They soaked the boulders in oil and lit them aflame as King Ulest had instructed.

"Release," an Iminti general yelled from beneath a red steel helmet.

All at once, the soldiers threw the levers, and the counterweights swung free. Innumerable flaming spheres dotted the night sky, careening through the air and crashing into the horde of blights encroaching from the north. The ground lay strewn with the remains of twisted arboreal forms—broken and charred and smoldering—but their endless masses were undeterred.

The blights poured over one another, armed with crudely shaped spears, clubs, and stones. They overcame the fields—a sea of colorful orbs within their chests and eyes the only indication of their vast numbers.

With a new, more ominous threat incoming, the army of Vanyareign abandoned its standoff with those from Winterashe and turned toward a swarm to the west. Spears rained down on them and soldiers ran a trail of oil along their western flank and lit it on fire. A wall of flame ignited. The blights recoiled and gave the army time to ready their siege weaponry.

The archer corps of both armies merged at the rear of their repositioned formation, loosed flaming arrows into the blights' relentless advance. The older, more-gnarled of the woodland ranks ignited—thousands of animated infernos writhed in pain—as the arrows pierced their bark-like skin. "Fire at your own discretion," a human general of the queen's army said, as she coordinated efforts between both those from Winterashe and Vanyareign alike from atop a chestnut warhorse. "Let them think a new day dawns by the flames of our volleys."

The blight horde crashed headlong into the commingled armies. They barreled through the wall of fire where necessary despite the damage it inflicted on their own. The larger blights bludgeoned swaths of men with their great clubs and crushed others beneath their footfalls. Fresh growth consumed the fallen as the blights trudged forward. The smaller among them washed over the pike men that formed the front line. The blights tore armor and limb from the bodies of man and ran them through with crude spears. Those blights that were on fire willed themselves across the battlefield, grappled siege engines, and reduced them to tinder.

Behind the vanguard came the Soul Carriers, their bodies gnarled and covered in galls and lichens. They ambled onto the field, carrying Will-O'-Wisps in woven baskets over their shoulders. They crept amongst the dead and dying, waving the soul cages over each body. The Soul Carriers hovered over the dead for a moment, the Will-O'-Wisps' essence intensifying. They drew a mote of purple ether from each body's chest. The gobs of energy swirled as they drew closer to the wisps, which consumed them, and guaranteed the souls would never reach Kalmindon and give power to the gods of man.

Those unfortunate enough to still have life in them when the Soul Carriers came calling suffered greatly as the Will-O'-Wisps pulsed lightning into their sullied forms and sent them writhing to their untimely deaths. The wisps tore the souls from these bodies as well. They left only charred corpses behind and moved to the next victim.

A horn bellowed. Cavalry countered the attack, the fragile line in need of reinforcement. The mammoth riders of Winterashe were the first to heed the call, thundering into the front lines, soldiers diving out of their path. The mammoths trampled everything in their way as they charged. Splinters sprayed across the battlefield as their victims shattered beneath them. The blights' spears and clubs bounced off the mammoths' armor as blade-covered tusks thrashed through the chaos.

The winter wolves, bears, and horses followed. Their riders hacked at the innumerable enemies that ambled between them with battle axes and long swords. The winter wolves tore into the blights and made light work of their brittle physiques—the blights' internal glow dissipated when torn apart in fanged mouths.

Having driven the dragons off, the manticore and eagle riders that circled Castle Forene joined the battle, drawn by the trebuchet fire below. They dove out of the night sky, lifting the enemy into the air, tearing them apart and scattering some to the wind, while dropping others into the fires that raged throughout the battlefield.

No matter the valiant effort, more blights came; they were an endless supply of fodder that had grown for a millennia awaiting this auspicious opportunity. They dragged winter wolves and horses to the ground. They overcame even the mammoths with their sheer numbers, toppling the magnificent beasts and thrusting their spears into their soft underbellies.

They plucked manticores and eagles from the sky with club and rock. Their victory was inevitable.

The armies fell back to Vanyareign's towering walls. Laudin, having emptied his quiver, drew his scimitar and joined King Ulest and the Three in hand-to-hand combat. King Ulest and Roen fought back-to-back, Tedarrin bursting with a flash of amber light each time it drew life from the blights at King Ulest's hand.

Myka and Veien stood beside one another, unaffected by the death toll swelling around them. Blights passed through their incorporeal forms, turning a sickly black upon contact. The sisters smiled when each blight they touched was reduced to a pile of ash on the earth around them.

A cry of despair caught Laudin's ear. He spun to see a mammoth topple, a Winterashe soldier pinned beneath it. Blights surrounded him. Roen ran across the field, hurdling bodies as he dashed to the struggling man's side. The first two blights he took from behind, driving his sword through the first and taking the second's head off with a backhanded swipe of his blade. Laudin charged after him.

The remaining three blights turned to face Roen, chortling as they spread out, their spears at the ready. The first lunged. Roen's blade cut its spear in half. He spun and cleaved the creature across its torso. He came before the pinned soldier and took a defensive stance against the remaining two blights.

He parried the attack of the next, as yet another blight appeared upon the mammoth's body behind him and leaped down onto his back. The impact forced Roen to one knee. The two blights before him seized the opportunity to impale him with their spears.

Roen fell back against the mammoth beside the pinned soldier whose dead eyes stared up at him. Roen coughed up blood as Laudin took one blight to the ground with a swipe of his scimitar. He spun through the other two, ending them in one sweeping arc.

A Soul Carrier approached as Laudin dashed to Roen's aid. It waved its Will-O'-Wisp over the dead mammoth rider and relieved him of his soul. Roen tried to raise his sword, but the Will-O'-Wisp sent a surge of electricity into his chest, sending him writhing against the mammoth's matted hide.

The Soul Carrier turned to Roen and held the Will-O'-Wisp over him. Roen pushed back against the toppled mammoth, as if inches would matter, but the wisp made no further attempt at wresting the soul from his body. Its carrier hissed in contempt and the wisp sent another shock into Roen's charred and smoking form. Dissatisfied, the Soul Carrier moved on.

King Ulest came to Laudin's side and dropped to his knees. "No. How can this be?" He smeared the sweat-soaked hair from Roen's face and held him by the temples. He tried to stir Roen awake, but there was no response.

Laudin looked back to Myka and Veien. The ghostly figures stood on the battlefield as though lost among the frenzy of war. Their forms faded in and out, their tether to this world waning as their brother lay dying in their uncle's arms. Beyond them the beaming forms of Umhra and Gromley ran from the north gate onto the field. Laudin held his breath. A glimmer of hope amid enormous loss fluttered in his stomach. He made for his friends.

Laudin cut his way through the blights roving between them, grabbed Umhra, and spun him into a firm embrace. He then turned to Gromley and held him by the shoulders, a lump in his throat. "I don't know how you come to stand before me, but I can't express how happy I am that you are."

"Tell me that in the morning," Gromley said, surveying the battlefield as it collapsed around them.

"Dragons led an assault on Castle Forene," Laudin said, "then the blights came from the north and west. There's no way we can hold them off—they must number in the millions."

"I can buy us some time," Umhra said, "but I'm afraid there or too many of them for me to put an end to this. On my signal retreat to Castle Forene. I will meet you there."

"I will remain by your side," Gromley said.

"No." Umhra took a step toward Gromley. "The others will need you. Organize the retreat. Secure safe quarters for as many as you can. The castle won't hold them all and proves not to be the stronghold we believed. We will need a plan of escape. I'm certain Shadow will know what to do. May the gods be with you both." Umhra ran off in the onslaught's direction, carving his way through swaths of blights until the fog of war obscured the gleam of his armor.

"C'mon, our path lies apart from his," Gromley said, pulling Laudin's arm, "I now see him in a different light. No longer is he merely a Paladin, or even a man. He has crossed over into the world of gods."

Laudin nodded. "King Ulest is still on the field. We should see to his safety in getting to Castle Forene."

"Lead the way." Gromley followed Laudin back into the fight—a new, persistent light emanated from his resurrected form. They fought their way back to King Ulest. Gromley's war hammer came down with prejudice upon the blights he encountered which left a trail of pulverized carcasses in his wake.

To Laudin's amazement, those soldiers that lay injured on the ground in the radius of Gromley's aura were healed and brought back to their feet. Laudin felt revitalized, watching this miracle, and poured everything he had into making a last stand before their inevitable retreat.

They returned to King Ulest and Roen, the faded visages of Myka and Veien standing close by, staring blankly at their brother as his lifeblood poured onto the ground.

King Ulest sat beside his nephew's body, tucked against the underbelly of the mammoth and out of sight of the blights in the area. He gasped as Gromley approached. "Lord Strongforge, I am glad to see you among the living. I was certain we had lost you. Please know the Orc's actions were not on my behalf."

"Now is no time for such platitudes, King Ulest. We must get you to Castle Forene. It is only a matter of time until the blights overrun us."

"Can you heal him?" King Ulest asked, his gaze returning to Roen. "I will give you anything you ask—he is as much a son to me as my own."

Gromley stepped over them but his aura had no effect on Roen. He kneeled and placed a hand upon Roen's forehead. A celestial light coalesced beneath his hand but there was no response. "I am afraid he is lost. His soul has departed. Though his last acts seemed to have been honorable, there is a pall of deceit that obscures his view of Kalmindon. He has no home there."

King Ulest pressed his forehead to Roen's and wept.

Laudin turned to Myka and Veien, solemn expressions on their faces. The sisters clasped hands and faded from sight.

King Ulest stared down at Roen, placed his hand upon a bloodied cheek. "Foolish child. Had I not taught you the dangers of pride and zealotry?" He turned back to Gromley. "The fault rests with me. I have taken responsibility for him since he was a child . . . made him steward of my western realm. Seemingly, I failed in my duty in steering him to better judgement. Roen merely worked in what he misguidedly thought were my best interests."

Gromley's eyes shifted from Roen to King Ulest, who kneeled in the mud created by Roen's blood. "His soul may not be fit for Kalmindon but you, King Ulest, have proven yourself honorable. I wish there was more I could do."

"King Ulest," Laudin said. "There will be a time to mourn your loss, but we must get you to safety. Alert your men of our plan to retreat to within the capital. We will lay the groundwork of Vanyareign's evacuation once we reunite with the regent. Gromley and I will remain until Umhra's signal."

"And how should I recognize the signal?"

"I'm certain that won't be an issue."

▲

Umhra carved a path through the mayhem, his chest heaving, his arms burning. He made light work of the blights who had the misfortune of coming within Forsetae's reach, but there were far too many of them for such a base response. Nearing the front lines of battle, soldiers from Winterashe and Vanyareign alike ran for their lives as blights poured through their broken formation unabated. Those who stayed to fight had peeled back to skirmish on the periphery. It was obvious there was nothing they could do to slow the blights' offensive. A lost cause.

The dead and dismembered cluttered Umhra's path. Their horrific wounds begged for attention, but he could not afford to give it to them. A middle-aged man, his dark hair having receded from the crown of his head, grabbed Umhra's leg as he passed. "If the gods walk among us," he said as blood poured from the stump of his left leg, "then I know Kalmindon awaits my soul." He fell limp.

"May you know Vaila's love, brother," Umhra said. He pressed onward. "May we all know her love this day." He swallowed to stifle his grief.

He stepped before the deluge of blights, his rhodium armor shone as a gleaming beacon amid a sea of despair, and hoisted Forsetae overhead despite his weary muscles. He inverted the blade and thrust it into the earth—falling to his knees—until he buried the cross guard in the trampled soil.

Blights poured over him, their spears shattered against his impenetrable armor, their claws splintered as they raked at his back. He huddled beneath them, drawing in their power, and that of Evelium, as the weight of the masses atop him forced him to the earth.

He wrenched Forsetae sideways, imposed himself outward. Blights flew off him in every direction as a clap of thunder bellowed across the battlefield. Calls for retreat arose as countless blights, many of them shattered hulls of their prior selves, rained from the night sky and a burst of preternatural energy buffeted the armies. Freed from battle, the able soldiers ran toward Vanyareign.

The earth shook, sections of the capital's walls crumbled into piles of rubble under its force. Where Forsetae had punctured the earth, a jagged crack formed between Umhra and the pursuing blights. Inconsequential at first, it grew, until it spanned nearly the circumference of Vanyareign and Mount Orys.

Umhra envisioned the crack as an unbreachable crevasse. He twisted Forsetae within the earth and the chasm broadened. Pulling the sword from the ground, the land on the other side of the divide thrust upward to the heavens and the waters of the River Torrent now flowed into a great fall.

The next wave of blights poured over the fissure's edge and tumbled into the darkness of Umhra's crevasse. Some clung to the edge of the newly formed cliff face. The assault came to a sudden pause. The blights probed the crumbling lip of the ridge that held them at bay. A large and ancient looking blight came to the precipice and screeched in defiance.

With the armies of Vanyareign and Winterashe retreating into the capital, Umhra stood alone before the blight horde as the sun rose and brought a pallet of pastels to the eastern sky. Assured the chasm had stalled the attack, Umhra turned back to Vanyareign and took to the sky toward Castle Forene on grey angelic wings.

He cleared the face of the escarpment and looked back over his shoulder to get a better sense of how his obstruction would hold up against the impatient mass of blights. To his surprise, they had backed away from its edge and were dividing into two packs, creating a wide, open path back as far as his keen eyes could see.

It would hold for now. For now. He raced for Castle Forene, hoping to reunite with his friends. Together, they would find a way to defend Vanyareign, or at the very least, get as many of the city's remaining inhabitants as possible to safety before the blights could find their way within its walls.

CHAPTER 42

I can't put my finger on it, but there is something about this
Umhra the Peacebreaker that Lord Morrow has hired to
uncover my plot. I look forward to understanding him better
as I peel the flesh from his body.

—*Telsidor's Missives*
Diary entry dated 23rd of Vasa, 903 AF. Unearthed from the
Ruins of Anaris, month of Emin, 1156 AT

—▲—

"Here, you fools," a raspy voice called from the doorway of a small home in the Osprey District, "Those foul creatures are everywhere."

Talus spun, Aquila drawn in his left hand, Alessa's hand in his right. The sky overhead burned. Smoke billowed from Castle Forene beyond the city walls. Their carriage lay toppled a half-block away. Dead horses and guards were strewn across the street. Another group of blights blocked the way forward. Talus peered into the darkness of the agape doorway.

"Hurry, now," the voice said, "I can't keep it open for long."

Talus and Alessa ran for the door, avoiding the blights' attention. Talus let Alessa and Turin enter first, took one more look around, then ducked under the lintel and joined them within the humble abode.

The door closed behind them, seemingly of its own will. They found themselves in a small room lit by a single candle that sat upon a crooked wooden table along the far wall. The room overflowed with baubles and glass jars filled with herbs and other substances. Piles of books littered every free surface and numerous sets of shelves along the walls. From the ceiling, a variety of mushrooms grew, taking full advantage of the cool, damp conditions.

"Hello?" Talus scanned the room for the source of the voice that welcomed them to this relative safety. "Thank you for inviting us in. There is no safe path back to the castle."

A little man, small for even a Farestere, came out from a dark corner, a ragged book under his arm. Shocks of frazzled white hair sprouted from the sides of his head—his crown speckled with liver spots. The thick glasses he wore made his eyes look comically large and exaggerated the deep wrinkles in his face.

He tilted his glasses down on his nose and peered at the pair and the infant in Alessa's arms while he stroked an orange and black lizard that rested on his shoulder. "Welcome, yes," he said, "an evil wind is in the air. The streets aren't safe."

"Evil, indeed." Talus wiped a bead of sweat from his forehead with his forearm. "Dragons attacked the castle, and now the city is teeming with what I can only assume are blights."

"Dragons, you say? Well, then we are lucky to be in here," the elderly Farestere said, leaving Talus unsure if he understood the gravity of the moment. "I want nothing to do with dragons."

"Excuse me for not properly introducing ourselves. I am Talus Jochen, High Guardian of the Queen and General of her army. This is Alessa Elmont, mother of the queen and, in her arms, is Queen Turin Forene." Talus grimaced at his careless disregard for discretion. "And you are?"

"I am Indrisor." He came forth and inspected his harrowed guests, his brow raised.

"She, the little one . . . she has been touched by the gods," the little man said, pointing a crooked finger at Turin, "She possesses a power few can understand."

"She is your queen, Sir Indrisor," Talus said, "Address her with the proper respect."

"Yes, the little one. I'm sure I do not offend her, and it isn't often I get to call one 'little'."

Talus took a step toward Indrisor. Alessa stopped him with a gentle tug on his wrist. "It's okay, Talus. Our evening has been exciting enough already. Indrisor, was it?" She stepped forward and extended a hand to their host.

"Yes. Indrisor. Not Lord, not Sir . . . just Indrisor."

"And you, Indrisor, are a wizard, are you not?" Alessa asked.

"If there were wizards left in this world, I might be known as one. In this day and age, I am just Indrisor, an eccentric old man. Come . . . please, sit."

Alessa looked up at Talus, raised her eyebrows playfully, a crooked smile on her face. Indrisor brushed a pile of books onto the floor, clearing a small chair for her. She accepted the chair and sighed. She smiled at Indrisor, then at Talus, and burst into tears. "This is all too much," she said between sobs.

Talus dropped to his knees before her and pushed her hair from her face. "It's going to be alright," he said, his tone gentle but unpolished. "I don't know how, but it seems like Turin can defend herself just fine. Did you see how the blade froze atop her?"

"Froze atop her, you say?" Indrisor asked. "As though the blade refused to strike the little one?"

"Yes," Alessa said, looking at Indrisor for something more. "An Orc chieftain struck down upon her with his blade this very night. He was unable to will his weapon to her flesh, despite his great strength. Our friend gave his life intervening on her behalf."

"Is this the first time she's shared her gifts?"

"No," Alessa said. "When we were on a ship heading for

Shent, we came under attack by a Tursas. She quelled its anger, and it retreated."

"I've read about this." Indrisor lit up. "Let me show you."

He turned around in a circle, his goggled eyes darting from one book to the next as if trying to recall which tome had enlightened him to Turin's abilities. "Yes, yes. Here it is. *A Traveler's Guide to the Odd and Obscure* by Sentina Vake." The book appeared in his hand and he flashed the binding in their faces.

Indrisor opened to a page two-thirds of the way through. "Here we are, yes." He ran his index finger across the pages. "When the great adventurer Sentina Vake traveled to the southern continent of Elandril, she met a young man in Jidun'In with grey skin and blackened rings about his golden eyes—much like the little one." Indrisor looked up from the book and offered an awkward smile at the pair.

"They referred to this young man as an Adyti, or boundless one. He was conceived of man, but their clerics claimed the gods had touched his soul. It seems, yes, that he was an adolescent when Sentina encountered him and he showed a proclivity for magic that was not tethered to a god, nor learned through books. This magic was innate—a part of the young man since birth. A sorcerer. The rarest of magics."

"Go on," Alessa said. She shifted to the edge of her seat.

Indrisor turned the page and continued. "He was adept at alchemy, able to change the form of materials, matter shifting at his will. The four kings of Elandril, who did not understand the young man's powers and found him a threat, had tried time and time again to have the young man assassinated, but to no avail.

"It would seem the accounts of these assassination attempts each state that, even as a young child, this Adyti was impervious to weapons, poisons, and illness."

"What became of him?" Alessa asked, "Why have we never heard of this young man? It seems that one with his abilities would be destined for greatness."

"The passage does not say. Maybe, yes, one of her later writings would complete the story. I could never find a copy of her other works, unfortunately."

Indrisor's lizard puffed out its black throat, little barbs sticking out in all directions in a show of alarm. It hissed at the hovel's sole window.

"They approach," Indrisor said, stroking the lizard's back. "They know we are here."

The window shattered and a small blight crashed into the room. Books and trinkets scattered everywhere. Talus drew Aquila and cut the intruder in two. More poured in through the window.

Indrisor pulled on Alessa's hand. "Come, we must get to my pocket." His face was twisted with worry.

Not seeing any other means of escape, Alessa followed the odd little man to the back of the room and beneath the table upon which the candle sat.

"Come now, hero," Indrisor said, "I believe I know a way to get the little one to safety."

The wooden door exploded as an enormous blight bludgeoned it with its club. The small room was quickly being overrun.

"Talus, hurry," Alessa said. Her voice sounded farther away than possible in such a confined space. "This is . . . amazing."

Talus took the head from one last blight, dashed for the table, and slid beneath it. Expecting to hit the wall, Talus slid through the darkness but not across the rough-hewn wooden floor or Indrisor's home but one of cold, smooth stone. As darkness gave way to lantern light, Talus tumbled to a stop. He found himself in a vast library with bookshelves that reached up to a ceiling sixty feet above and ran for as far as the eye could see.

Alessa and Indrisor waited for him at an ornate stone table in the middle of the room, their entrance seemingly much more graceful. Talus scrambled to his feet and took a defensive stance, Aquila held out before him.

"They can't come here," Indrisor said, "I have wards against such intruders. Only those I care to invite may enter. Unfortunately, we cannot go back there, no. The capital is no longer safe."

"What is this place?" Talus asked, keeping Aquila at the ready despite Indrisor's assurance.

"As I said, Hero, this is my pocket. My very own dimension. I have built it stone by stone over my many years. It is my life's work."

"It is quite impressive," Talus said, "Please call me Talus."

"Oh, this is just the library, Hero, there are many more rooms." He pointed at the various doors interspersed among the bookshelves. "I must insist you stay with me, however. I would not want either of you getting lost."

"Indrisor," Talus said as he sheathed Aquila, "I need to get Queen Turin and her mother to Castle Forene at once. The others of our party will be concerned for her well-being on this harrowed night. Is there another way out of your pocket than back through your home in Vanyareign?"

"Of course," Indrisor said, as though the question was absurd. "Who would build a pocket dimension with only one means of egress? That would be absurd."

"Excellent. May we head to one of the other exits, then? One close to Castle Forene if possible."

Indrisor placed his lizard on the shoulder of his red tunic and rubbed the scruff of his chin. "I'm afraid my home was the closest door to the little one's home. Our choices are disparate, but once we choose one, we should be able to get word to your friends."

"Disparate might not be a bad thing, given the circumstances," Alessa said, "What are our choices?"

"Well," Indrisor said, "there is the door to the Isle of the Twelve Mines."

"No," Talus said, "The dragons have already claimed Mount Anvil as their own."

"Unfortunate— then, how about Marabyth?"

"Anything closer to home?" Alessa asked. "I don't think we mean to abandon the kingdom."

"I have a small cottage on Maryk's Cay. We would be only a stone's throw from Anaris."

"Perfect," Talus and Alessa said in unison.

"Not the most adventurous of choices, but if it's what you wish." Indrisor shrugged. He looked at each of the doors along the far wall, touched his index finger to his lips, and muttered to himself. "Yes, yes. That's right," he said, "Second door to Maryk's Cay, third room exit by light of day."

Talus looked at Alessa—who seemed to enjoy this adventure and Indrisor too much, given the circumstances—and raised an eyebrow. For him, a night of dragons and blights was more than enough. He found little in the way of patience for an eccentric wizard, despite now owing him a life debt. He had to admit, the alternate dimension that reached across Tyveriel was quite impressive. Nobody thought any of these things still existed—vestiges of a bygone age. Then again, there were no known Paladins remaining until Umhra walked into King Arving's throne room just over two years ago. Since that day, Talus's mind had opened to the possibility that the old ways hadn't entirely left Tyveriel, as so many had thought. Tonight, this gave him hope that not all was lost.

"Come, come. Follow me," Indrisor said. "We have a bit of a journey ahead of us."

Indrisor walked to the second door, pulled a book on the shelf beside it. The door opened, and he stepped into the next room. Talus and Alessa followed close behind. In stark contrast to the warmth of the library, the hallway they entered was lit by a harsh, artificial light with no discernable source that forced them to guard their eyes for a moment. The floor was spongy underfoot, as though they were walking across the fenland. It was a reflective metallic color, matching the curved walls and ceiling which undulated as they progressed.

"A temporal bridge like this connects each room. They allow us to travel great distances in a matter of steps. Tread carefully, however, tearing the bridge will send us spiraling into an endless abyss of time immaterial."

"And you fashioned this, yourself?" Alessa asked, her eyes wide with wonder as she scanned the membranous tunnel.

"Yes. My life's work. A lonely life it has been. Come, we exit to the sitting room ahead."

The hallway ended abruptly in a dead end, a wall of reflective semi-solid metal standing in their way. Indrisor reached out with his right hand and pushed through the wall's surface, looked back over his shoulder at his guests.

"Now we must push back through to the physical plane. A bit ineloquent, yes, but functional."

He drove his other hand into the wall, which resisted at first and then gave way. He continued forward, slowly absorbed by the quivering wall, leaving Talus and Alessa alone on the temporal bridge.

"Do you trust him?" Alessa asked.

"I know better than to trust almost anyone," Talus said. "I don't, however, see that we have a choice at this point."

Talus took Alessa's hand and stepped through the wall. "It's cold, but there is solid footing on the other side."

"Then let's have at it," Alessa said.

Talus put his shoulder into the wall and pushed through the membrane, emerging in a room of wood paneling lit by an enormous stone fireplace, a door on each wall. In the center of the room, Indrisor sat in a leather back chair. The wizard smiled as he waited for his guests to arrive.

"Very good, yes," Indrisor said, "I did not tolerate the travel so well my first few times. Jumping such a distance in so few steps can leave one's stomach behind for a moment, if you get my meaning."

Talus nodded, his stomach roiled but he was too proud to admit it. "So, which of these doors do we take next?"

"We are technically in Travesty right now. If we were to go through the door on the left, we would exit into a small home I own near the market district. The door straight ahead leads to a dead end. You don't want to see what awaits you there. The door to the right leads to the observatory. Beyond the observatory lies Maryk's Cay."

"We will have to cross another bridge like the last?" Alessa asked.

"You are a quick study, yes. The little one is lucky to have such a mother."

Indrisor popped up from his chair and made for the door. They crossed another bridge identical to the last, and came to a room made of glass. The cosmos swirled around them in all directions, an endless expanse of galaxies and deep space.

"My favorite room," Indrisor said, walking to a glass door at the far end of the room, "There is so much more to life than Tyveriel. I hope to visit other worlds someday."

Alessa gasped and turned slowly as she followed. "This is amazing . . . you are amazing."

"Time and focus, my dear. That's all it takes. Most don't give enough of either to anything in their lives. It's a shame we are in such a rush. I've spent years in this room . . . and here I can offer you only but a moment."

"Yes, a shame," Talus said, slack jawed. "We should get to Maryk's Cay as soon as possible."

"Maybe another time, then." Indrisor opened the door, not to the dark void of space but to a quaint, sun-filled room. "Welcome to my cottage on Maryk's Cay. From here we can send word to your friends that the little one is safe."

Alessa and Talus stepped into the room. It was clean and airy, with oversized windows overlooking crashing waves of the Sea of Widows from atop a bluff. Wind buffeted the little wooden building, whistling as it lashed its façade. The room was plain, its walls whitewashed, which made it feel bigger than it was. Place settings for three sat upon a simple wooden dining table beneath a pair of the windows, a basket of fresh bread as its centerpiece. A hearth heated the room as it cooked the contents of a large cast iron pot hung over its flame that blanketed the room with the aroma of fresh herbs and onions.

"Please, make yourselves comfortable," Indrisor said, "I'm sure you are both weary from the day's events. We are safe here."

"Indrisor, thank you for helping us," Alessa said, "It took great courage to open your door to us and I am sorry for the trouble we have brought upon you."

"Not at all." Indrisor smiled. "I am just grateful I was in Vanyareign last night. If you would like to put the little one down, there is a bed in the back room, yes."

"I would appreciate that." Alessa took Turin into the bedroom, leaving Talus and Indrisor alone.

"May we get that message to Regent Avrette? She must be worried sick."

"Of course, Hero. Let's not waste another moment."

CHAPTER 43

The primordial gods' objections went unheard. In turn, they revolted against the Great Creators.

—The Gatekeeper's Abridged History of Tyveriel
Vol. 1, Chapter 2 – Unearthed from the Ruins of Meriden, the month of Anar, 1217 AT

—▲—

Laudin sat in the tower's window watching the first of the titans come into view just after sunrise. The behemoth had awoken from its slumber and torn itself away from the Seorsian Mountains where it had hidden itself for ages. Its course set Vanyareign in its sights.

Its physique was almost entirely of stone as old as that of Tyveriel itself—a rotund monstrosity on six stout legs. Five yellow oval eyes arched across an amorphous head boasting the jagged maw of a snapping turtle.

The titan trod forward, earth and tree falling from its back. Each step it took set off a stronger tremor throughout the capital. Countless blights poured forth from the Wistful Timberlands to the west and surrounded their gargantuan ally.

Laudin ran down the narrow spiral staircase and barged into the throne room where his companions awaited him. "A titan approaches from the west," he said, his lungs burning. "We have a few hours at most to evacuate the capital before it breaches Umhra's chasm."

"You have your orders, general," Regent Avrette said. "Complete the evacuation of the capital with immediacy."

One of the two generals in the room, a tall Evenese man with long red hair, saluted and dashed from the room.

"Regent, we must leave," the second general said, cracking his knuckles against a gloved palm. Regent Avrette stood at the table in the throne room, ignoring the advice. "I will not leave this castle until I know that either Queen Turin is safe, or there is nothing else we can do to save Vanyareign. It's the last I'll hear on the matter . . . I will not change my mind." She looked up. Exhaustion and defeat plagued her face. "General, take the Elders Syndicate and anyone else wishing to leave. Head south with the others. The Barrow's Pact will see to my personal safety, I assure you."

"As you wish, Regent," the general agreed without hesitation, "King Ulest, will you be joining us?"

"If it is all the same to the regent, my contingent would like to remain at her side."

Regent Avrette nodded to the general and dismissed the Elders Syndicate, who eagerly followed the general along with a few others in the room.

A great horn bellowed twice, calling upon the remaining citizens of the city to evacuate, the heavy military presence given instructions to lead them south and east away from the blight onslaught.

"Umhra," Regent Avrette said as the doors to the throne room closed, "you said one of the dragons is, in fact, the undead Mesorith?"

"I vanquished him in the Burning Wood," Umhra said, "But, in order for him to have been brought back from the dead, there must be a phylactery of some sort to hold his soul. Until we destroy that vessel, he can be reanimated. The bigger problem is the other dragon. While I am well equipped to deal with the undead, a living dragon is another story. I am untested against such a foe and have been told a Mystic would not fare well in such a confrontation."

"You can bring people back from the dead," Gromley said. "Surely, you can stave off a dragon."

"You were not dead. I believe only a god could wield such power. I merely provided you a path back to us. As to the dragon, at best, I can buy us time, as I did with the blights. Once that monstrosity of theirs gets here, I'm afraid there is little we can do to save the capital."

"Modig Forene was victorious the last time these forces combined to rule Evelium, and so shall we," Lord Morrow said, standing from his seat and pounding the table.

"Yes, after a conflict that lasted a millennium," Regent Avrette said, "I have no intention of letting this drag on any longer than need be. We must figure out a way to put an end to their aspirations soon."

"The child," Umhra asked, "you were saying earlier she possesses innate powers?"

"Yes," the regent said, "an Orc chieftain struck out at Turin, and an unseen force repelled his weapon from harming her."

Gromley stood at the mention of his would-be killer and turned from the conversation. Shadow came to his side, put an arm around him.

"What's that sound?" Laudin asked. The entire gathering turned to face a whirring sound which grew from outside the castle. The wall exploded behind the Raptor's Throne, sending stonework careening across the room. Umhra summoned his armor as a boulder collided with him and shattered against his glowing form. He held up his hands and slowed the momentum of the explosion, steering a large stone away from Regent Avrette, and into the wall behind her.

An immense serpentine head appeared in the burgeoning hole in the castle's façade, its grey scaled form a ghost amidst the smoke and rubble. With rage in her eyes, Silyarithe roared and wedged herself into the room.

"Kneel before the Grey Queen, or I shall devour you all."

Shadow kicked the stone table over and pulled the regent behind it with him. Silyarithe released a shower of purple plasma across the room and the others dove for protection. The initial blast sundered the Raptor's Throne, hurling its pieces across the length of the throne room and shattering against the gold doors that marked the room's formal entrance. The doors dented outward, one coming free of its hinge.

Silyarithe's torrent set Lord Morrow aflame, caught with no cover in range. He cried out, but Silyarithe opened her mouth and consumed him before anyone could get to his side and pull him to safety. Regent Avrette screamed as she watched the Grey Queen devour her husband.

Laudin loosed two arrows at Silyarithe while Umhra rushed forward, braving the searing streak of flames that burned from the stone floor and summoning Forsetae to his hand. With a single leap, he engaged Silyarithe, slashing Forsetae across her face twice. The dragon reared up, the throne room's stone walls crumbling overhead.

Umhra drew in the energy around him, syphoning Silyarithe's inferno from the room, and released a concussion that forced Silyarithe to retreat.

The Grey Queen peeled away from the castle façade, lifted into the air over its battlements, and arched backward into a dive. Laudin rushed to the jagged edge of the gaping hole she had left and watched the Grey Queen open her wings and soar in a sweeping circle out of sight.

"Get to safety," Umhra said, his wings sprouting from his back, "Don't wait for me. I will buy you as much time as I can." He ran through the gap and flew into the air.

"You heard him," Laudin said, "Shadow lead the way."

Shadow nodded and placed his hand on Regent Avrette's shoulders. She held her right hand out, reached for her beloved husband, her gaze fixated on where he stood just moments before. Tears streamed down her face, the purple glow of Silyarithe's fire reflected off her cheeks.

"Regent," Shadow said. "Jenta." He shook her to garner her attention, her wild eyes darted to meet his. "We must go. Come with me, I know a way to safety."

"What of everyone else?" She asked, her tone distant.

"We can't worry about everyone else right now. We must leave so we may live to reorganize and fight another day."

Regent Avrette nodded, wiped tears from her eyes only to have them replaced with new ones. She stood and allowed Shadow to guide her from the room, looking over her shoulder at the place where Espen should have been until it fell out of sight.

The castle was empty, a broken shell of its former glory. The building crumbled around the party as Shadow led them down into its undercrofts, Laudin picking up the rear. By the time they reached the huge iron doors that led to the dungeon, the thunderous footfalls of the titan grew close and shook the structure to its very core.

Shadow picked the lock at the entrance to the abandoned dungeon and ushered the group inside. He ran through the guards' quarters, threw open a door, and held it for everyone to pass into the prison.

"Hurry now."

"What are we doing down here?" King Ulest asked. "We will be trapped."

"I know a way that leads into the caverns beneath the mountain. From these caverns run two sets of tunnels; one set leads out to the River Torrent, the other into the depths of Sepyltyr. From there, I can get us almost anywhere."

"Sepyltyr? Surely, this is madness."

Another titan footfall shook Castle Forene's foundation, this one followed by a resounding crash that betrayed the proximity of the behemoth.

Naivara ran through the doorway, her arm around the regent as if protecting her from the entire world. "Shadow, do what you must. I fear this mountain won't stand much longer."

Shadow let the door slam behind them, locking them in the dungeon. He led the group past the prison cell and unlocked the prisoners as the party progressed. Everyone ran down the hallway where Shadow had led Talus. Shadow sprung the lock to the interrogation chamber and led everyone inside.

"You two go first," Shadow said. "The descent can be treacherous for the untrained. Naivara will follow with Jenta, and then the rest. Nicholas and I will go last. At the end of this tunnel, there is a drop. Be cautious."

Laudin nodded and slipped into the hole Shadow had exposed by removing the stone.

▲

Shadow prodded everyone forward. Gromley followed Laudin down the hole. For a moment, Gromley sat at the edge of the opening and gauged whether his broad shoulders would fit into the tunnel. Squeezing into the narrow passageway, he fell out of sight.

Naivara stepped up, her arm still around the regent's shoulders. "Wait for her at the bottom," Shadow said, "You will probably have to fly her down to the floor of the cavern the tunnel opens into. And steer clear of the pools. They prove to be quite dangerous."

"We will all need rest when we get down there," Naivara said, "The regent most of all."

"I know," Shadow said, "As soon as we are safe."

Naivara followed Gromley into the hole. Shadow took Regent Avrette by the shoulders and looked her in the eyes. "Jenta, can you follow Naivara down the tunnel? It will be a difficult descent."

The regent nodded, her pale face streaked with tears and grime. "I can," she said, her voice weak.

"Go then, time is precious."

"Yes, it is," Regent Avrette said. She dropped before the interrogation table and shimmied into the darkness.

The others followed, the few prisoners they had picked up along the way included. When he and Nicholas were alone, Shadow put a hand on his friend's shoulder. "I want you next to Jenta at all times," he said. "If we get into any trouble down there, I want you to whisk her away immediately. Delivering her to safety is our top priority. We will need her if we are to maintain this fragile peace with Winterashe and reassemble as many of us as we can to fight the Grey Queen and her blights."

"You have my word. I will keep her close to my side every waking moment. Where are we heading?"

"I know of a tunnel through Sepyltyr that will bring us as far as Willow's Notch. From there, we will head south to Farathyr. There is a cave system just west of the town that Laudin told me would be large enough to accommodate those that survive and heed our call. Modig Forene used the same caves as a refuge during the War of Dominion. Laudin says there are still structures in place."

"Sounds like as good a place as any," Nicholas said, "I'll keep an eye on Jenta. If we get separated, I will take her to Farathyr."

The room shook as the titan took another step toward Mount Orys. Nicholas crawled into the tunnel and Shadow followed close behind, not bothering to seal their means of escape. It wouldn't matter to the titan, the blights, or the Grey Queen. They had already won.

CHAPTER 44

At the rear of their vast army stood an entity unlike any I had seen before. At its will, the blights poured forward with reckless abandon.

—*The Collected Letters of Modig Forene*
Letter to Admiral Kellan Essl dated 20th of Ocken, 997 AC. Unearthed from the Ruins of Vanyareign, month of Ocken, 1301 AT

—▲—

The titan's foot crashed down just shy of Umhra's chasm. The earth shook, a plume of dust rose into the air. The capital was in a state of unbridled frenzy when Silyarithe landed in the Grand Bazaar. The evacuation order underway, people ran in every direction—a panicked mass of refugees. They poured through the park to hasten their escape through Vanyareign's south gate.

Silyarithe spun in a tight circle, setting the Grand Bazaar ablaze in purple flame. The firestorm incinerated hundreds of people on contact, while those on the periphery of the crowd screamed in terror and scattered as their flesh burned. The myriad shops that encircled the park became spokes of flame spreading outward to the Grand Concourse.

Umhra set down within Silyarithe's ring of fire just as the mountainous titan set its giant foot into the city. Its next step shattered the city's west wall, throwing rubble nearly as far into the city's heart as where he now stood. Buildings toppled as the shower of rock rained from the sky.

With the titan behind her, Silyarithe didn't seem as imposing as she had in the confines of the throne room at Castle Forene. A few of her scales had broken or become dislodged during the night's exploits—superficial wounds, but wounds, nonetheless.

Umhra knew the titan would only matter if he could rid Tyveriel of the Grey Queen. His gaze trained on Silyarithe, whisps of blue ether raised from his form. His armor reflected the heliotrope firestorm around him.

Forsetae's voice resonated in Umhra's mind. *She is a formidable beast, but no worse than the guardians we have faced. The wound on her chest. Thrust me into it and she will fall, as her father did upon my blade before her.*

Silyarithe stretched her sinuous neck and roared at Umhra. Umhra walked toward her, Forsetae kept low at his side. His pace quickened with every step until he was at full stride.

Her tail lashed out at him as soon as he came within range. He leaped over the attack, which careened into a burning stand of trees beside him and tore them from the ground. The trees soared through the smoke-filled air like massive flaming arrows.

Silyarithe spun, followed the momentum of her tail, a wake of destruction in its path. She batted Umhra with an open claw. The crushing blow sent Umhra airborne. He crashed through the front windows of the Marwyn Homestead. She jumped forward and wedged her claws into the building's façade. Pulling her forelegs apart, she tore the Marwyn Homestead in half, the domed sky light at the center of the parlor shattering into countless shards of stained glass which rained down upon Umhra.

Umhra flew out of the shower of dust and debris and

plunged Forsetae into Silyarithe's exposed chest where a scale had fallen the night prior. The sword sunk deep within her. She screamed at the heavens in pain and rage.

Silyarithe reared up onto her hind legs. Umhra clung to Forsetae as she lifted him into the air. She scowled at him, as one would upon finding a tick burrowed into their skin.

"It will be a bit harder than that, I assure you." With a swipe of a claw, she flung him from her torso into the rubble below.

Purple blood pouring from the wound, she charged at Umhra. Umhra scrambled to his feet and dodged the first swipe of her claw. He countered with a slash from Forsetae, which rang off one of her fangs as her jaws snapped shut just before him. Forsetae shattered, leaving nothing in Umhra's hand but the hilt and a short, jagged shard of its blade.

His mind flashed back to Wicked's Pass and the ogre that attacked him as a child. He shook his head clear as a second claw crashed down upon him and pinned him to the ground. The marble floor cracked beneath him.

She bore down through gritted teeth, his rhodium armor stressing under the pressure and the foundation of the Marwyn Homestead groaning. He let go of Forsetae's hilt, the shattered blade dissipated into wafts of blue ether. He grabbed the dragon's immense claw in both hands—Silyarithe snarling above him and his armor giving way to her will.

He strained against her full weight, as hopeless as it all seemed. He drew upon the energy around him and space bent inward upon them. Just as his armor was set to fail, he released a blast of collected energy, and leveled the remaining walls of the Marwyn Homestead and crushing countless blights that now roamed the streets in pursuit of the retreating masses.

Silyarithe stood her ground, undeterred by the force of the blow. Her lips curled ready to finish her work. Her tongue lolled out and licked Umhra's flesh. "I will savor the taste of you." Umhra's heart quickened within him. Once again he summoned Forsetae, only the broken handle heeded his call.

He focused on the ruined blade as Silyarithe's full weight came down upon him. The rhodium of what remained of the blade flowed into a slim dagger. Crude, but useful.

Umhra thrust the dagger into Silyarithe's foot. The Grey Queen released him for a moment, tore her foot free of the newly formed blade. Umhra rolled to his knees. Hot blood streamed from his nose and ears, his battered armor retracted, and his wings sprouted from his back. With one leap, he shot up into the sky above Vanyareign. Silyarithe snapped at the fleeing Mystic with outstretched jaws. Just missing, she took flight after him.

With one last step, the titan struck Mount Orys head on. Castle Forene toppled and the mountain broke in two as Umhra turned northwest with as much speed as he could muster. His eyes stung and his mind raced. Not everything Spara had told him was a lie. Mystics were not equipped to oppose dragons. With his sword destroyed, he had but one hope left.

Silyarithe chased after him, arcs of purple light danced in her mouth as she grinned menacingly, keeping pace. They streaked over the Ilathril Mountains. Umhra stretched his lead and dove low to the range. He weaved around its jagged, snow-capped peaks, careful to keep Silyarithe in sight behind him while taxing her as best he could.

Taking a hard turn precariously close to the rock face, he dove into the darkness of a cavern that yawned like a gaping mouth below him. He flew past the crystalline walls of pale green quartz and followed the winding river back to the sleeping Vendarithe's lair, forced to walk the last stretch of the river as the tunnel narrowed.

He entered the cavern, the purple glow of the Waystone now steady and vibrant. Vendarithe paced the far wall, her rose gold scales glimmered in the reflection of the fire that raged in her maw.

"Tell me, Umhra the Peacebreaker," she said, drool cascading from her mouth as she spoke, "What has woken me from my Long Sleep? Tyveriel trembles mercilessly."

Umhra slowed his pace, unsure how to approach the restless dragon. As she stood, she looked even larger than she had when he saw her last—twice the size of the Grey Queen and, obviously, in no mood to be trifled with.

"Two of your kind. The lich that was Mesorith and a grey dragon, who have amassed an army of blights and have destroyed Vanyareign. The trembling you mention comes from one of their great titans, which has leveled Mount Orys."

"Mesorith and the Grey Queen are not of my kind," Vendarithe said, her tone deteriorating into a hiss. "Are you that naïve to not know the differences that lie between us?"

"I wouldn't have come to you if I were unaware of the disdain the gold dragons of old held for their chromatic brethren. I meant no offense."

A great plume of smoke billowed from Vendarithe's nostrils. "And what would you have me do about the mighty King of Dragons turned lich and his fabled daughter?"

"You needn't worry about the lich," Umhra said, "at least not for now. I dispatched him temporarily with little effort. The Grey Queen, is another story entirely. I faced her and narrowly escaped with my life."

Vendarithe stepped forward, brought an enormous eye to Umhra's level. "I told you the powers of a Mystic could not best a dragon. You are lucky to be here before me, and luckier that I, for some reason, find your death undesirable."

"I am most grateful for that. And for the wisdom you imparted upon me as to the limits of my power. As a sign of my appreciation of your tolerance, I had the Grey Queen follow me here. At this very moment, I suspect she waits for me at the mouth of your cave, daring not to follow me below the surface."

"Oh, how very smart of you, Peacebreaker." Vendarithe sighed. "Unfortunately, not a complement I would pay many of your kind."

"So, will you fight the Grey Queen?"

"You assume correctly that I am bound by a code that supersedes the one holding me in this cave. I cannot sit here idly as that scourge goes unchecked. The conflict between chromatic dragons and those of my lineage precedes even the Age of Grace. If I do not intervene, she will lay claim to Tyveriel and pursue dominion of the other realms as well. This, I cannot allow."

"I was hoping you'd say that."

Vendarithe grinned, her teeth were a flawless set of serrated death. She whispered a few words in a language Umhra was unfamiliar with and transformed into a human woman. In this form, she was almost as tall as Umhra, her long straight hair was the same hue of her tan skin flecked with gold. Her eyes were oversized on her face—their irises, ruby red. She wore a simple linen shirt and leather pants that clung to her thin frame, with gold boots rising nearly to her knees.

"I had no idea." Umhra laid his astonishment bare.

"There is much you do not know of my kind," she said, her voice no longer a thunderous baritone, but a cool, swaying timber too eloquent to present as natural. "We had so much more to offer humanity than our scales, teeth, and claws. Unfortunately, that sentiment was not shared by the races of man. They drew no distinction between the black and the gold, the red and the silver. To them, we were all enemies destined for extinction. Alas, such things no longer matter, as I believe my time in this realm is nearing an end, Umhra the Peacebreaker. The last Waystone is no longer in need of my protection. I consider my charge fulfilled. Perhaps, we shall cross paths again."

She drew in a deep breath as though she inhaled the sweet air of freedom and walked toward the river.

"Wait," Umhra said, eliciting a slight glance over her shoulder, "Are you saying you can't beat her?"

"What I'm saying is that I have little to lose and much to gain, and while I may not deliver to you victory over the Grey

Queen, I can deliver to you exactly what you need."

Vendarithe stepped into the cool water of the rushing river and followed it out of sight, leaving Umhra alone in her lair—the Waystone unguarded for the first time in two millennia.

▲

"I smell your stench, Mystic," Silyarithe growled into the mouth of the cave, "The blood I drew from you is thick in the air. Come out and face me. There is no sense in delaying the inevitable and I grow weary of this game."

Water splashed in the darkness below, steps drew closer.

"Yes, come," Silyarithe said, staring deeper into the abyss.

The splashing stopped, giving way to the beating of wings. Not the small, feathered wings of the Mystic she had chased into the cave, but the great reptilian wings of an ancient gold dragon.

Vendarithe burst from the darkness, biting into Silyarithe's neck and lifting the smaller dragon into the sky with little effort. She thrashed her head, the serrations on her teeth slicing through the Grey Queen's scales and into her flesh. Dark ichor poured from the wounds—the taste long forgotten by Vendarithe's tongue.

Silyarithe grasped onto the gold dragon's mouth with both claws, pried her jaws open, and pulled her neck free. With her hind legs, she kicked against Vendarithe's chest and arched backward, freeing herself from her adversary's grasp.

Vendarithe's tail whipped across the Grey Queen's back. Bones cracked under the force of the blow.

Silyarithe spiraled out of control and plummeted toward the forest below. She spread her wings wide. Arresting her fall, she looked up at Vendarithe, who blotted out the sun from above as she hovered in anticipation. Silyarithe dashed south toward the Seorsian Mountains. To defeat such a formidable opponent, she would need help.

Vendarithe gave chase. Keeping herself at a higher altitude

than her quarry, the gold dragon gained ground on Silyarithe with each beat of her immense wings. All too soon, Silyarithe felt the cool shadow of the larger dragon slip over her back.

Silyarithe collapsed her wings and dove for a slight break in the canopy below. As she disappeared into a bank of clouds, Vendarithe plunged after her, like a golden meteor falling from the sky.

Silyarithe neared the break in the canopy and unfurled her wings. They caught the air, and slowed her descent. Vendarithe struck her at full speed, once again grabbing her neck in her mouth as she careened into the forest floor. Despite her speed, she landed sure-footed and used her momentum to spin and throw Silyarithe into the woods before her.

Silyarithe tumbled to the forest. The earth erupted in a shower of trees, stone, and dirt. Vendarithe roared and followed the path of destruction into the darkness. Trees rumbled like thunder as she forced herself further into the forest. Even the sturdiest snapped as she barreled forward.

Silyarithe rested before a monolith of black stone. A pool of blood gathered beneath the lacerations on her neck as the golden dragon came upon her. Vendarithe lowered her head and inhaled.

"I would have thought this more a challenge," she said, brandishing a hooked talon and bringing it to Silyarithe's throat. "The Grey Queen, indeed."

"Who are you to enter this hallowed wood without my permission?" A voice as old as Tyveriel itself asked.

Vendarithe turned an eye to the interruption. Where the monolith stood was now an entity made of black stone. It pulled its feet from the earth and stepped between Silyarithe and the intruder.

Countless glowing orbs came to light around Vendarithe. Together, they brought the darkest recesses of the forest floor and the canopy above to life with an eerie glow.

"I am Vendarithe the Gilded Death," she said with a hiss, "I am here only for the Grey Queen. I have no interest in the wars of blights and men. Nor am I interested in the aspirations of a primordial god."

"That is most appreciated," the Aged One said, "but the Grey Queen is my sworn ally and her safety our concern."

The blights closed in, chortling to one another. Vendarithe bared her teeth, a fire igniting within her. "I will burn you all to ash."

"Do as you wish," the Aged One said, "from the worst fires grow the strongest of forests. You may burn us until you exhaust yourself and yet there will be more behind the incinerated. As long as I will it, your demise will be their sole purpose."

The first wave of blights dropped from the trees onto Vendarithe's back and worked their spears into the gaps between her scales. From each side, the others charged, crawling over one another in their frenzy to draw the ancient dragon's blood.

Vendarithe unleashed a torrent of fire upon the Aged One and then spun, setting the blights and the surrounding woods ablaze. She shook, blinded by fury, her red eyes glowing. She threw as many of the blights from her back as possible and beat her wings to break through the canopy that kept her from open sky and salvation.

The Aged One stepped from the flame, its form glowing like a hot coal. It held up its arms and the foliage overhead grew, branches tangled together to form an impenetrable ceiling that forced Vendarithe back to the ground.

The blight horde attacked again, pouring over Vendarithe until only sporadic glimmers of gold flashed through the writhing mass. The Aged One held its hands out wide and, again, raised them overhead. Trees shot up from the earth, one running through each of Vendarithe's wings, and a third through the center of her chest.

In one last fit of rage, Vendarithe threw the blights from her back and thrust her head into the air, lighting everything she could on fire. She tried to push up onto her feet but failed—

her wounds too great. She collapsed, smoke billowing from her nostrils.

Silyarithe approached, limping. Blood dripped from her mouth and she placed a talon beneath Vendarithe's jaw and tilted her enormous head so their eyes met. "If only you weren't so overconfident, you would have had your way with me. Stupid fool. Return to your Fae realm and tell your brethren that Tyveriel is mine and, when the time is right, I shall come for the lot of you."

She ran the talon down Vendarithe's throat. The gouge ran deep. Blood flowed to the forest floor. Silyarithe opened her mouth wide and bit the exposed flesh, tearing it from Vendarithe's still living form.

The plumes of smoke ceased, Vendarithe's ruby eyes faded to a dull pink.

CHAPTER 45

And so, we depart this mortal world. This crude experiment.
How I shall miss it.

—*The Tome of Mystics*
Unknown Origin. Unearthed from the Ruins of Oda Norde,
month of Bracken, 1320 AT

—▲—

Shadow dropped from the wall into a shallow puddle of murk, quickly stepping back from its edge. He dusted himself off and looked around the cavern, counting the faces that looked to him expectantly. "Good, looks like none of you are any worse for the wear. From here we have two choices. One tunnel leads out to the River Torrent. You can avoid the assault and rejoin the armies and other survivors who the regent instructed to head southeast toward Farathyr. Or you may join the Barrow's Pact and the regent who will take the other tunnel at the far end of the cavern. This will take us through the Sepyltyr as far as Willow's Notch, avoiding the blights and dragons altogether."

"The Sepyltyr?" One of the freed prisoners asked. "I'd rather take my chances on the surface than with the evils lurking down there."

"Exactly why I gave you the option. I realize neither option is of our choosing, but they are the only choices we have. You are free to go your own way."

The prisoner looked at the others and then to Regent Avrette, who stared ahead unaffected. "Regent? Is this well with you?"

"Yes, yes," Regent Avrette said, "Go the way you choose. Be well. Be safe."

The prisoner nodded. "Thank you, Regent. Anyone with me?"

A few of the others nodded and followed the prisoner down the tunnel. Watching them disappear from sight, Shadow addressed the rest of their party. "I don't pretend this trip is going to be easy. A few of us know our way through the Sepyltyr. I, myself, lived there for the first winters of my life. It is fraught with terrors, but I promise if you put your faith and trust in the Barrow's Pact, we will see you through to the other side. I'd rather take our chances with the potential dangers below than the known dangers above. I believe it is the best way forward. Let's go."

A jagged, foreboding hole in the cavern wall came into view as they ran. One after the other, the party climbed onto a shallow ledge that led to the opening and scrambled into the adjoining tunnel.

They collapsed onto the cold, damp floor, heaving from the exertion. The earth shook and large portions of the cavern caved in behind them, cutting them off from the path back. A plume of dust enveloped the party.

Shadow climbed to his feet and walked along the tunnel a bit, peering into the darkness ahead. A persistent breeze pulled at him from below, as though the Sepyltyr beckoned him into the depths. He sighed.

"I know we are all tired, but we can't sit long," he said, returning to the rest of the party.

The group nodded; Laudin helped Regent Avrette to her feet. Gromley retrieved an orb from his satchel and held it in the air before him. It came to light and its soft glow unveiled a narrow path delving through the volcanic rock of Mount Orys. He let it go, setting it adrift before the party.

Another light—unexpected—joined it, this one a cool blue in the form of a small Farestere man standing in the middle of the party.

"Good, good," the avatar said. "It looks like I found my way to you, yes. You were difficult to locate. Great magic surrounds you."

"Who or what are you?" Gromley asked, stepping forward, one hand on his holy symbol.

"My humble apologies. I am Indrisor, or at least an astral projection of him."

"Is that name to have meaning to us?" Gromley asked.

"No, no, I suppose it would not unto itself," the avatar said, "The hero asked me to get a message of import to the regent. Is she among you?"

"The hero?" Gromley asked.

"The one that calls himself Talus," the avatar said, "Is the regent among you?"

"I am." Regent Avrette stepped toward the avatar. "What news do you carry from Talus? Is the queen safe?"

"Those questions are one and the same. The little one is quite safe. As well as her mother, should you be inclined to care. We escaped Vanyareign and are now in Maryk's Cay."

"That news is most welcome, Indrisor. I cannot fathom how you've traveled to Maryk's Cay so quickly, nor do I understand what magic brings you before us now, but we have not been as fortunate. We are on our way to a safe location. I shall send word when we get to our destination so we may make arrangements to reunite with the queen. I'm told this will take us some time, though, and the path is daunting."

"I will do as you wish, Regent. Rest assured, the little one is safe. Nothing will find her here. I bid you good luck on your travels and I await your word."

The image flickered and then vanished. Regent Avrette sighed, a glint sparkled in her eye. "Well, not all is lost," she said with a hint of her normal enthusiasm, "but we have lingered too long already. Shadow, will you lead us forward?"

"Of course."

Shadow set off down the tunnel, Gromley's orb hovering just behind him, casting his shadow across the glossy black stone. He glanced over his shoulder to account for everyone and nodded when he saw Laudin pulling up the rear—a row of trudging bodies between them.

The path soon took a distinct downward slope, carving its way through the base of Mount Orys in a sweeping arc to the south. King Ulest lost his footing which sent Regent Avrette to the wall for support. Dirt crumbled down to the floor.

"I hope they evacuated the city," Regent Avrette said. "I can't stand to think we are abandoning so many good people."

"None of that will matter if you don't survive," Shadow said. "Those who make it to the Amari Caverns will need your leadership more than ever. To that point, we must hurry. I'm not sure how long the mountain will hold, and we are far from beneath it."

Their pace quickened, the tunnel falling away from them. Coming to a sharp turn, the rock shifted from the pure black volcanic stone of Mount Orys to a midnight-blue, marking their arrival in the Sepyltyr. Shadow slowed the party, a hand cautioning them as he crept to the apex of the turn in the path.

He peered around the corner, having heard something shambling about in the darkness. Here the path widened into a small cavern, a gelatinous yellow substance clung to the ceiling and walls. At the center of the room were three figures covered in patches of coarse dark blue and black fur—matching the surrounding stone. Each had four arms and two long, slender legs with large clawed feet.

They huddled around a fourth creature that lay motionless on the floor of the cavern. They carved into it with elongated fore claws on their two lower hands. They ate the flesh, grabbing large chunks with their free hands and forcing the meat into their gluttonous mouths.

Shadow turned back to the party, motioning with a finger for them to be quiet, and pulled his daggers from his belt. He held them with a throwing grip and turned back to the cavern. When he peered back into the room, he found himself staring into an abhorrent face with four sets of fiery orange eyes and spider-like mandibles.

Shadow rolled his eyes, knowing what was coming next. The creature grabbed him with two hands and threw him into the room where the others of its kind waited. Shadow slid across the stone floor, the yellow substance burned his skin where he came into contact with it.

"A little help," he yelled as the other two Boryths lunged at him, their sickle like fore claws at the ready.

"Nicholas, keep the regent safe," Laudin said, drawing his scimitar and meeting the first of the Boryths in battle. King Ulest drew Tedarrin and joined him, a fourth Boryth deflecting the first of his blows.

Naivara and Gromley ran to Shadow's aid as he struggled on the floor with the two other fiends. "The coating on the walls is acidic," he said, parrying their attacks with his daggers.

Naivara transformed into a black drake and leaped across the room, tackling one of the Boryths from Shadow's chest. The momentum carried them to the back wall of the cavern and they splashed into a puddle of the ooze. She pinned the creature to the floor—the acidic jelly not affecting her scaled body—and snapped her jaws down on its shoulder.

The Boryth hissed back at her. Its two small arms were tipped with barbed spikes and unfurled from its abdomen. They jabbed into Naivara's underbelly. She released the Boryth's arm and bit into its face. She thrashed her head, tossing the Boryth about like a raft in a storm. The Boryth's neck snapped, and its body tore free with a spray of gore and tumbled to the floor. Naivara dropped the head and growled.

Gromley uppercut the other Boryth standing over Shadow with his war hammer and sent it careening across the cavern. The creature hit the wall, grabbed on with his claws, and skittered up into the dark recesses of the ceiling.

Gromley hoisted Shadow to his feet with one hand, and placed his other on his platinum medallion, a blue light burgeoning in his eyes. He cast a bright light throughout the cavern, revealing the Boryth as it crawled across the ceiling, looking for advantage or escape. He focused the light into a single beam of energy, following the creature's path. Catching up to it as it neared a hole in the cavern roof, the light intensified, causing the Boryth to wither as though the light drew the vitality from its form.

The Boryth screeched in pain as the light seared its flesh. It tried to escape the gleam's wrath, but Gromley followed its last few steps. The creature released its grip and fell to the floor with a thud, splattering some yellow jelly upon Gromley's armor. Gromley recoiled against the acid, but it sloughed harmlessly from him.

Shadow and Gromley ran back to the tunnel, rejoining their party as King Ulest spun around Laudin's back and drove Tedarrin into a Boryth's exposed chest. The sword pulsed, amber ether drifting from its blade as it pulled the life force from its victim.

Laudin followed, thrusting his scimitar through the final Boryth's face and out the back of its skull. He pulled his blade from the corpse and wiped the ichor from it with his cloak. "Not uncommon, unfortunately," he said, looking to Regent Avrette, who stood beside Nicholas a safe distance back.

"Thank you all for your concern for my well-being," the regent said, "I assure you, however, I am no fragile flower in need of tending."

"Not for a second does anyone here consider you to be any such thing," Shadow said, walking to the regent's side "It's just that our kingdom has lost so much today, and we dare not risk it losing you as well. Who will rule on behalf of the queen in these trying times, if not you?"

"Yes, Jenta," King Ulest said, "Your safety is paramount. I have no experience with the Sepyltyr either, but I gladly step in the path of anything it throws at us for you."

Regent Avrette nodded. "Well, I should like to help, nonetheless. At the very least, I don't need a babysitter. No offense, Nicholas."

"None taken."

"Now, we must press on," Shadow said. "We have a long trip ahead of us, rife with untold dangers. Please be careful as we cross through the cavern ahead. The yellow matter that covers the ceiling and walls is quite acidic. Naivara awaits on the far side of the cavern, having taken the shape of a black drake. Please don't let her startle you."

In single file, the party followed Shadow across the cavern, finding Naivara at the entrance to the next set of tunnels. She put a shoulder to Laudin as he came up beside her, sending him off balance.

He smiled, returning the nudge, and continued into the darkness at her side.

CHAPTER 46

To stay hidden, I have assumed a myriad of identities over the
ages. My current suits me quite well. I shall keep it for as long
as it keeps me safe.

—Entry from Aldresor's Journal
Undated. Discovered in the Tower of Is' Savon, month of Riet,
1444 AT

Umhra collapsed to the floor of Vendarithe's lair, exhausted.
He couldn't remember a time when he'd been more tired
. . . when he'd felt more pain. Every muscle and bone in his
body yearned for rest. He sat, contemplating his next move as
the sounds of the two dragons engaging in battle reverberated
through the chamber. His mind darted between assisting
Vendarithe in a battle she seemed to hold little hope of winning,
to rejoining his friends and seeing them to safety, to returning
to Vanyareign and destroying the titan and whatever blights he
had the power left in him to do away with.

He sat up and summoned Forsetae to his hand. The shorn-
off hilt heeded his call, and the rest of the famed blade clattered
to the stone floor in shards. He rubbed his chin.

"Any thoughts?" he asked aloud, hoping the sword would

reply as it had since the day he claimed it as his own in the bowels of Telsidor's Keep.

Silence.

He allowed Forsetae to dissipate, the shattered pieces turning to wisps of blue smoke that clung to the ground for a moment and then vanished. He was disgusted with the vast breadth of his failures. Spara's deception stung worse than any physical harm he'd endured. "How could I have been such a fool?" Pounding the ground with an already battered fist, he tried to stand but collapsed back to the floor.

The sounds of the dragon battle faded out of earshot. Umhra sighed and hung his head.

"Why the long face, my champion?" A familiar voice said from the river's edge.

Umhra looked up and saw Vaila standing before him, her image composed of the restless, swirling waters coursing along the far wall of the cave. She stepped forward and held out her hand for him to take. "Come to me."

He rolled to one knee and forced himself to his feet—her presence giving him strength he didn't know remained. "I'm afraid the Grey Queen was too much for me. With all the power you have granted me, how is it I am so inadequate when it comes to her?"

Vaila tilted her head. "I would hardly say inadequate. Was it not you who chased her from the castle, saving your friends' lives? Were there others waiting in line to battle her within Vanyareign's walls? Was it not you who was cunning enough to lead her here to the gold dragon—the only creature in Tyveriel equipped to best her? You did everything you could, and more than anyone else dared. You are a most miraculous creature, Umhra the Peacebreaker, but you are not a god and should not put the expectation of being one upon yourself."

Umhra took Vaila's hand, and her form shifted from one of swirling water to the one he held in his arms in Pragarus. Her powder-blue skin radiated of its own, the light bounced off her diamond gown and danced along the walls of the cavern like thousands of Fae Hobbs.

She smiled. "I cannot stay long. The world of mortals is not the only realm on the brink of war."

She led him to the edge of the Waystone. Its purple glow intensified as the god who built it and imbued it with her own power neared. Underlit by the Waystone, Vaila cast no shadow across the lair. Nor was her flawless form blemished by its harsh glare.

"What would you have me do?" Umhra asked, exasperated. He looked for answers in Vaila's eyes.

"I would have you free your mind of the troubles that plague you and find your way back to your path forward. This self-pity is but a tributary to your intended course."

Umhra chewed at his bottom lip. "I helped her . . . Spara. She played me for a fool and I was all too willing to let it happen, thinking she was teaching me things I would not have figured out on my own. I brought her to this gate, having paved the way for her with the power that grew within me. The power you so graciously gave to me. Not only did I fail my people in their hour of need, but I failed my god as well."

"You have failed nothing but your own expectations." Vaila took Umhra's other hand, holding both of his and hers. She ran a finger over the abrasions on his knuckles. "It was Spara's destiny to reach Kalmindon. Even I wasn't sure how or when, but it was inevitable, just as was the arrival of the Grey Queen. But you are wrong to think your journey at her side wasn't of significant benefit to you and our cause. Her greatest mistake was sharing with you the power of the Waystones and entrusting you to the gold dragon. What desperate acts rage awakens."

"And yet, I am not strong enough to do anything about it."

"You are everything you need to be, Umhra." Vaila's image flickered. "It is true, there is nothing you can do about the Grey Queen, but there is much yet you can do for Tyveriel. There is one Waystone left and its Guardian has perished, not to return from the Fae. Use the stone's power as you see fit. It belongs to you, alone."

Vaila's form flickered again, once again taking on the fluid form by which she had arrived, and then splashed to the floor, leaving Umhra alone at the edge of the last Waystone. He pondered Vaila's words, rubbing the back of his neck.

He held his left hand over the stone and again summoned Forsetae. The sword materialized—its grip familiar and comforting in Umhra's hand. The power of the Waystone held the shards of its shattered blade suspended in the air before him. Umhra, admired the beauty of the jagged pieces of rhodium as they slowly arranged themselves in the proper order, as though willed to find their way back together.

The light of the Waystone surrounded Forsetae, intensifying further in the gaps of its form until the blade itself glowed. Threads of light reached from one shard to the next and drew the disparate pieces together. Sparks jumped from the blade's surface as it was refashioned.

The light faded to its normal radiance, leaving Forsetae reformed in Umhra's hand. Umhra turned the blade over, inspecting its flawless surface and smiled.

Welcome back. I thought I had failed you as well.

A familiar voice calls me back from beyond the veil. I was lost to you, Peacebreaker. The beaches of Kalmindon beckoned my soul. How is it I return to your side?

Umhra was relieved at the voice's return and the warmth of Forsetae's energy coursing up his arm. *How doesn't matter. What matters is that you have returned. Thank you.*

Their remains unfinished business. Forsetae's tone was inquisitive— hopeful. *You still have use for me.*

Always. Umhra pulled Forsetae from the Waystone's aura and flourished it at his side.

He walked the perimeter of the Waystone and made toward the river, intending to return to his friends. As he left the Waystone behind, he noticed a familiar thrumming in his right ear.

He turned back to the Waystone, took a step closer. The pulsing grew stronger. With each step, the annoyance intensified until becoming so strong that it forced him down to one knee. "Bah," he said, gripping the right side of his head with his free hand. He shook his head, trying to rid himself of the discomfort.

Umhra forced himself to his feet and reversed his grip on Forsetae. Hoisting the blade overhead, he prepared to thrust Forsetae into the Waystone and sever the last thread that tied Kalmindon and Tyveriel together.

He hesitated, his weary shoulders shaking at the weight of the sword. He stared at the center of the glowing stone. The carving on its surface was that of a pyramid covered with swirling wisps of wind. He glanced at the icon hanging around his neck—an identical match.

Forsetae's voice once again resonated in his mind. *Your wisdom far exceeds your age, Peacebreaker.*

Umhra lowered the blade and held a hand toward each of the passages that allowed entrance to Vendarithe's lair. Tightening his grip on Forsetae and making a fist with his right hand, he bore down.

Rock fell from the lair's roof, splashing into the river that ran along the back wall of the cavern and clattering along the stone floor. As Umhra imposed his will on the passages, they both collapsed, cutting off any means of accessing the cavern.

River water pooled before the new obstruction. Umhra nodded and returned his attention to the Waystone.

Dust hung in the air in the stone's glow. Umhra stepped onto the Waystone's surface. The Waystone's light intensified, its energy pulling at Umhra's form. Cautiously, he walked to the stone's center, the radiance of the stone building with every step. He stood upon the pyramid . . . his pyramid. The light coalesced, following the outline of his icon, and shot up to the cavern ceiling.

For a moment, Umhra's thoughts darted to the gate to Pragarus, recalling how its energy torturously lashed him as he traveled between plains. This time was different—welcoming. It was as though he was being beckoned home after a long, tiresome journey.

His heartbeat slowed. His wounds healed. He let his mind open to the idea of ascending to Kalmindon. The Waystone's light flickered erratically, its aura weakening with each pulse, until leaving Vendarithe's lair in utter darkness. Umhra vanished.

▲

The party crossed a narrow bridge of midnight-blue stone, delving deeper still into the Sepyltyr as cave fishers hung their luminescent lures overhead, patiently waiting for their next meal. By the light of the drift globe they trudged, exhausted but reluctant to rest in such an expansive cavern.

From upon a small crag which broke the path, Shadow assisted the others to climb beyond the obstruction. Sweat stung Shadow's eyes as he reached for Regent Avrette's hands. She ducked beneath a cave fisher's lure and accepted the help, scrambling up the steep incline.

The regent safely stepped on the elevation beside Shadow. Gromley dropped to one knee, placing a hand precariously close to the edge of the bridge to right himself. Rock crumbled into the darkness below.

Naivara came to his side and dropped to her knees before him, grabbing him by the shoulders to steady him.

"What's wrong?" Laudin asked from the rear of the group.

"I don't know," Naivara said, the group closing in around Gromley, "He's having some kind of fit."

Gromley fell prone, his eyes rolled back in his head, his body convulsed.

"Do something," Shadow said in desperation, looking at Nicholas.

Nicholas dropped to Gromley's side and placed a hand on his forehead.

As Nicholas focused on his ring, Gromley's convulsing ceased. "Umhra," Gromley said, winded but otherwise, fine, "He's ascended to Kalmindon."

ACKNOWLEDGMENTS

Writing and publishing your debut novel is an experience fraught with challenge and self-doubt. It is a lonely process of navigating murky waters and making difficult decisions. While, in many ways, writing a sequel is much harder (there are expectations now), I am grateful to now be part of a wonderful community of indie authors, bloggers, and other bookish folks with whom I can share the journey. To all of you who have read Paladin Unbound, shared your thoughts and enthusiasm, and been there for me while I was writing Mystic Reborn, I thank you for your friendship and support.

It's been a long road for Susan Brooks at Literary Wanderlust. As my editor, she has pushed me to become a better storyteller every step of the way while allowing me the creative flexibility to manifest Umhra's story as I see fit. As my publisher, she's been a tremendous advocate for the Archives of Evelium reaching the public. Susan, I cannot thank you enough.

We are all fortunate to have Omer Burak Onal and Thomas Rey return to AoE with more outstanding artwork. For Mystic Reborn, Omer brought to life (or unlife as the case may be) one of my favorite scenes for a vivid and iconic cover. Thomas built upon his map of Evelium in Paladin Unbound to share the entirety of Tyveriel to accompany the scope of the book. Thank you both for being wonderful artists and wonderful people.

Of course, it all starts at home. A special thanks to my wife, Missy, for her unending support of my writing. AoE would never have materialized without inspiration from my sons, Wyatt, Owen, and Henry. You guys amaze me every day. I couldn't love you more.

Finally, I'm also fortunate to have a mother, two sisters, and many dear friends who have been my biggest cheerleaders throughout the creation of these books. Thank you all for your love and encouragement.

ABOUT THE AUTHOR

Jeffrey Speight's love of fantasy goes back to an early childhood viewing of the cartoon version of *The Hobbit*, when he first met an unsuspecting halfling that would change Middle Earth forever. Finding his own adventuring party in middle school, Jeff became an avid Dungeons & Dragons player and found a passion for worldbuilding and character creation. While he went on to a successful career as an investor, stories grew in his mind until he could no longer keep them inside. So began his passion for writing. Today, he lives in Connecticut with his wife, three boys (his current adventuring party), two dogs, and a bearded dragon. He has a firmly held belief that elves are cool, but half-orcs are cooler. While he once preferred rangers, he nearly always plays a paladin at the gaming table.

Mystic Reborn is his second novel which follows his successful first release, *Paladin Unbound*, an Archives of Evelium Tale.

CPSIA information can be obtained
at www.ICGtesting.com
Printed in the USA
JSHW022012250123
36837JS00002B/11